SHE WHO SLEEPS
MOON OF MADNESS

SAX ROHMER

INTRODUCTION BY CURTIS EVANS

Stark House Press • Eureka California

SHE WHO SLEEPS / MOON OF MADNESS

Published by Stark House Press
1315 H Street
Eureka, CA 95501, USA
griffinskye3@sbcglobal.net
www.starkhousepress.com

SHE WHO SLEEPS
First published in hardback by Doubleday, Doran & Company,
New York, and Cassell, London, copyright © 1928.

MOON OF MADNESS
First published in hardback by Doubleday, Doran & Company,
New York, and Cassell, London, copyright © 1927.

"Sax Rohmer: The Flapper and the Princess" copyright © 2024 by
Curtis Evans

ISBN: 979-8-88601-122-7

Book design by Mark Shepard, shepgraphics.com.
Proofreading by Bill Kelly.

First Stark House Press Edition: December 2024

SHE WHO SLEEPS

New York socialite Barry Cumberland is racing along the back roads one evening when he sees the woman of his dreams—right before wrecking his car. While recovering he is haunted by this dream woman. He tries to find her to no avail. Then his father, a famed Egyptologist, shares with him a recent find of monumental implications. Danbazzar, a fellow historian, has discovered a papyrus that points to an unopened tomb of a 3,000-year-old Egyptian princess—who supposedly has been preserved alive! Barry, his father and Danbazzar sail for Egypt to unearth this ancient princess. For Barry it is personal, for there on the papyrus is an image of the princess—and she looks just like his dream girl!

MOON OF MADNESS

Nanette is flirting her way toward adulthood, and Decies is one of her many admirers. In fact, all the young men love Nanette. So Decies is surprised that when she does fall in love it's with the much older Major O'Shea. Nanette and her parents are vacationing, but O'Shea is on the island of Madeira on a mission—to scout out a group of sabotaging Reds. Unfortunately, his efforts are constantly subverted by the well-intentioned Nanette. It begins with De Cuna who is after some secret photos that O'Shea needs to send back to England. Then the nefarious Macalister becomes involved, and Nanette is kidnapped. Decies is at his wit's end trying to rescue her. All Nanette wants is to get O'Shea's attention—but this time she has gone too far!

TABLE OF CONTENTS

SAX ROHMER: THE FLAPPER AND THE PRINCESS

By Curtis Evans

Sax Rohmer, one of the "big three" of English thriller writers who came to greatest prominence around the time between the First and Second World Wars (the other two being Edgar Wallace and H. C. McNeile, aka "Sapper"), was prosaically born Arthur Henry Ward to a native Irish Catholic clerk and his spouse in the northern industrial city of Birmingham in 1883. Having adopted the tony but fictitious "Sarsfield" as his middle name, Arthur Ward moved to London, where he wrote sketches for music hall performers. In 1909 he married Rose Elizabeth Cromwell Knox, a member of a noted theatrical family. One of her brothers, an acrobat known as Teddy Knox, became one half of the celebrated English comedy team Nervo and Knox.

However, Ward did not achieve his own breakout success until, in his thirtieth year, he published, under the pen name Sax Rohmer, his debut novel, *The Mystery of Dr. Fu-Manchu* (1913). This novel introduced to the world one of the great supervillains of twentieth-century crime fiction: Chinese criminal mastermind Fu Manchu (the initial hyphen was later dropped), the so-called "Devil Doctor," a mad scientist and megalomaniacal menacer not only of nations but of western civilization itself. If Sapper was celebrated for his public-school hero Hugh "Bulldog" Drummond and Edgar Wallace for his amazing prolificity and the general fecundity of his imagination, Sax Rohmer over his forty-five-year crime-writing career was most renowned as the creator of Fu Manchu. Even Arthur Conan Doyle's evil genius Professor Moriarty, archnemesis of Sherlock Holmes, had never achieved his own series.

Making his appearance little more than a decade after the Western nations' violent quashing of the anti-foreign Boxer Rebellion in China, Sax Rohmer's "yellow peril" crime thriller immediately captured the

Western reading public's rapt attention. "One of the most remarkable recent additions to modern sensational fiction," trumpeted one awestruck English reviewer in 1913, who avowed that with Fu Manchu "the author personifies, in one diabolical character of giant intellect, the Yellow Peril." Knowing a good thing when he saw it, Rohmer made Fu Manchu the villain in two successive novels, *The Devil Doctor* (1916) and *The Si-Fan Mysteries* (1917). (In the United States the Fu Manchu trilogy was published under the punchier titles *The Insidious Dr. Fu-Manchu*, *The Return of Dr. Fu-Manchu* and *The Hand of Dr. Fu-Manchu*.) A fifteen-part silent film entitled *The Mystery of Dr. Fu-Manchu* followed in 1923.

No doubt with characteristic dramatic license, Sax Rohmer himself later claimed that he had been inspired to write the first Fu Manchu novel when he asked his Ouija board—no one should be without one— how to make a fortune and the planchette obligingly spelled out the word "Chinaman." In Rohmer's case, it is apparent, the razzle-dazzle music hall showman never really left the stage. In fact, it has been plausibly argued that the character of Fu Manchu owes its inception not to an unsubtle supernatural hint from a Ouija board but rather to the real-life personage "Chung Ling Soo," aka William Ellsworth Robinson, a purportedly Chinese stage magician who began performing in his guise on London stages in the early twentieth century. (Robinson is alluded to in the 2006 Christopher Nolan film *The Prestige*.) In a bizarre twist reminiscent of a Sax Rohmer novel Chung Ling Soo was fatally shot in 1918 during a performance of his version of the bullet catch trick, which he called "Condemned to Death by the Boxers."

Around the same time, Fu Manchu vanished from Sax Rohmer's crime writing for fourteen years, not appearing again until 1931 with *The Daughter of Fu Manchu*. Over these years Rohmer published eighteen crime novels and short fiction collections, many of them, including some of his best-known works (*Brood of the Witch-Queen*, *The Quest of the Sacred Slipper*, *The Green Eyes of Bast*), were packed to the rafters with Orientalism and fantastic, supernatural situations. However, other books are reminiscent of the more down-to-earth detective fiction of Arthur Conan Doyle, of whom Rohmer was a great admirer.

The two Sax Rohmer novels paired in this volume, *Moon of Madness* and *She Who Sleeps*, were successively published in 1927 and 1928 and well-received by reviewers. *Moon of Madness* is an espionage thriller, with a Hitchcockian "MacGuffin" (secret papers) and the villains this time around are beastly, bearded Bolsheviks rather than scheming, pigtailed Chinamen. There are stolid Western good guys and a flapper nymphette named Nanette who dazzles all the men around her and inevitably is imperiled by villains. (Rohmer evidently was inspired to concoct the character of Nanette by a much younger superfan of the same name with whom he commenced a romantic affair quickly kiboshed by his wife.) If the plot occasionally gets a bit sticky as their ocean liner perilously crosses the Atlantic on route to London, it is definitely lively as well. The *Wilmington Morning News* allowed that although "the book does not have the same Edgar Allan Poe touch of [Rohmer's] earlier work, in which a Chinaman was always hovering somewhere in the background, it is equally as good and probably the best thing on the season's list of mystery stories.... The book is filled to the brim with exciting incidents...."

To my mind *She Who Sleeps* is the more intriguing of the two tales, having more of the authentic, exotic taste of Sax. Just a half-dozen years before its publication, Lord Carnarvon's famed archaeological expedition in Egypt's Valley of Kings discovered and opened the fabulous tomb of Pharaoh Tutankhamen, sparking a wave of Egypt fever over the Western world, in decorative arts and architecture as well as popular literature. Heightening the public fever was the fact that Lord Carnarvon in 1924 bizarrely died at age fifty-six from an infected mosquito bite, leading to the inception of the press myth of the Pharaoh's fatal curse upon all interlopers in his earthly resting place. *He who robs the graves of Egypt . . . dies!* an Egyptian character would dramatically intone in the Fifties Hammer Studio horror film *The Mummy*. When reading *She Who Sleeps* one can readily see how Sax Rohmer, who carefully cultivated his own mystical public persona, drew on the facts and fictions of the "King Tut" expedition in writing the novel.

Like that of *Moon of Madness,* the plot of *She Who Sleeps* is constructed around a bewitching female. It seems that a Western archeological expedition in Egypt is set upon opening the tomb of the princess Zalithea and recovering from it nothing less than the lost princess herself, who, according to a recently discovered ancient papyrus, should be in a perfect state of preservation, having been placed in suspended animation during the reign of Seti I, over three thousand years in the past. With this plot Sax Rohmer recalls not only the real-life King Tut expedition but H. Rider Haggard's famed fantasy novel *She,* about a beautiful immortal woman, Ayesha, an uncanny two-thousand-year-old sorceress from a lost African civilization. This hugely influential work inspired a host of pulp imitators down through the decades, including Cornell Woolrich's 1950 pulp novel *Savage Bride,* recently reprinted by Centipede Press.

Once the formula for revivifying Princess Zalithea is carried out, what will happen? Will *she*, rather incredibly, actually come to life again? And then what? Did our protagonist, Barry Cumberland—privileged son of one the expedition organizers, John Cumberland, a New York millionaire antiquarian Egyptologist—really have some sort of strange, mystical prevision of Zalithea on the balcony of a country house in New York, or is the love-smitten Barry just increasingly going, to use a technical term, bonkers? What does Danbazzar, John Cumberland's commanding Arab antiquities agent, know? This is an entertaining tale, about which more cannot be said without spoiling its teasing twists and turns.

A reviewer in the *Cardiff Western Mail* aptly summarized the book's, and the author's, virtues, writing: "Mr. Sax Rohmer has exploited successfully a line of mysterious romantic eastern stuff which makes up very well, and business in his booth at the bazaar is always brisk. There are no villains so villainous, no mysteries so mysterious, no ingenuity so ingenious as his. His latest novel [has] mystery that keeps one on tenterhooks, adventures that stir the reader and, of course, the immeasurability of the desert sands…. Sax Rohmer is always a master in the way of plots."

As mentioned above, Sax Rohmer would return to the Fu Manchu series in 1931 and the next year would see the release of the film *The Mask of Fu Manchu*, starring, in the title role of the Devil Doctor, a heavily made-up and hugely fingernailed Boris Karloff, fresh off *Frankenstein*, and, in the supporting part of his sexily sadistic daughter, Myrna Loy, of future *Thin Man* fame. Despite its expense the film was an international hit at the box office, cementing Rohmer's fame as Fu Manchu's creator. Fu Manchu tales would predominate in the author's output thenceforward through American entry into World War Two, culminating in *The Island of Fu Manchu* (1941), with some notable exceptions like the novels *The Bat Flies Low* (1935) and *White Velvet* (1937).

Unlike Edgar Wallace and Sapper, both of whom sadly would not survive the decade of the Thirties, passing away at the untimely ages of fifty-six and forty-eight respectively, Sax Rohmer remained active after World War Two, reviving the Devil Doctor in novel form after seven years in *The Shadow of Fu Manchu* (1948). In spite of the author's dedicated efforts, however, the Asian criminal mastermind, whose poisoned roots ran deep in the colonial Edwardian era, seemed more of an anachronism during the Cold War and the rise of Communist China, when James Bond was rather more the thing. From Rohmer's hand there also came some entertaining non-series tales of mystery and imagination like *Hangover House* (1949) and *The Moon Is Red* (1954), yet Fu Manchu would rise again in a couple of novels which the author published at the end of his life: *Re-Enter Fu Manchu* (1957) and *Emperor Fu Manchu* (1959).

Rohmer died at the age of seventy-six in 1959, after contracting, rather ironically, the Asian flu during the worldwide pandemic of 1957-58, and was interred with his parents at St. Mary's Catholic Cemetery in Kensal Green. The credulous might deem this more supernatural revenge from the East, a sequel to Ching Ling Soo's weird demise and King Tut's mystic vengeance upon Lord Carnarvon. (Death does come in threes, they say.) For Rohmer's legion of loyal fans, however, the author was deserving not of death curses but rather the most lavish of laurels.

—September 2024

Curtis Evans received a PhD in American history in 1998. He is the author of *Masters of the "Humdrum" Mystery: Cecil John Charles Street, Freeman Wills Crofts, Alfred Walter Stewart and British Detective Fiction, 1920-1961* (2012), *Clues and Corpses: The Detective Fiction and Mystery Criticism of Todd Downing* (2013), *The Spectrum of English Murder: The Detective Fiction of Henry Lancelot Aubrey-Fletcher and G. D. H. and Margaret Cole* (2015) and editor of the Edgar nominated *Murder in the Closet: Essays on Queer Clues in Crime Fiction Before Stonewall* (2017). He writes about vintage crime fiction at his blog The Passing Tramp and at Crimereads.

SHE WHO SLEEPS

SAX ROHMER

CHAPTER I

A FLASH OF LIGHTNING

Barry Cumberland pushed on through a growing darkness. There seemed to be an unfamiliar quality in this darkness which he first noticed when, quite mechanically, he stooped to switch on his headlights, and in doing so saw the time by the clock in the car. He slowed down for a moment, on a crossways, and stared into the west.

A great cloud, black as the pall of Avalon, was draped before the sinking sun.

As he watched, it crept farther and farther up the dome of blue, like a velvet curtain drawn by giant hands. Through a gap in the trees which had closely beset the path for some distance now, Barry looked down into the valley along which his route lay to the highroad and New York.

Three hundred feet below, perched apparently on the edge of a ravine, he saw a house. Some rent in the curtain of the storm had allowed a ray like a searchlight to break through and to shine upon a sort of turret which crowned the building. Shrinking behind guardian walls and overhanging yet lower depths, the effect was that of a drawing by Sidney Sime. Beyond, the road zigzagged, disappeared into shadow, later to reappear in the form of a bridge, until it finally became lost to sight before the plain was reached.

The moving curtain blotted out the light. Where a fairy castle had been, eerily illuminated, came blackness. He looked ahead sharply, accelerated, and knowing the violence of these sudden storms in the mountains, prayed that his Rolls would deliver him from treacherous byways before the blinding rain began.

He had only himself to blame if he should be stormbound. For no reason that he could have defined he had left a cheery crowd at the club, with never a word of farewell, urged by a sudden irrational impulse to reach home in time for supper. Such abrupt changes of plan were characteristic of Barry, annoying to his friends, but in no way destructive of his popularity.

A young man endowed with good looks, charm of manner, and John Cumberland for a father is not dropped socially merely because nature has designed him for a poet in a material age.

Through this ever-growing darkness he drove on; and although the route was one which normally carried little traffic, it seemed that this evening not a soul rode or walked upon the length of it. But loneliness dovetailed with his mood. He welcomed it. And so, when a sharp bend leading to a long descent set the storm behind him, he thought of it as a pursuer. He took the slope in breakneck fashion. It was a race against the pursuing darkness.

Presently came a dangerous turning which he remembered. But he had possessed the Rolls—a birthday present from his father—long enough for it to have become a part of him, responsive almost to a thought, nearly to a mood.

He checked where a ragged fence appeared suddenly ahead like a barrier and negotiated a tortured figure S which brought him out above a sheer drop. Beneath lay meadows where late corn showed speckled gold in the crawling shadows. Down, the road led, and still down. A gallant ray from the stifled sun alighted momentarily upon white walls of a building far ahead. He was aware of a flowered porch, a window, a low roof.

Vaguely he recalled this little home. Something had drawn his attention to it upon the outward journey from New York. Then it was blotted out like a house of dreams; but he was losing nothing on the storm. The race grew more and more real.

Some classic analogy cropped up in his mind; a fragment of half-forgotten studies which he could not identify. He became a mortal defying the gods. But from this flight of imagination he came sharply back to earth. The house by the roadside passed—and even now he was bearing down upon it—what lay beyond?

Jim Sakers, his pilot on the outward run, now was many miles behind, probably dancing; happily unconscious of the fact that his friend, bareheaded, in dinner kit, was racing for New York, a victim of moods, pursued by the storm.

There was a bridge, Barry remembered. They had passed a Studebaker on it; very nice navigation, for the bridge was narrow. Yes! Here was the bridge. The Rolls went booming across it at fifty-five. And now Barry sighted his first pedestrian: an old man with a clean-shaven upper lip and a tufty white beard. He wore blue overalls, a huge plaid cap which would have suited Harry Lauder, and smoked a very short pipe. Pausing, he stepped hurriedly aside as the bareheaded madman swept by in a cloud of dust. His cap went up like a Scotch balloon.

Barry clenched his teeth. The shadow was gaining upon him. Oh for a long, straight turnpike where he could open up. But memory warned him that there were many tortuous miles in which no such race track offered. Now came a long sweeping curve which he recalled clearly, tree bordered on the one side, and, on the other, outlining an outcrop of primitive sandstone, where sparse vegetation and scattered rocks formed an isthmus around which his route lay.

Here for a moment he could glance aside. The black curtain was still gaining. The storm promised to win.

Into a cutting he plunged, high-banked, tree-topped, through the blackness of which his headlights carved like a gleaming scimitar. Some little animal shot across the blade of silver. He resigned himself to his mood, wondering in what way he differed from his friends, what barrier it was that would intrude at times between him and those enjoyments for which others never lost zest.

In the games and amusements to which they devoted much of their lives he took part; and most of the things that Barry Cumberland attempted he did well. His sports record was good, but not excellent. He was happy in athletic pursuits, but could never screw up any enthusiasm for pot hunting. Cards frankly bored him. He danced well, except when abruptly, unaccountably, his dancing mood left him and he experienced a sudden longing for the silence of imaginary forests.

The girls about whom other men raved stirred him but slightly. They were all too true to pattern. The thought of home life with any one of them was definitely objectionable.

He took a sharp bend at dangerous speed, wondering if, during a long-projected but never accomplished tour of Europe, he should meet a girl having power to arouse that curious state of unrest which he had sometimes noted in his friends and vaguely wished he could experience. No doubt he was a visionary. He had often been told so. Perhaps the influence of his own home might be to blame.

It was only reasonable to suppose that an establishment which is less a residence than a museum of Ancient Egyptian antiquities, should contribute something to the character of one born and reared in it. Those almond-eyed, slender priestesses, so alluring, so aloof, had possibly played a part in disabusing his mind of any romance in connection with the girls of that very modern set to which he belonged. Since childhood they had looked down upon him, from wall paintings, vases, bas-reliefs, those cloudily robed, sinuous Egyptians, whose long eyes were wells of feminine secrets; who had never smoked or tasted cocktails, but who lived in a mysterious world which for some reason he identified with the deep notes of an organ.

Yes, it was their mystery that appealed to him. Mystery was what he sought, but never found, among the women of his acquaintance.

The road became a high ledge, a thread encircling a bowl of shadow. The gradient grew dangerously steep, and Barry checked speed almost unconsciously.

His musing had carried him many miles. Startled, he became aware of the fact that he could recall no point of the route from the spot where he had passed that solitary pedestrian. But the black cloud had won; for a darkness like night had fallen all around him. He must think what lay at the bottom of this winding road, and how they had approached it. He seemed to remember that there was a fork; that they had come out upon the valley side by one of three ways. But by which of them?

He slowed down more and more as he reached the bottom of the slope, which now turned sharply eastward out of the valley. He had been right. Three roads opened before him. His decision was promptly made. He swung into the middle route, confidently giving the Rolls her head again. On he raced, along a smooth avenue, overshadowed, and so dark that midnight might have come.

During that momentary check he had heard the booming of thunder, away behind him in the west. The avenue began to curve south. It seemed to be unfamiliarly narrow. More and more southerly it inclined, until at last came a crossroad. He pulled up, hesitated, and knew definitely that he had made a wrong choice. It was the north fork he should have taken. Therefore he turned left into the crossing, presuming that it must bring him out upon his proper route.

Going was very bad. The Rolls bumped and shook from stem to stern. But he pursued his way and swore under his breath when he found that this road also inclined to the south. But now, through an opening in the trees, he saw yet another crossway. Left again he swung, pursued by louder rumbling of thunder. Rain was beginning to fall.

Suddenly, his head lamps flooded a high wall. He wondered, but drove on; when—blinding, awesome—the lightning came . . . and he saw Her!

There was a stone-faced house not twenty yards ahead, and on a balcony high up before an open window she stood. She wore some kind of cloudy robe—a jewelled girdle—the dress of a Theban priestess! One hand upraised rested against the sash of the window, the other upon the curve of her hip.

She had long dark eyes which seemed to be watching him, and her lips were parted in a slight smile. . . .

"I am dreaming," he said aloud. "An Egyptian princess!"

Save that it seemed to live, the beautiful figure was one of those out of a dim past which had watched over him from childhood!

And now the wheel was wrenched from Barry's grasp—he was aware of a cry—a loud, splintering crash—a sickening blow on the skull—of no more. . . .

CHAPTER II

THE DIVIDING LINE

Very slowly Barry Cumberland opened his eyes—took one look straight before him—and then shut them again quickly.

Something was wrong. He could swear he had been sitting but a moment before with his back against the giant pillar of an Ancient Egyptian building, staring at a window high up in a temple wall. In the moonlight he had seen a beautiful priestess standing at this window; and he had been waiting patiently—patiently—for a black cloud to pass, a cloud that had suddenly obscured the moon and hidden the slender figure.

Yes, those were the facts, he felt fairly confident. He opened his eyes again. He saw a small, very clean white room; and he was lying in a very clean white bed. He seemed to be propped up in some way, and he experienced great difficulty in moving his head, together with great disinclination to do so because of a dull pain above his eyes.

There were some medicine bottles and cups upon a glass-topped table, and there was a tall white screen of some very glossy material. The only spot of colour in the room was a bowl filled with red roses, which also stood upon the table. He wondered idly what was behind the screen, and then closed his eyes once more.

There was some mistake. No doubt the explanation was simple enough, but his brain seemed to be tired, physically tired. He found himself incapable of grappling with the problem. In one respect, of course, he must have been wrong: In regard to the Egyptian temple. He had never been in Egypt. In his idea that he lay in this unfamiliar white room, no doubt he was wrong, also; although the red roses were suspiciously like the handiwork of his Aunt Micky.

Without Barry becoming aware of any movement, a cool hand was presently laid upon his forehead.

For the third time he raised weary lids—and found himself looking into a pair of kindly eyes, their kindliness magnified by the glasses which their owner wore. A white-capped nurse was bending over him! She was entirely dressed in white, too. Everything in the place seemed to be white, except the roses, which were red, and the nurse's eyes, which were blue.

"Ah!" she said, speaking in a low, soothing voice which yet had a note of gaiety in it, "so you have decided to wake up."

Barry Cumberland tried to say Yes, but only achieved a whisper. Great heavens! He had never felt so cheap in his life! What was it all about?

"Don't bother to talk," the soothing voice went on. "When you have had another little sleep you will feel ever so much better. I have brought you a drink."

She held a glass to his lips. He drank, looking into the kindly, smiling eyes; and fell asleep again.

The next time he awoke, the nurse was sitting in a chair beside him, reading. Presumably it was night, for a silk-shaded lamp was lighted upon the table at her elbow.

Barry stirred slightly and turned in her direction. She looked up at once.

"Good-evening," she said; "is there anything you want?"

"No, thank you." His voice was very low, but at least he could make himself understand. "Except—where am I?"

"In the first place, you are quite all right," she replied in her gentle way. "You were thrown out of your car, you know, and really had—a most lucky escape. In the second place, you are in the Elizabeth Foundation Hospital."

"Thrown out of my car?" Barry muttered. "Elizabeth? How did I get to Elizabeth?"

The nurse looked at him doubtfully, stood up, and:

"I am not at all sure that you should be allowed to talk yet," she said in a tone of authority. "At any rate, it is time for your medicine."

She measured out a dose from a graduated bottle on the table, and held it to his lips. He drank, watching her, and vainly trying to grab at any one of a thousand ideas that were dancing wildly through his brain. Yes, of course!—there *had* been a crash! He remembered, now. He had been driving the Rolls—when was it? Some time earlier in the evening, no doubt. And there was something about Egypt. Had someone been talking to him about Egypt? He could not capture this idea at all.

As the empty glass was set down:

"Please tell me," he asked, and found that he had already more control of his voice, "did I crash near here?"

"Some little distance away," the nurse answered, resuming her seat and smoothing a white apron with sensitive fingers.

Barry considered this reply for a long time. His brain was working with unfamiliar and amazing slowness. Then:

"Was I alone?" he inquired.

"You were alone in the car—yes."

"You are sure there was no lady with me?"

"Quite sure."

"Then how do I come to be here?"

"You were brought here by someone who found you."

"Do you mean a friend?" Barry asked.

And as he spoke an explanation came to him of that extraordinary pressure about his skull for which he had hitherto been unable to account. His head was tightly bandaged!

"I am afraid you are talking too much," the nurse said with gentle sternness. "It is contrary to Dr. Barton's orders for me to allow you to talk. But I will answer your question. The man who brought you was a stranger, and his finding you a pure accident. And now please close your eyes and stop thinking about it."

Barry smiled, and, in regard to closing his eyes, obeyed. But he did not stop thinking about it. He lay there endeavouring to capture those maddeningly elusive ideas which scampered about his mind like so many rabbits. Yes—he had crashed in the Rolls. He had been bound for New York. He remembered so much, clearly. He could not remember why he was bound for New York, nor from where; but New York had been his objective. He opened his eyes.

"How was I dressed when I was brought in?" he inquired.

"You were wearing your dinner clothes," the nurse replied distinctly, raising her eyes from the book which she had resumed reading. "Please ask no more questions, because I shall be unable to answer them. In ten minutes I am going to turn the light out and leave you. So try to get to sleep."

"Thank you," said Barry, and continued his reflections.

He had been wearing his dinner clothes. Where on earth could he have been coming from? He opened his eyes, another point having occurred to him which might help to throw light upon the problem. But, slowly turning his head aside and noting the firm little chin of the girl as she bent over her book, he hesitated and did not ask the question. Nevertheless, he determined to remain awake until he had the facts in order. With which idea firmly in mind, he immediately fell asleep again.

When next he awakened, morning sunlight flooded the room, and he saw, standing beside the white-capped nurse, a cheery-looking, gray-haired man, having a very ruddy complexion.

"Good-morning, Mr. Cumberland," said the cheery man in a cheery voice.

"Good-morning," Barry replied—and, in the act of speaking, knew that he was himself again and that he had not been himself during those earlier conversations with the nurse.

He raised his hand to his bandaged skull. It was singing and throbbing, but that curious dull pain had gone.

"My name is Dr. Barton," the other went on. "Feel better?"

"Rather!" said Barry. "What the deuce happened to me? Did I try to take a high jump or something?"

"Not exactly," Dr. Barton replied, sitting on a rail at the end of the bed and addressing Barry over his shoulder. "You seem to have tried to climb a tree."

Barry grinned feebly.

"How's the Rolls looking?" he inquired.

"That I can't tell you," was the reply. "I understand it has been towed to a garage some miles from here."

But, even as he listened to Dr. Barton's answer, Barry's mind had been actively at work. A phantom that had been haunting him took human shape. He recalled every circumstance that had led up to the accident. His smashed car ceased to interest him. His own condition became a very trivial matter. One thing, and one thing only, he wanted to know, and:

"I remember it all clearly," he said. "I had lost my way. One point I *must* clear up."

"Well, get busy with it," the genial doctor directed, "because we are going to have you out of bed, presently, and see how you feel on your feet."

"Splendid," Barry replied. "What I want you to tell me is this: the exact spot at which the crash took place."

Dr. Barton shook his head.

"I haven't the faintest idea!"

"What!" Barry exclaimed. "But whoever brought me here must have known where he found me!"

"No doubt," Dr. Barton admitted, "but he didn't think it necessary to mention the fact."

"Perhaps you don't understand," Barry went on patiently, "that it's rather important. Could you possibly ring up this Good Samaritan and arrange for me to see him?"

"We *could*—if we knew his number."

"Didn't he leave it?"

"He left nothing!" was the astonishing answer. "He drove you here in a Studebaker—it was a Studebaker, wasn't it, Nurse?" The nurse confirmed his statement with a nod; and: "In a Studebaker," Dr. Barton continued, "at somewhere around ten o'clock. Dr. Perry was in charge and admitted you. You looked like a serious case, you understand. You're not, but you looked like it. Who you were we found out from your cards, license, and whatnot. Then this dark horse in the Studebaker faded out."

"Faded out?" Barry echoed.

"Precisely!" Dr. Barton inclined his head in solemn fashion. "Faded out. He didn't leave so much as his best wishes."

"Do you mean you have no means of tracing him?"

"None whatever," the nurse assured him. "Dr. Perry told me he was a rough-looking man. I was on duty that night. And no one was more surprised than Dr. Perry when we learned that he had driven off."

"You see, it looked suspicious," Dr. Barton explained; "and we have been manhandled by the police about it. I mean, there was nothing to show that you had not been assaulted and robbed."

Barry stared at the speaker unseeingly. He was thinking again.

"Whoever towed my car to the garage," he mused aloud, "will tell me where I was found—or where the car was found."

"I am sorry," Barton declared, "but he won't! The garage telephoned here the same night to say they had the car. We had a police officer on the premises at the time."

"Well?" said Barry eagerly.

"A man driving a Studebaker towed the car in," Barton went on; "said it was the property of Mr. Barry Cumberland and that Mr. Cumberland would settle with them for repairing it. Then he faded out."

"Leaving no name?"

"Leaving no name."

"Was this last night?"

Dr. Barton glanced at the nurse, smiled, and then:

"It was on *Wednesday* night," he returned. "You were semiconscious for forty-eight hours! And now, stop talking. I've got my work to do. Stand by, Nurse."

"One moment!" Barry pleaded. "My father?"

"Your father has been in constant touch. We advised him at once. He is downstairs now, waiting to see you."

CHAPTER III

A WEEK LATER

"She might have stepped down from that painting!" said Barry, pointing to a reproduction of part of a wall of the great temple at Medinet Habu, above the carven mantelpiece of the library.

His father nodded and smiled, but not unkindly. He was strangely like his son, except that John Cumberland's curly hair was gray and Barry's curly hair was brown.

At the present moment Barry did not look his best, owing to the fact that a patch of the said curly hair was very neatly shaved and the corresponding portion of his skull decorated with unattractive surgical dressing.

They both possessed fresh, healthy colouring and steadfast gray eyes. Both were virile, real, and would have been unusually handsome except that both had "the Cumberland nose," which was quite frankly tip-tilted. But, in spite of it, there were many girls in New York who invariably referred to Barry Cumberland as good-looking. And indeed he was, as his father still remained.

No two men could have seemed more strangely out of place in this setting. John Cumberland might have passed for an old-fashioned English squire; Barry was as typical a young man of today—sane, fit, keen—as one could find anywhere in the English-speaking world. Yet this library more closely resembled one of the Egyptian rooms at the British Museum than the favourite haunt of a prosperous man of affairs.

Egypt—unaccountable though it appeared to his friends—was John Cumberland's hobby; a hobby in which he had sunk a not inconsiderable fortune; in which he had sought, and ultimately found, it would seem, consolation for the loss of Barry's mother, who had died when Barry was seven years old.

Today the Cumberland Collection ranked as the second finest of its kind in the United States. It was representative of Egyptian civilization in all its phases—save that it contained no mummies. It was not confined to the library, but overflowed into practically every room in the house. Yet nowhere were there any mummies. This was a concession to Aunt Micky, John Cumberland's sister, who acted as the widower's housekeeper and hostess.

Whereas the loss of his wife had occasioned a wound to John

Cumberland's heart that only time had healed, the loss by his sister of the dissolute Count Colonna had left her a grateful if somewhat embittered woman. The later years of her married life had been years of hidden misery, during which she had realized to the full that, if she had married a title, Colonna had married a dowry. Time, however, had sweetened her even as it had healed her brother. She tasted the strange fruits of our modern orchard with astonishment but without dyspepsia, nevertheless firmly declining to remain under the same roof with a mummy.

"This girl on the balcony seems to have made a tremendous impression upon you," said John Cumberland, keenly watching his son across the library table.

"I can never forget her," Barry declared; for between these two was that rare comradeship which makes secrets unnecessary. "I don't mean that I have fallen in love at first sight, or anything ridiculous like that! But I have an intense curiosity to know who she is."

"You are quite sure," his father went on, carefully selecting a cigar, "that the order of events was: the girl and the crash?—not the crash and the girl? You see what I mean, Barry? You have always had an interest in these things—" he waved his cigar vaguely in the direction of the library walls—"which I suppose I have encouraged. You had it in mind to get back here to supper, and so it is just possible —"

"I quite see what you mean," Barry interrupted: "that the girl on the balcony was the beginning of delirium *after* I had banged my head? Well, of course, it's impossible to explain how I know it, but you are wrong. I certainly saw her. And what adds to my certainty is the curious behaviour of the people who took care of me afterward."

"You mean the man who brought you to the hospital and the one who towed your car to the garage?"

"Why, certainly!" Barry replied. "As not a thing was stolen, either from me personally or out of the Rolls, why should these people have deliberately kept in the background?"

"I see your point," said his father slowly; "but I rather think there was only one man concerned."

"I believe you are right," Barry agreed; "and I believe that this man was acting for the girl I saw at the window!"

John Cumberland looked up, fumbling for his lighter.

"Now," he confessed, "I don't entirely follow you."

"I mean, Dad," Barry explained excitedly, "that she must have seen me. She was looking at me. If I saw *her*, she certainly saw *me!*"

John Cumberland lighted his cigar.

"Now I begin to follow," he nodded. "You mean that she didn't want you to trace her?"

"Exactly!"

"You are sure she saw you? A flash of lightning such as you describe would have a very blinding effect."

"It did," Barry admitted ruefully, "in *my* case! But the crash took place less than twenty yards from the spot where she was standing."

"Yes," his father mused; "probably you are right. You think that she sent this mysterious man with the Studebaker to your assistance, had you taken to the hospital in Elizabeth, and then had the Rolls towed to a distant garage, with the idea that you would be unable to find the spot later? Rather a hazard. How was she to know that you were unfamiliar with the neighbourhood?"

"She might have thought it worth a chance, at any rate."

"But the object?" John Cumberland exclaimed. "What could be the object? Was she very inadequately dressed? I mean was she likely to feel ashamed of having been seen in such a condition?"

"Why, no," said Barry reflectively. "She was very strangely dressed, and, as far as that goes, scantily. But in these days that wouldn't upset her. There's some mystery about it—of this I am certain. Tomorrow I am going exploring. I wish you could come."

"Unfortunately I can't," was the reply. "I have two important conferences. But if you go, let Hemingway drive you. You have had a devil of a knock on the head, my boy, and you shouldn't overtax yourself."

Barry, however, had planned to go with Jim Sakers, who claimed to know the country like the palm of his hand. And on the following morning the two made an early start, beneath a cloudless sky which lent the towering buildings of New York an unfamiliar ethereal quality.

Jim Sakers, in appearance and in temperament, was as different from Barry Cumberland as a Gruyere cheese is different from an ivory Buddha. He was dark and of a lovable ugliness; practical to a degree that his friend sometimes found irritating; invariably good-humoured; and frankly ignorant of everything that could not be dealt with on Wall Street. An enthusiastic sportsman to whom the Arts were an awful mystery, he, withal, regarded the moody Barry more tenderly than Horatio looked upon Hamlet.

Once extricated from the crossword puzzle of New York's traffic and clear of Hoboken's shores, they began to make speed, Jim commenting continuously upon sights by the way, as was his manner, Barry answering only in monosyllables and being entirely wrapped up in his own thoughts. Presently:

"When we get to the house," he said, "I propose to call."

"Cheers!" cried Jim. "I hope the Egyptian princess keeps a good cellar.

But what for?"

"To thank her for looking after me. I shall take it for granted that she did."

"Wait until we find the house," Jim warned; "and then, wait until we get in!"

Barry smiled lightly.

"Of course we shall find the house," he asserted. "You know the way, don't you?"

"Absolutely," Jim assured him, "as far as the forks. I simply couldn't go wrong. But from there onward, I am entirely in your hands. You say you took the middle road?"

"Yes," Barry nodded. "The middle one."

He became lost in thought again, paying so little attention to his companion's cheery remarks that presently these ceased, as mile after mile was left behind and New York seemed to become very remote, in the peace of the countryside that they were traversing.

And now, undaunted, Jim began to sing, loudly.

"Dear one, the moon is waiting for the sunshine—"

"Shut up!" Barry implored. "Don't sing. Or, if you *must* sing, sing the right words. It isn't 'the moon'—it's 'the world.'"

"Oh!" Jim stared. "I don't believe it. But, anyway, I like 'the moon' better."

"The tune is all wrong as well."

"You're too blamed particular!" said Jim.

Engaged in this argument they came sweeping down a long, straight road, turned sharply to the right, and Jim pulled up.

"Behold!" he cried, and pointed.

Barry could not conceal his excitement.

"Gad!" he muttered. "It looks all different, now. But, yes, that's the road."

"Middle one, boss?"

"Yes."

"Very good, boss."

Jim grinned cheerfully and swung around into the thoroughfare indicated.

"Tell me when to stop, boss!" he shouted. *"Dear one, the moon ...'"*

He sang lustily, and inaccurately, for half a mile or more; until:

"Here we are! Left!" Barry shouted.

Jim obediently turned into the narrow way indicated by his companion, raced along it, and then:

"What's this?" he exclaimed, and pulled up sharply. A barrier confronted them. "We've got into a private road! And it's closed for repairs. Look!" He pointed to the board which clearly stated this fact. "It's been closed for a long time, too, from the look of it. You've muddled the contract, you poor nut!"

Barry sat staring blankly ahead. At last:

"Try back," he suggested. "I can't make this out."

Jim grunted, backed out to a gap, turned, and retraced the path to the high road. Slowing up:

"Now, boss," he demanded, "what next? Where's the princess?"

Barry, who had been sitting with knitted brows, looked up sharply.

"Jim," he declared, "that *was* the right road—and it was open on the night I drove along it!"

"We might park the bus and walk," Jim suggested helpfully.

"No," Barry replied; "I don't feel fit enough. Besides—"

"Well?" Jim prompted.

"Why was the road closed? There's a mystery here, Jim, and I shall never solve it by blundering in like a bull at a fence."

"Then what do we do now, boss?" Jim demanded.

"Go home!" was the reply.

"Right!" said Jim, and headed east for New York. "*Once upon a time,*" he recited, in a loud singsong, "*there was a princess . . .*"

CHAPTER IV

SHADED WINDOWS

In the days that followed, Barry Cumberland resigned himself to waiting. He was soon practically fit again, however, and he made up his mind to employ his first morning of freedom in a methodical search for the scene of his accident.

Working from the nearest base where he could garage the convalescent Rolls, he set out on foot; and in something less than half an hour had reached the barricaded road. He had come alone. Jim Sakers's open scepticism upon the subject to which he usually alluded as "Barry's princess" had begun to jar upon the victim's sensitiveness.

He made a slight detour through close-set trees and came out upon the private road twenty yards beyond. There was nothing to show that anything in the nature of repairs was taking place, and he proceeded confidently, looking about him in quest of some landmark. He found none. But presently an opening appeared on the left. Barry turned into it, pulled up, and suppressed a cry of triumph.

Hitherto completely hidden by embracing woods, a house lay forty yards back from the road. Its grounds were surrounded by a high wall, and its construction was memorable because of a turret which crowned the easterly wing of the building.

Barry stood watching it for a time, and groping for another memory which the sight of the house provoked, but which nevertheless eluded him. He realized from its situation that upon the southeast it must look sheerly down into a valley. When, and where, before, had he seen such a house? Try how he might he could not remember. Had he seen it in a dream? Surely he had looked down upon it from a great height! But when? Had the vision been prophetic—an omen? If so, an omen of what?

He advanced slowly. He bent, studying the road and the unkempt shrubbery on his left. The track was altogether too deeply rutted to have retained any imprint by which the passage of his own tires could be identified.

But now, in the very shadow of the building, he pulled up sharply, staring. There was a tree stump some four feet out from the wall, its bark newly gashed in a rather peculiar manner. The undergrowth about here, too, had an odd appearance. It was dying in patches.

Stepping back to the middle of the road, he looked up across the wall. He found that he was staring directly at a window of the house beyond— a window before which a small balcony projected!

He had made no mistake! Here it was—at this very spot—that he had crashed! Dr. Barton had been nearer to the truth than he knew when he had declared, "You seem to have tried to climb a tree." Exhilaration came. This provoking mystery was about to be solved.

Passing along the entire length of the wall without coming to any gate, Barry reached the corner and looked across a sloping lawn beyond which stone steps led down to a sunken garden. Far below lay the bowl of the valley through which ran the high road to New York. A semicircular path swept around before the long, low porch of the house, which, as he immediately noted, appeared to be deserted. All visible windows were shaded. There was no evidence of life whatever about the premises. His hopes fell to zero.

Stepping onto the porch, which looked very dusty and unswept, he pressed the bell and waited, lighting a cigarette.

There was no response; not even the barking of a dog. A second and a third time he rang with equally negative results. The thing was growing more and more extraordinary.

Since this road, now closed, clearly led to nowhere but the house, if he had imagined that figure of a girl at the window, by whom had he been taken to the hospital?

Baffled, but not beaten, he walked down the steps again. He had noted a path which clearly led to a garden at the back—a garden concealed behind that high wall against which he had crashed. He turned into it, passed under the very window in which the girl had stood, and came out at the rear of this house of mystery.

He paused in sight of the garden. Beside him was a door. It was partly open—and from beyond came an unmistakable sound of clattering pots and pans!

Barry raised his hand and rapped sharply. The sounds ceased. A minute passed in silence. Barry rapped again, more loudly.

The door was suddenly opened—so suddenly, he realized, that the woman who now stood before him must have crept forward to peep at the intruder. He found himself confronted by a truly formidable female, built for cargo rather than for speed. Her arms appeared to be wet to the elbows, and were, in the words of Jim Sakers, to whom Barry later gave an account of the interview, "as per specification. See 'Village Blacksmith,' page 1." Her muscular hands rested upon her hips. She was iron-jawed, and her regard was a challenge.

"Good-morning," he began. "My name is Barry Cumberland."

The woman did not reply.

"I could get no answer to the bell," he went on, "and came around in the hope of finding someone at home."

"There's no one home but me."

"Can you tell me when they will be back?"

"Who?"

"Well—particularly the lady. The lady whom I really came to thank for her service—"

"Say it again."

"The lady who witnessed an accident which took place outside this house two weeks ago."

The Amazon stared in silence, until:

"Forgive me," said Barry patiently, "but did you hear what I said?"

"I heard."

"Then why don't you answer?"

"I don't know what you're talking about."

"But a lady *does* live here."

"Does she?"

Barry was torn between laughter and indignation, but he feared an assault might follow any manifestation of either; therefore:

"I think I told you that my name was Barry Cumberland?" he said in his most amiable manner.

"You surely did."

"You may have heard the name?"

"You said it twice."

"Hang it all! At least you must know I mean no harm. I want to thank the owner of the house for taking care of me when otherwise I might have died on the roadside."

"There's no one home."

"So you have told me! But surely I can communicate with him somewhere? What is his name?"

"Brown."

"But there are so many Browns! What is his first name?"

"John."

Barry, stifling his rising anger, drew out a pocket case and pencil. Solemnly he noted the name "John Brown"; then:

"And at what address can I write to Mr. Brown?" he asked.

"I don't know."

"I mean, is it anywhere in America, or has Mr. Brown gone to Europe?"

"I don't know."

Apparently by accident, a ten-dollar bill dropped from the case, and Barry held it out insinuatingly. Thereupon, with suddenly dilated nostrils, the formidable guardian of the empty mansion slammed the door in his face! He distinctly heard a bolt being shot.

"Well, I'll be damned!" said he.

There are some situations from which retirement in good order is the only possible course; and Barry Cumberland recognized the fact that this was one of them. Returning his wallet to his pocket, he began to retrace his steps.

"What the devil does it mean?" he muttered.

Of the woman's antagonism there could be no doubt, nor of her loyalty to her employer. "John Brown!" Of course, it was a fabrication. She was lying, deliberately. Her instructions plainly were to give no information—and she had followed them to the letter.

The object of it all defied his imagination, but he was more than ever certain that the girl at the window overlooking the garden had been real and no figment of delirium.

As he walked slowly out to the road again, his mind was busy with possible theories. He had learned much but little. Suspicion created by the barred road was strengthened by what he had found at the house. For some unfathomable reason, the girl at the window and those associated with her were peculiarly anxious to avoid meeting him.

But the longer he considered the problem, the more hopeless it became. He determined to consult the local real estate people, to endeavour to trace the ownership of the place, and to identify this "John Brown" who was so pointedly anxious to avoid him.

CHAPTER V

BARRY IS HAUNTED

"In short," said Jim, "the princess may be described as still at large?"

"Shut up about 'the princess,'" Barry retorted. "At least I have found out that the woman didn't lie. The house actually belongs to someone called John Brown."

"Then, in private life, the—the lady—must be a Miss or a Mrs. Brown. Not a romantic name. But what did the realty sportsman tell you about this mysterious citizen Brown?"

"Very little. Said he had never seen him. And, for your enlightenment, there is no Mrs. Brown and no Miss Brown."

"Odder and odder. Have you thought that she may have been the daily help bound for a fancy-dress orgy?"

"I have not."

"Well, think about it. Sherlock Holmes would have thought about it at once. Another theory. Mr. Brown may be a bootlegger! A third theory—"

"I don't want to hear it!"

Jim Sakers looked at Barry reproachfully.

"You are not tackling this thing in the light of pure reason," he protested. "The proper method is to think of every possible solution, jot 'em all down, and then pick out the right one."

"Go to blazes!" said Barry.

He had begun to cultivate a sort of New Jersey complex, and was forever driving out into the hills which had been the scene of his strange and unfortunate experience.

One afternoon he drove as far as the club from which he had been returning when the accident had occurred. He had no particular purpose in view, beyond that of travelling over the now familiar route. The golf course was thickly dotted with players, but none of his intimate set seemed to be in the clubhouse or on the tennis courts. He smoked a reflective pipe on the veranda, watching long drives and short drives from the first tee, and then set out for home again.

Rain threatened; indeed, was only checked by a high wind. And at a point in the descending road which seemed to be peculiarly familiar for some reason, he pulled up and sat staring as one who has seen an apparition.

A long-dormant memory awoke.

Through a rift in the driving clouds sunlight poured suddenly upon a building halfway down the slope beneath, surrounded by high walls and having a curious turretlike structure at one corner!

Good heavens! It was *the* house—her house; and he had first seen it under very similar conditions on the evening of his crash! The clouds swept on, and shadow came where there had been light—just as had happened before.

He had not dreamed it, after all. But, nevertheless, his first glimpse of the building had been in the nature of an omen. Considering the fact that it lay a mile or more back from the main road, his subsequently coming to disaster under its very walls was at least an amazing coincidence.

Automatically he took out his case and lighted a cigarette, all the time watching the mystery house nestling there far below in its enclosing gardens. Once he glanced away. It was to see what prospect offered of sunlight again flooding that part of the landscape. Even as he looked back, the desired effect came about. Some quality in the atmosphere seemed to bring out details very sharply; and the result was that effected by a reducing glass. He saw the house as through the lens of a camera.

Smoke from his newly lighted cigarette rose before his eyes. Abruptly he tossed the cigarette away, and watched—watched; eagerly, fixedly.

A tiny but clear-cut figure in the distance, a girl moved in the walled garden!

She appeared to be gathering flowers. . . . The shadow of a cloud crept across and across; until once more the picture was blotted out.

Barry's heart gave a great leap. At crazy speed he swept down the valley road, taking one keen bend on two tires. Of his going he afterward remembered nothing. When, for the second time, he stepped upon the porch of "John Brown's" house, he recalled the remark of a girl he had once overheard: "Barry Cumberland is picturesquely mad," she had said.

"She was right," he reflected and pressed the bell.

The place looked as it had looked before. All the windows were shaded. There was dust on the porch. No one answered his repeated ringing.

In a state bordering upon stupefaction, he went to that side path which led to the garden. He found only a barred gate, at which he stared in unbelieving wonder. Beyond, he could see the door where he had held his interview with the unrelenting caretaker. But all around was silence. Today there was no rattling of pots and pans.

Could it be, as his father had hinted, that imagination was playing tricks with him? Had the vision at the window indeed been the outcome of an injury, and was this phantom of the garden an aftermath of it—a second illusion—a mirage? Back along the ill-kept road he walked to the barrier, where, heedless of possible loss, he had left the Rolls.

What ailed him? Was he going mad? Was his interest in this house and its occupants due to frustrated curiosity? If so, did this fully explain his waking and sleeping dreams of a dark-eyed girl in a cloudy robe, watching him from a high balcony?

Barry was taking Aunt Micky to dine that evening at a restaurant on Forty-seventh Street, which legitimately enjoyed the reputation of owning a good cellar. Jim Sakers was joining them, and bringing Jack Lorrimer. Jack was Barry's cousin. She was very pretty, having missed the Cumberland nose. Following dinner, they were going to see the most improper play on Broadway. The event was in honour of Aunt Micky, who occasionally indulged in what she termed "a night of pure sin."

Having dressed, Barry was sitting smoking in the library when she came down. He had been studying the figure of a slender priestess from the temple at Dendera.

"Well, young Cumberland," came a deep female voice, "dreaming again?"

Barry turned—he was seated on the edge of the library table—and smiled at the speaker. Countess Colonna was a woman of medium height, sturdily built, and deep-chested, as were all the Cumberlands. Her crisp gray hair was closely bobbed; her unflinching steel-gray eyes looked out from under thick, dark eyebrows to tell the world that a dissolute husband had not crushed her spirit. She had been handsome in her youth. The Cumberland nose in a woman was not unattractive.

Her dress was somewhat masculine, consisting of a smart dinner jacket with white silk waistcoat—the latter cut moderately low—a short black skirt, black silk stockings, and chic black shoes. That she had hitherto refrained from wearing trousers Barry regarded as a concession, for which he was duly grateful.

"Hello, Micky," he said—"all set?"

"Surely," his aunt replied, lighting a very large cigarette and replacing the lighter in the pocket of her jacket. "I have always avoided your speak-easy, young Cumberland, because I don't want to be mixed up in a raid. But, as I don't care for whisky with dinner, I have fallen."

"Splendid," replied Barry, laughing. "We shall make you a complete sinner yet."

"I aim to be," said Aunt Micky, "on my 'night.' The night over, there isn't a better citizen in the United States than Michael Colonna."

"There isn't a better sport in the world," added Barry affectionately.

"Pity you never married again, Micky."

"Don't be a damn' fool!" was the reply.

As they came down the steps to the street: "Hello!" said Barry, "why have we got the big car?"

"John has taken the other," his aunt replied.

She wore a French cape, red-lined, with which in the high wind she was struggling valiantly.

"Where has he gone?" Barry asked, as Hemingway held open the door of the car.

"He is dining with the man Danbazzar," Aunt Micky answered, getting in.

"That means he's spending money," Barry mused as he dropped down upon the seat beside her. "What is it this time? A scarab or half the side of a temple?"

"Can't say." His aunt shrugged her shoulders. "Don't like Danbazzar. Fascinating man, but don't like him."

"Oddly enough, I have never met him," Barry said. "But I know he has done business with Dad for years."

Presently the car pulled up before an ordinary-looking chop house, and Barry jumped out, helping Aunt Micky to alight. She stared in through the open windows, beyond which rows of tables might be seen, some already occupied; she glanced up at the signboard and looked into the narrow doorway.

"Hardly Ritzy," she commented.

"Not to look at," Barry admitted. "But the wine is *bon*; so are the liqueurs."

"Ah, well," his aunt mused, "sin leads our footsteps into strange bypaths."

They went in. Barry had reserved a table to which a very gentlemanly Irishman conducted them.

"Haven't my friends arrived, Pat?" Barry inquired.

"No, Mr. Cumberland. But you are a shade early."

Barry glanced at his watch and then at the clock. "You are right," he agreed. "What about two special cocktails?"

"Precisely," his aunt inquired, ignoring all offers of assistance and throwing her cavalry cloak across the back of a chair—"precisely what is a 'special cocktail'?"

"It is clearly indicated tonight," Barry assured her.

"Then let it be brought," said Aunt Micky.

The cocktails had just been served and Barry was studying the menu when Jim appeared in the open doorway, staring from table to table in quest of his party. Beside him stood a pretty girl wearing a very modern dance frock, a fragment of silvery gauze. Barry stood up, waving, and Aunt Micky shaded her eyes with her hand, a mannerism indicating disapproval. She drew a deep breath as the new arrivals approached, Jack Lorrimer observed of many observers.

"H'm," she murmured—"silver currency coming in again. Young Lorrimer has a dollar in front, a dollar behind and no change. Barry, the girl's nude!"

"Shut up, Micky!" said her embarrassed nephew. "Hello, Jack! Hello, Jim! They are bringing your cocktails."

When everyone was seated, Aunt Micky shaded her eyes again, surveying Jack from shingled nut-brown hair downward to the table edge.

"Are you liking my frock," the girl asked, "or hating it?"

"Neither," was the reply. "I am looking for it."

Jim applauded softly, and Jack turned to Barry for sympathy, leaning forward so that two curly heads were very close together.

"Do you see anything wrong with me?" she pleaded.

Jim watched in tragic disapproval, then rested his hand upon Aunt Micky's shoulder.

"Look at them!" he said—"admired, self-satisfied—pink and white. Micky, we brunettes must hang together!"

The dinner turned out a great success.

Aunt Micky followed a routine on these occasions: drinking red wine because of its pleasing resemblance to blood, eating a prodigious quantity of celery, taking the blue-plate item in the menu regardless of its constitution, and winding up with rum omelette in flames, because it was "so hellish."

The notorious play bored her.

"I am going home to read in bed," she declared, as they waited outside the theatre for the car. "I shall read *The Sorrows of Satan,* by Marie Corelli."

They dropped her at the Cumberland town house, an old-fashioned mansion in one of those sections of the big city where a few historic families still linger. A tired-looking person was smoking a slightly used cigar and supporting the iron post which decorated a neighbouring corner. As the door closed and Barry came down to reenter the car, the weary man saluted him.

"Bloated capitalist," Jim murmured; "living in constant terror of the honest but starving burglar. Your wretched treasures guarded night and day by detectives—"

"Yes," said Barry, laughing, and directing Hemingway through the tube. "It seems funny to me. Because I can't imagine the most hard-working burglar staggering away with a couple of hundredweights of granite sphinx on his back."

"I much prefer the detective's life," Jim continued irrepressibly. "The detective's life is the life for me. 'All forms of shadowing undertaken. Divorce and blackmail our specialties. Order your armed guards by telephone. One to five thousand—in uniform—at a moment's notice. Our watchword: Shoot to Kill. Telegraphic address: Confidence, New York'—"

"For the love of Mike," Jack implored, "be quiet for five minutes!"

The car threaded its way through Fifth Avenue, and, at the very moment of its turning into that thoroughfare sacred to prohibitive prices, a traffic signal checked them. A French limousine shot past ahead, its occupants clearly visible. They were two; and as the man was seated on the off-side, Barry had never a glimpse of his features. But the girl wore a curious black veil, of a fashion neither Oriental nor Spanish.

She had apparently just raised it, but dropped it again swiftly on seeing another car so near. Yet she failed to veil quickly enough to prevent Barry obtaining a glimpse of her face. He uttered a loud cry. To the astonishment of his friends—even Jim was silenced—he wrenched open the door and leaped out into the street!

He ran three or four paces and stood there like a madman, right in the traffic fairway, glaring after the retreating car! Its number was indistinguishable. He turned, staring back at Hemingway, who was regarding him with deep concern.

"Am I really going mad?" he muttered.

The girl in the car was the girl of the balcony!

CHAPTER VI

DANBAZZAR

The abstracted mood of Barry during the remainder of the evening was too noticeable to pass without comment. His dance partner, Naomi, a girl friend of Jack's grew very petulant, until Jack was really sorry for her. This wouldn't have mattered, but Jack showed it. Whereupon Naomi became furious.

Barry knew that he would not lack successors, however, for a lot of their crowd were there, and Naomi was what Jim termed "a star looker." Accordingly he excused himself early on some imaginary pretext and started for home. He had let Hemingway go, and he taxied back.

He longed for the solitude of his own room—for reflection.

He wanted to argue this thing out with himself once and for all. He wanted to know if he had been purposely mystified by the occupants of the hillside house, or whether he was succumbing to a delusion. This he must determine, for his highly sensitive nature demanded it. The family physician had warned him that the blow to his skull had been a severe one, and that he must on no account overtax his brain for at least a year to come. Somewhat belatedly he began to take this warning to heart.

Had it been a covert intimation that he was threatened with insanity?

The detective on duty at the corner saluted him again as he discharged the taxi. Jim Sakers's words returned to his mind while he fumbled for a key. He remembered too that his father had advocated a long vacation abroad.

What did this mean? Should he regard it as confirming his worst theories? Or did his father suspect that there was some deep plot afoot? Reared from childhood in an atmosphere of luxury, he had never hitherto appreciated, in all its significance, the fact that he was the son of a millionaire.

As he was passing the library he heard voices; one of them unmistakable, the other deep, resonant—equally unfamiliar.

John Cumberland as a rule retired early, and Barry paused, wondering whom this late visitor might be. Curious, he rapped and opened the door.

He looked down the long rectangular room. The Cumberland library was one of the acknowledged "sights" of New York, but to Barry it was a commonplace. It was lined with relics of that wonderful civilization which flourished under the Pharaohs. Its very atmosphere was reminiscent of the Nile land, of the indescribable smell of Egypt.

His father was seated in the big armchair, looking up at a wall painting from Medinet Habu. Facing him, and seated on a corner of the library table—a favourite perch of Barry's—was a man of arresting appearance.

He was in dinner kit, but in lieu of the more regular black bow displayed a stock. His hair, brushed back from a fine brow, was silver-gray; his head leonine; the pale chiselled features were of Moorish severity. He wore a short moustache and a small tuft beneath his lower lip, of that kind once known as an imperial. He was built massively, imposingly. His eyes, which at Barry's entrance had turned in the direction of the door, were light brown and, in their piercing regard, resembled the eyes of an animal. He stood up, revealing his height, which Barry estimated to be more than six feet.

"Hello, Barry!" said John Cumberland. "Glad you looked in. I should like you to meet Mr. Danbazzar."

Danbazzar raised his hand in a slow, majestic movement, and:

"I am delighted to meet Mr. Barry Cumberland," he replied, and his voice possessed a deep organ note. "But you forget, Mr. Cumberland"—turning to the elder man—"that I lay no claim to the title of Mister. I am Danbazzar; neither Danbazzar Esquire, Sir Danbazzar, nor Lord Danbazzar; merely Danbazzar."

He came forward, extending his hand.

"Mr. Barry Cumberland, I hope you and I will be friends, as your father and I have been for many years."

Half attracted, half repelled, Barry took the extended hand—and experienced a mighty grip, which greatly reassured him. He smiled.

"You can be sure of it, Mr.—I beg your pardon—Danbazzar," he returned. "I heard voices. That was why I came in."

Danbazzar inclined his head graciously and placed a chair.

"Perhaps you would like to sit here?" he said. "We are discussing a matter upon which I think your father would welcome your views."

Barry sat down, and:

"Is that so, Dad?" he asked. "What's the big argument?"

"There's no argument, Barry," was the reply; "there isn't room for any. It's a proposition, and it's up to me to say Yes or No."

"Precisely," Danbazzar murmured; and resumed his seat upon the corner of the library table.

He had an odd trick of tensing and then relaxing his lips. He did it now, looking from the older to the younger man. Then, from a box upon the table, he selected a cigarette, lighted it, and reflectively blew a puff of smoke toward the dancers and other ladies of Pharaoh's golden court displayed upon the wall above him.

Barry, his mind full of his own affairs, settled down rather reluctantly to listen.

"I am afraid this is going to be right over my head," he confessed. "But it's bound to be interesting, so fire away. What is it all about?"

Danbazzar waved his cigarette in the direction of John Cumberland, and the latter, smiling, replied:

"It's a deal in Egyptian antiquities, Barry, as no doubt you surmise. But in a new kind of antiquity—different from any Danbazzar has ever offered me before; different in every way."

"You are right," boomed the deep voice. "No such proposition has been made to any living man, I should guess, since the days of Rameses the Ninth."

Danbazzar imparted a quality of awe to this extraordinary statement which was not without its effect upon Barry. He found himself studying the large, well-shaped hand holding a lighted cigarette and discovered a curious fascination in a little scarab ring on the fourth finger. As one does upon meeting a man of whom one has heard much, he endeavoured to sum up his impressions of Danbazzar and to compare the result with what he had hitherto learned about him.

He was reputed to be the agent of an individual or a syndicate in Egypt, and it was rumoured that his activities had more than once attracted official attention. Certainly, he had been the medium through which many rare antiquities had reached collections of wealthy connoisseurs, and indeed, more than one public institution. John Cumberland's museum had been enriched by not a few items obtained in this way. And since the export of such antiques was contrary to the laws of the Egyptian government, and their importation subject to a heavy tax by that of the United States, it was only reasonable to suppose that Danbazzar was a smuggler. But he was master of his subject, a fact to which the names of his patrons testified. His nationality was unknown.

"It is some years since we have met," John Cumberland pursued, "On the last occasion, if I remember rightly, you brought me—"

He pointed to a very beautiful enamelled casket enclosed in a glass case.

"Correct," Danbazzar nodded. "There are only two of that period in existence, and the other is in the Louvre. I had the honour to supply it to France, as I told you at the time of our deal."

"Yes, I remember," said John Cumberland. "And now, Barry—" turning to his son—"I have been given first refusal of a proposition which, if it matures, will win me a place among the *real* Egyptologists; let me in on the ground floor, in fact."

Danbazzar raised his hand, checking the speaker.

"One moment, Mr. Cumberland," he interrupted, and turned to Barry, fixing upon him a penetrating glance from his extraordinary eyes. "You quite understand that what you are about to hear must not be mentioned in any shape or form to anyone now outside this room?"

"Quite," said Barry, almost startled by the intensity of the speaker's gaze. "You may rely upon me."

He glanced at his father, and realized that he was labouring under the influence of intense excitement. His voice, his colour, his movements betrayed him.

Enthusiastic though John Cumberland had always been upon this subject, Barry could never remember to have seen him quite so roused before. He felt, suddenly, that he stood upon the verge of something momentous. The shadow of Ancient Egypt at last was reaching out to touch him. He experienced a momentary shrinking, followed by a thrill of anticipation, communicated, possibly, from father to son.

"I have seen a papyrus tonight, Barry," John Cumberland went on, "which even my limited study of the subject"—he acknowledged with a smile Danbazzar's gesture of denial—"shows me to be unique. You shall see it presently, if you wish—that is, with my friend's consent."

Consent was given in a gracious gesture.

"It may mean little to you, but it has meant much to me. I foresee that reproductions of it will occupy a place in the library of every student of Egyptology. It will be more sought after than the Papyrus Harris, or the Papyrus Ebers. The discovery of the Rosetta Stone, itself, will almost be dwarfed by the publication of the Danbazzar Papyrus—"

"Mr. Cumberland!" Danbazzar's voice broke in imperiously. "You have heard my proposition with all its conditions. If you accept them, the papyrus shall be known as the 'Cumberland Papyrus.' Upon this I insist. It is no more than your due. By your efforts its authenticity must be established."

"A minor point," John Cumberland assured him. "My share will be that of a backer. You are the discoverer."

"Not of the sarcophagus," was the reply. "This has yet to be discovered, and can only be discovered by your help."

"Tremendously thrilling!" said Barry, standing up restlessly and lighting a fresh cigarette; "but, as I expected, right over my head. Does it mean a job of exploration or something?"

"It does," said his father, looking at him.

"Might I take a peep at this papyrus?"

Danbazzar bowed gravely, and from the other side of the library table took up a large portfolio having double locks. He opened it carefully and spread out a stained fragment, some three feet in length, part of which was clearly missing and other parts of which were defaced by curious stains.

It bore rows of figures of a type quite familiar to Barry, but nevertheless meaningless, and some of the colouring retained much of its original freshness. It seemed to deal with the inevitable subject of burial, but upon one figure, perfectly preserved, he fastened his gaze as if hypnotized. It was that of a slender girl, more delicately drawn than any he ever remembered to have seen. But that which held him enthralled was the resemblance, the uncanny resemblance, of this figure to the girl of the balcony.

Allowing for the conventional methods of the ancient artist, it might have been her portrait! He heard Danbazzar speaking.

"My own translation is here," he was saying, indicating a manuscript which he held in his hand. "I have asked your father to have it checked by any two authorities he may select. But the theory that I have based upon this is the point that will interest you."

"It will startle you out of your life!" John Cumberland interjected.

Barry looked up.

"What *is* the theory?" he asked, looking from face to face.

"The theory is," Danbazzar replied, "that unless some unforeseen accident occurs, or has already occurred, we shall shortly be in a position to learn some of the secrets of Ancient Egypt from the lips of one who lived there!"

CHAPTER VII

ZALITHEA

"I should be glad," said John Cumberland, "if you would just run over the main facts again for Barry's benefit."

Danbazzar inclined his head in that courtly manner which was his and glanced aside at the younger man.

"Quite so," Barry agreed. His original purpose was forgotten, for here apparently was an even deeper mystery than that which had been puzzling him. "At the moment I simply don't know what to make of it all, so please start right at the beginning."

Danbazzar took up a position before the mantelpiece. Barry could not help thinking that the background suited the figure. The man had the majestic presence of a Pharaoh.

"The facts," he began, speaking slowly and impressively and emphasizing his statements with graceful and unfamiliar gestures, "are of a sort which you would be justified in doubting if you met them in a Sunday newspaper. My reputation, though, gives them a greater value. But in spite of a life devoted to these subjects, I'm not infallible, and I won't consent to go any further, as I have already told you, Mr. Cumberland"—turning in the latter's direction—"until two other opinions have been taken."

"Your proposal is fair and reasonable," was the reply; "and I have already agreed to it."

"Very well!" Danbazzar resumed. "The story starts from five years ago, when I was paying one of my periodical visits to Egypt, and when I discovered"—he pointed—"this papyrus. I won't bore you with particulars of how it came into my possession as Mr. John Cumberland has these already. Nor can I account for its presence in the place where it was found. Enough to say that I recognized it to be genuine and immediately set to work to decipher it. I tried to restore, as far as possible, those parts which had become defaced.

"A first glance had shown me that it was not the ordinary ritual buried with most mummies. A very short study proved that is was unique—unique in every way—and that it dated from the latter part of the reign of Seti the First."

"When did he reign?" Barry asked.

"Roughly, about thirteen hundred and sixty years before Christ!"

"Good heavens!" Barry stared again at the fragment with its amazing freshness of colouring; "then this thing is something over three thousand two hundred years old?"

"Precisely," Danbazzar nodded. "In other words, it dates from a time when the art of mummifying human bodies had reached a very high state of perfection. One day, perhaps very soon, you will see the mummy of Seti himself in the Cairo Museum. You will never forget the majesty of his features preserved by that lost art for over three thousand years. I mention the fact of the high development of the art of the mummy maker at this period, because the contents of the papyrus show that this had been achieved by long years of study, and that even more extraordinary results were looked for by a certain group of students closely associated with Pharaoh's court.

"I found it to consist of two parts. The first, fortunately, almost complete, the second, as you see, with a great part missing. How much is missing I can't even surmise, but I should say that from this point"— he bent forward and laid a long finger upon the papyrus—"to the end where it is torn covers a period of some two hundred and eighty years. It bears the names, or as we should say, the signatures, of six generations of priests.

"The first and shorter part, written toward the end of Seti's reign, if I'm not mistaken, states that in accordance with the wishes of a certain learned high priest of the Temple of Amen Ra at Thebes and with the consent of Pharaoh, an attempt was made to prove that not only the physical frame but human life itself could be preserved indefinitely under peculiar conditions."

"What!" Barry exclaimed incredulously—"that a living person could be mummified and remain alive?"

"This priest," Danbazzar replied, "referred to in the papyrus—his name would mean nothing to you—believed that he had perfected a process for accomplishing this! It was all an outcome of that peculiar egotism which belonged to the Ancient Egyptians. And in this way, no doubt, he interested Pharaoh in his experiments.

"You get what I mean? The statues and records which had preserved for posterity the principal events of earlier reigns weren't good enough to tell coming ages of the greatness of Seti the First! To *his* glory a *living witness* should be left behind to testify to the ancient grandeur of Egypt. This is stated at the beginning of the papyrus, which then goes on to relate that a beautiful captive, attached to the person of the Queen, was selected for this high honour."

"High honour!" cried Barry. "You mean she was selected to be put to death!"

Danbazzar smiled slightly.

"As it is stated that she was of great beauty and bodily perfection," he admitted, "it is just possible that an element of jealousy entered into this selection. At any rate, for whatever reason, this girl was chosen, and she is referred to in the writing as Zalithea, a Princess of Unu, taken captive in the wars of Seti. As Egyptologists have never succeeded in identifying this island of Unu, we can't even guess at the nationality of Zalithea. But she possibly came from the neighbourhood of Cyprus.

"Now—" he paused, raising his finger—"the nature of the process by which this suspension of life was induced, and that by which it was to be ended, or the subject awakened, is not mentioned. This papyrus"— he lowered his finger and pointed again—"is no more than a brief statement of the fact that, in accordance with the wishes of Pharaoh, Princess Zalithea was selected for this high honour and laid in a certain tomb under the guardianship of a group of priests appointed as custodians.

"Certain funds were set aside for the upkeep of the small temple attached to the tomb, and one of the most extraordinary experiments ever attempted by man had begun."

"But," Barry objected, "while I'm not in a position to dispute the genuineness of this writing, it's—well, what shall I say?—it's really a nightmare—the dream of a madman—who unfortunately had power enough to carry it out and condemn this poor girl to a living death! Thank God we live in an age of *real* civilization!"

His father caught his eye, and:

"Don't judge until you have heard all the facts," he said. "The civilization of Ancient Egypt was more real, and higher, than you appreciate."

"That is true," Danbazzar resumed, unmoved by Barry's criticism, "as the second part of the papyrus bears out. This roughly covers the reigns of seven kings. In the ages that have since gone by, time has reduced the whole of the papyrus to a more or less uniform colour. In fact, some of the earlier colouring is brighter than the later, but here"—he stepped forward to the table—"we move from somewhere around 1365 up to somewhere about 1200 B.C. It was the duty of the priests, to which they were sworn, to examine the sleeping Zalithea at certain periods which I estimate to have been fifty years apart."

"You mean to awaken her?" Barry demanded.

"Surely!" said Danbazzar. "They were entrusted with a certain formula by means of which, in the belief of its inventor, the sleeping woman could be aroused from her trance. It was their duty at specific dates to record the results. Here we have five such records, covering a period of some two hundred and fifty years, as I estimate. Each, as you see, is confined within a ruled space, and every one is undoubtedly the work of a different scribe and possesses recognizable characteristics of the period in which it was written. Each also bears what we may term the signature of the chief priest in office at the time, and the accounts, while the wording varies slightly, all tally. The last, or the last to be preserved, states as the others state, and is attested by three witnesses, priests of the temple, that at this time *the Princess Zalithea was still living!*"

"Good God!" Barry exclaimed. "It simply isn't credible! Don't misunderstand me! I am not doubting your translation or the genuineness of the thing! But there must be some mistake!"

"You are entitled to suppose so," Danbazzar admitted. "It was because I supposed so myself that I allowed several years to elapse before making the proposition that I have made tonight to your father. During those years I have not been idle. A trusted agent of mine in Egypt, working upon such information as I could give him, had been searching—secretly, of course—and twelve months ago his search was rewarded."

"What was he searching for?" Barry asked

"He was searching for the tomb of Zalithea. You see, it would be unlikely to attract the attention of the ordinary excavator, its historical importance being slight—except in relation to this papyrus."

"Do you mean that he found it?" Barry demanded amazedly.

"He found it!" Danbazzar replied. "There *is* such a tomb!"

"Do you understand, Barry?" said John Cumberland excitedly. "Do you understand what this may mean?"

Barry in bewilderment looked from his father to Danbazzar and then stared down at the papyrus on the table.

"I worked on it all last winter," Danbazzar went on quietly. "I opened a way in—and I found myself checked by a great stone portcullis."

"You mean," said Barry dazedly, "you spent last winter in Egypt, actually excavating?"

"Actually on the job! I got away with murder. I had no permit to dig. But I've explained my system to your father. I'd hoped to go back this season; but funds won't allow. It's going to be ruinously expensive to complete that excavation. But the man who *does* complete it will make a name for himself."

"If," John Cumberland went on, "she remained alive for three hundred years, Barry, why not for three thousand?"

"But, Dad," said Barry, "this is raving lunacy!"

"It seems so," Danbazzar admitted gravely; "but five generations of learned men whose names we have here testify to the fact. Are we to assume that they were all liars? If so, with what object did they lie? I found the tomb—unopened, untouched!"

But Barry's attention had wandered again, and the words reached him but vaguely. He was staring intently at the graceful figure in the papyrus which aroused such strange memories. And now, turning to Danbazzar, and resting his finger upon that part of the record:

"What does this mean?" he asked. "Is it a symbol?"

"No," was the reply. "You will notice on the right of the figure what looks like a cartouche. I have been unable to identify it, though. Translated, it means, 'She Who Sleeps but Who Will Awaken.' For this reason I take the figure to be a portrait of the Princess Zalithea."

CHAPTER VIII

SPECIAL OPINIONS

"The last time the man Danbazzar was about," said Countess Colonna, "the result was that a motor lorry and ten men arrived. The front doors were taken off their hinges and a stone figure as big as the Statue of Liberty was carried into the library."

"I don't think it will happen this time, Micky," Barry assured her.

"I hope not," was the reply. "I don't like Danbazzar. I always imagine him living in a harem."

"I haven't met the sportsman," said Jim Sakers, "but I am going to crash into the University Club tonight and look him over keenly. If I don't approve, Barry, I shan't hesitate to advise you to drop him. On the other hand, I may be favourably impressed. And as is only fair to him, if this should prove to be the case, I shall relieve your mind at once and let you know."

"Thanks," Barry replied. "I shall be in a frightfully unsettled state until I have your opinion."

"That's quite natural," Jim agreed; "but I promise not to keep you in suspense."

"It occurs to me, young Sakers," Aunt Micky broke in, "that you and I are being deliberately kept in the dark about this thing. Young Cumberland here has a secret eye. It's his left!"

Barry laughed.

"You hit the nail on the head, Micky," he admitted. "Danbazzar has come across with a proposal about which I have promised to say nothing. It's a very queer business—more than queer, in fact; but tonight I shall know more about it. Dad has invited him to join us at the University Club with Dr. Rittenburg of the Smithsonian, Horace Pain, the big Oriental man, and Dad's old friend, Dr. Blackwell of Yale."

"What a wild party!" Jim commented. "I suppose you are going on to the Earl Carroll Vanities after dinner?"

"On the contrary," Barry assured him, "we are going on to Danbazzar's place."

"You can't delude me," cried Jim scornfully. "I see Dr. Rittenburg and Professor Blackwell dancing far into the small hours of the morning in some small but costly cabaret. I can see you all, haggard-eyed, flushed with wine, a really shocking Six, taking breakfast at Child's on Fifth Avenue as the morning sun peeps in upon the end of your debauch. Barry, I'm sorry, but you are making the pace too fast."

The dinner turned out more successful, however, than Jim had predicted. Barry's father had never before so taken him into his confidence in regard to this hobby of his life, and under different circumstances he would certainly have come prepared to be bored. As it chanced, the company proved to be so amusing that he was amazed to find how quickly the time passed.

Horace Pain, the celebrated Orientalist, was all that he had expected of him; a dry, slow-spoken scholar, whose only enthusiasm was for his subject. But Dr. Rittenburg proved to be a comedian who would have rejoiced Jim's heart. He was a round little man—a study in curves. His red face was round, his bald head was round, and he wore very round glasses. He and Professor Blackwell succeeded in keeping the party in a state of continuous laughter; for Professor Blackwell, tall, gaunt, and saturnine, had a fund of wit, as Barry knew, which seemed to be inexhaustible.

Danbazzar, too, was a delightful companion. There seemed to be few spots in the world, civilized or uncivilized, that he had not visited, from the headwaters of the Amazon to the monasteries of Thibet. The real purpose of the meeting was not touched upon, however, until the party had adjourned to the library of the club. Here, as they took their seats in an alcove, Barry observed Jim. Faithful to his promise, he had "crashed in."

With an exaggerated air of secrecy, based upon the Charlie Chaplin tradition, he crept around the gallery above, turning his back swiftly whenever one of the party looked up, and apparently searching for some book which he always failed to find. Crouching low behind the rails, so that only the top of his head and his eyes were visible, he peered down intently. This amazing piece of pantomime was only interrupted by the decision of the party to adjourn serious discussion to Danbazzar's apartment.

But, as they quitted the club and got into John Cumberland's big car which waited outside, Jim Sakers, his face buried in an evening paper, hat brim pulled down over scowling features, stood beside the steps watching intently.

Danbazzar's apartment, Barry had always been given to understand, contained a number of literally priceless objects, every one unique and irreplaceable, and any one of which he could have sold over and over again for incredible sums. Used to the orderly neatness of his father's collection, he came prepared to find something similar, although probably on a smaller scale.

The address proved to be situated amid some of the loudest noises of New York. He had thought vaguely, before, that it was an odd spot to live in. But he had not allowed for the fact that Danbazzar lived on the roof. Here, like a priest of Bel, high above all the buildings surrounding him, Danbazzar from a cloudy silence looked down upon teeming streets, thousands of lighted windows, dwarfed sky signs.

His apartment was virtually a bungalow from the porch of which one stepped into a sort of Japanese garden, with flowering vines and tortuous, spiny cacti. A large pond was approached through a loggia and peopled by golden carp. From little arbours around the wall one might look down upon a muted New York. An Arab servant, who apparently knew not one word of English, attended upon the guests; and presently they entered a large, low room, in which the famed collection was housed.

Here, Barry had a shock. The value of the statuettes, vases, mummies, caskets, items of jewellery, and other nameless relics of Egypt he could not dispute. But instead of being formally lined up in wall cases and cabinets, they were littered about the place in the utmost confusion.

A magnificently painted sarcophagus had been converted into a cupboard to contain bottles of Scotch whisky, old brandy, champagne, and other material comforts. Cigar butts disfigured the polished floor. There were books and papers lying about anywhere and everywhere.

The effect was that of a second-hand dealer's establishment in which somebody had been trying to rope a steer. He was unable to conceal his amazement, and:

"Did you ever see anything like it, Barry?" his father said, speaking in a low voice.

"Never!" he confessed. "Are these things really valuable?"

"Valuable!" exclaimed Dr. Rittenburg, who stood near. "There is a fortune in this room."

Danbazzar cleared a space upon a large table and set out the papyrus.

"Now, gentlemen," he said in his courtly manner, "let us get to the business of the evening. I have given you, Dr. Rittenburg, and you, Mr. Pain, an opportunity of examining and testing this piece of writing. I await your opinion."

"I have anticipated it," said John Cumberland, in a voice that betrayed suppressed excitement.

Horace Pain removed the cigar from between his teeth, cleared his throat, and:

"I know Professor Rittenburg's opinion," he said, "and he knows mine. The papyrus is undeniably genuine. It has points of resemblance to the Turin Papyrus which I shall presently point out, as I have already pointed them out to my friend Dr. Rittenburg. Respecting the claims of its writer, or writers, I shall have nothing to say. This is outside my province. As, I take it"—turning to John Cumberland—"it is outside yours? I mean, your interest, like mine, is in the writing itself, not in what it states."

"Partly," John Cumberland replied, glancing swiftly in Danbazzar's direction.

"Well," Pain went on, in his dry, hard voice, "I mean to say that a parallel is the medical papyrus in Berlin. No one would think of making up a prescription from it. You agree with me, Professor?"—turning in the direction of Professor Blackwell.

"I agree with you entirely," was the reply. "It contains among other things a prescription for a hair restorer which, I will guarantee, would turn Paderewski bald in a fortnight."

"Exactly," Dr. Rittenburg agreed. "I look upon this business of the sleeping Princess as a sort of religious ritual, Cumberland, similar to the worship of the Apis Bull—only kept up for political reasons to delude the people, and to preserve the immortal name of Seti. Something of that kind."

"Quite beside the point, gentlemen," Danbazzar's deep voice broke in. "The fact that the papyrus is genuine and, in your opinion, dates from the time of the Pharaoh mentioned in it is the thing of interest to Mr. Cumberland and to myself."

"Of this I am certain."

Dr. Rittenburg nodded his round head vigorously.

"So am I," Horace Pain admitted. "Of course, its publication will create a profound sensation, and the museums of the world will outbid one another to get it."

"They will bid in vain," Danbazzar replied. "Mr. John Cumberland has acquired it."

"Ah!" exclaimed Dr. Rittenburg. "But of course you will publish a reproduction? Every student in the world is entitled to access to such a discovery."

John Cumberland smiled happily. No triumph that his business had offered or could offer compared with the thrill of such a moment as this.

"In due course," he said, "but not yet."

Whereupon a debate arose concerning certain papyri, with the mere names of which Barry was unacquainted, and their points of resemblance to this one. Much excellent old brandy aided the debate. The two experts disagreed fiercely; but at a late hour, Dr. Rittenburg and Horace Pain having departed quite reconciled:

"Now," said John Cumberland, "with Danbazzar's consent, I shall discuss this matter with you, Blackwell. Your province is rather physiological than archeological. We have had expert opinion on the papyrus itself, and now we should like to have your opinion upon the feasibility of the claims made in it."

The silent Arab replenished the guests' glasses, except the Professor's; for Blackwell, who was already lost in thought, waved him aside. The distinguished scientist was a tall man, though not so tall as Danbazzar, and built bonily. He was clean-shaven, with a long strong nose; and from his high brow, hair which was beginning to go gray was carelessly brushed back. His clothes would have fitted someone else better than they fitted the Professor, and he wore a low double collar with his dinner jacket, allowing free play to an enormously developed Adam's apple.

His eyes, behind the thick pebbles of his glasses, resembled two interrogation marks.

"I never jump to conclusions," he began, thoughtfully selecting a cigar from a box which Danbazzar slid across the table in his direction.

The box was an Ancient Egyptian curiosity, but Professor Blackwell had not even noticed the fact: his thoughts were elsewhere.

"Life," he went on, "considered in the abstract, is the one thing of which Science knows nothing. Adolf Weisman maintained that duration of life is dependent upon adaptation to external conditions. We may take the case of what is sometimes termed 'mummy wheat.' Personally, I cannot vouch for these stories."

"*I* can," Danbazzar said gravely. "I myself have seen grains of wheat taken from a tomb of the fourteenth dynasty cultivated."

"Did they yield any crop?" the Professor inquired.

"No," Danbazzar acknowledged. "They shot up a very tender green to a height of six inches and then died."

"Quite, quite," murmured the Professor, "but the life principle was present, you see—dormant, but present. There is the case of a toad imprisoned in a rock cavity for several generations, vouched for by persons of repute, and I once examined, in India, a fakir who claimed the power to unhitch his spirit from his body. Under these conditions he presented every appearance of death and existed without visible wasting for a long period unsustained by food or drink of any kind. The question really is whether the tissues could be preserved over so long a period as this"—nodding toward the papyrus—"indicated."

"If for three hundred years, why not for three thousand?" John Cumberland demanded.

"Quite, quite," the professor murmured; "but unfortunately this fact rests upon what I may term 'hearsay.' The people who wrote it have been dead for some little time, you must remember!"

There was a short silence, broken by Danbazzar.

"Have you ever seen the mummy of Seti the First?" he demanded in his deep, impressive tone.

"Yes." Professor Blackwell looked up slowly. "Curiously enough, I was thinking about him. He, of course, dates from somewhere about the same period as Princess Zalithea, and the preservation in this case is remarkable. But the system of mummifying employed on Seti could not be employed on a living person. It is very interesting, though—very interesting. A German physiologist whom I met in Berlin recently—I forget his name, but he was a knowledgeable man—was anxious to attempt some experiment of the kind, in a small way, upon a hypnotized subject. The difficulty, of course, was to find the subject."

"Naturally!" said Barry, laughing.

The Professor glanced aside at him over his spectacles. And then:

"I pointed out to my German acquaintance," he went on, "that normal processes of decay would proceed under these conditions quite inevitably. And if there is anything in the extraordinary claims made in this papyrus, I can only assume that some formula must have been invented to check these processes. Of course, it is frightfully empirical. One dare not raise such a thing seriously before modern science. It would spell ruin."

"Nevertheless," said Danbazzar, "you are right—there was such a formula."

"Ah!" exclaimed John Cumberland, "if only we could recover it."

"I *have* recovered it," Danbazzar replied calmly.

"What!"

"I acquired it at the same time that I acquired this other papyrus. It is locked in that safe over there."

"That settles it," said Cumberland, standing up. "My other plans are made. What do you estimate it would cost, Danbazzar, to finance the expedition?"

"Two hundred thousand dollars," was the prompt reply.

"Be ready in a fortnight," said Cumberland. "I must start then or postpone the journey till next season."

CHAPTER IX

EGYPT BOUND

"Some people are so indecently lucky," Jim Sakers protested. "It has been my ambition from childhood to visit the interior of the Sphinx."

"You poor nut!" said Barry. "The Sphinx is solid. You mean the interior of the Pyramid!"

"Not so hasty," Jim rebuked him, "not so hasty, my friend. My ambitions are not the ambitions of an ordinary man. Any fool can visit the interior of the Pyramid if he's lucky enough to get to Egypt. Nothing so commonplace as that appeals to me. I said, and I repeat, that it has always been my ambition to visit the interior of the Sphinx. I hope I make myself clear."

"You expose fresh views of your ghastly ignorance at every turn," Barry said. "If you can think clearly for two minutes, concentrate on what I'm going to say. Everybody seems to think that I need a vacation, and Dad has decided to pay a visit to Egypt and to spend the beginning of winter there."

"Lucky, lucky man," Jim murmured.

"He is keen for me to go with him," Barry went on; "and as I have never been out of America yet, the idea rather appeals—"

"Rather appeals!" Jim echoed. "Oh! the blasé youth of this generation! I should cheer for an hour without stopping if my honoured parent could be induced to get out of touch with Wall Street for a weekend!"

"In brief," Barry pursued patiently, "the idea that I am trying to drive into your thick skull is this: I am going to Egypt, and I am going next week."

"This is dreadful," Jim declared. "Think of the broken hearts in New York. Besides, what about the Princess?"

"It is about the Princess," Barry returned, "that I want to speak to you. Several people, yourself included, have tried to convince me that I'm suffering from a delusion where this girl is concerned. But I am just as certain as ever that I have seen her, definitely twice, possibly three times. What I want to ask you is this: Once in a while, when you are in that neighbourhood, see if you can find anything out."

"You mean," Jim suggested, "drop in on Mr. Brown and say that I have called about the electric light, or the installment due on the Ford, or something of that kind?"

"Something of that kind," Barry agreed. "Do it your own way—but just keep a sharp lookout. And if you should pick up any information, send me a cable. I can't give you the route. When we get to some place up the Nile where we are going to camp, I shall have to let you know."

"Consider it done," said Jim. "And now, *I* have a request to make. Bring me back a large bottle filled with the sand of the unchanging desert. By sprinkling this in my bathroom and walking about in bare feet, I shall be able to imagine that I am a son of the mysterious East. Ho, there! Fatima, my dark-eyed ship of the desert!"

"The expression 'ship of the desert,'" Barry interrupted, "usually refers to a camel!"

"I am talking about a camel," Jim assured him. "The affection of the Arab for his camel is an historical fact."

"You are thinking about his horse!"

"I am not thinking about his horse!" Jim cried. "The Arab I am talking about *has* no horse, he has a camel."

And now: "What's the row?" demanded a deep voice.

Aunt Micky intruded, carrying a large hatbox.

"Hello! Micky!" Barry exclaimed. "Been shopping again?"

"Yes," was the reply; "it has just arrived. The best that Dobbs could do for me."

Opening the box, she produced a sun helmet of dazzling white, decorated with a puggaree band in silver, violet, and maroon.

"Great shakes!" Jim exclaimed. "Is this for Barry?"

"It is," Aunt Micky returned firmly. "It is most important that he should not expose his skull to the rays of the sun. John always wears a helmet in the East."

"I know he does," Barry admitted ruefully, contemplating this "creation," "but the one he wears is a decent sort of putty shade—and without ribbons. However! Is it the right size?"

He tried it on.

"Really smart people," Jim commented, "wear a feather—a small, neat feather—stuck in the band just above the left ear. I am told that everyone will be wearing them this season. Didn't they tip you this at Dobbs', Micky?"

"They tipped me a lot of things," Micky returned, lighting a cigarette, "and there are lots of things I could tip *you!*"

"I know it," he said; "my ignorance is appalling. But on one point Park Avenue is agreed. I *do* know how to dress. Further, I don't merely put on my clothes—I wear them! Allow me, Barry."

He raised his hands and settled the helmet at an angle over Barry's right ear, then took a step back to contemplate the result.

"Better," he muttered, "better. That is the British Army rake. Of course—" again grasping the helmet and tilting it forward—"there is the Rajah rake, very popular in India, and *also*—"

He was about to take further liberties when Barry gave him a playful but powerful punch in the chest.

"And *also* there is the complete limit," he said, "and you reach it every time, Jim."

Taken all around, however, the period of preparation was an exciting one for Barry. His father was an experienced traveller and, under his guidance, Barry acquired all sorts of equipment for the journey. On the advice of Danbazzar, most of the camp gear, the firearms, and the impedimenta of the excavator, they were picking up in London. Danbazzar had prepared a formidable list of these, and Barry discovered a great fascination in merely reading it.

The papyrus had disappeared into Danbazzar's great safe, and Barry often wondered if his imagination had played him tricks in regard to the portrait of Princess Zalithea. He had abandoned hope of ever seeing this girl of dreams again; but Fate had one more curious experience in store for him, and it came about in this way:

Professor Blackwell was leaving for Europe a week ahead of them, and later joining the party in Egypt. Bound to strictest secrecy regarding the nature of the expedition, his scientific curiosity had been greatly aroused, and he had consented to be present at the opening of the tomb when that time came.

The steamer sailed at midnight, and Professor Blackwell had dined at the Cumberland home prior to joining her. Barry and his father went on board with him, inspected his stateroom, ascertained that his baggage had arrived safely, and then:

"There is no point in waiting," said the Professor. "We don't sail for another twenty minutes or so, but it is my custom on these night sailings to turn in. I leave unpacking until the morning. I hate all this fuss and bustle!"

"As you like, Blackwell," said John Cumberland. "See you in Cairo—or, if you have gone up the river, in Luxor. Hope you have a nice crossing."

Barry and his father came down the gangway, turned to wave to the tall, gaunt Professor at the top, and then made their way along the pier toward the staircase. They reached the street level at practically the same moment that the elevator started up.

Through the iron grille of the car a girl was looking out, apparently directly at Barry.

He stopped dead, stared at the ascending elevator, and then, with no explanation to his father, turned and fled back up the stairs like a man demented!

His behaviour was so extraordinary that a Customs official intercepted him at the top.

"Kindly stand aside!" Barry said breathlessly. "I have seen someone I want to speak to—*must* speak to!"

"Go easy, go easy!" The man persistently intruded his burly form. "Wait a minute! Who are you running away from?"

"I'm not running away from anybody!" cried Barry angrily. "Let me pass! I want to go on board."

"Go easy!" the man repeated. "You can't go on board. The last visitors are just coming ashore. In three minutes the gangway will be cleared —"

And then John Cumberland, even more breathless than Barry, arrived on the scene.

"What's the matter?" he asked; and, to the man: "It's all right," he explained. "My name is John Cumberland. My son has seen someone he thinks he knows."

"You can guess who it is!" the latter returned. "And I've lost her again!"

Slipping past the mystified Customs officer, he raced out along the pier.

Beyond exciting amusement and astonishment among the onlookers, his reward was nil. Of course! He was too late! And he was sure, absolutely sure, that this time he had not been mistaken! Could it be that she had gone on board the liner?—that she was leaving America—still unknown, elusive to the end!

He was prevented from reaching the gangplank. The order "Clear away!" was given as he ran up. Realizing the hopelessness of the thing, he turned and went back to where his father waited. His manner was constrained.

As they drove home, John Cumberland was very sympathetic, but secretly was glad to think that the journey to Egypt would prove a powerful distraction, which he considered his son badly needed. He was growing more and more anxious about this odd obsession of Barry's.

> We are no other than a moving row
> Of magic shadow-shapes which come and go,
> Round with the sun-illumined lantern held
> In midnight by the Master of the Show.

The Master of the Show had many more queer tricks and illusions in store. But neither Barry nor John Cumberland, being poor mortals, could peep behind the scenes. The ensuing week passed like a feverish dream, so magically does time dissolve on such occasions—and the night of their departure for Egypt came.

A tremendous crowd of friends turned up to see them off, Aunt Micky more iron-jawed than usual, and full of dark theories respecting missing baggage (which was really safely on board, of course).

"Clean your teeth in Vichy water," was her last injunction to Barry. "Once you are out of England, all water is poison."

Then came the final shouted farewells, Danbazzar, Barry, and John Cumberland standing at the rail as the liner crept out of her dock. Much cheering and waving of hats. Great excitement, to be followed by depression. And over it all came a clarion cry from Jim Sakers, standing bareheaded far below, a megaphone upraised.

"Don't forget, Barry!" he bellowed—"a bottle of the Unchanging Desert! I am an Arab brave and free!"

CHAPTER X

CAIRO

From the balcony of Shepheard's Hotel, Barry fascinatedly watched the life in the street below. This was Cairo!—real yet less than his imaginings concerning it.

Vendors of fly whisks, of scarabs incredibly old, of necklaces from the tombs of queens, of red slippers, of all sorts of Birmingham ware, clamoured in a group beneath him. They poked their offerings through the railings at his feet. The instinct of these people was wonderful. His father was never solicited in this way. One glance the sidewalk merchants would give him, smile sadly and pass on. While of Danbazzar they seemed to be positively afraid.

The passers-by absorbed his attention. He had learned to pick out the residents from the tourists, to recognize the curious air of detachment, that quiet fatalism which is the seal of Africa. He had also grown used to the *tarbûsh* worn by the British officers. At first he had mistaken them all for Turks. But he was not yet entirely reconciled to the presence of laden camels and smart automobiles in the same street.

In some of the cars he had glimpses of veiled women, whose long dark eyes provoked him. Whenever such a *harem* car went by, he craned forward eagerly, vaguely expecting to meet the glance of eyes that he knew.

During the journey, he had torn himself free in a measure from this strange infatuation, but Egypt had revived his dreams.

He had dressed early this evening, and now, sipping a cocktail, sat waiting for his father to join him. It was too hot yet for the big tourist invasion, but the advance guard was already in possession. Guide books were in evidence at several tables in his immediate neighbourhood. To whatever government, Turkish, French, British, or Egyptian, the people may from time to time acknowledge obedience, everybody knows that Egypt really belongs to Thomas Cook & Son.

Tonight, Danbazzar was expected back from Luxor, where he had been to select a base of operations and to check the information furnished by his agent. This agent, Hassan es-Sugra by name, had met him there four days earlier and was returning with him to Cairo.

John Cumberland's excitement had been intense all day, and Barry's little less. Never, until now, had Barry fully understood the hold that Egypt and the things of Egypt had over his father. It was a complete, an absorbing passion. The John Cumberland of New York was barely recognizable in this keen, alert, bright-eyed man to whom the African air was an elixir of youth, and who now crossed the terrace and joined him.

"Well, Barry," said he, "has the spell of the Nile got hold of you yet?"

"It has, Dad," Barry admitted, looking at the healthily tanned face of the speaker; "I'm simply dying to start. I went again today to look at the mummy of Seti; and even now I find it hard to believe that this man ruled over Egypt, a civilized country, at a time when Europe was peopled by savages, and when the American Continent was probably a mix-up of mountains, forests, swamps, and rivers. That man was no savage, he was a ruler of great power and intellect."

"Certainly he was," John Cumberland agreed, nodding to an acquaintance coming up the steps. "We are very proud of our new wisdom, Barry. I wonder how much of it is in advance of the old?"

"I hadn't been altogether able to believe in your hopes of success," Barry went on, "but the figure of Seti is beginning to make me share them. There he lies in the flesh for everyone to see. I looked at him yesterday for nearly half an hour, and I realized that he had known, probably had many times spoken to, the Princess Zalithea! Dad, I'm just crazy to be on the job! Isn't Danbazzar late?"

John Cumberland glanced at his watch; then:

"No," he replied. "The train got in about ten minutes ago. He should be here at any moment now."

And even as he spoke an *arabiyeh* pulled up at the steps and Danbazzar got out.

He wore a white drill suit, the coat cut tunic fashion and buttoning close up to the neck. His light gray felt hat with its very wide brim awakened in this Eastern scene memories of the West. His pale skin had assumed a deep, even tan, and, with his aquiline features, he looked more truly of the Orient than any of the Cairenes about him.

His gaze sought and found John Cumberland on the terrace, and he raised his right hand in a slow, graceful gesture. A second traveller descended from the carriage and followed Danbazzar up the steps.

This was an aesthetic-looking Egyptian, black-robed and white-turbaned, slender, with small delicate features and the gentle eyes of a gazelle. He carried an ebony cane and possessed a curious dignity, utterly unlike that of Danbazzar, yet in its way equally impressive.

John Cumberland sprang up eagerly and extended his hand.

"Is everything all right?" he demanded.

"Everything is fine," Danbazzar replied, and, turning, greeted Barry. "I want you to meet our Chief of Staff, Hassan es-Sugra. What I don't know about the Valley of the Kings, Hassan can tell us."

Hassan saluted profoundly, and Danbazzar now gave him permission to be seated. Discreetly, he took a chair a little removed from the others and waited to be addressed.

John Cumberland glanced around to make sure that he could not be overheard; and:

"How many men have you got?" he asked.

"Hassan has engaged fifteen," was the reply. "Most of them are already in Luxor."

"No suspicion has been aroused?"

"Absolutely none," Danbazzar assured him. "So far, there hasn't been a single hitch."

"I take it these men are living in Luxor at present?" Barry asked.

"Yes. In the native quarter, where most of them have friends; for they are all excavators and used to the work."

"We will have cocktails in my room," said John Cumberland. "One never knows who may overhear us."

The party went upstairs to Cumberland's suite, which overlooked the romantic gardens of the hotel, and cocktails were ordered. Hassan es-Sugra was a devout Moslem, one who had made the pilgrimage to Mecca. He drank coffee, which, when the waiter presently appeared, he took with him out on to the balcony, bowing deeply as he retired.

"That's a mysterious fellow!" said Barry.

Danbazzar fixed the speaker with his piercing regard, and:

"You're right," he agreed. "He's quite a lot of mystery. But he holds some kind of position in the Moslem world that gives him complete control of the natives. He's the best man at the job in Egypt. He can get things done that you or I couldn't manage if we spent a million dollars. Yes, sir, Hassan es-Sugra is worth his weight in gold, and he knows the game from A to Z."

"Good!" commented John Cumberland. "I know the type and I believe you. Wasn't he with Flinders Petrie at one time?"

"The tomb?" asked Barry Cumberland eagerly. "It has not been disturbed?"

Danbazzar stood up, and slowly crossing to a side table, dropped ash into a tray. He turned and:

"It's absolutely untouched," he replied. "The entrance where I reclosed it is almost hidden by sand. You can rest easy." He paused impressively. "No one has disturbed her."

"Gad!" Barry brought his hand down upon his knee. "It sounds almost too good to be true! But how did Hassan identify the tomb in the first place? How was he sure? How can *you* be sure?"

"You can take it I made sure before I started," Danbazzar answered calmly, "but, anyway, Hassan never makes a mistake. You remember the cartouche in the papyrus? It was not that of any Pharaoh or any member of any known royal family. It was clearly meant to represent Princess Zalithea."

He stooped over the cane table at which John Cumberland and his son were seated. With a pencil he roughly outlined upon a newspaper which lay there a design of four figures.

"We're agreed," he said, glancing up, "that its meaning is: 'She Who Sleeps but Who Will Awake.' Both Mr. Pain and Dr. Rittenburg have checked this."

"Well!" said Barry eagerly.

"Well!" Danbazzar replaced the pencil in a breast pocket of his tunic. "This same inscription is cut in the rock before the entrance of the tomb!"

"I have sometimes wondered," said John Cumberland, "why it has been overlooked so long."

Danbazzar stared at him for a moment, and then:

"Have you stopped to think," he asked, "how many tombs there are in that valley? Why should those few people with powers to excavate open an obscure one? What's more, the tomb is in an unfrequented spot, almost due north of the Tombs of the Queens and on the edge of the western valley, more than half a mile from the Tombs of the Kings. The nearest place ordinary tourists ever visit is the tomb of Queen Nefertari and that of Seth Ra, the wife of Seti the First. This was about where I figured to find it. Seven miles farther west, and about a mile and a half north of the caravan road from Farshut to Kurna, Hassan has put up our men. There's a small Hawwara village there, and the Sheik is a good friend of mine."

"When do we start?" cried Barry eagerly.

"I can see no reason," Danbazzar replied, "why we shouldn't leave for Luxor in the morning. We shall be wise to take every advantage of the slack season before the tourist rush begins."

Barry watched the speaker fascinatedly. During his short stay in Cairo, he had been out to visit the Sphinx, that long-cherished ambition of Jim's; he had penetrated to the interior of the Great Pyramid, and had wandered through the fascinating bazaar streets of the Mûski. He had known the whole indescribable atmosphere that creeps over the most modern and garish hotel in Cairo when night drops its cloak upon Egypt. Now, it seemed to him, watching Danbazzar, that of all the mysteries that the Nile has known, this man was the greatest.

"And now, I suggest that we consult with Hassan," Danbazzar went on.

He stood up, clapping his hands sharply. From the shadowy mystery of the balcony, Hassan es-Sugra entered, a slim, impressive black figure. He bowed low upon the threshold.

CHAPTER XI

LUXOR

The Nile was high. Much of the Memnonia was impassable. The Colossi sat lonely in the midst of a great lake, when Barry came to Luxor. In this way he saw the City of the Sun under advantageous conditions.

The Winter Palace Hotel, whose impudent modernity aspires to dwarf the majesty of the great temple, was in a comatose state. Its palatial suites which later in the season would echo Wall Street quotations, its public rooms where, anon, much talk would be heard about the situation in the English coalfields and the cheery optimism of Mr. Baldwin, these were empty. Empty was the dragomans' bench before the entrance. No guttural German voices were raised in argument against the soft music of Arabic impostors, relative to the cost of donkeys from Kurna to Dêr-el-Bâhari. The tourist steamers were missing; yet Barry did not miss them.

Sighing wearily at the end of her summer sleep, the City of the Sun looked wistfully down the Nile from which at any time now invasion might be expected.

Barry had conceived something very like friendship for Hassan es-Sugra. The man fascinated him. Delicate in form and features, soft-spoken and mild-eyed, slow of movement and speech, invariably unruffled, Barry had detected beneath the velvet surface an indomitable will, and something else.

On the evening of their arrival, leaving Danbazzar and John Cumberland at the hotel poring over rough plans, Barry had set out with Hassan to view the celebrated spectacle of Karnak by moonlight. The evening was oppressively hot. The sky looked like a dome of lapis lazuli. The moon was such a moon as gave birth to Isis; fronds of palms seemed to be carved out of ebony; and the whiteness of the buildings was dazzling. Plaintive notes of a reed pipe crept up from the river, with more distant throbbing of a *darabukkeh*.

A great zest of life, an eagerness to inhale, as it were, the unfamiliar perfume of this strange land, possessed Barry. He hurried as though bound for his father's New York office. But:

"Sir," said Hassan, in his soft, caressing voice, "there is no need for haste, and the evening is hot."

Barry pulled up and glanced aside at his companion. The gaze of the gazelle-like eyes met his own. Hassan smiled.

"Always," the speaker went on hesitantly yet with perfect expression, "always the gentlemen who come from America and from Europe are in so great a hurry; particularly the gentlemen from America. Yet there is so much time, and life in Egypt is very beautiful for those who will rest and enjoy it."

Barry laughed.

"No wonder you always look so cool," he commented. "Now I come to think of it, I have never seen you hurry."

Hassan extended his slender brown hands, his ebony stick held lightly between the first and second fingers of the left.

"What is there to hurry for?" he asked softly. "We are all going the same way. Why should we try to pass one another? Everything that life has to give us is ours tonight. Let us enjoy it, for tonight will never come again."

Barry stared curiously at this survival of the Arabian philosophers, but checked his eager steps and walked on sedately beside the dignified Egyptian.

Spots of interest were pointed out by Hassan, and, as they moved through the streets, it became apparent to Barry that his companion possessed many acquaintances in Upper Egypt by whom he was held in high esteem.

A most notable demonstration of this came when they passed a café in the native town. A number of men sat smoking outside. Five of them, on sight of the approaching figure, sprang up and performed a graceful Arab salute with the right hand. All were fine types, tall muscular fellows, and different from the townsmen surrounding them. Hassan es-Sugra gravely returned their salutation, but they remained standing until the café was passed.

"Who were those men, Hassan?" Barry asked.

"They are some of our excavators, sir," Hassan replied. "Most of them are already at the camp: these are late arrivals who go tomorrow."

Barry glanced curiously at the delicate, almost effeminate face of the speaker, and he wondered, as he had wondered many times before, how Hassan es-Sugra had inspired, and how he retained, the profound respect of these men.

And so, pursuing their leisurely way, they presently found themselves on the ancient road to Karnak, formerly bordered by Sphinxes throughout the mile of its length. The silence now was broken only by the distant note of a pipe, the faint throbbing of a drum. Barry grew silent, too, awed by the sleeping past upon which he intruded. At that point where the road turned left into the Avenue of the Rams he sighted the great shadowy ruins and hastened his steps.

"It is fortunate, sir," Hassan said, laying one slender hand upon Barry's arm to check this impetuous increase of pace, "that we have been able to begin while the Nile was in flood."

"Why is that?" Barry asked.

"Because," Hassan replied, "the tomb, which is on high land, can only be approached from above at this season and is cut off from those routes along which people generally come. We are less likely to be disturbed."

At the entrance to the Temple, the *Ghafir* appeared, mysterious, out of a bank of shadow. Barry, a law-abiding citizen, had been given to understand that he must show his ticket here, but Hassan es-Sugra waved him aside, saluted the guardian, was saluted deeply in return, and they entered the great, silent building.

Again Barry found himself glancing curiously at the face of his companion, delicately beautiful in the moonlight. He was learning a lesson that anyone susceptible to truth learns in Egypt. He was learning to look with less satisfaction upon the hurriedly grasped successes of modern life, and to experience an unpleasant sense of inferiority in the company of this dignified, placid, yet majestic Arab.

Those who are sent to govern in these lands must be of a type immune from such impressions. Barry had too much poetry in his nature to be blind to some strange spiritual calm possessed by Hassan es-Sugra (whom Aunt Micky would have briefly classified as a heathen), the secret of which has been lost during generations of feverish endeavour.

He found himself amid a forest of vast columns; statues looked down upon him scornfully; and all about him upon painted walls were those Pharaohs and gods whom the imagination of Pierre Loti has depicted as eternally signalling to one another. Bats haunted high, shadowy places, and the note of some night bird sounded eerily.

Hassan es-Sugra walked through the mysterious darkness as confidently as Barry would have walked along Fifth Avenue, until they came to the Great Hall, most awe-inspiring of all the Egyptian monuments. He seemed to know every inch of the place. The hieroglyphics held no mystery for him. Raising his stick he pointed to an inscription, translating slowly:

"I did the best I could for the Temple of Amen, as architect of my Lord. I placed obelisks, their height reached to the world of heaven. A propylon is before the same in sight of the city of Thebes; and ponds and gardens of flourishng trees. . . ."

"Who made this inscription, Hassan?" Barry asked.

"He was the First Prophet of Amen," was the reply, "in the reign of Rameses the Second, who was the son of Seti the First."

Barry did not reply. A new idea had possessed him; a new magic had invested the building. Here, in this vast, wonderful temple-place, SHE must have walked—the Princess Zalithea!—the beautiful, mysterious girl of the past who was so like that other, who lived, who surely lived, in the present! His blood tingled, impatience claimed him, and, suddenly turning to Hassan:

"When do we begin to excavate?" he asked abruptly.

"I hope, sir, the day after tomorrow."

"Good!" said Barry.

The magic of Egypt had got into his veins. He knew that whatever else life might hold for him, wherever Fate should guide his steps, always until the end he would hear it calling him—calling him back to the Nile.

Later that night in the almost deserted lounge of the hotel he got into conversation with a very bored young man whose job was connected with the Irrigation Department. In a less virulent case this young man could not have failed to prove a perfect antidote.

"Dead-alive hole, this," he declared, "out of the season. Did you stay long in London?"

"A week," Barry replied.

"Lucky man!" sighed the other. "I would cheerfully sell all Egypt, if it belonged to me, for a week in London. See any new shows?"

"One or two."

"Gad! I'd see one every evenin'! And after the show I'd go on to the Kit Cat, first night; the Embassy, next night; Ciro's, third night. And so forth."

"Really?" said Barry. "That's odd! The life in London or New York or Paris seems to be much the same. I've been fed up with the usual round for years!"

"I've never had a chance to get fed up," the other declared plaintively. "I went straight from Oxford to the war, straight from the war to hospital, and straight from hospital to this blasted hole."

"Don't you get a vacation sometimes?"

"*Sometimes* is right," said the other.

Barry laughed at his acquaintance's pessimism and ordered another drink. As the waiter brought it:

"You are not here for fun, are you?" the irrigation man inquired wearily; "because there's nothing funny about Luxor."

"No," said Barry guardedly. "My father and I are here on a job of work."

"You are not goin' to try to Americanize Egypt, are you?" the other suggested.

"Not exactly," Barry replied. "Dad has a scheme for exploiting the old caravan road to the Dakhla Oasis."

"What for?" drawled his acquaintance. "Nobody wants to go there!"

"They might," Barry returned, "if the journey were easier."

"Goin' to build a hotel there?"

"I don't quite know, but we are starting out tomorrow to prospect."

"Good luck!" murmured the irrigation gentleman, raising his glass. "If I'm still alive when you come back you might bring me a few dates. They are the best dates in Egypt. I don't think they grow anything else."

Their chat was interrupted at this point by the sudden appearance of Professor Blackwell, expected that evening from Assouan and evidently newly arrived.

"Ah! Professor!" cried Barry, jumping up. "Glad to see you! Does Dad know you are here?"

"No," the Professor replied, dropping into an armchair. "I have only this very moment come in."

Barry introduced the Professor to the irrigation expert, who presently, however, having offered to buy more drinks, withdrew to what he termed his "fly trap," nodding gloomily to Barry as he went.

"Don't forget the dates," were his parting words.

Going back to their rooms, Barry ushered in Professor Blackwell. John Cumberland, who was seated at a table studying some maps, stood up gladly to greet him. Danbazzar, his broad back to the room, was staring out of the open window across the Nile to where, sharp in the moonlight, the Libyan Hills were outlined against the sky. He turned, fixing his penetrating regard upon the new arrivals; and:

"Hassan tells me," Barry began eagerly, "that we start operations on Thursday. Is that correct?"

"It's surely correct," came Danbazzar's deep voice. "I don't know who's been giving public recitations, but it looks like some of our plans have leaked out. Yes, sir, we start on Thursday."

CHAPTER XII

THE CAMP IN THE DESERT

Barry now entered upon a period of existence widely different from any he had known. Danbazzar's camp was in the neck of a *wâdi* on the north of the caravan route from Thebes to Farshût. Further north, and visible from the tents, on the summit of a mountain stood an ancient watchtower, used in the days of the Pharaohs by the tomb guard. All about were remains of stone huts which had probably been the quarters of these guards. On the right, above terraced, desolate hills covered with debris of abandoned excavations, rose the stately mass of El Kurn, the Horn.

Here in this weird quarry to which no one ever penetrated, they had their base of operations. The native excavators, in charge of a headman who proved to be one of the group that had been seated outside the Luxor café, had their quarters several miles distant, in a sort of tumbledown village principally inhabited by dogs. Native life in the towns had offered novel features, but the conditions prevailing in this desert village surpassed anything Barry could have imagined. An entire absence of sanitary arrangements was the outstanding novelty; next to which he never got used to the spectacle of a considerable family, a number of dogs, chickens, and sometimes a donkey, residing happily together in one apartment which could have been covered by a full-sized dining table.

They reached camp at dusk, although they had crossed the river in the morning, having travelled by a circuitous route over high ridges and through gloomy passes, to find that a native cook had prepared dinner and that Hassan es-Sugra, who had gone ahead, was waiting to receive them.

Before attacking the meal, Barry, tired though he was, climbed the side of the *wâdi* and stood on the edge of a small plateau, looking out to the rosy haze that marked the course of old, distant Nile. The unforgettable dusk of Egypt was falling. Rocks showed like black smudges on a gray canvas, and the sky was passing through an amazing transformation of delicate blue to shell pink, which, by some natural magic, combined to form the violet afterglow which is not the least of this country's beauties.

From below came a faint clattering of cooking utensils, and a dog was howling somewhere, probably in the village where the workmen were quartered. The great adventure had begun. Tonight he was to see for the first time the tomb of Princess Zalithea!

He uttered a deep sigh, which was a sigh of contentment, and climbed down the steep descent again to the camp.

They dined inside one of the tents, Danbazzar deeming it unwise to court attention from any chance travellers upon the ridge above.

Barry stooped and entered the little canvas dwelling which was to be his home for some time to come. It presented a spectacle, on that first night, which was always to remain with him as an odd memory.

Plates of steaming tomato soup (Heinz tinned variety) were set upon the small square table, which even boasted a white cloth. The cook, a big, bearded fellow from the Fayyum, his magnificent teeth revealed in a constant grin, was just placing loaves and a pitcher of water upon the hospitable board.

Danbazzar, wearing a white shirt open at the neck, riding breeches, and gaiters, seemed utterly appropriate in that setting. His pale skin had assumed an even, dark tan, his magnificent composure was an unspoken retort to Barry's sudden idea that this was some solemn farce—a dream from which he would presently awaken. John Cumberland, also coatless, sat on the right of the table. He seized a loaf and began to carve it vigorously, looking up as Barry entered.

It was hard to recognize the John Cumberland of New York in this sun-baked adventurer, and the only member of the party who seemed out of place was Professor Blackwell, who faced his friend across the table. He wore a black alpaca jacket and had omitted to remove his sun helmet. He was gazing in gloomy disapproval at a large beetle of the *Scaraboeus* family which appeared to be attracted by the odour of his soup.

"Well, Barry!" John Cumberland greeted him. "What do you think of our new quarters?"

"First rate!" was the laughing reply, as Barry took the vacant chair. "If we go on in this style we shan't starve."

Professor Blackwell bent toward him; and:

"There's plenty of liquor," he whispered in his ear, "but all these fellows are strict Moslems, and we should lose their respect, so Danbazzar informs me, if they knew we drank anything stronger than water."

The soup dispatched:

"Stick your head out and tell Mahmoud we are ready for the chicken," said John Cumberland.

Barry nodded, stood up, and stepped outside the tent. The camp kitchen had been established in a sort of cave in the side of the *wâdi*, suspiciously like the entrance to a partially opened tomb. The glistening, smiling face of Mahmoud, the cook, showed in the reflected light. He smiled as he cooked and sang soft Arab love songs.

Before the entrance to this little tunnel, leaning upon his ebony cane, Barry saw Hassan es-Sugra, reflectively studying the efforts of the chef. At the same moment he detected a faint, sweet sound. From a great distance it seemed to come—above and beyond—a rhythmic, silvery jingling. He had just opened his mouth to shout "Mahmoud," when Hassan turned toward him and raised his hand in warning.

Night now had fallen, swiftly, blackly.

Ebon shadows lay in the *wâdi;* above, on crags and terraces of the mountains, were gleaming high lights where the moon shone. The musical sound went on uninterruptedly. Danbazzar's precautions had been justified.

Spiritually transported to the realms of the Arabian Nights, Barry stood, silent, listening. Camel bells! It was the sound of camel bells! High above on the mountain ridge a caravan was passing on its way from Thebes to Farshût....

After dinner, pipes and cigars being lighted, they held a council of war, seated around the table in the tent. At this council Hassan es-Sugra attended.

"Although no precautions have been neglected," said Danbazzar, "there appears to be suspicion about the object of our journey in certain quarters. I had an interview yesterday with the secretary of Mudîr of Luxor. We have known each other for some years, and he gave me a big dose of advice about the route beyond El Kharga."

Danbazzar paused, tensing his lips so that his abbreviated beard stuck out truculently, a peculiar mannerism which Barry had noted before. Then:

"The Mudîr's secretary was most hospitable," he went on, "and so anxious for our comfort that I'm dead sure he knew I was lying. He knew we had no more intention of visiting the oasis than he has."

"But how could the truth have leaked out?" John Cumberland asked.

"What about these people in the village," Barry suggested, "where the men are quartered?"

Hassan es-Sufa extended his palms and softly intruded with a remark.

"They are of the Hawwara," he explained, "or claim to be. They owe allegiance to their own sheik, and he is my friend. No, it will be some of the workmen, while in Luxor, who have been talking."

"Then what can we do?" John Cumberland demanded.

"I could thrash two or three of the men," Hassan suggested gently, "until I found one to speak the truth."

Barry stared in amazement at the aesthetic face of the speaker, thinking that he jested; but no smile appeared. This was apparently a firm offer.

"No!" Danbazzar's deep voice broke in. "It would do no good. If this fellow Tawwab suspects anything—"

"Exactly," said Professor Blackwell uneasily; "that is just what I am wondering. If he suspects anything, what will he do? Inform the Inspector of Antiquities?"

Danbazzar knocked ash from his cigar. The scarab ring upon his finger twinkled in the lamplight. He stared fixed at the Professor; then:

"He is an Egyptian," he replied. "What would he gain by that?"

"Ah!" John Cumberland exclaimed. "*Gain!* That's the answer—*bakhshish!*"

"Under the present government," said Danbazzar gravely, "always!"

"Well!" Cumberland shrugged his shoulders. "I came prepared to pay! Is it safe to start?"

"I was about to ask the same question," declared Professor Blackwell, raising his gaunt and ungainly form from the low camp chair in which he was seated.

"Yes."

Danbazzar spoke deliberately, and without betraying any of the excitement which the Professor had been unable to conceal, which obviously possessed John Cumberland, and to which Barry was a restless prey. He turned to Hassan es-Sugra.

"Hassan," he directed, "make sure that all's clear."

Hassan saluted deeply and went out of the tent.

"It's a bit of a scramble," Danbazzar warned. "Everybody in fibre shoes, and don't forget your flasks."

Their preparations were complete when Hassan returned with the news that the road was clear; whereupon, they set out.

The route they followed was merely a native path and not one of the roads ordinarily used. For a goat or a barefooted Egyptian it was navigable enough, but what with leaping over chasms of unknown depth and scrambling up narrow funnels composed of crumbling rock, brittle as a cracker, it was not all that might have been desired by a party of townsmen out for an evening stroll.

At last they came out on the hummock of a hill, and below them, magnificently outlined in shadow, lay the Valley of the Queens. Above towered that strangely shaped mountain once sacred to the goddess Hathor. Breathless, Barry leaned upon a block of stone, listening to a duet in hard breathing contributed by his father and Professor

Blackwell. Danbazzar's cigar glowed in the shadows of a neighbouring rock, and Hassan es-Sugra exhibited no evidence of fatigue.

Awhile they paused there, and then set out again, Danbazzar and Hassan leading, John Cumberland and the Professor following, Barry bringing up the rear. Thus they went, except where broken formation of the ground necessitated single file.

By what sailing marks the pilots traced their course was not apparent. But through the desolation of this land of tombs they passed, the way twisting and turning, their route being sometimes upward and sometimes downward, until at last:

"Here it is!" said Danbazzar.

Barry's weariness departed; his heart leaped.

They stood before a sheer rock face, its irregular surface pitted with openings. Above a mound of drift, Hassan es-Sugra began to dig with his stick, clearing sand and rubbish away. Barry watched him abstractedly: he was fighting to conquer the reality.

Somewhere here, deep in the heart of this rock, she lay, the princess of long ago! She whose picture, portrayed in the papyrus, was a vivid representation of the girl he had seen on that balcony in faraway New Jersey! Here! somewhere in this ancient mountain where she had lain for thousands of years.

What was the link? What did it mean? Useless! His mind refused to grapple with so monstrous a problem.

"See!" Hassan es-Sugra turned, extending his palms. "The cartouche, sirs! As I found it a year ago!"

A ray from Danbazzar's electric torch shone on to the rock. All bent forward eagerly.

"Quite! Quite!" murmured Professor Blackwell. "Yes, it is the same, unmistakably!"

Deeply carved in the surface, it was there for all to see—the curious sign which translated, meant: "She Who Sleeps but Will Awaken."

CHAPTER XIII

THE EXCAVATORS

Nothing succeeds like impudence. The original plan had provided for work at night only; but the flooded state of the Nile Valley was so discouraging to tourists and interruption of labours in the remote spot where the tomb was situated so unlikely that Danbazzar at the outset decided upon day shifts and night shifts.

Now definitely launched upon this unlawful project, a sort of unholy joy fired the party. It was even shared by Professor Blackwell.

The plan of operations was worthy of its inventor. The entrance to the tomb lay in a fairly deep recess; and Danbazzar had constructed, in convenient sections, a huge screen—practically a piece of scenery. The material for this accounted for the presence of several strangely shaped cases among their baggage for which Barry had hitherto been unable to account.

Set in place before the entrance to the tomb, with top pieces and side pieces, or wings, it was joined with sand and rubbish to the rubble of the valley path. When lovingly finished by Danbazzar—seated upon a light scaffold—with odd dabs of paint applied to a wet surface upon which sand had been thrown, the result was magical. While it slightly altered the conformation of the landscape, it was utterly impossible to detect the presence of this screen even by the closest scrutiny. One would have had to tap it to learn that it was of wood and canvas, and not of rock.

Access to the interior was gained by an ingenious door, low down at one corner. This door was in reality a shallow box filled with rubble and cement and opening upward. In the space between the screen and the rock there was ample room for work, which was carried on by lantern light. With two men always on duty, one at the high end of the valley and one at the low, to give warning for operations to cease, detection was next to impossible, short of treachery on the part of an employee.

On the morning that this screen was completed, Danbazzar, paintbrush in hand, stood surveying his work with the pride of an artist. He turned to Barry, who stood beside him and:

"Some illusion, I think!" said he.

"It's simply amazing!" cried John Cumberland.

"I worked behind that screen, sir," said Danbazzar, "for three months, and not a soul but my men ever knew I was there! The last month I spent covering up what I'd found."

"I take it," said Cumberland, "we can soon demolish what you reconstructed?"

"Pretty soon," Danbazzar agreed. "But I had to make a sound job of it."

"Anyway," said Barry, "from now onward we are safe."

"As you say—" Danbazzar bowed as one who acknowledges applause and gave the signal for the scaffolding to be demolished—"the dangerous part is over. Rain is the worst we have to fear now."

He touched Hassan es-Sugra upon the shoulder.

"Hassan," he directed, "let the first party begin at three o'clock. You have my instructions. I shall be back at five."

Hassan saluted, and leaving Mahmoud in charge of the clearing-up operations, walked away, slow and stately, down the valley.

As it chanced, their belief in the artistic genius of Danbazzar was very shortly to be put to the test; for, returning to the camp, where they intended to remain during the heat of noon, they were met by a very courteous Egyptian official.

John Cumberland started at sight of the figure wearing the tarbûsh, but Danbazzar exhibited neither surprise nor alarm.

"Ah! Mr. Tawwab!" he cried genially. "It was real good of you to hunt us up!"

Mr. Tawwab's smile was noncommittal.

"The Mudîr felt anxious about you," he explained; "and learning that you had not yet started for the oasis, suggested that I should see you."

"We are honoured and delighted," Danbazzar declared. "Allow me to make known to you Mr. John Cumberland and Professor Blackwell—Mr. Barry Cumberland. This is Mr. Ahmed Tawwab, secretary to the Governor of Luxor. Coffee, I believe, is prepared. You will join us, Mr. Tawwab?"

"Certainly."

The Egyptian bowed, and they all entered the tent which served as dining room, office, and council chamber.

Danbazzar entered last, behind Barry, and, in his ear:

"Mischief!" he whispered.

The boring ceremony of coffee and cigarettes, which is indispensable to any piece of Arab business, having been duly performed:

"The Mudîr," Mr. Tawwab explained, turning the gaze of his languorous eyes upon Danbazzar, "learns from the Mudîr of Asyut, that a considerable party of Hawwara Arabs, led by a sheik of the Hamman family and plainly meaning mischief, has been reported from El Kharga, in the Great Oasis. It is perhaps a political or a religious demonstration, but the Mudîr thought it wise to advise you that there may be danger."

"Convey my thanks to His Excellency," said Danbazzar gravely. "We are all most indebted."

His deep voice was lowered to a sort of caressing purr; which, however, resembled that of some large member of the cat family.

"But," Mr. Tawwab pursued, rolling a cigarette between his flexible fingers, "I understand that you are a fairly large party, and, of course, you can make choice. He will be glad to learn, nevertheless, that his information was correct, and that this warning has reached you before your setting out."

Mr. Tawwab having presently departed:

"What does this mean, exactly?" John Cumberland demanded.

"It means, sir," said Danbazzar grimly, "that our screen was only erected in the nick of time! We shall be watched!"

"What!" exclaimed Professor Blackwell with alarm; "but we may be arrested!"

Danbazzar turned his strange eyes in the speaker's direction, studying him silently for a moment; then:

"Before that time comes," he replied, "we shall be invited to *pay*. But if we can get through without paying, all the better."

"Do you believe the story of the Arabs?" Barry asked.

"No," Danbazzar answered promptly, "I don't!" His fierce eyes grew very reflective. "Nor do I believe that Ahmed Tawwab came from the Mudîr at all."

"I don't follow," said Barry. "What is your idea about it, then?"

"My idea is," Danbazzar answered, "that Mr. Tawwab has discovered the identity of your father and has simply called as an ordinary matter of business. He has got wise that we're here with some secret purpose, and he's going to make us pay. It was against grafting of this sort that I budgeted when I mentioned the price for the expedition, Mr. Cumberland."

Undeterred by these vague threats, operations were commenced that day. A tiny opening, a mere crevice, had been left by Danbazzar in the reclosed entrance, some ten feet above, and to the left of the inscription on the rock.

The first party set to work to enlarge this, and two guards were placed where they could command all possible approaches. By nightfall, enough had been done to show that this indeed was the entrance to a narrow, sloping shaft, carefully closed at the top with stone blocks.

John Cumberland's excitement became intense. Professor Blackwell experienced much difficulty in persuading him to sleep. Throughout the afternoon and the evening not a soul had appeared in sight of the excavation, and the first day promised well for the enterprise. Barry only deserted the job when a night shift of excavators came on duty, walking back, tired but mentally exhilarated, to the camp with Hassan es-Sugra.

As they pursued their way through moonlight and shadow down to the little *wâdi*, Barry glanced many times at his silent companion. The wonder of it all swept over him—the insanity of their dreams; the almost incredible fact that less than a month before he had been leading a rather empty life in New York.

Now, he was walking through a vast cemetery peopled with kings and queens, princes, princesses, councillors, of a glorious civilization which the desert had reclaimed long ages before the name of America was known to men!

The stillness seemed to become oppressive. Not even the bark of a dog could be heard. And tonight no camel bells jingled on the ancient caravan road. Barry spoke at random.

"How long, Hassan," he asked, "should it take to reach the tomb?"

"It is doubtful, sir," was the reply. "Perhaps, if the stones are not too hard to be broken, only a few days, for we have many men at work. Perhaps longer; and then, we do not know if the passage is clear beyond the first portcullis. Sometimes there are two; sometimes three. And, at the bottom of the shaft, the entrance to the funeral chamber will have to be broken."

"But the way in from the top? The part you closed up again last year?"

"That should be easy, sir. Perhaps by tomorrow. But there is still all the shaft."

"Is that a long job?"

"Always," Hassan replied, "it is a question of the conditions. Sometimes the air is so bad that men cannot work in these tombs."

"A question of Kismet, eh?" said Barry.

"Kismet, yes!" Hassan es-Sugra smiled in his sweetly grave way. "If it is written that we succeed, we shall succeed. If not"—he shrugged his shoulders—"no matter!"

Dog tired, Barry undressed and threw himself upon his camp bed. He shared the tent with Professor Blackwell, and his last waking recollection was of the sonorous snores of that weary scientist.

He seemed scarcely to have closed his eyes before he was awakened by a stray beam of morning sunlight. Someone had raised the flap of the tent. He opened his eyes. Professor Blackwell was still sleeping peacefully; but the bearded, grinning face of Mahmoud appeared in the opening.

Mahmoud had a little English; and:

"Sir!" he said. "I come to tell you. They make a small opening—too small for me. But this morning Hassan es-Sugra goes through!"

"What!" Barry was out of bed in one bound. "You mean he has gone into the tomb?"

"He goes in, Effendim, and comes out again!"

"Where is he?"

"He is there, in the valley."

"What!" came a harsh, sleepy voice.

Professor Blackwell turned over on his elbow. "They've reopened the tomb, Professor!" Barry cried excitedly. "They've reopened the tomb!"

"Impossible!" the Professor muttered, sitting upright. "I never heard of such a thing!"

"But Hassan es-Sugra has been in! Mahmoud has told me so!"

"Oh, yes!" said the Professor, fumbling under his pillow for his glasses. "Quite! Quite! Of course I was forgetting that it had been opened before."

Mahmoud departed, grinning broadly, as Barry made a grab for his clothes.

John Cumberland and Danbazzar were not in camp; and, having hastily disposed of hot coffee and biscuits, Barry and the Professor started for the excavation.

They had actually come out onto the plateau looking down upon the valley, when both pulled up dead, exchanging a swift, significant glance.

Unmistakable upon the still desert air, the note of a police whistle reached them! The guards were armed with these, but this was the first time there had been occasion to use them.

"Damnation!" Barry muttered. "Who can it be? Come on, Professor, let's hurry!"

To the great discomfiture of the older man, they performed the remainder of the journey at a fairly rapid trot. And, coming out of a narrow ravine which opened some twenty yards above the site of the excavation, they almost literally ran into Mr. Tawwab!

He was standing not more than a dozen paces from Danbazzar's screen, smoking a cigarette and looking about him curiously.

CHAPTER XIV

THE HAUNTED VALLEY

Prone upon a high crag Danbazzar lay, watching a horseman making his way down the slope of a distant valley and heading in the direction of the Nile. At last:

"He's gone!" he said, and looked back over his shoulder.

John Cumberland heaved a great sigh of relief and, standing, stretched his cramped limbs. One long last look Danbazzar took at the receding figure, and then the two climbed down to the path below where Professor Blackwell and Barry awaited them.

"Do you think I got away with it?" the latter asked.

"No!" Danbazzar said promptly—"not entirely. Your explanation that we had gone out for jackal was good."

"Excellent, in my opinion!" Professor Blackwell murmured. "You are really an accomplished liar, Barry."

"Well," Barry explained, laughing, "I knew we shouldn't find you in the camp, and some sort of explanation had to be offered. I spoke loudly enough for you to hear me behind the screen, so that if he insisted upon staying till you returned, your story would correspond with mine."

"Unfortunately," said John Cumberland, "he must have heard the whistle."

"He did!" declared the Professor—"although he never once mentioned it."

"That is why I know he didn't believe you," Danbazzar added. "I shall go into Luxor on Monday and talk business to Mr. Tawwab." He turned to Barry. "You haven't heard the good news yet! Can you imagine that I was forced to stop work last year within a matter of hours of breaking through that portcullis?"

"What do you mean?" Barry cried.

"They cleared the entrance," his father replied excitedly, "which Danbazzar had reclosed, without difficulty. You see, Barry; we are provided with the very best and latest gear. They set about the portcullis, and Hassan found a flaw in the rock itself beside this otherwise immovable stone door."

"Why didn't we find it last year!" boomed Danbazzar. "I figured that portcullis was a long, tough job!"

"They worked on it all night," John Cumberland went on, "enlarging it—"

"Have you actually been in!" cried Barry.

"No," was the reply; "the opening isn't big enough. But Danbazzar and I were looking along the passage when we heard the whistle!"

"Hassan has been down," said Danbazzar. "There's an obstruction twenty feet below, but he reports the air is fairly good."

"But what's the obstruction?" Barry asked.

"I fear another portcullis," said Danbazzar. "But the roof of the shaft seems to have collapsed at this point, or partly collapsed, and Hassan is uncertain whether there's another portcullis or not. It may be a month's work, or our job may be nearly finished. Remembering the purpose for which it was constructed, I look for a simple tomb. I should be surprised to find wells or dummy passages."

"Could I possibly get through?"

Danbazzar looked him over briefly; and:

"No!" he replied, "but we have dropped a light into the shaft and you can look down. The men are at work again now."

Excitement rose to fever pitch. Constant relays of skilled excavators could not work fast enough for John Cumberland or for Barry. By nightfall, the hole beside the mighty stone door which closed the passage had been appreciably enlarged. But whereas their first success had been due principally to a flaw in the rock tunnel itself, progress beyond this stage was a matter of patient drilling and chipping.

Danbazzar's optimism was shown to have been excessive. Hours went by in constant work; blazing days and nights of ceaseless toil; but still the great portcullis defied them. Hassan es-Sugra, with the smallest men of the party, had attacked the lower obstruction. But conditions were bad. Both air and proper light were lacking. Since they could not be relieved, their progress was necessarily slow. And, meanwhile, the main gang chipped and chipped patiently at the rock tunnel surrounding the stone door.

By Monday success seemed to be in sight; and as Danbazzar set out for Luxor to interview Mr. Tawwab, he gave orders touching the work on the lower passage. And so, this day, which it was written should be a memorable one, wore on.

When the wonderful curtain of dusk was drawn over the valley, Danbazzar had not returned from his interview with Mr. Tawwab. Barry pictured him patiently drinking numberless cups of coffee and smoking scores of cigarettes.

Mahmoud had been out for quail in the morning, and the savoury odour of his cooking increased the appetite of the party, already keen enough at the end of an arduous and exciting day. Having performed their somewhat limited ablutions, they assembled in the tent over a surreptitious cocktail, perforce without ice.

"It seems to me," said John Cumberland, "that this thing has developed into a race. The man Tawwab is out for blackmail. That's clear."

"Can we keep him off until we succeed, or will he hold us up?" murmured Professor Blackwell. "Success might come almost any day. What is beyond that further obstruction no one can pretend to guess. But as to what it *is*, from my scanty observations—for the light was very bad—I have formed a theory."

"What's your theory, Blackwell?" John Cumberland asked.

"It is this," the Professor continued: "That first portcullis blocking the passage was built to be raised—I am sure of it."

"I believe you are right," said Barry; "and it worked in deep grooves."

"Quite! Quite!" The Professor nodded. "By what means such a vast lump of rock was lifted, I leave to the greater knowledge of Danbazzar to explain. I am no Egyptologist. But I think the obstruction twenty feet down, from what I can see of it, is, or was, a second portcullis. The broken pieces look of about the same thickness as that at the top."

"But why should the second be broken and not the first?" Barry demanded.

"Which brings me to my theory," the Professor continued. "I think the second portcullis, at some time when it was raised, fell and was shattered."

"By jove!" John Cumberland exclaimed. "You may be right!"

"I am almost sure I am," the Professor said. "I think I can see one of the deep grooves it worked in. If this is so, it should be fairly easy to clear the debris, and, unless there is a third portcullis, intact, why should we not then find ourselves in the actual burial chamber?"

"It's possible," his friend admitted. "Let's hope you're right."

"There are no inscriptions to be seen on the walls of the passage," Barry remarked.

"No," said the Professor; "but I understand that this is usual. Am I right, Cumberland?"

"Quite right. But we may look for something very *un*usual in the chamber itself."

They were all feverishly restless, but as their presence at the excavation merely interfered with the work, for this restlessness there was no proper outlet.

Dinner concluded, and Mahmoud having cleared the table, the Professor and John Cumberland, shirt sleeves rolled up and cigars lighted, settled down to poker. Barry, pipe in mouth, sauntered out into the *wâdi* vaguely wondering why Danbazzar had not returned.

Without consciously intending to do so, he found himself following the familiar path, to which he no longer required a guide. On he went and down, until he came to that little ravine which opened into the valley just above the tomb. In the nick of time he remembered the usual routine and clapped his hands sharply three times.

Had he forgotten, the result would have been a blast of a police whistle and the suspension of operations!

The ingeniously screened working lay in deep shadow. He could see neither of the guards, but, standing there, silent, he could hear vaguely, deep in the heart of the rock, a sound of regular muffled blows. He was tempted to open the sand trap and to penetrate to the scene of activity, but overcame the impulse and turned right, walking up the valley to where it came out on the shoulder of a hill. Here, squatting under a curious mass of rock roughly resembling a giant skull, was one of the guards, who stood up as Barry approached.

"Lêltak sa' îda!" said the man, saluting him.

Barry echoed the words, to which he was now becoming accustomed, and passed on. The guard re-seated himself under the rock.

He determined to walk up as far as the ancient caravan road which crossed the crest above, a spot from which, Danbazzar had informed him, the view by moonlight was remarkable. He had counted, however, without the natural difficulties of the route. The path which he had intended to follow disappeared into midnight gullies and twined about upstanding crags. The shadowy places might be full of pitfalls. Barry paused, looking up at the ridge sharply outlined against the clear blue of the sky.

Perhaps, after all, discretion was the better part of valour. He might quite easily break his neck if he attempted this climb in the darkness. He stood there for a while looking about him, and knocking out his pipe upon the heel of his bass-soled shoe.

These slopes above and below he knew to be literally honeycombed. This weird place, almost unreal in its colouring under the moon, was no more than a vast necropolis. A month before, with New York's life pulsing around him, the thought of this desolation and of being lonely amid it would have been appalling. Yet so adaptable is human nature that already he was growing accustomed to these haunted solitudes.

He began to refill his pipe. Upon a ridge fifty yards away, sharply outlined in the moonlight, a slinking shape appeared for a moment and as quickly disappeared. A jackal! Only the night before one had visited Mahmoud's pantry, had succeeded in some mysterious fashion in opening the door, and had absconded with a cold chicken, a portion of a tin of sardines, and a piece of cheese. Another, even more original in his tastes, had stolen one of Professor Blackwell's slippers.

Barry determined to return to the camp by a circuitous route which he knew, and which would bring him out at the lower end of the *wâdi*. Having satisfactorily lighted his briar, he set out, now walking more briskly and wondering if the night shift at work in the tomb of Zalithea had succeeded in penetrating to the second portcullis.

Danbazzar, an old hand at the business, had arranged a sort of bonus system which was a constant urge to the men, and effectively abolished any possibility of slacking. If the shift which changed at twelve o'clock or that which changed at four should be in a position to report that their immediate objective had been gained, they were instructed to awaken Danbazzar, or in his absence John Cumberland.

Barry, stepping out briskly upon the comparatively clear path which he had chosen, conjured up a vision of the chamber in which, if their hopes should be realized, they would find Zalithea.

Prior to their final departure from Luxor he had visited several characteristic tombs under the guidance of Hassan es-Sugra. He imagined that the chamber of the sleeping princess would be different from any of these. His impatience was so great that he could scarcely contain himself. He doubted if even his father's enthusiasm was greater than his own. Danbazzar, whatever he felt, revealed little. Hassan es-Sugra seemed to be removed from all human emotions.

Coming to the lowest point in his descent, about half a mile below the excavation, he paused, looking about him.

By moonlight the place was different. But he recalled that it did not matter which of the several paths to the left he took, since any of them would ultimately bring him to his destination, and if one should prove impassable he could always return. Crossing a flat-topped mound, he descended the slope beyond and saw beneath him a rugged bowl dotted with minor ruins, probably of those stone huts which occurred in the Valley of the Kings. He stood looking down. It might be wise to avoid this valley, which no doubt contained pitfalls and across which he would have to climb rather than walk.

Then, as he hesitated, suddenly he saw something—something that caused him to shrink back, to inhale sharply—to wish he were not alone.

A figure was moving in the deep shadows of the hollow—a figure definitely horrible in such a place at that hour. It presented the appearance of a tall, gaunt man! There was a faint light, too, a fitful, elfin light which rose and fell—rose and fell—among the ruins!

All the old confidence with which Barry had walked through this place of the dead now deserted him. He recognized that he was afraid—and was ashamed of the recognition. But he retraced his steps swiftly, never pausing or glancing back until he had regained the main path.

Then, from behind him, far behind him, came a sound. . . .

Someone or something was climbing up from the bowl of the little valley!

In the profound silence of that place the noise was clearly audible. A jackal was out of the question; for no four-footed creature is more silent than a jackal in its comings and goings. He stood still, listening intently. Footsteps!—unmistakably those of a man and not of any four-footed beast!

Immediately facing him where he stood was an irregular mound of rock and sand, outlined on the right by the silver of the moon, but a place of ebony shadows on the left. He crossed into the shadows and waited. Nearer and nearer came the approaching footsteps. Whoever was coming up from the valley of the ruined huts was about to enter that narrow gully through which Barry had walked!

Half a dozen reasonable explanations presented themselves, but his mind rejected them one after another. Eeriness touched him with a cold finger. He watched the vague slash in a wall of darkness, which, from his present position, represented the entrance to the gully. Now, the one who approached was coming along it. In another moment he would be out. Three more paces must bring him into the light.

Barry's heart was beating rapidly. He was afraid—and did not know of what he was afraid.

And now he realized that the one who walked had cleared the gap, although he could not yet see any movement in the shadow. A second— two seconds—three seconds elapsed . . . and a man came out into the moonlight.

It was Danbazzar!

CHAPTER XV

THE HAWWARA

Automatically Danbazzar's hand dropped to his hip, the first intimation Barry had of the fact that he carried arms; then:

"All right!" cried Barry, and stepped out of the shadow, conscious of an almost ridiculous sense of relief.

But, for a moment, Danbazzar did not move. "What are you doing here!" he demanded—for it was less a question than a demand.

Barry experienced a momentary vague resentment.

"If it comes to that," he replied, "what are *you* doing here?"

Danbazzar smiled and came forward, shrugging his broad shoulders and dismissing the matter with a slow, graceful wave of his hand.

"I believe," said he, "that we have both got the 'jumps.' *I* am here because my donkey boy refused to come beyond the end of the valley at this time of night. And as we have no accommodation for a donkey, I let him return to Kurna. As a matter of fact, I helped him start!"

"I see," said Barry, meeting the fixed stare of those strange eyes. "For my part, I was taking a walk because I couldn't sleep. But weren't you prowling about in the hollow down yonder?"

"I was," Danbazzar replied gravely. "I had an idea that someone was hiding there, watching me—and I won't be spied upon."

"That's odd!" said Barry; "because *I* had a notion I saw someone there about five minutes ago."

"Is that so? What was *your* impression—a tall thin man?"

"Yes," Barry nodded, "unpleasantly like an unwrapped mummy!"

"Humph!" Danbazzar lighted a cigarette. "Very queer! Evidently you're not aware of the fact that that little hollow is supposed by the Arabs to be haunted!"

Side by side they proceeded up the slope, Danbazzar heading confidently for the camp. He seemed to know these desolate hills as he knew every street and every alley in Cairo. For Danbazzar, Egypt had few secrets.

"However," said Barry, "if we really saw anybody, it was probably some harmless eccentric who lives alone in one of the ruins."

"It may have been," Danbazzar murmured, "or it may not! What news of the tomb?"

"They are still enlarging the opening, but except for Hassan and the younger Said, no one has been through yet."

"I'm very anxious," Danbazzar declared.

"You can't be more anxious than I am!" cried Barry.

"Possibly not," the other admitted, "but my anxiety may be different from yours. I have spent several hours today with Mr. Tawwab."

"Yes," Barry prompted eagerly—"what do you think he knows?"

"I don't think he knows anything. He's just guessing. But he takes it for granted that we're digging somewhere—for something. We're going to be watched, or intimidated, or both!"

"Intimidated!" Barry echoed.

"Exactly!" Danbazzar nodded in his slow, grave fashion. "I practically made Tawwab an offer in the roundabout ceremonious fashion which alone they understand. He intimated with equal circumlocution that he didn't think the price high enough. I told him in a complimentary speech of fifteen minutes to go to the devil. He pressed on me several cups of coffee and nasty musk-scented cigarettes. Then he gave me to understand in the course of twenty minutes or more that I had his official permission to go to hell likewise. We parted perfectly good friends, though. It was a question of terms. But I think he holds the winning card."

"What do you mean?"

"Well!" Danbazzar shook his leonine head. "Mr. Tawwab reverted to the story of these Hawwara Arabs reported from El Kharga. I thought it was just plain lying when he spoke of it at first, but as he came back on the matter today I knew there was more in it. He informed me, with deep regret, that a party of the Hawwara had been reported on the caravan road some five miles south of Araki."

Coming from moonlight into shadow at that moment, Barry met the glance of the speaker's eyes.

"Do you mean," he asked, "that they are coming in this direction?"

"That's what Tawwab implied," Danbazzar admitted. "They must have come from the Farshût road, and now they're heading our way. He professed to be much concerned about our safety, pointing out that at this season our camp was a very lonely one. It's true enough that, after leaving Kurna, except for a few scattered houses we're pretty well isolated."

"But what do you think he was driving at?" said Barry. "These Arabs are surely peaceable enough?"

"As a rule they are," was the reply, "but a wave of fanaticism will sometimes pass through a tribe, or a section of a tribe, and then they go Mad Hatter. However, I certainly know why Tawwab kept coming back to it."

"Why?"

"To drive the price up! He was good enough to mention that his relations with the sheik who seems to be at the head of this mysterious movement have always been of a most cordial character."

"The devil take it!" Barry muttered. "Why can't he mind his own business!"

"Well," Danbazzar smiled, "departmentally speaking, this *is* his business! If he handled it properly we should find ourselves under arrest tomorrow! No!"—he shrugged his broad shoulders—"Mr. Tawwab holds the cards. We'll play as long as we can play, after which we must *pay*."

A beam of light shining out across the bottom of the *wâdi* and the unmistakable rattle of poker chips signified that John Cumberland and the Professor were still at their game. The appearance of Danbazzar, however, broke it up, and, eagerly listened to by the party, he gave a detailed account of his visit to Luxor.

"I can't imagine any reason for the Arabs coming in this direction," said John Cumberland, when Mr. Tawwab's warning had been repeated to the party.

"There can be only one reason," Danbazzar returned gravely.

"What is it?"

"This camp!"

He tensed his lips in a grim manner, reaching across for the bottle of Martell Three Stars, his favourite beverage in moments of reflection.

"Of course," Professor Blackwell broke in, "they may assume that we have large sums of money in our possession."

"They would assume rightly!" Barry remarked. "Can you count on the men, Danbazzar?"

"On the excavators?" the latter inquired, pouring out a drink and turning his eyes toward the speaker. "On every man of them."

"We haven't arms enough to go round," John Cumberland murmured. "Oh! it's unthinkable, anyway."

"All the same," said Barry, "I suggest we mount guard in future—here as well as at the tomb. And as it's too late to make any other arrangements tonight, I think we ought to take watches ourselves. What do you say, Dad?"

"I agree," John Cumberland replied quietly. His face was very grave. "This is something I had not counted upon."

Professor Blackwell raised his gaunt form, ducking his head to avoid contact with the sloping roof of the tent.

"I appoint myself first guard," he announced. "I'll take the Lee-Enfield."

"As you like," said Danbazzar.

With the heel of his riding boot he pushed a long wooden chest in the Professor's direction.

Stooping, Blackwell unlocked the box. It contained a moderately extensive collection of arms. And he selected a rifle of the British service pattern. The Professor was an old campaigner; and, having charged the magazine with care, he lighted a fresh cigar, and, nodding to the others, strolled outside the tent. His footsteps might be heard receding along the *wâdi*.

"For many reasons, I hope we break through in the next three days," Danbazzar went on, ending a short, uncomfortable silence.

He nodded his massive head in the direction of his own tent, which lay to the south.

"It took years to collect the ingredients mentioned in the formula. Some of them are perishable. One oil I got from Persia six months ago is already changing colour under the influence of climate. Besides, if these things were destroyed, God knows when I'd assemble them again."

"But you have the case well hidden," said John Cumberland.

"It's buried in the sand under the floor of my tent, but I don't feel too happy about it, all the same."

"The papyrus!" cried Barry eagerly—"you have that with you?"

"Not on your life!" Danbazzar returned. "No, sir, I have a photograph of it, and one of the formula as well. The originals are in the vault of my New York bank."

"Yes," John Cumberland nodded, turning to Barry. "I thought I had mentioned this to you."

"No, Dad; I imagined we had them with us."

"And now," said Danbazzar, standing up, "I'm going along to look at the work. If that second portcullis is broken, there's no reason why we shouldn't be down to the mummy chamber tomorrow. We're reaping the benefit of what I did last year. It would be better if you both remained in camp till I return. We shall have to follow some rule of this kind for the present."

He took a small repeater from his pocket and dropped it in the arms chest, taking in its place a heavy revolver. When he had gone, John Cumberland looked at his son rather blankly.

"I hope and believe, Barry," said he, "that this thing is a big bluff. If it isn't, I shall feel inclined to withdraw."

"Withdraw!" cried Barry. "You surely wouldn't do that!"

"I'm not thinking of the danger," the older man went on quietly, "but of the impossible position we should find ourselves in if we definitely came to blows with these Arabs. The whole plan would be exposed. I can't afford to take that risk, even if Danbazzar can."

"You are thinking of the Egyptian authorities?" suggested Barry slowly.

"I am." His father nodded. "Imagine the disgrace if we were arrested! No. If it comes to shooting, this party must break up. We could only hope to return at some future time, when the district was more settled."

"I never heard of such a thing." Barry declared. "Of course, I know nothing of the country. It's most unusual, isn't it?"

"Most unusual," John Cumberland agreed. "I confess I can't understand it. But I don't like it."

In short, Mr. Tawwab's conversation with Danbazzar had created an unpleasant feeling of tension.

"I'll take the next watch, Dad," said Barry; "you might as well turn in. If nothing happens, we shall have a busy day before us tomorrow."

John Cumberland hesitated for a moment, and then stood up.

"You are right," he agreed; "I will. Good-night!"

"Good-night, Dad."

For a few minutes afterward he could hear his father talking to Professor Blackwell at the top end of the *wâdi*. Then came silence again. He lighted a cigarette and helped himself to a nightcap, reflecting that he might as well have two- or three-hours' sleep, although the novelty and excitement of the situation were by no means conducive to easy slumber.

Presently, however, he got up and walked in the direction of his own tent. Outlined against the sky beyond he could see the gaunt figure of Professor Blackwell, rifle on shoulder; and:

"Is all well, Professor?" he called.

"All's well!" cried the Professor, his voice echoing eerily from wall to wall of the *wâdi*.

Barry turned in fully dressed, and lay on his bed for some time listening, although he did not know for what he listened. Somewhere in the distance a jackal howled—a second—a third—a fourth—a fifth: a regiment of jackals. Then silence fell. Once he heard a distant voice. Finally he fell asleep. . . .

He dreamed he was standing in the tomb of Zalithea. He was alone, and had reached the place by no visible entrance. On his right, against the wall was a wonderful gold sarcophagus. He found himself in a dreadful, pent-up condition. He was utterly panic-stricken. His heart was beating like a hammer. For the lid of this sarcophagus, which was hinged, was slowly, slowly, very slowly opening!

Then he saw a hand appear, and in the semi-darkness of the painted tomb chamber a light shone out from the interior of the sarcophagus. It grew brighter and brighter. The hand grasping the lid was a gaunt, long-fingered hand. He did not know what to expect. He was in that curious state in which one realizes that one is dreaming, yet is horrified by the incidents of the dream.

The lid had opened nearly wide enough to reveal the occupant, when Barry shook off the horror of the nightmare which had him in its clutch and sat suddenly upright.

A sharp sound had awakened him. He was bathed in cold perspiration. And, as he leaped from his bed to the sandy floor, this sound was still echoing in the hills around. He knew, in the very moment of awakening, what it had been.

The crack of a rifle! And now, here was an explanation of his half-waking dream.

Professor Blackwell was holding the tent flap aside. Outlined against reflected moonlight he bent, looking in. Barry heard dim voices.

"What is it?" he demanded hoarsely.

"Ssh!" the Professor warned. "The Arabs!"

CHAPTER XVI

THE HOLE IN THE WALL

The position of the moon had cast the greater part of the *wâdi* into deep shadow. There was a gap in the irregular wall nearly opposite to Barry's tent through which a certain amount of light came, but right and left of it lay ebony darkness.

As he came out and joined Professor Blackwell:

"There's a party of Arabs up on the caravan road!" said the latter in a low, urgent voice.

"Where is my father?" Barry whispered.

"Here I am, Barry!" came a reply out of the darkness. "Speak softly. Voices carry for miles in this place."

Barry groped his way in the direction of the speaker.

"Is Danbazzar here?" he asked.

"I'm right here!" Danbazzar answered in a harsh whisper; then, speaking more softly: "Who fired that shot?" he demanded.

"I don't know," Professor Blackwell returned. "It came from high up in the mountains. It must have been one of the Arabs."

"I wonder!" murmured John Cumberland. "I make the time half after two. The second shift comes on at four. So that no one is likely to have been moving—unless one of the watchmen may have seen something."

"*Sssh-ssh!*" came a warning. "Look!"

High on the ridge above them, like some spirited ebony statue, the figure of a horseman appeared, a magnificent silhouette against the deepening blue of the sky! A moment he remained there. Then—no sound reaching their ears—he disappeared magically, as he had come!

"I want someone to go up to the excavation." It was Danbazzar speaking in a suppressed undertone. "Shall *I* go and leave you in charge, Mr. Cumberland, or—"

"I'll go!" Barry volunteered promptly. "You may be wanted here."

"It's just possible," Danbazzar went on, "that something may have gone wrong there. It is also possible they mayn't know the Arabs are here. Order everybody to stay under cover except the guards. All work to be suspended till further instructions. Got it clear?"

"All set," Barry replied promptly.

"Be careful, my boy," said John Cumberland; "and don't forget the signal, or our own men may attack you, if they are on the *qui vive*."

A big muscular hand grasped his.

"Here," said Danbazzar, "take this."

He found a service revolver thrust into his fingers. Thereupon he set off, rejoicing in the adventure yet wishing that Jim Sakers could have been there to share it with him. He moved with great caution. In this desert stillness, the slightest sound was audible for miles. . . .

At some points in the journey, the *wâdi* left behind, that ridge along which the caravan road ran was visible; at other points it became lost to view. But always Barry slunk in the shadows, sometimes dropping prone and wriggling for several yards, in order that he might take advantage of some narrow belt of shadow; ever conscious, when the dangerous ridge was in sight, of the possibility of being seen, or worse—

of being shot.

Yet the very shadows that befriended him held their own terrors. Some spies of the fanatical Arabs might lurk there. But without sight of the band, and having heard no sound to indicate the presence of any living thing on the plateau above, he came to that midnight gully which opened out immediately above the tomb.

Peering from the end of it, he clapped his hands very softly.

An answering signal came from the top of the slope. He surmised that the guard at the lower end was out of hearing. Mentally reviewing what he knew of the course of the caravan road, he determined that from no point upon it was this valley visible.

He surveyed the rocky face of the mountain before him, his glance travelling along uninterrupted by any oddity due to Danbazzar's screen—that miracle of camouflage. He crossed and hurried to the trap, pausing a moment before he raised it.

Very softly he clapped his hands again. An answering signal came from beyond the canvas.

Gently he lifted the shallow box of sand, turned, and groped with his foot for the first of the wooden steps below. Finding this, he stood upon it, ducked his head, and lowered the trap. He took three steps, walking backward, then turned, and stared up a little incline.

Above him, a lantern was set upon a heap of debris in the yawning entrance to the tomb. And where dim light shone upward upon his ascetic face stood Hassan es-Sugra, smiling with gentle melancholy. No sound came from the depths of the tunnel.

"Hassan!" said Barry. "The Hawwara Arabs are here!"

Hassan bowed gravely and extended his hand to help Barry up the slope.

"I know, sir," he replied. "We heard the shot, and I ordered everyone to be silent."

"Did they fire at one of the watchmen?" Barry asked, scrambling up beside the speaker.

Hassan shook his head slowly.

"No," he said, "I do not know why the shot was fired, but everything was stopped until news came from outside."

His gentle eyes, which were so like the eyes of a gazelle, held a curious light. Later Barry determined that it had been an indication of excitement. Now, squatting about among the debris of the excavation in the curious artificial cave created by the screen, he saw a group of workmen. Some chewed, one of them was smoking, and they all regarded him with glances in which only smiling curiosity could be read.

He stared down into the haunted depths of the shaft, and then back again to Hassan es-Sugra.

"It was written that we should succeed," said Hassan.

"What?" Barry demanded, conscious of a new tingling in his veins.

"It was the work done last year," Hassan continued calmly, "which made it possible. It we had known, sir, with a little more time and trouble we could have completed. The second portcullis is broken. I cannot say how it was broken. But we have made a way through."

"Well!" Barry cried. "What's below?"

"A small square chamber," Hassan replied, "without any decorations. On the right is a doorway. It has been closed with square blocks and cemented up. We have removed one of these blocks without great difficulty. When the warning came I had just shone the light of a torch through the opening, sir, which the workmen had made."

"Yes!"

Barry grasped his arm hard.

"It is the burial chamber," Hassan went on calmly. "A great granite sarcophagus is there, untouched."

Almost too excited for speech, Barry pointed, and Hassan, gravely inclining his head, took from beneath his robe a pocket torch.

Stooping, he led the way down the shaft.

At the side of the first portcullis was an irregular opening wide enough for a man to squeeze through. Hassan went first and then so directed the light of his torch as to assist Barry to follow.

"Now, sir," he said, as the latter joined him in the lower part of the tunnel, "be careful here. The roof has fallen. It is this, I think, that broke the second door."

Bending forward, and at one point going on all fours, the two pressed on. Presently, climbing through a gap not more than eighteen inches high, over a mass of broken granite which seemed to have fallen from a deep cavity in the roof, Barry suddenly remembered Professor Blackwell's theory about the second portcullis.

The heat in the lower part of the shaft was oppressive, but having proceeded for another twenty feet the descent ceased. They found themselves in a small, square chamber hewn out of living rock, some three paces across, and perhaps nine feet high.

At first glance the wall upon the right resembled that in front and that upon the left; but the trained eye of Hassan es-Sugra had almost immediately detected the trick. It was plaster covering square blocks— in part at least. This plaster had been chipped away—it was several inches in thickness—over a space of a square yard or so. Beams of wood and all sorts of excavators' implements lay about the apartment.

And, presumably by means of these, one of the blocks had been forced into the chamber beyond. The effect was that of a small square window in a very thick wall.

"Take the torch, please," said Hassan, "and shine it through and a little to the left."

He passed the torch to Barry. And the latter was surprised to find that his hand was shaking slightly. Hassan es-Sugra smiled.

"Triumph is sometimes terrible, as well as defeat," he said.

Barry grasped the light and thrust it forward into the opening. A beam shone out before him, upon a rose sandstone sarcophagus! The covering was accurately in place. Clearly no human hand had touched it for centuries.

He experienced a curious choking sensation. He turned the light slowly, so that the beam moved along the top of the sarcophagus lid and beyond, upon the wall of the chamber.

The wall was brilliantly and beautifully painted. Immediately before him, slightly to the right of the sarcophagus, the disk of white light came to rest. Barry could feel his heart thumping against the rough stone upon which he rested. He was staring at a symbol in high relief, exquisitely coloured. It was that which meant: "She Who Sleeps but Who Will Awaken."

CHAPTER XVII

MR. TAWWAB COMES TO TERMS

"In my opinion," said Professor Blackwell, "the whole thing might be described as a demonstration."

John Cumberland nodded.

"I agree with you," said he.

"You are right," Danbazzar confirmed, "and we'll have proof of it in the next few hours."

"In what form?" Barry asked.

"A visit from Mr. Ahmed Tawwab!"

Danbazzar tensed his lips, looking fiercely from face to face. The anxious night was ended, and in the light of early morning this was a somewhat haggard company. Danbazzar with Hassan es-Sugra had been up onto the crest and had explored the Farshût caravan road for some five miles northwest of the camp, but had found no trace of the Arabs. It was possible that they were still somewhere in the vicinity, but Danbazzar considered this unlikely.

"We'll drive right on!" he boomed. "I wouldn't check now for a million dollars! The work below can't be heard in the valley, and all we have to watch for is that we're not seen coming or going."

"Mahmoud tells me that two or three of the men are nervous," said Barry.

"What about?" his father inquired—"the Arabs?"

"Yes."

"They'd better keep their nerves out of sight!" roared Danbazzar's great voice. "If Hassan sees any signs of nerves he'll knock stars out of them!"

"A most surprising character," Professor Blackwell murmured.

"He's the most efficient headman, sir," Danbazzar assured him, "at this kind of work that ever came out of Egypt. We're surely lucky to have him."

"Quite!" said the Professor. "I quite agree."

Mahmoud, grinning cheerfully, appeared with steaming coffee, and as the sun crept up into the sky the vapours of the night disappeared. Triumph was in sight. The discovery of the granite sarcophagus, alone, in John Cumberland's opinion justified the expedition.

"Even if it were empty," said he, "its existence confirms the authenticity of the papyrus."

"It won't be empty," Danbazzar asserted confidently. "That lid has never been moved since a Rameses reigned in these parts. When early tomb robbers have been at work, it's generally found smashed. Certainly they would never have taken the trouble to put it back again."

"There is another possibility," Professor Blackwell interrupted. "I believe it was Dr. Rittenburg who mentioned it: the possibility that the story of Princess Zalithea was merely a sort of religious ceremonial. I am disposed to share his theory. I seem to recall that no bull has ever been found in the Apis mausoleum. The sarcophagi are all empty."

John Cumberland, behind the speaker's back, pulled a wry face.

"True enough, Blackwell," he admitted; "but then the lids had all been moved!"

"Quite, quite!" the Professor said. "The parallel is not exact, I agree."

"There's no damned parallel at all!" boomed Danbazzar. "Inside this granite sarcophagus there's a wooden sarcophagus, and in that there's a mummy!"

"How long will it take to remove the other blocks?" Barry asked excitedly.

"We ought to be in tonight!" was the reply. "It's an easy job. That doorway was only temporarily walled up—as we might have expected."

"And what about lifting the lid?"

"We have a set of jacks for the purpose, Barry," his father replied. "They are in the cases that were shipped from Birmingham to Port Said. It is this sort of heavy gear that makes our position so dangerous. If Mr. Tawwab saw those jacks, for instance—"

"Quite!" said Professor Blackwell, and poured out another cup of coffee, to which he added a finger of rum.

Danbazzar had brought some mail across from Luxor, including a cable for Barry from Jim Sakers, which had infuriated the former to the very limits of endurance. It was conceived as follows:

Called on Mr. Brown yesterday afternoon. Door was opened by Princess. Recognized description. Height five eight. Age fifty-two. Weight thirteen ten. She carried a rolling pin at beginning of interview and threw it at end of same. Congratulations. JIM.

There was also a letter from Aunt Micky touching briefly upon the principal causes of dysentery in hot climates and emphasizing the claims of Vichy water as a dentifrice. There was much home chat about mutual friends, and then a brief postscript which read:

Avoid Nile boils. I had one on my honeymoon.

Barry hurried back to the excavation, his father accompanying him. Danbazzar had a number of arrangements to make in regard to the transport of necessary implements to the tomb, and it was considered desirable that one representative of the party should remain in camp. Therefore Professor Blackwell remained.

And so it happened that late in the afternoon, while the Professor sat in the shade before his tent, studying through a magnifying glass a number of small bones from the arm of a mummy, neatly arranged upon a sheet of white paper, he started suddenly and looked up from his task.

The cause of his disturbance was a distant shot. It came from somewhere between the camp and Kurna, and ordinarily it would not have aroused especial interest. This morning it had a particular meaning.

Professor Blackwell placed the specimens inside the tent, and, standing up, clapped his hands sharply. An Arab appeared from the kitchen. In the absence of Mahmoud, who was a specialist in the kind of work now going forward in the tomb of Zalithea, this man was preparing the midday meal. But he had other duties; and, as he saluted the Professor:

"Danbazzar Effendi!" said the latter, and pointed southwest.

The Arab saluted again and set off at a steady trot along the *wâdi*. Professor Blackwell peered into the kitchen. He found nothing more formidable going forward than the slow stewing of a sort of vegetable ragout; and so he contentedly lighted his pipe, which had gone out.

Already the morning was uncomfortably hot, and Professor Blackwell's costume must have occasioned some little comment had he seen fit to wear it before a class of students at Columbia. It consisted of canvas shoes, B.V.D.'s and a sun helmet. The more exposed parts of his person presented a glistening appearance, occasioned by the presence of a certain pungent oil with which he anointed himself against the onset of mosquitoes and sand flies.

About half an hour later Danbazzar appeared, followed by the Arab messenger. His was a picturesque and attractive figure. His great height and breadth of shoulder appeared to best advantage in such attire as he wore now: A very clean white shirt with sleeves rolled up above the elbow, the low pointed collar unbuttoned, white breeches, and tan riding boots. He wore also a soft felt hat, wide brimmed, light gray in colour, and he held a cigar between his small, strong-looking teeth.

"You got the signal?" he asked abruptly.

Professor Blackwell nodded.

"Half an hour ago," he replied.

"Then we can expect him almost any time," said Danbazzar.

"Have you got everything ready to be moved up to the tomb?" the Professor asked.

"Yes." Danbazzar nodded. "I'm only waiting to get the measure of Tawwab. Then I'll shoot it all along."

They were apparently deep in conversation and quite unaware of the presence of any stranger, when presently Ahmed Tawwab strolled into the *wâdi*. He was smoking a cigarette and looking about him, as one who lounges in Bond Street, or idly glances at the notices in the lobby of his club.

Danbazzar suddenly saw him, and:

"Why! Mr. Tawwab!" he exclaimed, and jumped up. "Look, Professor, who's here!"

"Surely, Mr. Tawwab?" the Professor murmured. "How fortunate you find us at home!"

Mr. Tawwab agreed that Fate had indeed been very kind, coffee was prepared, and a perfectly meaningless conversation began. After a long time:

"Mr. Cumberland and your other young friend will be returning shortly?" Mr. Tawwab inquired.

"Probably in an hour or so," Danbazzar assured him. "They are visiting one of the more interesting tombs."

"Ah! the tombs—Yes. I thought they might be shooting."

"Shooting?" Danbazzar echoed. "No, I don't think so; not this morning."

"I thought I heard a shot," Mr. Tawwab explained, "down on the edge of the swampy ground, to the left of the road. You know the spot I mean?"

"Quite!" murmured Professor Blackwell. "Quite! It might have been one of our fellows after quail."

"Sure it might," Danbazzar agreed. "We're devils for poultry in this camp."

"You are wise, however, in delaying your departure," said the Egyptian.

"How is that?" Professor Blackwell asked politely.

"Well," Mr. Tawwab extended his palms apologetically, "it is not to our credit to say so, but the whole of the country west of the Nile, from here across to Farshût or even further north, is in a somewhat disturbed condition. In fact"—he sighed reflectively—"the Mudîr, I am sure, would feel more happy if you would return to Luxor."

"That would cheer him up, would it?" said Danbazzar.

"It would be most agreeable to him," Mr. Tawwab assured the speaker.

"Much as we are indebted for the offer," said Danbazzar gravely, "I fear that to return to Luxor would interfere with our plans."

"We should never forgive ourselves," Mr. Tawwab murmured, "if you were molested in any way. Even if you were not harmed personally, your property might be destroyed, or stolen. I dislike to think of it."

"So do I," Professor Blackwell declared.

"We know rather more about the nature of the disturbance," Tawwab pursued evenly, "than when you called upon us. It is a matter concerning the collection of certain revenues. Concessions demanded by the Sheik Ishmail we are not, as a matter of fact, prepared to grant. But, oddly enough, the negotiations have been left practically in my hands, as I know the Sheik Ishmail quite intimately."

"I rather thought you did," said Danbazzar, with a large, amiable smile.

He exchanged a significant glance with Professor Blackwell, and the latter, by a prearranged plan, stood up glancing at his wristwatch.

"I have a few notes to make on the subject of those mummy bones," he murmured, "and there's only just time before lunch. Perhaps, Mr. Tawwab, you will excuse me for a few minutes?"

Mr. Tawwab also stood up and bowed most ceremoniously as the Professor departed to his own tent. This haven reached, Blackwell produced the paper of small bones again, and ostentatiously spread them upon a table before his door.

The interview between Danbazzar and Mr. Tawwab occupied an inordinately long time. Two relays of coffee were requisitioned, and at intervals Danbazzar's great voice was raised in a manner rather unparliamentary. But as the debate was throughout conducted in Arabic, Professor Blackwell could only assume that the question was one of terms.

It was ultimately settled amicably, however, Mr. Tawwab expressing his profound regret that he could not wait for the return of Messrs. John and Barry Cumberland. But important official business demanded his speedy reappearance in Luxor.

As Danbazzar walked beside him along the *wâdi*, one large hand laid caressingly on his shoulder, the contrast between his slight Egyptian figure and the great bulk of his companion was notable. Professor Blackwell derived an odd impression that Danbazzar would have loved to twist Mr. Tawwab's neck.

Having escorted him to where a servant waited with two horses, Danbazzar threw a stump of cigar upon the sand and selected a fresh one from several which he kept loose in the breast pocket of his white shirt. He bit off the end and spat it out reflectively, standing, a huge, picturesque figure, staring after the horsemen.

When presently he rejoined Professor Blackwell:

"How much?" the latter asked, standing up to greet him.

"Ten thousand piastres for the first week," Danbazzar replied calmly, and critically surveyed the end of his lighted cigar, which he extracted from between his teeth apparently for no other purpose; "twenty thousand piastres for the second week; forty thousand piastres if we stay over into a third, and so on. In other words, if we stayed for three months we'd need to send an SOS to Mr. Rockefeller! That's our rent, and we've got to pay it!"

"Quite, quite!" the Professor murmured. "Five hundred dollars for the first week, a thousand dollars for the second, and two thousand dollars for the third, or any part of the third, during which we remain here. Is that the figure?"

"You said it."

"And suppose John Cumberland declines to submit to this extortion?"

"Let's suppose." Danbazzar dropped down upon a small packing case which sometimes served as a chair. "In the first place, we'd be raided tonight by some scurvy bunch of Arabs in the pay of Tawwab. If we came out smiling, from tomorrow onward we'd be watched so closely the game wouldn't be worth the candle. He would then threaten official interference. And if we kept right on smiling, there'd also take our excavation and take our shirts! They'd also take our excavation and every damn thing they could find in it! The real shape of our job in the valley shown up, Mr. Tawwab would next suggest, say a hundred thousand piastres to let us go home to America. Alternative—send us to Cairo for trial! Professor"—he extended his palms in an extravagant imitation of Ahmed Tawwab's favourite gesture—"he has walked away with my check on the National Bank of Egypt for ten thousand piastres. We've got a clear week."

"Do you think he will stick to his bargain?"

"Certainly not!" roared Danbazzar, and brought his hand down with a resounding bang on the side of the box, so that it emitted a drumlike note. "If we were ready to move in three days, it would make no difference. He'd want at least another fifty thousand piastres to let us leave Luxor."

"It is expensive," the Professor murmured.

"It *would* be," Danbazzar returned, "if we paid it."

CHAPTER XVIII

THE LOTUS SARCOPHAGUS

The sun was casting its last shafts of gold across the fringe of the Libyan Desert when Barry Cumberland stepped over the threshold and entered the tomb of Zalithea. He had pleaded for this privilege, and it had been granted to him. Danbazzar and John Cumberland followed, Professor Blackwell hard upon their heels; and Hassan es-Sugra, smiling in gentle triumph, brought up the rear.

Sweat-grimed workmen crowded the outer chamber. . . .

No inscription of any kind appeared upon the sides or lid of the great granite sarcophagus, but the walls were very beautifully painted. The atmosphere was so oppressive as to be almost insupportable.

There was something awesome in this sudden silence which had succeeded upon clamour. Danbazzar was the first to break it.

"The name of Princess Zalithea," he said, his deep voice oddly hushed, "occurs, as you can see, in several places." He directed the ray of his torch from point to point. "Much of the decorations—such as the procession of boats, the Sem-priest in his mystic trance, the funeral offerings, and so forth—are quite conventional in character. You will notice, though, that the Lotus constantly occurs, as well as the Ankh, emblem of eternal life." He shone the light all around. "There are other important points, too," he mused, "which we can look into later. Be very careful. Touch nothing."

Barry, wholly absorbed in his own peculiar reflections, was passing around the sarcophagus; feeling its surface with his fingers; peering into the tiny crevices between the lid and the lip. Meanwhile, Danbazzar and John Cumberland were bending almost reverently over a strangely shaped, squat table on which were salvers, bowls, curious-looking phials, and a number of tall, slender lamps.

"Observe," said Danbazzar, a note of triumph in his deep voice: "*these are not the usual funerary offerings!*"

Professor Blackwell's long bony fingers were extended toward one of the phials, but:

"No, no! Blackwell!" cried John Cumberland excitedly. "Don't touch it! Touch nothing! It may crumble!"

The Professor withdrew his greedy hand reluctantly.

"And I wonder what that casket contains?" he murmured.

The casket to which he referred, an exquisitely carved object, stood by itself upon a sort of pedestal, some little distance from the table and beside a long, low couch, the legs carved to represent the feet of a leopard. Danbazzar almost imperiously waved him to silence. Then, turning his back to the sarcophagus, the table, and the pedestal, he addressed them as a speaker addresses an audience.

"The casket, gentlemen," he said, "as well as the bowls and bottles, contains the ingredients mentioned in the formula! I have seen enough already to tell me my preparations are complete. Presently, Professor"— he turned to Professor Blackwell—"maybe you can assist me in checking these; but the task of preserving many of the fragments is going to be a delicate one. We mustn't forget they're three thousand years old."

"It is almost more than I can believe!" declared John Cumberland rapturously.

Barry, one hand resting upon the sarcophagus, faced him, and:

"Dad," he said, "it's *altogether* more than *I* can believe!"

"What?" Danbazzar demanded. "That here before us, perished but recognizable, lie the ingredients of the formula as they were prepared by the last priest to wake Zalithea, for the use of his successor?"

"No," Barry replied: "*that's* hard enough—but what I cannot believe is that the woman who is the centre of this incredible story lies *here*, in this sarcophagus!"

"Personally, my mind is open!" Professor Blackwell asserted, glancing around him. "There is no other entrance to this chamber?"

"None whatever," Danbazzar confirmed.

"Therefore," the Professor went on, shaking perspiration from his high brow, "we are the first explorers, since this amazing ritual came to an end for reasons which, probably, we shall never know." He glanced aside at the sarcophagus. "It's uncanny," he murmured, "the thought that inside those walls of granite— But, no! I stick to my opinion!"

"How long will it take to raise the lid?" Barry interrupted.

John Cumberland, hot, tired, met his son's glance with one fired by no less enthusiasm.

"With the aid of the apparatus which we have with us, Barry," he answered, "not long. You agree, Danbazzar?"

The latter, who was less excited than the others—always excepting Hassan es-Sugra—bowed in his old-world manner.

"We'll have that lid off in an hour!" he declared. "But before we start there are quite a lot of precautions we have to take. . . ."

Two hours later the gear for lifting the great granite lid was brought from its hiding place; and everything was put in order for the operation, the result of which would prove or disprove Dr. Rittenburg's theory (now shared by Professor Blackwell) that Princess Zalithea was a myth; that no such person had ever existed; that the tradition was a priestly invention designed to impress the vulgar mind.

Ever distrustful of Ahmed Tawwab, guards armed with rifles had been placed at selected spots northwest of the camp along the caravan road to Farshût; these reinforcing the ordinary guards in the valley.

The wildest excitement prevailed among the party. Apparently, as well as Barry could make out, apart from the problematical contents of the sarcophagus, the objects found in the tomb were in many ways unique.

There was an exquisitely embossed bowl, which, he learned, was of pure gold. The figures upon it were apparently different from any found hitherto. Professor Blackwell succeeded in identifying seven of the substances found, in the vials and the casket, as identical with those mentioned in the formula possessed by Danbazzar. One or two defied speculation, or the Professor's knowledge, until Danbazzar enlightened him as to their nature. Whereupon he recognized them, but raised his voice in doubt respecting the possibility of obtaining these at the present day.

"I *have* obtained them!" Danbazzar assured him. "When the time comes, you shall see them. Oh! I've been busy, Professor. Where the Ancient Egyptians got these things God only knows! They can't have had a colony in Russia in those days."

"Russia!" the Professor echoed.

"I said Russia," Danbazzar affirmed. "One of the ingredients—the one we have been arguing about—I ultimately got from Russia!"

"You refer to the substance which you tell me is of mammalian origin?"

"Precisely."

"Mammals have been found in Africa," the Professor murmured. . . .

And so in the atmosphere of excited debate and unceasing toil the day wore on.

Hassan es-Sugra never left the tomb. It would have been impossible for any workman to remove a grain of dust from it and escape the scrutiny of those gazelle-like eyes. Barry's enthusiasm was such that the tedious methods employed by Danbazzar for raising the lid of the sarcophagus tortured him to the borders of frenzy. At one point:

"Why all these precautions?" he cried. "It would need a steam hammer to crack that lid!"

"Surely it would," Danbazzar returned gravely. "What's the big point?"

"The point is," said Barry, "that you are making a perfectly preposterous fuss about lifting it—as though it would matter very much if we dropped it!"

"I see!" Danbazzar spoke softly, regarding the younger man through half-closed eyes. "If you were lying in a stone chest next to hermetically sealed, and somebody dropped half a ton of granite on top of it"—his voice suddenly rose, booming around the enclosed chamber—"where in hell do you think you'd be?"

"Good Lord!" Barry was startled. "Of course! You are quite right!"

"You'd be dead of concussion!" Danbazzar shouted. "Thundering concussion! This is my business—and I'll do it my own way!"

He was formidable in his sudden anger, and Barry realized that he had committed an unforgivable *faux pas*—that of criticizing an artist in the practice of his profession. . . .

The coming of dusk found the raising gear in place to Danbazzar's satisfaction, at which point he cleared the tomb, leaving Hassan es-Sugra on guard in the outer chamber.

"The eight o'clock shift will start the lifting," he pronounced. "We all want dinner, so we'll all have it."

John Cumberland, sweat-grimed but happy, looked up from the task which he had been performing side by side with the Arab workmen. Barry leaned up against the rugged masonry beside the opening and mopped his forehead with a very dirty handkerchief.

"It's torture to quit," he declared honestly, "but you are right, Danbazzar. I am dead tired. Aren't you, Dad?"

"I am!" his father admitted. "I would give a big price for a real hot bath before dinner!"

"It would be most acceptable," declared Professor Blackwell.

"Association with these very worthy natives adds to one's knowledge of humanity but results in so many fleas!"

They returned to camp in the *wâdi*, taking turns in the portable bath supervised by the grinning Mahmoud. This was a rare luxury, for water had to be brought a great distance, and inadequate though these baths might be, they were keenly appreciated by the party.

All brought keen appetites to dinner, which was well up to Mahmoud's standard. Having reached coffee (into which they were forced to pour their cognac, lest Mahmoud should see the bottle which they kept concealed in the sand, or, worse, smell the glasses):

"Tonight," said Danbazzar, selecting a cigar, "the lid of the sarcophagus will be raised."

"What then?" cried Barry.

"There'll be an inner sarcophagus," was the reply, "probably of sycamore and elaborately painted. Our next task will be to raise that, which won't be difficult. Nor will the opening of the wooden lid; but—" he paused, carefully lighted his cigar and rolled it between his fingers for a moment—"I'm going to give orders, and in these orders you are included, Mr. Cumberland."

"I am at your service," said John Cumberland. "You know more of this business than I do."

"Very well," Danbazzar went on. "The raising of the second lid will be easy. But it won't be raised until I say the word."

"Why?" cried Barry.

Danbazzar turned to him.

"Because," he answered, "the raising of that lid will be the first critical moment. We don't know what we shall find. We don't care to think what we shall find. But we have to suppose that there is a woman there—in what we might describe as a trance. Now"—he performed a slow, impressive gesture—"according to the formula, as you'll remember, Mr. Cumberland, there must be no delay between the opening of the sarcophagus and the beginning of the ceremony for waking the sleeper."

"Good heavens!" exclaimed Professor Blackwell. "Is this some strange dream?"

"It may be," Danbazzar admitted, "but we have to suppose that it isn't. Also, we have to suppose, or rather to remember, that the Princess Zalithea, if she's there and still living, last saw this world in the days of the Pharaohs!—according to my calculations, about the time of Rameses the Ninth. Let's put ourselves in her place. If we aren't all crazy—if those old priests weren't all crazy—she will suddenly find herself surrounded by a group of wild-eyed devils—I include myself— wearing fantastic clothes and speaking a barbaric language! Now this can't be. Think a minute!"

"I follow you entirely," said Professor Blackwell. "Quite! Quite! And I see what you are about to propose."

"Good for you, Professor!" Danbazzar nodded appreciatively. "We've got to dress the part, and I came prepared for it."

"What!" Barry exclaimed.

"Yes, sir," Danbazzar went on; "when we take that lid off, we have got to be dressed like Ancient Egyptians!—and we have got to be silent! Leave the talking to me. I have the outfit. Does everybody agree?"

Everybody agreed. . . .

They did not linger long over their coffee, but hurried back to the excavation.

Guards were posted as on the previous night. Excitement ran higher than ever. They worked, and the Arabs worked, under the direction of Hassan es-Sugra, like men whose lives depended upon their speedy success.

But the eight o'clock shift had returned to quarters and the twelve o'clock shift were near to their time of departure, before the great lid was raised high enough to enable them to explore the interior of the granite coffin.

Not one of the party was wholly master of himself. Barry experienced an unfamiliar desire either to laugh or to cry. But, composure regained, light was directed into the interior. . . .

It contained a magnificent wooden sarcophagus, highly gilded and painted. The lid, which was in relief, represented the figure of the occupant—a girl, clad in a gauzy robe, her hands clasped upon her bosom and holding a Lotus flower. The Ankh—symbol of life—was at her head and her feet. The presentment was wonderful—uncanny.

Barry's mood changed. He felt suddenly sick. He believed that he was likely to swoon.

The eyes, the hair, the full lips, the slender, cloudily clad figure! This was madness! He stood upright, his hand on his brow. Perspiration was dripping into his eyes.

It was *she!* It was the girl of his dreams! More, far more than a coincidence, this was a miracle—or a delusion!

CHAPTER XIX

THE VOICE IN THE VALLEY

The hours that followed were feverish hours. They were marked by at least one strange event.

Barry's excitement grew so intense that the mere idea of sleep was out of the question. If he had had his way, the wonderful painted lid would have been torn off and the occupant revealed within a very few minutes of its discovery. But Danbazzar sternly took command. The tomb was cleared; the triumphant workmen were sent off to their quarters; all operations were suspended until morning. And on this point Danbazzar proved adamant.

In view of the advanced state of the work, and of what interference at this critical step would mean, he determined to supplant the ordinary guards. It was arranged that John Cumberland and Barry should take a dog-watch (two hours) at the high and low ends of the valley; then Hassan and Danbazzar; and finally Professor Blackwell and Mahmoud. All would be armed.

"It'll take me right through the first spell," said Danbazzar, "and most of the third, to collect up the stuff I want to get along. Maybe I'll make more than one journey each time, and Hassan can help."

"Don't forget the signal!" Professor Blackwell warned. "We are all tuned up above concert pitch!"

And so, beneath a glorious moon that painted the Valleys of the Kings and Queens with silvern mystery, Barry and his father began the first watch. Wholly animated now by the spirit of adventure, they tossed for positions—and Barry got the low end.

Shouldering his rifle, he marched down the slope; and, his post reached, gave himself over to reflection. The first idea to claim his mind was a grotesque one. Here were a group of eminently respectable Americans mounting armed guard over a tomb that belonged to the Egyptian government! True, they had evidence pointing to the possibility that it contained a living woman; but to pretend that they were in any sense actuated by the motives of a rescue party would be sheer hypocrisy.

The spot, if somewhat inaccessible, was nevertheless open to the public. He experienced momentarily the sensations of one who claims a certain mound in Central Park and posts sentinels over it.

Then, swiftly, his thoughts changed. Zalithea! To no living soul had he breathed his conviction that Zalithea—if she really lay under that painted cover—had already appeared to him, perhaps in visions, but apparently in the flesh! He knew that he had not spoken of this because he had not dared. Even now he was afraid to think of the painted figure, afraid to face the question: What does it all mean?

He tried to banish these ideas. They definitely disturbed him. And the morrow would show—what?

Resting his rifle against a rock, he filled and started a pipe. The flame of the little gold lighter—a parting present from Jim Sakers— made grotesque shadows. He remembered that at this point he was no great distance from the haunted valley where he had seen the mummylike figure moving.

The thought was unnerving. He imagined that gaunt, half-human shape creeping toward him, secretly, through the darkness. In the little hollow were ruins of those huts which had been built in a remote age for the accommodation of the tomb guards.

If the spirit of such a guard could revisit that spot, how bitter—and how just—would be his resentment!

He toyed with this idea. And, largely because of an unpleasant tingling of his scalp which he was brave enough to admit to himself betokened approaching panic, he argued that the case presented peculiar and extenuating features. Here was no violation of the mighty dead. On the contrary, they were carrying on the labours of the priests who had begun this amazing experiment. They were attempting to make possible that dream of Pharaoh in which he had seen men of a future age listening to a story of his grandeur from the lips of one who had witnessed it!

From this convincing argument he derived much comfort. The supernatural dread which had threatened to claim him receded like a real presence—only to return suddenly, magnified a hundredfold.

Coming unmistakably from the direction of the haunted hollow, a sound broke the profound silence of the night—*a woman's voice!*

Utterly unexpected, wholly incomprehensible, it seemed to make Barry's heart stand still. No word reached him; merely the silvery tones. From a great distance it came—and ceased abruptly—almost as though the speaker had been silenced.

A woman—in that place—at that hour! The idea simply wasn't admissible. Yet he had heard her voice! His hands closed like a vise upon the rifle. He gripped his pipe between his teeth desperately. Compromise with himself was no longer possible. For this was no trick of his imagination. Beyond shadow of doubt he had heard a thing admitting of no reasonable explanation; and he was definitely, dreadfully scared.

Intently he listened, but could hear only a drumming in his ears. The tinkle of a camel bell up on the caravan road would have been as balm to his fevered mind; for it would have offered a possible solution of the mystery. But nothing stirred.

He longed to join his father, to tell him of the phenomenon. But he knew that he must not desert his post. Nor could he conscientiously convince himself that there was justification for blowing the whistle he carried—a signal that would summon John Cumberland.

And so he stood there, holding grimly onto his slipping courage—while minute after minute passed in profound silence, that great, deep silence of the desert which can almost be heard.

Hours seemed to elapse in this way. But, when Barry glanced at the luminous dial of his wrist watch, he learned that he had been on guard for less than half the allotted span. In the act of consulting the watch, his heart gave a great leap.

Another sound had broken the stillness.

Then he heaved a sigh of relief. It was the signal, higher up the valley. Someone had clapped his hands three times. Immediately, John Cumberland's voice came:

"Who's there?"

"Danbazzar," Barry heard.

After this, words became indistinguishable; but a human link had been established; he no longer felt alone with the shadows. And his dread slipped from him like a discarded garment.

He wondered, practically, if he should report the occurrence. He decided to wait until he was relieved by the next watch.

So the second hour of his duty wore on, uneventfully, and at last came the familiar signal again. Some conversation there was; then an interval of silence. Finally, he heard the voices of John Cumberland and Danbazzar drawing nearer as they walked down the slope. Coming around the last bend:

"Two more loads will do it," Danbazzar was saying. "I'll bring them up while Blackwell and Mahmoud are on watch. Then everything will be safely planted by daylight." As they came into view: "Hullo, there!" Danbazzar called. "All clear?"

"Yes," said Barry, "except that I heard a most extraordinary thing about an hour ago."

"What?" Danbazzar demanded sharply.

He bent forward, so that even in the darkness of the *wâdi* Barry could see the gleam of his fierce eyes.

"A woman's voice!"

"Eh!" John Cumberland exclaimed. "You must have been dreaming, Barry!"

"I wasn't dreaming, Dad."

"Where did it come from?" Danbazzar asked rapidly. "Which direction?"

Barry pointed.

"Down there—where we saw the mummy man."

"Good heavens!" said his father—"the haunted valley!"

He was acquainted with the story of the apparition seen by Danbazzar and Barry, and had even explored the hollow by daylight, but had found no evidence of human habitation.

"Strange," Danbazzar muttered, in his deep voice. "Did she seem to be speaking English?"

"I couldn't say. No words were distinguishable."

"Was it a young voice?" John Cumberland asked.

"Yes."

Danbazzar and John Cumberland exchanged swift glances. Then:

"Is it possible," asked the latter, "that some camping party has crossed?"

"No!" Danbazzar spoke confidently. "I'd have had news of it from Hassan. He knows everything that's arranged in Luxor. And there's no *dahabîyeh* up either. I can't account for it."

He stared hard at Barry.

"I heard it," the latter repeated.

"I don't doubt you heard *something*," Danbazzar admitted. "But I'm just wondering what it was. There are night birds that have a note not unlike a woman's voice. Some small animals, too, when a jackal gets them, squeal like hares. And the cry of a hare is very human. Did you know that?"

"I knew it," Barry replied, "although I never heard one. But this was no animal or bird. It was a woman a long way off, but unmistakably a woman."

The mystery unsolved, they presently parted; Danbazzar taking over the watch, and John Cumberland and Barry returning to camp. They exchanged greetings with Hassan es-Sugra, posted at the head of the valley, and then, silent for the most part, tramped on to the tents.

Professor Blackwell was very much awake. In fact, he had got Mahmoud to prepare coffee for them. Sandwiches consisting of Huntley and Palmer's biscuits, native butter, and bottled prawns were also in readiness.

"Highly indigestible," the Professor admitted. "But one or two extra nightmares count for little upon such an expedition."

The phenomenon of the mysterious voice was discussed at length.

"I vote for some kind of nighthawk," John Cumberland finally declared.

"It was no nighthawk," Barry assured him.

"H'm!" murmured Professor Blackwell. "I am consistently unfortunate at games of chance. But I venture to hope that on my watch I may draw the upper end of the valley and Mahmoud the lower!"

How this fell out, and what Danbazzar and Hassan had to report, Barry did not learn. Determined though he had been not to close his eyes until the night was ended, tired nature prevailed. Not even the prawns and coffee could keep him awake. He found himself nodding over his pipe. John Cumberland was deep in slumber in a chair, and Professor Blackwell's snores rang out sonorously upon the desert silence.

Barry aroused himself, and:

"It's no good, Dad!" he said.

John Cumberland started into wakefulness. The Professor snored on.

"We must turn in," Barry continued. "We are both dead beat!"

"You're right, my boy," his father agreed. "But who's going to wake Blackwell when the time comes?"

Barry pointed, laughing sleepily.

A cheap alarum clock, set for fifteen minutes ahead of the Professor's watch with Mahmoud, stood only six inches from the sleeper's head!

"The scientific mind," murmured John Cumberland—"always methodical. Good-night, Barry. I'm for bed."

"Good-night," said Barry.

Five minutes later he was fast asleep.

No dreams visited him tonight. He slept the sleep of utter weariness. A gunshot would not have awakened him. And the sun was high above the valleys where those who ruled Egypt in the golden past slept even more soundly than he, when a booming voice ended his slumbers.

"Turn out!"

Barry opened his eyes. Danbazzar stood looking into the tent. This extraordinary man, from his leonine head with its well-brushed gray hair down to his polished riding boots, was spruce as though the dust of deserts positively avoided him.

"We open the sarcophagus in an hour!"

CHAPTER XX

THE RITUAL

Barry looked around the square, rock-hewn chamber communicating with the tomb, and wondered why he felt no inclination to laugh. Had Jim Sakers formed one of the party, his mood might have been different; but, in the company of his father, Danbazzar, and Professor Blackwell, he found himself touched by awe.

They wore robes, sandals, and curious linen skullcaps which entirely concealed their hair. Danbazzar, so arrayed, presented an impressive picture. He did not look like an Egyptian priest, but he might have been a Pharaoh disguised as one, except for his moustache. The others, save for their deeply tanned skin, could by no stretch of the imagination have been mistaken for anything but American citizens masquerading.

Professor Blackwell, oddly enough, was more convincing than the rest. Without his spectacles, although he could see little, he had a distinctly hieratic appearance.

Hassan es-Sugra was not present. With Mahmoud he mounted guard in the valley, above.

A richly embroidered curtain hung in the now demolished doorway of the tomb chamber. The heat was almost insupportable; and the smell of some kind of incense which was burning on the other side of the curtain added to the oppressiveness of the atmosphere. This was *Kyphi*, mentioned in the "Papyrus Embers," and, according to Danbazzar, only twice hitherto prepared in modern times.

Danbazzar gave his final instructions.

"To the best of my knowledge," he said, "everything is ready. One essential oil—you know the one I mean, Professor—has changed colour since I had it distilled. I can only hope that its special properties, whatever they are, remain the same."

"It has no special properties that I am aware of," the Professor murmured.

"We shall see," the deep voice went on. "The seven lamps are ready to be lighted. You know when to light them and which lamps each of you must light. The last one, I light. The two unguents are in the bowls. You"—turning his piercing regard upon Barry—"will put the taper to the liquid in the perfume burner when I give the signal.

"The wine for the final draught, you"—indicating John Cumberland—"will pour into the cup onto the powder at the last moment—when she opens her eyes. I consider the wine to be the most doubtful item. It's Madeira wine, over a hundred and fifty years old, but I'm not sure of it all the same."

"That contained in the flagon found here was undoubtedly a similar vintage," Professor Blackwell said. "It was a grape wine. My microscope has convinced me of this."

"We can only hope you're right," said Danbazzar. "And now—the most important point of all. The sarcophagus I've had lifted out onto a sloping trestle. The implements for raising the lid are ready. The couch, described in the formula, is still serviceable, if we take great care. Directly the lid is off, she must be taken out of the sarcophagus and laid on the couch. I'll do it. From that moment on, no one must speak! No one must make a sound! Just do your jobs. And, for God's sake, don't bungle!"

He held the curtain aside, and the party filed into the tomb.

It presented a picture that time could never efface from the minds of those who saw it. Dimly lighted by an ancient lamp set upon a pedestal, the air was misty with clouds of incense arising from a tripod placed on the right of the doorway.

The lotus sarcophagus rested, slanting, near to the great granite box which had contained it for generations. Upon a low table were two bowls containing some kind of ointment; a metal perfume burner; a jewelled cup in which was some gray, powdery substance; a stoppered flagon; and a curiously shaped lamp. The table was set close to the head of a long, narrow, gilded couch, having legs carved to represent those of an animal, and found in the tomb.

Six other lamps were placed at intervals around the walls.

Danbazzar pointed to a bundle of tapers. They were made of some inflammable resinous substance.

"The moment I lift her out," he directed, "light those tapers at the brazier. The wrappings I look to find perished, and I shall set to work right away. Say all you want to say before I get the lid off. I shall work fast, even if I do damage. Once the thing is open—not a word from anybody."

He stooped over the sarcophagus, with its startling presentment of the occupant. His shadow, gigantic, moved upon painted walls and ceiling. A sound of wrenching, cracking wood broke the oppressive silence. . . .

Barry clenched his teeth hard. He glanced at his father. Even through the tan one could see that John Cumberland had grown pale. Professor Blackwell's gaunt features glistened with perspiration Barry wondered—as though newly faced with the problem—what he should do if the sarcophagus really proved to contain a woman! A sudden unaccountable conviction had come to him that it was empty.

The heat in the tomb seemed to be growing greater every moment. . . .

John Cumberland stepped forward, in response to a signal from Danbazzar. Together, they raised the painted lid and rested it upright against the nearest wall.

Through a mist that was not wholly due to the incense, Barry saw the figure of a woman lying in the sarcophagus!

The figure was swathed in saffron-coloured wrappings. The arms and hands were enwrapped also. But within a sort of aperture where the face should have been appeared a thin gold mask. He experienced a sense of suspended animation. He seemed to watch that rigid figure through a vast period of time. Then, casting an imperious glance around him, and raising a finger significantly to his lips, Danbazzar stooped.

Lifting the mummylike form, he placed it on the couch.

With a pair of surgical scissors he began to cut through the wrappings. . . .

A hand touched Barry's arm. He started wildly.

Professor Blackwell, his features strangely haggard, handed him a taper and pointed to the tripod.

Barry, by dint of a stupendous effort, regained control of himself. He remembered that it was his duty to light the first two lamps.

This duty he performed blindly. A sound of tearing linen seemed to fill the chamber. The perfume of the oil in the lamps began to mingle with that of the *Kyphi*. . . .

John Cumberland lighted two more lamps.

Barry turned and looked. Like lilies blooming in corruption, he saw two slender, exquisite arms peeping out from the torn and powdered wrappings . . . bare, creamy shoulders gleamed in the lamplight.

Danbazzar gently detached the gold mask and removed the turban-like swathings which confined a mass of short, wavy dark hair.

A pale, exquisite face was revealed, delicate as a Greek cameo. Long, curling black lashes rested on the youthfully rounded cheeks. The pouting lips seemed to smile. . . .

In on the hush of it burst a loud, harsh cry:

"My God!"

Even as he met a furious glance of Danbazzar's blazing, wild animal eyes, Barry did not realize that it was *he* who had cried out. But instantly came recognition of the fact.

He clapped his palm over his mouth, literally choking back the words he had been about to utter. John Cumberland had his hand raised in warning—a hand that shook wildly. Professor Blackwell lighted the last pair of lamps. His face looked waxen—ghastly.

Danbazzar, icily calm again, proceeded to carry out the singular formula. A wave of embarrassment swept over Barry, making his very scalp tingle. He turned aside.

But his heart was leaping—leaping . . . Danbazzar lighted the seventh lamp—and glared at Barry.

Barry plunged a taper into the brazier and applied the little tongue of flame to an oily liquid in the perfume burner. It ignited at once. Danbazzar, bending over the girl blew the aromatic smoke gently over her face.

At which moment, Professor Blackwell staggered toward the curtained doorway. John Cumberland, his face masklike, waved to Barry to assist the Professor. Danbazzar never even glanced aside, as Barry threw a supporting arm around the tottering man and helped him to gain the outer chamber. There:

"Air!" he whispered. "I must have air."

The task of getting him along the sloping passage was no easy one; for Professor Blackwell was heavily built. Especially it was difficult at the point where the roof had collapsed, since here he must negotiate an opening only about eighteen inches high.

But it was done at last. The Professor sank down in that little artificial cave created by the screen, and shakily produced his flask.

"Go back," he said in a low voice—"go back. You will want to see if —"

"I couldn't think of it," Barry returned. "Not until you feel better. Was it the heat down there, Professor?"

Professor Blackwell returned his flask to his pocket. Some trace of normal colour was showing again in his cheeks. From a hiding place beneath his priest's robe he produced his spectacles and set them in place. He made a very grotesque picture. Then:

"Not entirely," he replied. "That was not without its effect, of course. But I confess that my threatened collapse was not entirely due to it. Your training, Barry, has not followed the same lines as mine. You are not only a younger man, but you are plastic-minded. The sight of a person defying the law of gravity without mechanical aid, for instance, would not appall you?"

"It would certainly interest me."

"Quite, quite. There's the difference. It would horrify *me!* And today I have witnessed a thing that has knocked the keystone out of the structure upon which my professional life rests. Those scientific principles to which, as a sane man, I have adhered unquestioningly throughout my career have been ruthlessly destroyed. Either modern physiology is fit only for the scrap heap or the claims of so-called occultists are worthy of close examination."

"You think she is really alive?" asked Barry eagerly.

"Think!" retorted the Professor. "I *know* she is! Whether the madhouse treatment now being employed by Danbazzar will terminate her miraculous trance or not I cannot say. But, quite definitely, she is alive! Go back, Barry. *I* dare not!"

Eagerly Barry obeyed. He returned to the scene of the poor Professor's seizure in a quarter of the time it had taken to come out. Softly raising the curtain he entered the chamber, all but intolerable, now, because of the clouds of incense.

He found his father and Danbazzar bending over Zalithea, their expressions tense. The slender curves which it had seemed desecration to uncover were hidden beneath a fine Egyptian shawl, but it revealed the delicate lines of her slim, still body.

Barry feasted his eyes on that pale face. Zalithea! Speculation was ended. Doubt was done with. By some unsuspected gift of prevision, of clairvoyance—call it what he might—he had been enabled to see her, though she lay deep in this rocky tomb, long before he had ever set foot on the black soil of Egypt! It was, therefore, predestined. As Hassan would have said, "It is written." For this he had been born. Because of this wonder which was to come, he had never found his ideal woman but had dreamed of dark mysterious eyes which one day would beckon to him. . . .

A faint sigh broke the deathly stillness. Princess Zalithea raised her drooping lashes—and looked long and wonderingly into the faces bending over her. Then, without otherwise stirring, she turned her dark, beautiful eyes in Barry's direction.

Danbazzar, that man of steel, gripped John Cumberland's shoulder and indicated the stoppered flagon. Cumberland, making a visible effort to steady his hand, poured the old wine into the goblet.

Never removing that fixed, childlike look of inquiry from Barry, the girl allowed Danbazzar very gently to lift her up. He held the draught to her lips and spoke a few words in a language entirely unfamiliar to the others.

Zalithea, glanced swiftly up at him and swallowed the drugged wine.

Then once more she looked at Barry, smiled like a tired child, and lay back, closing her eyes.

Danbazzar pointed to the doorway. As John Cumberland and Barry tiptoed out, he extinguished the seven lamps, joining them in the outer chamber.

"She is now sleeping normally," he whispered. "She should wake in eight- or nine-hours' time—and resume life!"

He reeled, clutched at Barry, and:

"Get me out," he said hoarsely. "I'm through."

CHAPTER XXI

THE AWAKENING

Perhaps, in his heart of hearts, no one of the party—excepting Danbazzar—had ever really counted on success. Certainly, in their wildest imaginings, they had not schooled their minds to acceptance of the miracle; had not realized what success would mean.

Slowly, and by different mental processes, realization came in turn to John Cumberland and to Barry, as it had come, instantly, insupportably, to the scientific mind of Professor Blackwell. A girl who had lived during the reign of Seti I—a girl barely out of her teens—was living now. She must be, according to ordinary human computation, fully three thousand two hundred years old; but, according to all the laws of modern physiology, she was still no more than nineteen or twenty!

To the Professor, the problem presented was one of scientific faith. Acceptance meant destruction of his life's labour, the tearing up of every textbook written on the subject; it assailed the very throne of reason itself. Rejection, with Zalithea living, meant closing his eyes to the truth. For a long time he remained alone in his tent and could not be induced to see her.

John Cumberland's problem was, a legal one. To whom did Zalithea belong? Since she antedated any government of which documentary trace remained, surely not to the authorities at Cairo? The thought that a false step might result in her loss was terrifying.

But, if these two found their ideas chaotic, how infinitely more so were those of Barry. At one moment he was raised to a poetic heaven. In the next he found himself plunged in an inferno of such torturing doubts that he longed for the power to run away from himself.

Upon the realization of his shadowy ideal, the proof that the unknown might become known, had followed, what? A knowledge that he must either fly from Zalithea or learn to love her—and that she was, to all intents and purposes, a supernatural being!

Such were the early reactions of these three to a phenomenon—and a phenomenon in the form of an unusually lovely girl—which struck deep at the roots of human credulity; which forced them to accept the inacceptable, to remain sane though face to face with madness.

Danbazzar alone attacked the problem with confidence. A large Bell tent was set up at the lower end of the *wâdi,* and furnished, though simply, in Ancient Egyptian fashion. The necessary materials he had brought with him and Hassan es-Sugra supervised the work. His optimistic foresight had not stopped here. A messenger who had been dispatched to Luxor at dawn returned before midday with an elderly Arab woman.

"She has been standing by over a week," said Danbazzar. "Hassan engaged her. She's a trained servant and was seven years in the harem of the last Khedive. Remember!" he warned. "Hassan doesn't know what we found in the sarcophagus! Nobody outside of this party knows. Zalithea is the sick daughter of a friend of mine in El Kasr who has come down for treatment by Professor Blackwell. That's the story, and we've got to stick to it. The sarcophagus was empty."

Accordingly Safiyeh was installed, with her few belongings, in the new tent. A covered litter was extemporized and Hassan dispatched on a mission to Kurna.

Danbazzar, following two hours of profound sleep, had become his capable self again. Three visits he had made to the tomb, and reported that Zalithea slumbered soundly. John Cumberland's anxiety was intense. He had urged the immediate removal of the girl from that nearly unbreathable atmosphere but had been overruled.

"We'll stick to the formula," said Danbazzar truculently, "with or without your permission. She has to stay there eight hours. After that we have nothing to go upon."

They carried the litter up to the tomb, setting it close to the screen. Professor Blackwell mounted guard at the top of the valley and Barry at the bottom. They wore their ordinary working kit; but John Cumberland and Danbazzar had arranged to put on the Ancient Egyptian dresses under cover of the screen before awakening the sleeper.

That Danbazzar could make himself understood in the long dead language known to Zalithea had been already proved. It was one further item of evidence showing his knowledge of Egyptology to be masterful.

"I know very few words," he admitted, "and until today I couldn't tell if my pronunciation was understandable. Others have claimed to know how to speak the language. But no living man for a thousand-odd years back has been able to prove it! I shall have to try to talk to her. She is sure to be frightened. I expect she'll be as weak as a kitten. And it's going to be no easy job to carry her up past that broken door."

"Let me help!" said John Cumberland eagerly. Danbazzar shook his head.

"Just stand by with the litter," he directed. "The fewer strange faces she sees the better. I can manage alone."

But the wonder of Egypt's sunset was stealing over the Valleys before the litter was borne down the *wâdi* to the tent and a slight, muffled figure tenderly carried inside.

Barry was wild to see her. Danbazzar would not consent.

"She's frightened to death," he said, "poor little girl. When she saw old Safîyeh she just fell into her arms and hid her face against her."

Professor Blackwell looked up. They were seated in the big tent.

"I have been endeavouring to do as you requested," he said. "But to prescribe any routine or diet for such a patient is quite beyond my powers. I have somewhat recovered from the first shock, however, and I am prepared to give her an examination at any time that may be convenient."

"When she has bathed and recovered from the journey," Danbazzar replied, "I should like you to see her. I think I have made her understand that the High Priest is coming."

"The High Priest!" exclaimed Professor Blackwell.

"Well, you must remember," said Danbazzar, "the priests were the doctors in her time. And I figured out that someone must have looked her over on the other occasions."

Professor Blackwell clutched his high brow.

"I was about to say something insane," he murmured. "I was going to ask if she seems to remember her last awakening. It suddenly occurred to me that this took place roughly three thousand years ago!"

"Yet she *does* seem to remember it," Danbazzar declared.

"What!" cried John Cumberland. "You have gathered this?"

Danbazzar inclined his head in that graceful manner which was his.

"I'm not certain," he confessed. "But I think so. I realize I only know enough of her language to act as a link. From this we must build up and teach her English as though she were a child. Her difficulties are going to be worse than those of an ordinary foreigner. We shall never be able to find any analogies! The objects, the customs—all are different."

Hassan es-Sugra, it appeared, had been prepared for the coming of the mythical sheik's daughter. He expressed no surprise on his return from Kurna, nor did he inquire what had become of her escort.

He had been making certain mysterious arrangements for transporting the tomb furniture to some place of safety. Work was to be resumed on the shaft next morning, with the object of widening it sufficiently to allow of the removal of the sarcophagus, and the unusual wall paintings were to be photographed before the tomb was reclosed.

Meanwhile, Professor Blackwell had completed a professional

examination of his strange and beautiful patient. He returned to the tent where the other members of the party awaited him, in an indescribably puzzled frame of mind. Removing his skullcap, he lighted a cigar and fortified himself with a peg of whisky from one of the bottles buried in the sand.

"Amazing!" he declared; "quite, quite amazing! Her pulse, respiration, and temperature are absolutely normal! Her flesh is firm and healthy. Her hair is vigorous; her teeth are perfect. I could swear that her nails were manicured yesterday!"

"They were last manicured around 1360 B.C.!" said Danbazzar.

"There is a small scar under the hair just above the right ear which suggests that the theory—now generally accepted, I believe—that surgery was practised by the ancients is not without foundation. She is in extraordinarily good spirits. I twice caught her laughing at me!"

No one seemed very surprised, but:

"What about diet?" asked John Cumberland. "Surely she should be treated as an invalid?"

"Frankly," the Professor returned, "I see no reason whatever to treat her as an invalid. Apart from the fact that she seems to be rather tired, I can detect no abnormal conditions of any kind. She addressed me several times during the interview, but her remarks were naturally unintelligible. They seemed to afford her considerable amusement, nevertheless. And the old woman from Luxor must have gathered something of their gist. She, also, appeared to be highly entertained."

"Safiyeh can't possibly have understood one word," said Danbazzar quickly. "Arabic is the only language she speaks, except for a smattering of English; and we have told her that Zalithea talks Kabyle."

"Which," added John Cumberland, "judging from her style of beauty, she certainly never did!"

"We'll know one day!" said Danbazzar.

"You don't think there's any danger," Barry broke in, "of—of—"

He fumbled for words, and:

"Of her crumbling to dust, or something of that sort?" the Professor concluded for him. "Your frame of mind, Barry, is gradually beginning to resemble my own. Frankly, I cannot answer your question. According to my personal observation, the young lady is as healthy as she is beautiful. According to my training and beliefs, she ought to have been dead for three thousand-odd years!"

"What amazes me," Barry declared, "is her cheerfulness! Just think. Everyone she ever knew is long forgotten. She found herself in a tomb, buried alive, this morning. Yet this evening you say she is laughing!"

"Her laughter may have been hysterical," murmured the Professor, pulling up his robe for greater comfort, and revealing the fact that beneath he wore a pair of very soiled gray flannel trousers rolled up some six inches above his sandals. "No doubt a visit from a High Priest is somewhat awe-inspiring."

At the end of further discussion, a dinner menu for Zalithea was decided upon, and Mahmoud given the necessary orders. A new spirit of restlessness had descended upon the party. If they had solved their first great problem, another faced them.

Barry, having prepared for the evening meal, climbed the side of the *wâdi* to that spot from which on the night of their arrival he had watched the sun setting. It was not so long ago. It seemed an age. He knew that something had happened in the interval which marked the end of one phase of his life, the beginning of another.

Now that he had actually seen Zalithea, that vague dread which had sometimes troubled him when he had found himself thinking of the girl on the balcony had gone. Yet, he asked himself tonight, did not his recognition of this girl increase rather than solve the mystery?

Since it could not possibly have been Zalithea he had seen on that balcony in New Jersey, then in the garden of Mr. Brown's house, and later on Fifth Avenue, it must have been her living double!—this or, as others had suspected, a delusion. But why should he have suffered this delusion, not once, but many times, immediately prior to the night that the papyrus came into his father's possession?

Surely he was justified in believing that only some form of telepathy or clairvoyance could explain it . . . and that this explanation presupposed a mysterious bond of sympathy between himself and the girl he was destined to meet?

The Ancient Egyptians, he understood, believed in reincarnation. Since their wisdom was so great in such matters, as the extended life of Zalithea proved, quite possibly they were right. *She* had slept, miraculously, living on; but *he* had died in the ordinary way, and was now reborn—in the ordinary way!

He recalled, was ever recalling, how she had looked at him in the moment of opening her long, dark eyes. Death had effaced physical memory in his own case; only subconscious memory remained. But Zalithea, never having died, remembered! They had met before, in those remote days—and she remembered him!

It was an idea that first delighted and then terrified Barry. He had imagined, on that night in his father's library, that the shadow of Ancient Egypt was creeping out to touch him.

He had been right!

What this inexplicable discovery might mean to John Cumberland, to Danbazzar, to Professor Blackwell, he could only dimly foresee. But what did it mean to him?

This he could not foresee at all.

And then, as he began mechanically to climb down to the camp, the sound of a distant voice reached his ears. It was a laughing voice . . . and he knew that he had heard it before!

CHAPTER XXII

A SUMMONS FROM THE PRINCESS

"I have reached a decision," declared Professor Blackwell, "upon a point that has been worrying me." Dinner dispatched, they sat around the table in council, pipes and cigars going. Safîyeh had reported that her charge had found the soup, the fried chicken, the Château y'Quem—of which they had only three bottles—and the peaches entirely to her satisfaction.

"What point?" asked John Cumberland.

"Distinctly," the Professor resumed, "distinctly she is the property of the Department of Antiquities."

"What's that!" cried Barry. "What on earth are you talking about?"

"He's talking sense," Danbazzar's deep voice broke in. "There are no two ways about it. She is."

"Are you all mad?" said Barry. "You behave as though the Department of Antiquities were an orphanage!"

"Or a harem agency," prompted the Professor. "Yet the fact remains that they and no one else have a legal claim upon her person. We are no more entitled to remove her from the country, alive, than we should have been entitled to do so had we found her in what I may term a normal state. I mean dead. She is as much the property of the Department as the sarcophagus she lay in."

"I must agree with you," John Cumberland admitted. "Our difficulties are enormous. The more I think about them the bigger they get. For instance—since none of us dare testify that he was present at the discovery, how can we ever give an account of it to the world?"

"We can't!" said the Professor. "Distinctly and definitely, I for one should not consent under any circumstances to lend my name to a statement on the subject. In the first place, assuming I were safely out of the country before the issue of such a report, criminal proceedings would undoubtedly be taken by the Egyptian government! This applies to all of us!"

Some moments of uncomfortable silence followed, then:

"The fact is," Danbazzar stated, "the greatest find in Egyptology since the game began has got to blush unseen. I hadn't thought of it. I'll say so honestly. None of us had thought of it. But there it is all the same. The testimony of this bunch would carry a lot of weight in America. I don't say we'd go unchallenged. But we'd be taken seriously. We're not going to get the chance. We started working in the dark. We've got to go on that way."

"I wish, now," said John Cumberland regretfully, "that I had curbed my impatience and formally applied for a permit to excavate."

"You'd never have got it!" Danbazzar assured him. "You might as well apply for a pass-out check to heaven! And once you'd applied and been turned down, to come here as we've done would have been to ask for trouble. No, sir, I'd worked on it from that angle before I put up my proposition."

"Then where do we stand?" cried Barry in bewilderment. "What have we gained if our discoveries can't be published?"

Danbazzar regarded him fixedly across the table.

"We have gained knowledge," he replied, "that has been lost for thousands of years. With what we know, and what Zalithea can tell us when we teach her English, we're going to revolutionize archaeology, physiology, and psychology—to say nothing of chemistry!"

"It appears to me," murmured Professor Blackwell, "that this tent contains the nucleus of a sort of New Rosicrucian order. We are bound together by a living secret which none of us dare divulge. Our present access of knowledge is very great. What we shall learn in the future from this phenomenal girl is also sure to be valuable. But of what use any of it is going to be to the world during our lifetime I confess I fail to see."

Evidently nobody was very clear on the point, for not a suggestion was forthcoming; but:

"In one sense," said John Cumberland, "our course is unavoidable. We are committed to go on. Until we have got clear and reclosed the tomb, we aren't safe! Personally, I'm satisfied. Our very highest hopes have been realized. We have triumphed! That's good enough for me. Let the future take care of itself. My present big worry is the girl."

"Explain what you mean, Dad," said Barry.

"I will," his father agreed. "In the first place, as soon as we can make her understand how much the world has changed, we have got to get over to Luxor. Difficulty number one: How do we explain her to the folks in Luxor? Assuming we manage this and arrive in Cairo, how in the name of Mike do we get her a passport that will be accepted in

New York?"

"Passport?" murmured the Professor. "Quite—quite. The point had not occurred to me. Of course, a certain difficulty is bound to arise in regard to a minor whose legal guardians have been dead for three thousand years." He scratched his head furiously. "There are times when I doubt my own sanity," he declared.

Danbazzar flicked a cone of ash from his cigar. In the lamplight a queer green spark moved on the face of the scarab in his ring.

"Leave the story to me," he said. "The stuff, I can get away. It's part of my business. The girl we'll smuggle out nearly as easily. We've got to lie like bond salesmen, but we'll get her away."

"Fried chicken," murmured the Professor.

"What's that, Blackwell?" John Cumberland asked.

"I was reflecting," the Professor explained, "upon the fact that a princess who doubtless has dined in the palace of the Pharaoh Seti I this evening partook of soup canned in Pittsburgh. I think I shall go to bed."

He was as good as his word, departing almost immediately. Danbazzar set out to learn if the two guards posted in the valley were on the alert, and Barry and his father were left alone. Hassan es-Sugra, that unfathomable man, was sleeping in the entrance to the tomb to insure against pilfering.

As the sound of Danbazzar's receding footsteps died away in the *wâdi*:

"You haven't said much, Barry," John Cumberland remarked, after an interval during which he had been closely watching his son; "but I think you have quite a lot to say all the same."

Barry started, looking up. Then he began to knock out his pipe on the heel of his shoe.

"You mean, about—Zalithea?"

John Cumberland nodded.

"Well—I have!" Barry admitted. "She is the girl I saw twice in New Jersey and twice in New York!"

"I knew it!" said John Cumberland. "I didn't speak, when I saw it first. I was waiting. Now that we have actually found her, alive, it's a different matter. Barry—I think I can explain the whole thing."

"Then go ahead, Dad!" Barry invited.

"We have proof—living proof—that the Ancient Egyptians knew more than *we* know. If they were wiser in one respect, it's only reasonable to suppose they were wiser in others. Now, here's what I believe: you didn't see Zalithea in America. You had *prevision* of her! Danbazzar spoke of what we know, upsetting physiology and psychology. It's going to upset religion as well. I believe you had an incarnation in Egypt at the time of Seti I, and I believe Zalithea remembers you!"

Barry started up excitedly.

"Why," he exclaimed, "I had come to just that conclusion only tonight! It's unavoidable, Dad! There's no other explanation."

They discussed the problem at some length, with the result that they agreed upon the main issue while differing about minor points.

"Poor humanity's unanswerable question—the destiny of the soul—has been answered for *us!*" said John Cumberland. "I'm dazzled, Barry, by the magnificence of all these revelations. We have learned something, or are on the verge of learning it, which has taxed the greatest intellects in history."

When finally John Cumberland turned in, Danbazzar had not come back from his tour of inspection. Barry, feverishly restless, lighted a fresh pipe and strolled out into the *wâdi*.

The night was very dark. Leaving the door of the tent, he walked into a wall of shadow, until, around a natural buttress, he saw a patch of light upon the sand ahead. It came from the entrance of Zalithea's tent. Danbazzar was just coming out. He wore the priest's robe and linen skullcap. Barry paused: and in the next moment Danbazzar saw him.

"I was coming to get you," he called.

"Why? Is there anything wrong?"

Danbazzar joined him.

"No," he replied. "But old Safiyeh was hanging around to speak to me. She caught me on my way back. Come along and get into a robe."

"What!" Barry exclaimed. "Why?"

"Because Princess Zalithea wants to see you!"

Barry pulled up dead in his tracks. His heart began thumping.

"How do you know?" he demanded. "I mean, how did she make you understand?"

"Largely by signs," Danbazzar admitted. "My Egyptian is mighty limited. But I'm learning."

That old sensation of unreality, phantasy, came to Barry again. Urged by Danbazzar, he attired himself in the strange dress that they had adopted with the idea that it would be more familiar to the awakened girl. Then, not entirely master of himself, he walked back along the *wâdi*. At Zalithea's tent:

"Wait outside," Danbazzar directed. "Safiyeh will call you when I have made her understand you are here. I'll do my best as interpreter."

He went in, leaving Barry alone in the darkness.

Vaguely, a sound of voices came to him where he waited. The deep, subdued tones of Danbazzar made a marked contrast to the silvery note of that other voice! How well he seemed to know it!

Barry wondered why he was so nervous.

Suddenly the flap was drawn open, and the old Arab woman looked out, beckoning. Barry stooped and went in.

He found himself in a sort of tiny antechamber or lobby constructed of hanging tent cloths. An antique lamp hung from above. There were carpets on the sandy floor, but no furniture.

Safîyeh held one of the tent cloths aside and intimated that he was to enter. He stepped forward. Some hazy impression he had of a silver lamp, of embroidered curtains, of cushions, queer-looking inlaid chests, but these were an indistinct background into which the tall robed figure of Danbazzar merged appropriately. He was standing behind a cushioned divan, or native mattress.

Upon it, her cheek resting in her upraised hand, lay Princess Zalithea.

She was dressed in a manner which perhaps represented a compromise between the ancient and the modern Egyptian style. Her beautiful arms were bare to the shoulders, and she wore no jewellery of any kind. A sort of tightly fitting tunic and some sort of gauzy dress disguised in a measure the delicate shape which Danbazzar's scissors had so mercilessly revealed in the tomb. Her white ankles were bare, as also were her little feet. It was so that he remembered her.

Long, dark, heavily fringed eyes were raised to Barry as he entered. They were the deeply mysterious eyes that had watched him since memory began—the beckoning eyes of the women who lived upon the frescoes surrounding his father's walls—the eyes that had smiled down upon him from a New Jersey balcony!

How beautiful she was! But how pale and fragile. He found himself unable to believe Safîyeh's report that she had enjoyed the meal so carefully prepared for her. Those full red lips, though, spoke of health. He was hopelessly, speechlessly embarrassed, under the grave scrutiny of unreadable eyes. But how beautiful she was!

"Speak to her," Danbazzar prompted.

Barry bowed awkwardly.

"Princess Zalithea," he said, "I am deeply honoured."

She watched him, unmoved, for several moments more. Then, a slow, delightful smile revealed her little gleaming teeth. She turned her head slightly, looking up at Danbazzar. She spoke in soft, queerly modulated syllables. One word which might have been "Zalithea," but accented very differently from Barry's rendering, gave him a clue to her question. Danbazzar replied, slowly, haltingly; then:

"I think," he said, "she is curious about how you learned her name.

She seems to have recognized it. I told her that you were a very learned priest. She wants to know what you are called. Tell her."

Zalithea turned her disturbing glance upon him again, as:

"I am called Barry Cumberland," he responded.

Zalithea considered the words, then:

"Bahree?" she said—and nodded interrogatively.

"Yes—Barry; Barry Cumberland."

She smiled, shaking her head in bewilderment. She looked up at Danbazzar and addressed him again. He listened, interpolating hesitant questions, while Barry watched, fascinated. Presently:

"She understands that you are called Barry," he explained. "Cumberland is too much for her. Now, she is going to tell you how to pronounce *her* name properly."

Zalithea turned to Barry, and, laying one slender hand on her breast:

"Zal'ith-*eeah*," she said distinctly, and beckoned to him to approach closer.

He did so, almost trembling: the mad wonder of it all had seized upon him anew. Zalithea, in a sweetly imperious way, intimated that he should kneel. He obeyed, and she laid her hand on his breast. His heart was thumping wildly. She looked fixedly into his eyes.

"Bahree," she said, and smiled.

CHAPTER XXIII

AN ENGLISH LESSON

The sound of a distant shot came—from the direction of the Nile. Professor Blackwell looked up with a start. He was inclined to nervousness in these days. Breakfast was temporarily suspended.

"Mr. Tawwab has called for the rent!" said Danbazzar grimly. He raised his great voice, looking over his shoulder. "Mahmoud!" he boomed.

The grinning face of Mahmoud appeared in the opening of the tent. Danbazzar spoke rapidly in Arabic. Mahmoud saluted and departed.

"I've told him," Danbazzar explained, "to warn Safîyeh that they must keep under cover and then to go up and tell the guards, in case they missed the signal."

It was now Zalithea's custom to take exercise, veiled like a Moslem woman, early each morning and again in the evening. In a manner reminiscent of that adopted (by request) during the historic ride of Lady Godiva, not a soul was visible about the camp on these occasions.

Hassan es-Sugra, at a respectful distance, acted as escort. And he had his instructions touching prohibited areas. After a time, Zalithea had seemed to recognize where she was. At the first coming of this recognition—realizing that she was in the Valley of the Dead—she had been seized with terror. Danbazzar's linguistic resources had been taxed to the utmost to pacify her.

Ultimately he succeeded in making her understand that she had slept, magically, for a very long time; that Thebes (which she knew apparently as Amen) had altered beyond recognition; and that they wanted her to become accustomed to strange changes before taking her there.

Once having conquered her first natural terror, the girl accepted her situation with astonishing philosophy. A reaction came. Perhaps she had grasped the fact that a new lease of life had been granted to her— and that life was sweet. At any rate, she developed a strain of childish mischief at once delightful and disturbing. For Danbazzar's orders she had little respect, apparently; but that diplomat was quick to learn that for Barry she would do anything.

"I trust," said the Professor, nervously glancing at his watch, "that the young lady from Unu will subdue her high spirits while Mr. Tawwab is in camp."

"I'm going to send Barry along to keep her quiet," replied Danbazzar.

Whereupon Barry felt a hot flush rising to his cheeks and hastily stooped to load a pipe.

"A duty by no means irksome," the Professor murmured. "I confess that a woman of more than sixty is no longer attractive in the amorous sense. I had never imagined that one over three thousand could be. But I was mistaken. Indeed, all my life has been lived in error."

"In another three days," said Danbazzar, flashing a triumphant glance around the table, "we'll be through! All the stuff is where Mr. Tawwab will never see it. The photographs are finished. My drawings I can complete when I like. It's just a matter of building up the opening, now, and striking the screen."

"My notes are fairly up to date, also," John Cumberland added. "I have material for a book that publishers would fight to get."

"Quite, quite," remarked the Professor. "But except as a work of fiction you cannot publish it."

"I shall write it, nevertheless," the other assured him. "It will be in three volumes. The first volume will deal, exhaustively, with the history of the papyrus and the formula. It will bring the account up to the time of our arrival here. The second volume will be compiled from notes made on the spot. It will deal with the excavation and end with the discovery of Zalithea. The third volume will contain the story of her life during the reign of Seti."

"Admirable," the Professor agreed. "I shall be obligated, however, if you will refer to me in your *magnum opus* as Doctor X."

And now, a slender, mysterious, black-robed figure, Hassan es-Sugra bowed in the tent opening.

"Your pardon, sirs," he said in his gentle way, "but Mr. Tawwab comes. He will shortly be here."

"I vote we *all* see him!" cried Barry. "Why should we study his feelings? He's just a common grafter."

"In studying the sensibilities of Mr. Tawwab," remarked Professor Blackwell, "one would be studying the non-existent; a paradox. But our own position is not too secure."

"We don't have to jolt him," Danbazzar agreed. "We're not out of the wood. But Mr. Cumberland and I can talk business. It's just as well that he should show his hand with a witness here. I guess, Professor, you'd rather not stay. And I'm taking Barry along to the Princess."

"Why?" Barry demanded, laughing to hide his embarrassment.

"Because you may be able to keep her in order. Nobody else can."

"But I can't talk to her!"

"You've got to learn. Give her some elementary lessons in English."

The masterful Danbazzar had his way; and Barry found himself, a few minutes later, in the little lobby of Zalithea's tent. Danbazzar went in to announce him, and almost immediately Safiyeh appeared, holding the tent cloth aside and intimating that he should enter.

He found this wonder girl who was so distractingly human, this charming survival of a mystic past, stretched on the cushioned mattress, her head buried in her creamy arms rebelliously. Danbazzar stood looking down at her in an unfamiliar attitude of defeat.

"She's a bit up-stage this morning," he announced, "It's so darned hard to remember that she's a princess and probably used to a lot of ceremony. I thought I had her set about the robes. I tried to tell her that we only wore them on religious occasions, and that other times we dressed as we're dressed now. I had to tell her something, because she caught me on Monday, you remember, coming back from the tomb?"

"I do remember," said Barry. "But when I saw her, later, she seemed to be used to our queer costumes."

Danbazzar looked down at his white breeches and speckless tan riding boots.

"It isn't that," he explained. "She's got the idea that the robes are ceremonious and that we're slighting her by not wearing them when we come to see her."

Zalithea half raised her oval face, so that one dark eye peeped out over the rampart of her arm. A quick, disdainful glance she flashed over Barry, from his bare head to his dusty shoes; and hid her face again.

"That's that," sighed Danbazzar. "There's no time to go back. But wait outside and I'll have your robes brought down by Hassan."

They turned to go, when:

"Dan-bazz-ah!" said a clear, imperious voice.

Barry and Danbazzar turned, together.

Princess Zalithea was sitting upright, her arms outstretched, her hands resting upon the cushions on either side of her. From her pale, beautiful features all expression had been effaced. They were like an exquisite ivory mask into which a magician has blown the breath of life.

She spoke a sentence rapidly, her long, half-closed eyes turned sideways upon Danbazzar. He bowed in his graceful manner and replied very hesitantly. No expression stirred the girl's lovely face.

"I was right," he explained. "She considers that we've insulted her! I took all the blame and told her you had just come back from a journey and asked to see her right away."

Barry frowned, and:

"Is it necessary to tell her so many lies?" he asked.

"You bet it is!" Danbazzar assured him. "Look at her!"

Barry glanced, guiltily, toward the divan. He started. Zalithea was watching them with a stare of such murderous anger that his heart seemed to turn cold! He would never have conceived it possible that her youthful features could assume a look of such utter malignancy.

Watching her, fascinated against his will, he experienced again that awful tingling of the spine which he had known during his vigil in the valley on the night he had heard the strange voice. Definitely, he knew in this moment that it had been *her* voice . . . although she had lain buried deep in the heart of the rock! Yes, this girl-woman, this child-witch who had first seen the light in an island unknown to modern geography, was uncanny!

Danbazzar's deep tones broke in upon the silence; he addressed Zalithea in the musical, oddly monotonous language which Barry was beginning to recognize as that which the Pharaohs spoke. Then:

"Come on!" he said abruptly. "I can hear Tawwab."

He raised the tent cloth. Barry was about to follow him out, when:

"Bahree!" came softly.

He turned. Danbazzar had gone, dropping the curtain. He was alone with Zalithea!

Half fearfully, he looked at her. . . .

She was resting on her elbow, watching him, and her sweet lips were arched in a smile which revealed little gleaming teeth! Her eyes, widely opened now, were deep pools of contrition; her delicate nostrils quivered. She was on the verge of tears!

Barry experienced a dramatic revulsion of feeling. In his hard, modern, Western self-sufficiency, he had wounded the tender susceptibilities of this sheltered flower of the East. What did *he*, or Danbazzar, for that matter, know of courts and palaces? Much less they knew of the splendid ceremony of those old, dead days when Seti, from Thebes of the Hundred Gates, ruled a mighty empire!

He hated himself and hated Danbazzar. They had a princess among them, and they treated her like a chambermaid! They discussed her as though she were a marketable relic, to be bought and sold—this living, lovely revelation of the wonder that was Egypt!

Some remote ancestor who had known the meaning of homage came to life in Barry; seized him by the scruff of the neck and forced him onto his knees. Very near to Zalithea he knelt, his head bowed, waiting for pardon.

Instantly it was granted.

A little hesitant hand touched his hair; and he looked up. The girl's long, curling lashes, the most perfect he had ever seen, were wet with tears.

"Forgive me!" he burst out, forgetting that she could not understand. "I—he—neither of us—meant to hurt you!"

She smiled through her tears and touched his hair again.

"Bahree," she said, and made a quaint gesture which conveyed dismissal of the subject.

And then, very close together, in silence, these two remained for long moments, watching one another; the girl reclining on her cushions and the man kneeling beside her. In that odd hush, the suave tones of Mr. Tawwab were clearly audible as he entered the upper end of the *wâdi* in conversation with Danbazzar. A subdued booming was all that could be distinguished of the latter's responses. Both voices presently ceased. The party had met in the tent above.

Barry suddenly grew self-conscious. He was kneeling beside Zalithea and studying her raptly. It had occurred to him that this was the height of rudeness. True, she had suffered his scrutiny without complaint, but this did not excuse his bad form.

In a nervous endeavour to break the tension, and recalling Danbazzar's instructions, he touched a symbol embroidered upon one of the tent cloths draped beside the divan. It was the *crux ansata*, symbol of life; and:

"This," he said, "means Life."

Zalithea looked at it, then turned to him. She seemed to be trying hard to grasp what he had in mind; and finally:

"*Ankh*," she said.

"You call it *ankh?*" he asked eagerly; for he knew this to be the Ancient Egyptian term for the figure. Zalithea, listening and watching, smiled.

"*Ankh*," she repeated.

"Life," said Barry.

"Lie-ef," Zalithea whispered doubtfully.

"Life!"

She shook her head. And Barry realized how, tempted by the fact that he chanced to know its Egyptian name, he had chosen an object impossible to explain in pantomime. Zalithea, laughing now, stretched out a finger and laid it gently upon his eyelid.

"Eye," he said eagerly.

"Eye," she repeated.

She touched his ear.

"Ear."

"Ee-ah!"

So the first lesson began—a lesson in a science that was old even in Seti's days. Master and pupil forgot the passing of the hours in that enthralling study. Old Safiyeh, squatting patiently on her mat beyond the curtain, nodded as the sun climbed a blue highway toward the dome of noon. Innumerable cups of coffee had been drunk by Danbazzar, John Cumberland, and Mr. Tawwab, and entire boxes of cigarettes consumed. But still Barry said, touching Zalithea:

"Arm!"

And Zalithea, watching him, replied:

"Aah-em!"

When, at last, a substantial check having changed hands, Mr. Tawwab rose to take his departure, he showed a marked preference for a route through the lower end of the *wâdi*. Mr. Tawwab was an observant man.

Suddenly, raised voices disturbed the English lesson. Zalithea sat very upright, listening.

"If you don't mind, yes!" Mr. Tawwab was saying. "Your camp is so interesting. I should love to see your kitchen."

Placing a finger on her lips, Zalithea stood up. In her simple native dress Barry thought she was the sweetest thing he had ever looked upon.

"Zalithea," he murmured, "you are adorable!"

She paused, glancing down at him.

"Zal'ith-*eeah!*" she corrected; then: "You-ah-addorahble!" she added.

Before he realized what she intended to do, she had glided to the tent cloth, raised it, and gone out. He jumped up and followed her. He had recalled, tardily, the real purpose of the interview. His duty was to see that Zalithea did not make her presence known to Mr. Tawwab!

In the tiny lobby, old Safîyeh had scrambled hastily to her feet. Beside her mat was a bowl in which were some peaches which Zalithea had evidently rejected as overripe. Some of them, presumably, Safîyeh had consumed. The less desirable remained.

Mr. Tawwab's voice came from immediately outside. He had paused on his way down the *wâdi*.

"Surely a new tent?" he inquired smoothly.

"Sure!" boomed Danbazzar. "An English Bell tent, sir!"

"You have guests?"

"No, sir! We're hoping for guests—distinguished guests—and we're all ready. If ever you feel like spending a night with the boys, say the word!"

"I am deeply indebted," Mr. Tawwab assured him. "It would be delightful. But my duties do not allow."

"That's a pity," said Danbazzar.

They moved on, slowly—and Zalithea, ignoring Barry's restraining hand, pulled the flap aside and peered out. Over her shoulder, he could see Danbazzar, a great, towering figure, moving down the *wâdi* beside the slight, red-capped form of Mr. Tawwab.

Then, in a moment, it had happened.

Displaying a deadly aim, Zalithea hurled an imperfect peach at the retreating Mr. Tawwab!

It struck him on the back of the head, squashed liberally, and dislodged his *tarbûsh!* With a cry of mingled fear and anger, he turned. Barry dropped the flap and sank back, aghast. . . .

Zalithea, both hands held over her mouth, fled beyond the tent cloth. Safîyeh, horror-stricken, followed.

"Hell's bells!" roared Danbazzar. "Mr. Tawwab, I can't say what I think! It's that half-wit Said! Wait here, sir! Take my handkerchief ! By God! I'll—"

He ran back and burst into the tent in an apparent fury. Barry faced him.

"Zalithea?" Danbazzar whispered.

Barry nodded.

"Howl like fury!" Danbazzar directed—"not in English!"

Thereupon he broke into a flood of Arabic, and clapped his hands, simulating smacks. Barry yelled obediently.

"You son of a mange!" Danbazzar concluded—and went out. "He's crazy, Mr. Tawwab," he called. "Don't blame me. Blame the people that hired him to me. . . ."

CHAPTER XXIV

THE RETURN TO LUXOR

Work in the valley was ended. The tomb, stripped of its contents, had been reclosed so that even Mr. Howard Carter could not have found it. The workmen, well paid and happy, had dispersed to their homes. Most of them were men of the Fayyum.

Danbazzar and Hassan es-Sugra had contrived the transport of Zalithea from the camp in the *wâdi* to a carefully chosen suite at a Luxor hotel without provoking comment. John Cumberland's bank account had silenced any criticisms regarding the nature of his interest in the heavily veiled Moslem lady for whose accommodation he had arranged. The thing had run on oiled wheels, dollars being the lubricant; but since there is more grit in the world than there are dollars, this smooth running inevitably couldn't last.

Barry, whose dream woman had miraculously come to life, found himself in a frame of mind which he was sane enough to recognize as unique. The Zalithea he knew, the adorable, winning, childish, petulant, sometimes frightening girl, he was learning to worship. The Zalithea of the papyrus, the princess of unknown origin who had been captured by the troops of Seti in an unimaginable past, he fought to forget.

Advance guards of the Thomas Cook army had already established themselves in Luxor. A German party, some days earlier, and on the eve of striking camp, had penetrated to the *wâdi*. Their insatiable Teutonic curiosity was their only guide; Danbazzar's lurid profanity their only reward. Even the donkey boys had blushed.

But the incident had gone to prove that they had achieved their purpose only just in time. It was the tourist invasion which had checked Danbazzar a year before.

That remarkable man, whose resourcefulness knew no bounds, had long since set out, accompanied by Hassan es-Sugra, two camel drivers and a large sum of ready money, for the Great Oasis. Here he had arranged to meet a certain sheik of the Shorbagis from Dakhla and to obtain from him a document, suitably witnessed, authorizing John Cumberland to escort the sheik's daughter, Zalithea, to America for neuropathic treatment prescribed by Professor Blackwell.

"The Senussi," Danbazzar had admitted, "are the most dangerous fanatics in Africa. One of that bunch would be about as likely to send his daughter to America as to burn his whiskers for firewood. But nobody here will be any wiser, never having been to those parts, and the American consul, who is a Greek from Alexandria, doesn't know an Arab from an onion. We'll get her passport without any trouble."

Zalithea's balcony overlooked the Nile. Here she spent many hours every day, watching the varied life of the river front. Her bewilderment Barry found at once pathetic and delicious. The dragomans, who were now beginning to put in an appearance, she mistook for priests. The strangely garbed tourists she assumed to be foreign captives!

The advent of the first steamer from Cairo aroused such terror that Barry grew alarmed. He found himself utterly incapable of explaining this mystery, handicapped as he was. Automobiles, for some reason, frightened her but little. Indeed, she managed to make him understand at last that she wished to ride in one!

That once vexed question of dress had been settled. Zalithea understood that no slight was intended by the wearing of a lounge suit. She seemed to think that the Winter Palace was the palace of Pharaoh, and she tried to ask if the reigning monarch was absent at war.

She was extraordinarily observant. In the cool of the evening, with Safiyeh in attendance, and escorted by Barry or John Cumberland, Zalithea would walk along the bank as far as the old *shadûf*. The really fashionable crowd was not yet in evidence, but, nevertheless, she quickly noticed—since wealthy Moslem women rarely appear in public—that except among the lower classes veils were nowhere to be seen.

This problem was quite beyond Barry's power of explanation. But John Cumberland, in his practical way, set to work to solve it.

From Cairo one day stacks of boxes arrived and were duly carried up to Zalithea's apartment. Barry had just bought her a bundle of illustrated magazines and was watching her, fascinatedly, as she pored over pages of photographs showing society groups in various sun traps from Mentone to Miami.

What an exquisite profile she had! He wondered, was eternally wondering, where the island of Unu had been. Zalithea's long, narrow dark eyes were of a kind he had never seen among the modern Egyptians, but they were typical of the women depicted on the ancient wall paintings. Her profile, too, was purely aristocratic and bore a remarkable resemblance to that of the beautiful queen Ameniritis. His rapt study of the girl was interrupted by the delivery of the boxes.

Zalithea ran in from the balcony immediately, filled with childish interest. As box after box was laid on the carpet, her excitement grew intense. Stooping, she touched a label, looked at Barry interrogatively and then indicated herself.

"Yes," he said, "for you! All for you."

"Fo-ah you?"

"No—you! you are me! I don't know how to explain!" He rested his hand on her shoulder. "Me," he said.

Zalithea, watching him eagerly, touched her own breast, and:

"Me," she echoed.

"Yes !" Barry nodded. "For me."

"Fo-ah me."

She clapped her hands excitedly and indicated that he should cut the fastenings. Happy because Zalithea was happy, he obeyed. . . . and out from this box and from that, with a vast rustling of tissue paper, came frocks, stockings, hats, flaky, delicate underwear—priceless loot of Paris.

Never had he seen Zalithea so excited. Taking up piece after piece, she literally danced in her joy!

Then, crying, "Safiyeh! Safiyeh!" she gathered up a great armful of assorted garments and ran into her bedroom. She had apparently forgotten Barry's existence. But he walked out onto the balcony to await her reappearance. Knowing his father's thoroughness, he didn't doubt that John Cumberland would have found some way to obtain things to fit. Zalithea had been early introduced to shoes; so that this part of her equipment was comparatively simple. As for the other items, perhaps he had enlisted Safiyeh's aid.

Barry looked out across the Nile to where the Libyan Desert baked under the merciless sun. He could hear Zalithea's delicious, childish laughter and the harsher tones of Safiyeh. The miracle of it all crashed down suddenly upon his mind like a palpable weight.

This gay, light-hearted girl, whose laughter rang out clear as a bell, happily as a child's, had lain for three thousand years over yonder in the Valley of the Dead!

He picked up a magazine at random from the little table set upon the balcony. There were things he couldn't face—yet. He wondered if he ever would be capable of facing them. He dropped into a cane chair and began to scan the pictured pages.

In a section devoted to the doings of New York Society, he came across photographs of two or three people he knew. He stared at them as at the pictures of strangers. He felt that a great gulf had opened between himself and the empty life he had known. Upon one side of it were the old set, Aunt Micky, Jim and the rest; upon the other he stood, alone—with Zalithea.

Beneath, beside the river, moved men and women to whom Thebes meant sightseeing and sunshine—no more. He watched them as through a haze or as in a glass, darkly. Then, from a minaret at the back of the town, distantly, sweetly, came the voice of the *muezzin* raised in the *adan*, or noonday call to prayer:

"*Alla-hu akbar. . . . La illa-ha ilia Allah! . . .*"

"God is most great. . . . There is no God but God!" He listened to those words, which he knew, with a fresh wonder. For some reason they soothed his troubled mind. The passive attitude of Islam toward life was very wise, after all. He found himself thinking of Hassan es-Sugra, that grave, graceful philosopher, when:

"Bahree!" came a cry from the room behind him.

He turned. His eyes, dazzled by the blazing sunlight, at first could see little in the darkened room. Then, standing just within the doorway communicating with her bedroom, he saw Zalithea.

She wore a very up-to-date dance frock which displayed more of her creamy skin than Barry had seen since that unforgettable hour in the tomb when Danbazzar's scissors had stripped off the wrappings. With unfailing instinct she had selected shoes to harmonize with the frock, which was very short.

Manlike, he thought she looked exquisite—and showed that he thought so. The admiring, grinning face of old Safiyeh appeared in the doorway, as Zalithea, almost timidly, came forward into the room. The girl's wonderful, black-fringed eyes were set upon Barry with an expression of childish eagerness.

Something very unusual there was in her appearance, not due to her wholly different style of beauty, but to some irregularity in her attire which for a moment he failed to place.

Then, all at once, he saw what it was.

Zalithea's shapely creamy legs were bare! She had forgotten to put stockings on! Watching him anxiously, she spoke.

"Zal'ith-eeah I" she said. "You-ah-addorahble!"

CHAPTER XXV

SOCIAL AMENITIES

On the eve of Danbazzar's return, Barry ran into his acquaintance, the irrigation specialist, in the lounge of the hotel. "Hullo!" said that chronically bored person, dropping into a neighbouring armchair. "I've only just come in from Assouan, but I heard you were back. How's the oasis lookin'?"

"Splendid," Barry returned hastily, hoping that the other had forgotten about the dates. "Dry Martini?"

"Thanks," was the reply. "Rumour has it that a charmin' stranger has joined your party."

"Oh!" said Barry. "With which of her many tongues did Rumour whisper this news?"

"Tawwab," drawled the tired voice. "Nasty bit of work. Know him?"
Barry nodded.

"I have that misfortune."

He experienced a vague uneasiness. To the best of his knowledge, Mr. Tawwab's hold upon them was no more. But the man's insatiable appetite for *bakhshish* on a grand scale might inspire him to some new piece of interference. He wished Danbazzar were back.

Zalithea was dining downstairs tonight. It would be the first time she had appeared in public unveiled. Barry had reserved a discreet table, and when he had left Zalithea to dress, she had been wild with excitement. A French chambermaid had been detailed to assist. Inexplicably, the hotel seemed to have become filled up. The lounge was crowded. A number of visitors had arrived during the afternoon. He hoped Mr. Tawwab was not present.

"Our guest is the daughter of a friend of Danbazzar's," he explained. "Professor Blackwell is treating her for nerve trouble."

"I see," murmured the irrigator, sipping his drink and lighting a cigarette. "Danbazzar is the sportsman like a Moorish pirate?"

"Yes!" said Barry, laughing.

"Saw him when you were here before. Extraordinary lookin' bird. Do you grow 'em like that in America?"

"Not in large quantities."

"*Rara avis*, eh? Tawwab was tellin' me your girlfriend only speaks Kabyle. As I don't know whether Kabyle is a vegetable or an ointment I ain't any wiser."

"It would be quite a good thing if Tawwab attended to his own business, don't you think?"

"Rather. It'd choke him—which would be toppin'."

John Cumberland and Professor Blackwell came down shortly afterward, and the bored young man went off to join a friend who was dining with him. While they waited for Zalithea, Barry related what he had heard.

"Mr. Tawwab is a subject who was born to be poisoned," said the Professor. "I shall feel altogether more at ease when I find myself outside his sphere of influence."

"It's disturbing," muttered John Cumberland. "I fear he's up to fresh mischief. He hadn't counted on our slipping away so soon and covering our tracks. He probably considers we have bested him." He broke of, staring. "By Jove!" he exclaimed. "Barry! Did we dream it all? Look at her!"

Zalithea had just come into the lounge, cynosure of many eyes. She was a radiant vision in a zephyr-like Paris model. Whom John Cumberland had commissioned to buy it and what he had paid for it only John Cumberland knew. But he was satisfied. Marie, the chambermaid, had done her work well. As they made their way to the table, soft music of an orchestra stole through the hubbub. Barry thought that the lovely girl beside him whose eyes were lighted up happily must have heard other music and witnessed stranger banquets on this very spot . . . three thousand years ago!

That uncomfortable sense of unreality, a sort of veil through which he saw and heard imperfectly, descended upon Barry during the early stages of dinner. The irrigation man and his friend sat quite near and were at no pains to hide their admiration of Zalithea.

In fact, it gradually became apparent that the beautiful unknown was being widely discussed. Barry wondered if the story of the sheik's daughter had spread farther than they supposed. He began to cast off the Old Man of the Sea astride his shoulders—to disregard the inner voice which whispered—whispered: "Yes, she looks young and lovely. But you saw her in the tomb. You *know* she is the oldest woman who has ever lived."

He was fully and finally aroused by a waiter who handed him a folded note. It was from the young man at the nearby table, and it read:

"Where can I take lessons in Kabyle?"

The smiling impudence of his acquaintance appealed to Barry's sense of humour. He showed the note to John Cumberland and the Professor. Zalithea, while they read it, touched Barry's arm, and:

"Fo-ah me?" she said.

He laughed outright.

"Yes!" he nodded.

Zalithea held out her hand for the note. Professor Blackwell passed it to her. And she studied it gravely. It was at this moment that a high-pitched feminine voice made itself audible above the other voices.

"I really *must* just say how d'you do!"

John Cumberland started and looked over his shoulder. A very smart, hard-faced woman was making for their table. She seemed to be possessed of volcanic energy, and:

"Holy Mike!" said he. "Mrs. Uffington!"

"What!" Barry muttered, and glanced in the same direction. "Good Lord! All New York will have the story now!"

Indeed, it was the famous Mrs. Uffington, most intrepid of lion hunters: according to Jim Sakers, "The pride of Pierre's and uncrowned Pope of Park Avenue."

She swooped down upon them. Zalithea, dropping the note, fixed a stare of cold hostility upon the face of the newcomer.

"My dear John Cumberland!" she cried; "and if it isn't our very own Professor and Barry!"

They rose to greet her—without enthusiasm.

"I know all about you!" she ran on vivaciously. "John Cumberland, I know all about you! *What* will Micky Colonna say? But, my dear—she's lovely! I can't believe she's a coloured girl—can't believe it!"

"Princess Zalithea is a member of a very old and distinguished family," said Barry coldly. "Allow me to present you." He bowed to the girl. "Mrs. Dudley Uffington."

Zalithea did not move. Her unwavering stare never left Mrs. Uffington's face. It had an oddly quelling effect.

"She's rather queer, isn't she?" asked the lady, in a lower tone.

"She doesn't speak English," Professor Blackwell explained.

"No! I was forgetting. But of course I have heard all about it. Do you know who told me? Mr. Ahmed Tawwab—such a charming man, for an Egyptian. He is looking in later, and I must really *insist* that you and your delightful—protégée—join us for coffee. I shall expect you!"

And she was off.

"Phew!" said John Cumberland. "Here's a mess!"

"Since she finds Tawwab so charming," murmured the Professor, "I sincerely wish she would marry him—and settle here."

Zalithea, through half-closed eyes, watched the retreating figure.

"*Hafee!*" she hissed—or that was how it sounded.

Barry began to laugh.

"I find I am learning Ancient Egyptian!" he said. "You may be amused to know that, to the best of my knowledge, *hafee* means 'snake'!"

"Really!" said Professor Blackwell, glancing uneasily at the malignant face of Zalithea. "It occurs to me that our foster child can be definitely unpleasant. She should prove a revelation to the drawing rooms of New York. Dear me, it's all very extraordinary."

Any plans they may have had to evade the subsequent meeting were frustrated by the energetic Mrs. Uffington. She had a table waiting, with coffee, liqueurs, and cigarettes, outside, after dinner. She swept them to it. And as they entered the palm-screened alcove in which it was situated, Mr. Tawwab rose to greet them, bowing deeply. He was accompanied by a lean, square-jawed man having small, fierce eyes, a bristling moustache, and very large prominent teeth. He resembled a mad horse.

He was presented as Captain Quick.

Zalithea, trailing a light wrap, seated herself disdainfully on the very edge of a tall chair, staring straight into the eyes of the two men in turn as they were introduced, but giving not the slightest sign of acknowledgment. Mr. Tawwab appraised her, critically and ravenously. Captain Quick burst at once into a shouted conversation.

"This is amazing!" he cried. "Positively! Never would have believed you come from the Senussi country! Never! Was down there in 'nineteen. What's your part?"

Mr. Tawwab exchanged a swift, malicious glance with Mrs. Uffington. John Cumberland looked helplessly at Barry. Zalithea stared at the speaker as though she had not heard him. It was Professor Blackwell, husky in his embarrassment, who explained:

"Our friend does not speak English, sir."

"Oh, damn it! What a fool I am!" yelled Captain Quick. "Wait a minute! Wait a minute! I know the lingo. . . ."

Zalithea stood up, leaving her wrap on the arm of the chair.

"Bahree!" she said—and pointed to it.

Then, without so much as a glance at any of the party, she walked slowly, languidly, out of the alcove.

"Excuse me!" Barry mumbled.

He had flushed to the roots of his hair. Grabbing the wrap, he ran after the girl.

Zalithea, moving with an unfamiliar, swaying movement of the hips which he had always imagined characteristic of the women figured on the ancient wall paintings, was making for the entrance.

He came up with her, but she did not pause or glance aside. The night was perfect, and there were groups assembled before the hotel:

visitors, residents, vendors of many wares, and guides clamouring to conduct somebody, anybody, to the Great Temple by moonlight.

Barry was longing to walk through those mighty halls with Zalithea, but—incredible thought!—they had feared the memories which sight of that stately ruin might arouse in the girl. Karnak she had seen. And Barry could never forget her expression, in which sorrow, stupefaction, and horror had mingled. She had retired to her apartment, refusing to see anybody for a whole day afterward.

How he longed to be able to talk to her! If his own brain became so tumultuous when he thought of the history of this lovely, wayward, yielding, imperious girl, what deathly terrors must she know when realization of the truth was borne home to her?

Side by side they walked on through the scented night. He placed the wrap over her shoulders. She was following her favourite route— that to the ancient *shadûf*.

And so, presently, in silence, they were alone beside the Nile. Zalithea paused, resting against a crumbling wall and staring out over the whispering water. A boatman began to play a reed pipe. He played that age-old melody which surely the boatmen of Seti knew. Barry glanced at Zalithea. She was listening—intently.

Her lips were slightly parted, her lashes drooped. She looked beautiful. But—perhaps because of the Egyptian night and the music of the reed—she seemed unearthly.

A cold hand clutched his heart. Princess Zalithea! He was alone with a ghost!

She knew that music! What was she thinking? Whom was she remembering? Did it bring dreams of happiness—of love? Or did it magically cast her spirit back over the ages to the coming of that unnatural sleep?

Zalithea sighed, shudderingly. Turning, she put her hand in his.

Her hand was warm. The little slender fingers clung tremulously. At their touch, his ghostly imaginings fled. She was real, a girl of flesh and blood; not a phantom, but a living, lovely testimony to the wisdom of a past science. If only he could get used to that idea!

In silence, as they had come, they walked back; like two children, hand in hand. And standing in the entrance to the hotel were Mr. Tawwab and Danbazzar.

"I am most indebted to His Excellency," boomed the latter's great voice, "for this offer of his service. But the lady has been entrusted to me by her father, and I have just left the American Consul—"

"H'm," murmured Mr. Tawwab, his sly eyes lighting up as he saw the slender, approaching figure; "you have seen him tonight?"

"Sure," said Danbazzar. "All's clear. A few formalities in the morning, that's all."

"But," Mr. Tawwab interpolated gently, "as the young lady belongs to El-Kasr, you tell me, this matter does not concern your consul. El-Kasr is in the *mudiriya* of Minia!"

"I've seen the Mudîr of Minia, sir!" Danbazzar replied. "I arrived in Minia last night. That's where I've come from. Believe me, I know the ropes of your country, Mr. Tawwab, although I'm greatly obliged to you. Our consul has got to give me a visé for the United States, that's all. I've arranged the rest."

"The Mudîr of Minia is very obliging."

"Most obliging man in Egypt, bar none!" boomed Danbazzar. "Always was an obliging man."

Zalithea passed in to the hotel, Barry following. From a hidden bench a slim, black-robed figure arose, bowing low.

"*Lêltak sa'îda, effendim,*" said a soft voice.

Barry started, peering into the shadows; then:

"*Lêltak sa'îda, Hassan es-Sugra!*" he replied.

CHAPTER XXVI

IN NEW YORK

A month later, to a day, Barry from the boat deck of the *Berengaria* pointed out Ambrose Light to Zalithea. She clutched his arm to steady herself in the high wind, nestling, furry, very close to him. As he looked down at her he found himself thinking not of the camp in the *wâdi*, nor even of the tomb; not of the ancient wonders of Egypt; nor even of those few delightful days in Paris and the later joy of taking Zalithea around London.

He found himself thinking of Hassan es-Sugra.

Hassan had seen the party off at Luxor, bringing a great bundle of flowers for Zalithea. Where everyone else was hurrying and bustling, Hassan had walked calmly up and down the platform with Barry. His eyes, which were so like the eyes of a gazelle, had been sad. But his words, softly intoned yet laden with some deep significance, had remained with Barry like the haunting memory of a song:

"One day, sir, you will come again to Egypt. Some of your friends, now, will not be your friends then. You will learn to forgive me if I have failed you in anything and come and tell me so. For in the end understanding will be. There is one thing, sir, I have to say to you: they tell me the lady is of El-Kasr. It is not so. I cannot say where she is of. But this I know—she is not of Egypt. She is very sad at heart. If, one day, she tells you why, be not angry with her."

Then the train had moved out. Barry's last impression of Luxor was that of the graceful, black-robed figure of Hassan es-Sugra, his hand raised to his forehead in a parting salute.

"Be not angry with her. . . ."

He looked down at the bewitching face half hidden in fur. Sea breezes had whipped a delicious colour into the soft cheeks—down which big tears were falling!

"Zalithea!" he cried. "My dear! what is it?"

She looked up at him quickly, blinking tears away; then:

"Sorree," she whispered.

This word, "sorry," she had acquired in London, but he knew that she employed it in the sense of "sad." He squeezed her arm reassuringly. He had long since decided that her courage was miraculous—unfaltering. Now, he tried to imagine what supreme dread—what rankling doubt—what sorrow for some long lost one had broken it.

It was always so with him. In the most perfect moments of understanding it would come—that inscrutable curtain; the veil of an unimaginable past.

Once, and once only, he had tried to ask her what he longed so ardently to know: if she remembered ever having met him before. By some unsuspected law of preordination alone could he hope to explain those visions. Had he not seen her as he was destined later to see her—in the dress of Ancient Egypt? Had he not seen her as she looked during the early days in Luxor—veiled like the women of Islam?

He thought he had made her understand. But instead of answering she had turned her back and walked away!

Did the question transgress some strange law, known to her but unknown to him?

There were times when his brain reeled. And now, with the American coast in sight, she was weeping; she was "sorree." He wondered hopelessly what her thoughts were at this hour. "She is very sad at heart," Hassan had said. How clearly he recalled the words of that extraordinary man. . . .

And then, before Barry realized the passage of time, they were in sight of the familiar skyscrapers.

Zalithea's mood had changed. The child had come uppermost again. She clapped her hands gleefully, grasping Barry's arm and pointing to the skyline of New York.

"Fo-ah *me?*" she asked.

Barry nodded, laughing.

"I trust," murmured Professor Blackwell, "she is not labouring under the delusion that you are the king of this country!"

They speedily had evidence of Mrs. Uffington's activity. She was not prepared to lose the credit of discovering a beautiful Oriental princess who had been adopted by an American millionaire! Every ship reporter in the city was primed; camera men were there in flocks.

And Zalithea imperiously declined to see any of them!

She retired to her cabin, with old Safiyeh on guard in the alleyway; and all remonstrances were in vain.

For a considerable time she banned Aunt Micky, as well, until Danbazzar made it clear to her that Aunt Micky was John Cumberland's sister. She received her, then, very graciously. Aunt Micky was stupefied.

"She's a beauty, young Cumberland," she confided to Barry. "But who the devil *is* she?"

"The daughter of one of the minor rulers out there, Micky!"

"But she's not black! She's whiter than I am!"

"It isn't *my* fault," said Barry humbly. "Cleopatra wasn't black, according to all accounts."

"But this girl isn't an Egyptian."

"Neither was Cleopatra!"

"Young Cumberland—you have a secret eye! It's the right. I'll get the truth out of John!"

Out on the deck, Jim Sakers and pretty Jack Lorrimer were consoling each other. When, presently, Barry reappeared:

"This is the blackest hour of my life!" Jim declared plaintively. "I am despised—cast out—rejected. I feel like a falling stock. As though it isn't bad enough to be told that the coveted bottle of unchanging desert has been forgotten! No man with a heart could have overlooked my quart of eternal sand. Now, with my eyes bulging out of my head and my temperature at a hundred and four in the shade, I'm told, 'No fairy princess. Pass along, please. Stand clear of the gangway!'"

"Be patient, Jim," said Barry. "She feels very strange."

"*She* feels very strange!" cried Jim. "*I* feel completely extraordinary! Here are we—poor little sleepy Jack, who didn't go to bed until three o'clock, and tired-eyed Jim who had to get home after seeing *her* home—here are we, lured from our slumbers at an unearthly hour by false promises! ... Sand and sorrow!"

When Zalithea finally went ashore she was so heavily veiled that not a glimpse of her features could be obtained.

As a result, the most conflicting accounts were published. For a ship reporter whose imagination cannot penetrate a few yards of drapery is not worthy of his hire. "Veiled Princess for Cumberland Collection," was one good headline. "Daughter of Persian Pasha Says New York Like Paradise," another declared. "Harem Beauty Brought by *Berengaria*," was the line which appealed to Jim. But Barry's indignation was aroused by "Cumberland Cleopatra Here!"

A suite of rooms had been prepared, by John Cumberland's orders, in the furnishing of which, while a definite Egyptian note had been struck, the total leaned to modernity. For Zalithea he had conceived an affection which, when he tried to analyze it, seemed to be compounded of the paternal, the scientific, and—he could not otherwise define it— the maternal! She was his child in a sense not hitherto comprehended in human relations; and she was the embodiment of that second great passion of his life—Egyptology.

Lovingly he had studied her. He had noted her early acceptance of those mechanical things which at first had appalled her; her easy, youthful adaptability to wildly strange environment. A certain shrinking from her—involuntary, superstitious—of which for a time he had been conscious, left him utterly in the sunshine of her warm humanity.

Barry's attitude occasioned him many anxious hours. That the boy should lose his heart to this beautiful mystery was no matter for wonder. He had eyes, ears, imagination. And Zalithea would have inflamed any man of his age not made of wood or stone with whom she was thrown into contact.

Furthermore, that the meeting of these two was preordained, John Cumberland found it hard to doubt. He knew that Barry thought so; and he did not blame him. For what other explanation could there be of those strange pre-glimpses which he had had of her? He had never doubted his son's word.

But he had found something phenomenal in the story which had led him to look upon it as the product of an excited imagination. How little he had known, in those days, of the wonderful! How sceptical he had been!

From the big armchair in which he was seated in the library, he looked up at a wall painting from Medinet Habu. Quite clearly he recalled that he had been seated here, looking at this very painting, on the night that Danbazzar arrived, on the night that he had first set eyes upon the papyrus!

Somehow, the values of his possessions seemed to have changed, subtly, during his absence. That wall painting, for instance, no longer struck him as a priceless treasure, although he had often thought of it as such. The enamelled casket of Nitocris; the exquisite painted wooden figure of the priestess, Thent-Kheta; even the great inlaid throne of Osorkon from Bubastis—in some queer fashion they had lost colour in his eyes.

Almost as the fact dawned upon him, its explanation came, too. As those ancient priests had foreseen, a living testimony to the grandeur of the Pharaohs would outshine all others!

The library door opened, although there had been no knock; and Zalithea stole in.

John Cumberland jumped up and placed an armchair for her. Jim and Jack were coming on after a theatre, Danbazzar and Aunt Micky having joined them there.

Zalithea was wearing a frock which had been bought for her in Paris. She wore it exquisitely. It was a semi-Oriental creation, simple enough; but it set off her dark, lithe beauty to perfection. She rested one slender hand on the chair back for a moment, smiling inscrutably at John Cumberland.

Then she crossed to the Bubastite throne and seated herself.

"Yes?" she asked naïvely, her head tilted aside. And John Cumberland knew that it would be quite useless to say No, therefore:

"Yes, Zalithea," he agreed, "if you're comfortable."

She listened in her intent fashion, then:

"Zal'ith-*eeah* you-ah-addorahble!" she corrected.

John Cumberland sat down. Apparently Zalithea thought that this was the name by which she was known nowadays. He strongly suspected the identity of the tutor who had led her into this error.

"Barry!" he muttered, reaching for the cigar box.

"Bahree-I-love-you," Zalithea corrected again. "Geeve-me-er-kiss."

"You're learning the wrong things too quickly, young lady!" said John Cumberland. "Do you know where you are, yet?"

"Ah-addorahble!"

"I mean where you live. I tried to teach you yesterday. Your home?"

Zalithea wrinkled her smooth forehead.

"Darling," she replied.

"I know you're a darling," John Cumberland admitted; "but I think I shall have to take your education in hand myself. I'm afraid I have been neglecting you."

Zalithea, from the throne of the Bubastite king, smiled regally.

A considerable disturbance in the lobby now proclaimed the return of the theatre party. Barry opened the library door, and:

"Hullo!" he cried. "You're in there! I've been hunting all over for you. Here's the gang."

Headed by the Countess Colonna, the party entered. Jack Lorrimer was frankly nervous—an unusual condition—but highly curious. She had not yet met the mysterious Cumberland guest. Jim followed in with Danbazzar, an imposing figure distinguished from the rest alike by his great height and by the slight eccentricity of dress which he affected. His Egyptian tan suited his oddly Moorish type.

"Zalithea," said John Cumberland, beckoning to Jack, "I want you to know Jack Lorrimer, my niece, and"—he drew Jim forward—"Mr. Sakers. Princess Zalithea has very little English, so excuse her."

Zalithea, beyond a slight smile, offered no sort of acknowledgment. Barry, covertly watching his friend and his cousin, noted that the girl's queer aloofness had created its usual effect. He noted something else. Jack Lorrimer was very pretty (what Jim termed "A1 at Cupid's"), and Barry, like many another, had often wondered where the dividing line lay between prettiness and beauty. Tonight he knew that Zalithea was beautiful.

Jim's reaction to the lovely, cold vision on the throne was good to study.

"Delighted!" he said. "Been counting the hours until— No, of course, you don't know what I'm talking about! . . . Cooler this evening, I fancy. . . . Wrong again! How's Egypt looking these days? . . . Let me out, somebody! . . ."

Danbazzar stood at his elbow. He spoke to Zalithea in that monotonous language which no one else understood. Under half-lowered lids she watched him, and then replied briefly. He turned to Jim.

"She says you talk too much!" he translated.

Jim turned fiery red.

Barry laughed delightedly, and Professor Blackwell, who had just come in, endeavoured to console poor Jim.

"She is a young lady of very definite ideas," he said, groping with one large, bony hand for a dress tie which, having become unknotted, had evidently dropped off somewhere. "For instance, she has a settled belief that I'm funny!"

"Please, Mr. Danbazzar!" whispered Jack. "Ask her if she likes me!"

Danbazzar, whom nothing annoyed more than to be addressed as "mister," conversed briefly, and unintelligibly, with Zalithea; then:

"She is a little undecided," he announced. "She has got hold of the idea that you're a dancing girl and wants to know when you are going to begin!"

CHAPTER XXVII

ABOUT IT AND ABOUT

Danbazzar, in these days, was constantly at the Cumberland home. Next to Barry, it was evident that Zalithea preferred his society to that of anybody else. John Cumberland she respected, but he, for all his knowledge of the old, mysterious land in which they had found her, groped in vain with the strange tongue which she spoke and which Danbazzar alone understood. Nor was he so successful as his son in establishing a link of understanding. Perhaps because he did not speak the language of love, which is God's Esperanto.

Nevertheless, and largely with Danbazzar as interpreter, he had begun his ambitious work. The first and second sections of the book came within scope of his personal knowledge. He believed that they were, now, comparatively valueless without the third. Therefore, beyond arranging his bulky notes, he had done little in this direction. His interest was with Zalithea's story, and this she surrendered only in provoking fragments, imperfectly understood by Danbazzar.

For instance, urged on one occasion to describe Pharaoh's court, she became unusually voluble. Danbazzar looked puzzled, thought over what she had said for some time, and then:

"It sounds to me," he confessed, "uncommonly like backstage at the Metropolitan Opera House!"

And a day was to come when those words should recur to Barry Cumberland.

Social invitations hailed upon them. No door in New York was closed to Princess Zalithea. But She Who Sleeps was as capricious as she was lovely. Modern ideas of good behaviour she simply didn't understand. They had learned from painful experience, to consult her, *vide* Danbazzar, before accepting proffered hospitality.

She would inquire closely into the character of the household and the probable guests before consenting to go. More often than not she flatly declined to be present.

And they knew that social embarrassment would almost inevitably follow if Zalithea were urged against her will. This knowledge had come as result of a disaster at the apartment of a prominent member of Washington's diplomatic set who was entertaining in New York.

Zalithea, reluctantly, had agreed to go. She had looked radiant. She was the sensation of a brilliant gathering. Then, Mrs. Uffington had arrived. As that gushing lady crossed with extended hands:

"Bahree," Zalithea had said, in her imperious way.

Ignoring Mrs. Uffington, ignoring everybody, she had glided, a slender, stately figure, out of the room—and out of the building!

It was a moment which Barry sometimes lived over again, memory of which brought cold perspiration. He had been furiously angry with her, and had been unable to conceal his anger. Unmoved, apparently, as an ivory statue, she had sat beside him in the car, while he had poured out the vials of his wrath. Perhaps she had understood, perhaps she had not.

But when he saw her face, as they alighted before the door of his home, he would have given much for power to recall those words. Her beautiful eyes were glassy, like those of a tortured animal. Then, as she turned to run up the steps, he saw the long repressed tears gathering under the dark fringe of her lashes. . . .

She had refused to see him that night and for half of the next day. His father, and Aunt Micky, who had been left behind to face the appalling task of explaining, arrived later—and were denied admittance to Zalithea's apartments!

Danbazzar was summoned. Barry knew no sleep that night. He paced the big library, a man demented, knowing—if he had ever doubted it— that the happiness of this girl meant more to him than the opinion of every hostess in America; than any friendship; than anything in life.

Reconciliation had come. But they had all learned their lessons.

Invitations to the Cumberland home were eagerly sought for. It came to be regarded as a sort of mark of distinction to be honestly able to say that Princess Zalithea had consented to know one. What guided her in her selections and rejections, John Cumberland could never make out.

Slowly, provokingly slowly, Zalithea was learning English. There was no lack of voluntary (male) tutors. In fact, by painful degrees, the fact dawned upon Barry that he had to count not only with that intangible dread, his knowledge of the true age of Zalithea, but also with more than one rival.

"There's something I want to know, young Cumberland," said Aunt Micky on a certain afternoon when Barry was lounging in her private sanctum.

This room was notable chiefly because of the fact that it differed from every other in the house; it contained not a single Egyptian relic.

"What's that, Micky?"

Aunt Micky puffed reflectively at her cigarette; then:

"When is Zalithea going home?" she inquired.

"What!"

Barry sat up with a jerk.

"Don't get excited," she went on. "It's a perfectly reasonable question. And as I can't talk to the girl, and your father won't talk to *me*, I'm asking *you*. Have we adopted her?"

Barry laughed to hide his embarrassment.

"I suppose in a way we are responsible for her," he answered evasively. "What does Dad say?"

"Nothing!" Micky replied promptly. "That is, nothing sensible. He told me, only yesterday, that her history was so strange I should never be able to believe it." She took a fresh cigarette from the box. "He's very likely right," she added.

"No, Micky!" Barry protested. "Something has upset you. What is it?"

"It isn't one thing; it's several."

"Tell me one of them."

"In the first place, who is this girl?"

"It's very difficult to explain, Micky."

"Ha!" She lighted her fresh cigarette with the stump of the old one. "That's what John says—and Blackwell! You're all lying—all the damn' lot of you! You can't tell fairy tales to Micky Colonna! And where, exactly, does the man Danbazzar come in?"

Again Barry hesitated. It was hateful to lie to Aunt Micky. Hitherto, by skillful evasion, he had dodged the necessity. He determined to endeavour to do so again.

"Well," he replied, "Danbazzar is the only one of the party who knows her language. He knows—all about her father, too."

Aunt Micky stared at him hard; then:

"*I've* been in Egypt, young lad," she said, "and although I never went so far, I know where the desert Arabs live—and what they look like. This girl isn't one! Also, when Dr. Davidson called, why did old Blackwell hurry him away without seeing Zalithea?"

"I don't know, Micky."

"But *I* do! Because Dr. Davidson has just come back from a journey through Zalithea's home country, among the Senussi Arabs! Teach your grandmother to suck eggs, young Cumberland!"

"Does all this mean you don't like her?"

"I'd like her well enough if I knew who she was. But all I know is that she's a little impostor and the whole gang of you are backing her up."

"She isn't an impostor," Barry retorted hotly. "No! I didn't mean to be abrupt, but you don't understand, Micky. It's the rest of us who are impostors!"

Aunt Micky shaded her unflinching gray eyes with one upraised hand, a mark of disapproval; then:

"Liars! all the lot of you!" she commented. "I knew it. But what's the object? Is she wanted by the Egyptian police?"

Barry laughed.

"Not exactly," he replied. "But there is a likelihood of complications, all the same. You see, we brought a stack of stuff away. It's all at Danbazzar's place, now."

"What has this to do with Zalithea?"

"Well, in a way— Oh, I can't explain, Micky! What's the use of trying?"

"Tell me what your father told me yesterday—that I wouldn't understand—and I'll heave this inkwell at you!"

The interview left Barry in a very unsettled frame of mind. He simply could not foresee the future otherwise than through a storm cloud. As he came down into the lobby, Zalithea was just crossing. She was going out to dinner and a theatre with a party that included Monty Edwards, a moneyed undesirable whom Barry detested. She disliked parties but loved theatres, they had discovered.

She was dressed already, and made a sweet picture against a background depicting the wars of Rameses II.

Barry's heart jumped ridiculously; for she was so close to him that by extending a hand he could have touched her. He suppressed an impulse—which seemed quite natural—to take her in his arms and hold her and kiss her.

"Zalithea," he said, "you are adorable."

She paused, looking sideways at Barry. Her smile maddened him.

"You like?" she asked naïvely.

"Yes."

"Bahree-geeve me-er-kiss," she invited.

He felt a hot flush rising to his forehead. Truly his sins had found him out! At some time he had murmured those words, and Zalithea, who seemed so slow to learn many things, had seized upon them mysteriously. Perhaps the syllables chanced to resemble those of her own language.

"I shall have to, one day!" he said. "I shan't be able to help myself!"

The maddest impulses surged up in his brain. Her eyes were beckoning to him. But she was helpless—their guest—to be guarded and protected.

He laughed—quite mirthlessly—turned, and walked across to the library. He never glanced back.

Jim Sakers was calling for him later. They were dining at a club and doing nothing in particular; what Jim termed "a night of well-earned rest." Barry was looking forward to the evening with great interest, because he had determined, guardedly, to voice his difficulties to his friend and to get the opinion of this honest, worldly soul.

Of Zalithea he purposely saw no more. He heard the others arrive and heard the car drive off. A few minutes later Jim arrived.

At a corner table, placed before a high oak settle, they presently found themselves in one of the Bohemian clubs of which Jim was a member. And Barry began by outlining the position that Zalithea occupied in the Cumberland home.

"I gather," said Jim, "that your former flaming passion for the balcony princess has now been transferred to the Egyptian princess?"

"Don't be silly," Barry returned irritably. "I'm serious. Can't you understand that that was a vision of the girl I was going to meet?"

"No," Jim admitted, "I can't. I have seen Mr. Brown's house, and I have interviewed Mr. Brown's housekeeper. There's nothing visionary about either. Why should there be about Mr. Brown's balcony?"

"I don't know; but there is. It's utterly impossible that I should have seen Zalithea there. It's utterly impossible that I should have seen her on Fifth Avenue."

"You saw her twin sister."

"Her twin sister, if she had had one, would have been dead long ago—"

He broke off. He had said more than he had intended to say. Jim stared curiously.

"How so?" he inquired. "Do they drown one of twins in those parts? Which one do they keep? Who decides? Answer me that—the local witch doctor?"

"Forget it!" Barry urged, "and talk sense. You have seen Zalithea—many times, now—"

"Undoubtedly. She's A1 at Cupid's—a first-class risk—Bachelor's Bane, Incorporated."

"You know her rather imperious spirit."

"I do. She has practised hard on me."

"But *I'm* crazy about her, Jim! And I'm dying to tell her so! But how can I?"

"How can you? Easily. You're not dumb."

"She has scarcely any English."

"Press your hand to your heart and kneel at her feet."

"It isn't that. She's our guest. I have no right—"

"Cable the sable parent. Say, 'Dear Sir: With reference to your charming daughter—'"

"Jim! you're not helping me! And, anyway, that's not all."

Jim realized that his friend was really serious. He listened, without facetious comments, while Barry hesitantly outlined a hypothetical case. He spoke of a famous physician of the East who had discovered a method of prolonging life for several hundreds of years. He could not bring himself to speak of *thousands!* He asked him if he should expect the offspring of a marriage between such a subject and an ordinary mortal, to be normal.

But Jim was merely bewildered.

"Are you hinting that Zalithea's mother is three hundred years old?" he demanded, incredulously. "Is *this* the skeleton in the cupboard?"

His tone was sufficient for Barry. Jim would never understand. How could he be expected to understand? He was glad he had been no more definite; and he clutched at this straw gratefully.

"So we were led to believe," he replied.

Jim's stare became that of a man hypnotized; but finally:

"Does your father believe this?" he asked. "And old Blackwell, and Danbazzar—do they believe it?"

"Yes," said Barry. "*You* would have believed it if you had been there."

But he knew, now, that he could look for guidance to no man. He and those others who had entered the tomb of She Who Sleeps had entered a world controlled by laws other than those known to the rest of mankind.

CHAPTER XXVIII

A DOOR CLOSES

Barry returned home comparatively early. Neither Jim's airy philosophy nor his more serious sympathy, which was not without a salting of worldly wisdom, had lifted the cloud of despondency that had settled upon him. He felt utterly alone. Never, in the loneliest hours he had known in the desert, had he experienced anything quite like his mood of tonight.

He had fallen in love with a shadow—a mirage; the shadow had materialized; and now, the substance was less real than the shadow.

The whole thing seemed to have gone out of tune. The Zalithea he pictured as he walked along, the Zalithea who went to theatres and parties, was this the sleeping princess they had delivered from an Egyptian tomb? Could it be the same pale, slender girl from whose lifeless body Danbazzar had torn those age-old wrappings?

In short, where had delusion begun? Where did delusion end?

The tired man smoking a soiled cigar lolled on the corner as Barry approached his home. It occurred to him that it was the same cigar that he had always smoked. It was unreal.

Without removing the root, the man touched his hat as Barry went in and took out his key. John Cumberland kept early hours; and, except when entertaining, his household was abed by midnight. Barry did not expect to find anyone up.

On the tray in the lobby he discovered two letters. Neither was important, but he switched on the light above the table and glanced at them. As he stood there, dimly he could hear steamer whistles on the river. One of them, a deep-throated blare, he thought he recognized as the voice of the *Berengaria*. Even as his glance ran over the typed page, in spirit he had crossed again to Southampton upon that quest never to be forgotten which had led to Zalithea.

Then, thrilling in the stillness of the big house, came a soft cry!

Barry dropped the letter and turned, standing stock still, with clenched hands.

He stared across at the closed door of the library. It was from there the cry had come. All was silent, however, as he stepped quickly in that direction. But, as he reached the door, in a strangled voice:

"Bahree!" he heard; then, in a coarse, laughing tone:

"Don't be so silly!"

Zalithea was in the library—with Monty Edwards!

Barry flung the door open and walked in.

Across by the big, carved mantelpiece, with its overpowering decoration from the wall of Medinet Habu, Edwards had the girl in his arms. He was a thickset, coarse-grained type, whose boisterous good humour served as a cloak for a rather nasty animalism. At the wrong age for a man of his character he had acquired control of a fortune little less than that of John Cumberland.

Zalithea's lithe body was bent back like a bow as she strove to avoid his lips. Edwards, holding her fast, stooped lower and lower to the alluring, forbidden red mouth.

By what cunning strategy he had contrived to be left alone with her Barry neither knew nor cared. It was the colossal outrage of the thing that struck him dumb. The affront to him, to his father, was gross enough. But the affront to this delicate, guarded treasure of some long-forgotten court was beyond computation.

To his imaginative mind it appeared that Monty Edwards had disgraced irrevocably the name of American hospitality.

So swiftly did he act, in his white-hot anger, that Edwards, hastily releasing the girl, allowed her to sink down upon the carpet. He turned in a flash—and Barry stood before him dumb with hate.

Edwards's high colour fled. He spoke huskily.

"Hullo, Barry! Don't get mad. It was only fun."

Barry was murderously pale. For ten—fifteen—twenty beats of the library clock, he stood, quivering; then:

"Get out!" he said. "Get out while I can remember you're in *my* house."

Monty Edwards bandied no words with the speaker. He knew when a man was seeing red. Head lowered and lips unsteady, he passed Barry and walked out of the library.

Zalithea stood up, breathing quickly. But Barry never moved, never stirred a muscle of his tensed-up body, until the closing of the front door told him that Monty Edwards had left the house. Then he turned to Zalithea.

She was dressed as he had seen her earlier in the evening. She was pale but more utterly desirable than any woman in all the wide world. Her long, dark eyes were fixed upon him in a sort of wonder—questioningly—doubtingly. He unclenched his fists. No word was spoken. But Zalithea stepped forward as if bidden.

His arms went around her like steel bands. He uttered a queer, pent-up cry. He kissed her lips breathlessly, her hair, her eyes, her smooth, creamy neck. He was in the throes of a veritable madness. His long-repressed passion swept him away. . . .

When, at last, he released her, she fell back, raised her hands to her eyes for a moment; then, giving him one long look of indescribable intensity, as though she would imprint his image indelibly upon her mind, she ran out of the room.

Standing as she had left him, his back to the lobby, he heard the light patter of her footsteps as she raced upstairs.

Somewhere, above, a door closed softly.

And to that sound Barry found himself listening with a strained intensity. It seemed in some way to be an answer to a question—to a subconscious question that his mind was incapable of framing. Exhausted by the fiercest emotions he had ever known, he dropped into a big padded rest chair in which, evidently, Monty Edwards had been sitting. A still-smouldering cigar lay in the little Oriental tray attached to the chair arm.

Mentally, he was depressed. But his heart was singing. His former experiences might have led him to doubt Zalithea's sentiments. But he could not forget that she had returned his kisses.

For an hour he waited, hoping yet not expecting that she would come back. He lived again through the strange days and nights he had known since that evening when Fate had steered the Rolls into a private road—and he had seen a vision of Zalithea.

Imagination led him on. Once more he talked with Danbazzar and the others in the tent in the *wâdi* and walked beside Hassan es-Sugra through those silent halls of the Great Temple. So walking in spirit, with gods and Pharaohs beckoning secretly from moon-touched walls, he fell asleep. The cigar, in the tray at his elbow, smouldered on. In the still air of the library, a bluish pencilling of smoke stole straightly upward. It burned until only a powdery shell remained attached to a leafy stub. But Barry never stirred. The night sounds of New York did not reach him in his dreams. And the detective on duty outside the house wondered why the library lights were still burning when dawn's gray mystery crept over the city.

Through the shades, morning light was competing with the electric lamps when soft footsteps sounded on the thickly carpeted stairs. Barry slept on. The footsteps crept lower and lower . . . and Zalithea stood peeping in at the doorway.

She turned swiftly at sight of the sleeper, her fingers raised to her lips. Old Safîyeh's wrinkled face appeared in the lamplight. Then Zalithea looked again at Barry, his ruffled curly head resting on one shoulder. She watched him longingly, as a woman watches a sleeping child. Once she stole forward, but hesitated and went back. . . . Very softly she drew the door partly to.

The man on duty at the corner saw the two women come out and walk away. He was not surprised. They frequently went for a walk in the early hours of the morning, although he could not recall that they had ever set out quite so early before.

As the front door closed, Barry moved. The movement rasped his neck against his collar—and he awoke. Cramped, stale, heavy-headed, he stared about him. Swiftly memory reasserted itself.

He stood up, stretching his cramped limbs. Then he crossed and switched off the lights. The library clock registered half-past five. He went upstairs, pausing outside Zalithea's door and listening intently. He could detect no sound. He passed on, mounted to the floor above, and went to bed.

His next awakening was a tragic one.

John Cumberland burst into his room, with:

"Barry! Barry! Zalithea has disappeared!"

"What!"

Barry sprang out of bed, his eyes wide in sudden fear. John Cumberland's face was pale.

"She and Safîyeh went out at half-past five this morning. They have not returned. It's after ten o'clock."

Half-past five . . . what memory did this awaken? Of course! . . .

"But I was in the library at that time!" Barry cried. "They must have seen me!"

"Explain," said John Cumberland. "What were you doing in the library so early?"

Barry, very briefly, told the story, mincing no words, concealing nothing. As he spoke, he was dressing in feverish haste.

"The door was closed, I suppose?" his father asked dully.

Barry paused in his task. He looked up.

"By heaven," he said, "she must have closed it! Edwards left it open, and I fell asleep watching the lobby. But it was half to when I woke up!"

"Do you realize, Barry," his father asked, "that it was probably the shutting of the front door that awakened you?"

"I can't bear to think of it."

The house was in an uproar. Remembering that Zalithea knew next to nothing of the language, and Safiyeh little more, it was impossible to imagine their plight. In one fact, that Zalithea was not alone, Barry found comfort.

John Cumberland's private secretary was already in touch with the police; and, as Barry came hurrying downstairs, Professor Blackwell arrived.

"Cumberland!" he cried. "What's this they tell me?"

"She's gone, Blackwell," was the reply. "No news."

The Professor dropped into a lobby chair. "Somehow, I can't grasp it," he said pathetically.

"If she had been alone I should have feared an accident, but as Safiyeh is with her—"

"That's what I think!" Barry interrupted eagerly. "An accident is out of the question."

"This being so," the Professor went on, "what are we to conclude? Is Danbazzar here?"

"Expected every minute," John Cumberland replied shortly. "I naturally 'phoned there first, as she is used to visiting him."

"She had not been there?"

John Cumberland shook his head.

"Tell him what happened last night, Barry," he said, and hurried away.

Barry, hoping against hope that something in the occurrences of the night might suggest to the scientific brain of Professor Blackwell a clue to Zalithea's motive, gave him an account of the matter. At last:

"It may be some primitive reaction," the Professor murmured. "The psychology of Zalithea is of course an unknown quantity."

"You think she is frightened and so has run away?"

"Frankly, I don't know what to think."

"I can't believe she would voluntarily leave the house," Barry declared. "Just think. Where could she possibly go to?"

Professor Blackwell shook his head.

"That is a question I cannot pretend to answer."

At this moment Danbazzar arrived. As the door was opened he came into the lobby, a big, dominating figure. But his stock was not quite so perfectly knotted as usual, and his strange eyes held a very wild light.

"Still no news?" he asked.

The blank faces about him were sufficient answer.

"Have her apartments been searched to make sure there's nothing there?"

Aunt Micky, very stern-faced, came downstairs. "I have searched thoroughly," she answered. "But it might be as well if you looked, also."

Danbazzar bowed and walked upstairs. Barry followed.

In the suite of apartments which had been furnished for the use of Zalithea, a very faint perfume lingered. It caught Barry by the throat. It spoke to him intimately. It was as though he had buried his face in her fragrant hair; as though she were in his arms again.

The rooms were strangely appointed. They were scantily furnished in the Eastern manner, with little inlaid tables and cabinets, and many richly cushioned divans. Perforated silver lamps concealed the electric lights, and the windows were screened with *mushrabiyeh* work. The bedroom struck a more Western note, being equipped with a wonderful dressing table possessing wing mirrors and laden with every imaginable luxury of Paris.

There was no evidence of disorder or of hasty departure. The bleak chamber adjoining in which the old Arab woman spent a great part of her days afforded no better evidence.

Danbazzar crossed to a window and threw back the nearby *mushrabiyeh* screen. For a long time he stood there, looking out.

CHAPTER XXIX

THE HIEROGLYPHIC LETTER

A period of anxiety now commenced to which it seemed impossible to imagine any end other than the return of Zalithea. The idea that he should never see her again was one that Barry simply could not contemplate. The mystery of her disappearance baffled all conjecture.

Short of the theory of drowning both in the case of Zalithea and of Safiyeh, no feasible explanation presented itself. At John Cumberland's urgently expressed wish publicity was for long avoided. But neither police headquarters nor the private experts employed on the case could offer any hypothesis covering the facts.

Since Zalithea spoke no English and her companion very little, it was difficult to imagine how they could have gone far without attracting attention. Further, it appeared that neither had any money, beyond, possibly, some small change.

To Barry, every waking hour seemed like a week. He had fits of anger during which he bitterly reproached the girl for the pain which she was inflicting. Then, his mood changing, he would mourn her as dead. Every time the 'phone bell rang his heart leaped wildly. Hope and fear alternately gripped him, threatening to drive him mad.

Secrecy at last became impossible, if not unwise.

"There's only one theory that covers all the facts," said the detective in charge of the inquiry. "They must be in hiding; either because they want to hide for some reason, or because they are being detained."

"Detained!" cried John Cumberland. "By whom? For what purpose?"

"Well," was the reply, "such things have happened before, you know. It may develop into a demand for ransom. But my point is this: apart from the fact that the lady's disappearance is beginning to be talked about, we are neglecting a very valuable weapon, in a case of this kind, by avoiding publicity."

"I agree with you," Barry said.

"If these two are hiding somewhere," the detective went on, "offer of a big reward will tempt someone to give them away. If they've been kidnapped, offer of a reward is what the kidnappers are waiting for. I know it's going to make things mighty unpleasant for you, and you're in no sort of humour to be badgered by newspaper reporters. But it's all that's left. The cat's out of the bag, anyway. Hundreds of people know. You might as well tell the world."

Reluctantly, sick at heart, John Cumberland consented. The notoriety which he knew must follow was appalling to his sensitive nature. But anything that might lead to the recovery of Zalithea he was prepared to face.

And so, on the following morning, New York revelled in full details of perhaps the most romantic mystery that had ever spread itself over the city's front pages. Photographs of Zalithea there were none available. Those taken on the day of her arrival, showing her muffled in veils, were at a premium.

Danbazzar supplied a brief and strictly untruthful biography of "The

Lady Zalithea el-Aziza ed-Dhahir (daughter of the Sheik Mohammed Abd el-Ghuri, of the direct line of the last of the Khalifs and a descendant of the Prophet) entitled by Moslem law and usage to the designation, Princess Zalithea."

As this corresponded with the particulars entered in her passport, no doubts of its accuracy were entertained. A description of Safiyeh was also given. She was cited as a native of Cairo.

"This is going to reach Egypt," said Danbazzar gloomily. "And if I know anything about Tawwab, it's going to reach the Sheik Mohammed. If it's made worth his while, he's sure to say he never had a daughter. What happens next we have to wait and see."

The sensational report issued, John Cumberland and Barry entrenched themselves behind secretaries, refusing to receive any newspaper representatives. Danbazzar discreetly disappeared. So intense was the public curiosity aroused that Professor Blackwell was forced to cancel a course of lectures and to retire to the home of relatives in the Middle West.

Wild rumours were circulated freely. Anybody who had ever met Zalithea was interviewed and cross-examined. Thousands who had never even seen her claimed acquaintance for the sake of a brief moment in the limelight. Reports flowed in from places as widely removed as Marseilles and Hollywood.

At a cost appalling to estimate, John Cumberland had every one of them taken up and tested. All proved to be mare's nests.

Aunt Micky's life became a perfect burden to her.

If it had not been for her recognition of the fact that Barry was breaking his heart over the affair she would have fled long since. Instinctively she had known from the first that there was some secret in connection with Zalithea which she did not share. Her resentment had been sharpened by what she termed "this damnable publicity."

Save for very old friends, Jim Sakers, Jack Lorrimer, and a few others, society she had none in these days, but was compelled to hide like a fugitive from the tireless persecution of paragraph writers. . . .

Then, it happened—the inexplicable thing; the event that, while it aroused a momentary hope, did so only to dash hope to the ground again.

Barry and a secretary were going through the voluminous mail one morning. Barry's high spirit had quite deserted him. He looked physically ill, and was morose and silent. He hoped for nothing, in all these letters, but inquiries prompted by idle curiosity or lies designed to torture him. Then:

"Here is a letter addressed to you, Mr. Cumberland," said the secretary, "and unstamped. It must have been delivered by hand. It is marked 'Private and Personal.'"

Barry stretched apathetically across the table and took the envelope, upon which his name was neatly typed. It seemed to contain a quantity of correspondence and also some small, hard object.

He tore it open listlessly.

A large double sheet of some very thick, tough kind of writing paper was inside. And, as he pulled it from the envelope, a ring fell out upon the table. Barry's heart seemed to miss a beat. What change had come over his face he could only guess by the secretary's horrified expression.

"Mr. Cumberland!" she cried—and stood up.

But Barry motioned to her to sit down again. He was staring—staring—at the ring which he held in his hand. It was an oddly mounted and very perfect piece of lapis lazuli.

He had bought it in the Rue de la Paix for Zalithea!

Uttering a stifled moan, he dropped the ring, and, with wildly unsteady fingers, unfolded the thick sheets of paper.

They were covered with Egyptian hieroglyphics! One glance he gave at the writing, and:

"Quick! Quick!" he shouted. "Get my father!"

He sprang from his chair and began to pace the room like a madman. His brain was working feverishly. The letter was from *her!* . . . The letter was from *her!* Even if John Cumberland could decipher it, he could do so only very laboriously, perhaps inaccurately.

"Mr. Cumberland is coming," the secretary announced.

"Call Danbazzar," Barry directed.

"He is out of town. Mr. John Cumberland received a note from him this morning saying he would be away for two or three weeks."

"Of course," cried Barry. "I don't know what I'm talking about!"

He clutched his head, trying to think clearly. Horace Pain was abroad and not expected back for a long time. But Dr. Rittenburg had been home when they arrived. He had dined with them only two weeks ago at Danbazzar's apartment and had had a private view of the contents of the tomb when these had reached New York through some mysterious channel controlled by their host.

"Look up Dr. Rittenburg's number," he said. "Get him at all costs."

And the secretary was engaged with the directory when John Cumberland burst in.

Barry could not speak. He merely pointed to the ring and letter—and went on walking up and down.

"Good God!"

John Cumberland's voice shook emotionally. He was staring at the writing, pale-faced, incredulous.

"It's . . . from her!" Barry whispered. "She's alive! She's alive!"

"Come down to the library, my boy," said his father, regaining his own self-control in presence of the distracted Barry. "Wallis Budge can help us here. I fear my knowledge is not sufficient."

As they left the room:

"Dr. Rittenburg has gone out," the secretary reported, "but they have given me a number where they think I can find him."

"Tell him to come along at once," John Cumberland directed, "or, if he's engaged, put him through to me in the library."

A few minutes later they were engrossed in study of the extraordinary letter; and from the well-laden shelves Barry, at his father's instance, had taken Budge's standard work on the language of Ancient Egypt, Erman's *Egyptian Grammar*, and other handbooks on the subject.

"It's going to be a hard job for me, Barry," John Cumberland confessed. "But it would be easy for Rittenburg or Danbazzar. It's hieratic writing, of which I know very little."

"Is it—" Barry began, trying to steady his voice, "is it the sort of writing *she* might be expected to use?"

"Undoubtedly," his father answered. "It was the form of writing employed by the priests and scribes. The papyrus and the formula are written in this style. But the characters in both are much more carefully drawn."

"For heaven's sake, let's begin. Does it read from left to right or right to left?"

"That's the trouble," John Cumberland replied. "Sometimes it reads one way and sometimes the other!"

"Can you find any clue—or any word you recognize?"

"That's what I'm looking for," his father murmured, bending over the page of hieroglyphs. . . . And for the greater part of an hour he looked, seeking aid in his researches from the pages of Budge, Petrie, and others. But he had made no progress whatever when Dr. Rittenburg arrived.

As the library door opened and the round, red face of the distinguished Egyptologist was thrust into the room, Barry rose from the table with a cry of welcome. Dr. Rittenburg bent forward, his large, round spectacles shining as he peered in the direction of the students. As is the way of the human brain, an idea suddenly presented itself to Barry now, in this hour of intense anxiety—that Dr. Rittenburg was a reincarnation of Mr. Pickwick.

Greetings were very brief, and:

"I must ask you, Rittenburg," said John Cumberland, "to treat the matter about which we want to consult you as strictly confidential."

"Certainly, certainly," Dr. Rittenburg agreed. "Count on me. What's the problem?"

Barry held out the letter.

"This!" he replied.

Dr. Rittenburg glanced at him curiously, noted his condition of tremendous nervous excitement, then changed his large, round spectacles for a larger pair, equally round. He seated himself and bent over the writing.

John Cumberland and Barry stood before the high, carved mantelpiece watching him. Courtesies were forgotten. They had not even offered the doctor a cigar.

For perhaps five minutes he peered down intently; then:

"H'm!" he murmured. "Very curious, if I may say so. Very, very curious." He looked up.

"Can you read it?" Barry demanded.

"Certainly I can read it!" the savant returned brusquely. "But as I assume you have not asked me to do so merely as a test of my ability, may I inquire who wrote it?"

An eager answer was on the tip of Barry's tongue when his father checked him with a gesture.

"This is our real problem, Rittenburg," John Cumberland explained. "We have certain reasons for believing, or hoping, that we know the writer. But we look to you for internal evidence, in the letter itself, to confirm our hopes."

"I see," said Dr. Rittenburg, glancing queerly from father to son. "The internal evidence is here. And knowing what I already know of certain occurrences, I may say that this letter astounds me—literally astounds me!"

Barry could scarcely contain his impatience; but:

"While it is not perfectly formed in many places," the doctor went on, "it nevertheless contains phrases that are beyond the compass of the ordinary student. In fact"—he removed his spectacles and polished them with a pocket handkerchief—"I doubt if there are six people in the United States of America who could have written it!"

"Is it—signed?" Barry asked.

"Yes!" Dr. Rittenburg replaced his glasses and bent once more over the letter. "It bears a name which I should be tempted to translate in a certain way if I were not afraid that my knowledge of other matters is unconsciously prejudicing my judgment!"

"For God's sake, read it!"

John Cumberland was the speaker.

"Very well." Dr. Rittenburg cleared his throat and read: "'Because I can be with you no more I send the ring'"—he glanced up, and: "I am almost sure that 'ring' is meant," he said, and read on:

"'By this you will know. Do not lament me or look in many places. Forget. There is nothing else. My heart I leave behind!'"

Again Dr. Rittenburg looked up, and:

"To the best of my knowledge," he added, "the next, and final word, is *Zalithea!*"

CHAPTER XXX

MARGUERITE DEVINA

"The Moving Finger," which waits for no man, moved on. But Zalithea did not return. The police had relaxed their efforts. They had nothing to work upon. It was obviously impossible to place the hieratic letter in their hands. Nor did its arrival assist the investigations of the private agency employed by John Cumberland.

He allowed them to examine it, saying that the writing was believed to be in Princess Zalithea's hand. They tried to trace the maker of the paper and of the envelope which had enclosed it, but failed. Their final effort was directed to the discovery of the messenger who had put the letter in the box. A reward of five thousand dollars was offered. No one claimed it.

During these anxious days, Barry had not neglected the house of Mr. Brown. In a despairing effort, he had had the history of this country home examined—in vain. The property had changed hands during his absence in Egypt, and little could be learned of the former owner or of his associates. Agents had handled the transactions in both cases. The housekeeper—once interviewed by Jim Sakers—could not be traced.

The nine days' wonder lived its allotted span; and the world in general began to forget Princess Zalithea, who had flashed, a dazzling meteor, across the social sky of New York, and, like a meteor, had vanished.

But Barry did not forget. He was not of those who love and ride away. For him a dream had come true—a dream held like a crucifix through years of waiting. He had lived in a heaven of moments. He had been snatched back to earth. And he was lonely.

One faith he had. To this he remained true; it saved him from despair. Zalithea was alive; so was Safîyeh. Somewhere, they were together. And one day he would find them. Despite official evidence proving that no such persons had departed from the port of New York, a conviction was growing in his mind that Zalithea had returned to Egypt.

John Cumberland's anxiety, divided from the first, began now to centre upon Barry. Professor Blackwell, feeling that he might hope to walk the streets again without being accosted by newspaper representatives, had returned to his usual quarters. And one evening the two old friends dined together at the University Club, to discuss the question of Barry's welfare.

"Bob Sakers couldn't join us for dinner," said Cumberland, when the Professor arrived, "but he's dropping in later."

"Danbazzar is still away?"

"Yes," John Cumberland nodded. "The publicity attaching to this unhappy affair came very near home, I think. His apartment is shut up. I shouldn't wonder if he stays away for a long time."

"Quite—quite," murmured the Professor. "Of course, for my part, I confess I am floored. I don't dare to think about it. The whole thing, from that unimaginable moment in the tomb up to the time that you received this incredible letter, often seems to me to be unreal—a nightmare."

"Yes," John Cumberland agreed, "it doesn't seem real. But—" he sighed—"it has ruined Barry."

"Poor boy—poor boy. She was very lovely, Cumberland."

A long silence fell between them, until:

"Do you ever ask yourself," said John Cumberland, "if she was—natural?"

"My dear fellow," the Professor returned, "I have asked myself that question a hundred times! And I think it has been answered for us."

"How? In what way?"

"By her disappearance."

John Cumberland stared, and:

"I don't think I follow," he declared.

"If," explained Professor Blackwell slowly, "Zalithea was supernatural, certainly Safiyeh was not. But Safiyeh disappeared with her!"

His friend considered the words for some time, and at last:

"I see the point," he said. "It's a new one, I admit."

When, later, Jim Sakers's father joined them, he put the case before him bluntly.

"This thing has knocked Barry sideways," he told Robert Sakers. "In confidence, it's touch and go. Blackwell will bear me out."

"I have watched Barry," the latter admitted; "and I am certain that he's on the verge of a nervous breakdown. He is crazy to go back to Egypt, via London and Paris. We don't hope that he will find the girl,

Sakers; we don't expect so much. But I am quite positive that the journey will save him. Now—he can't go alone. It's out of the question. Jim is his oldest friend, and you can very well spare him for a month or six weeks—"

"I'm not asking you to stand the damage, Sakers," John Cumberland interrupted. "It wouldn't be fair on top of the inconvenience of losing your right-hand man."

"Leave that part out," said Robert Sakers. "Let's get down to dates."

And as a result of the conference which followed, some ten days later Jim Sakers found himself, with Barry, bound for Europe. His profound and ceaseless amazement, expressed at great length, was an antidote to poor Barry's melancholy—as it was designed to be.

New environment and the magic of sea breezes aided the cure; and after an idle week in London, during which Barry's restlessness seemed to have abated in a measure, they crossed to Paris.

The faithful Jim cabled an enthusiastic report home; and perhaps Barry, by this time, had begun to realize that the journey was intended to be a "cure" and to reconcile his overwrought mind to the idea of resignation. But what he did not realize, what neither of them realized, was that they were helpless in the "moving row" of which old Omar spoke, and that they were being danced impotent toward that inevitable end designed by "the Master of the Show."

Paris proved rather a setback. It provoked memories which brought about in Barry a relapse into melancholy. Jim worked like a Trojan to arouse him from his mournful apathy.

"Regard, oh, regard the glitter of the boulevard," he invited, as they sat outside a popular café in the sunshine. "Unknown to the old folks at home, in their sleepy village adjacent to the delta of the Hudson —"

"The Hudson has no delta," Barry murmured.

"Let that pass. But still unknown to them, whether they have a delta or not, here we sit sipping perfectly good wine at a price for which we could not obtain a cup of coffee in our little home town. Therefore, let us rejoice! And, lo! here come soldiers—complete with band! Let us cheer!"

A small party of infantry marched past, accompanied by a large band. Jim stood up, watching them enthusiastically and talking away all the time. Receiving no criticisms from Barry, he turned.

His flow of nonsense was checked.

Barry, pale as death, clutching the edge of the marble-topped table, was staring—staring—across the street, his ghastly features those of one who sees a ghost!

"Barry!" Jim gasped. "Barry!"

Barry did not stir. When he spoke his voice was a whisper.

"Jim," he said, "*I have seen her!*"

"What!"

"She has just gone into the perfumers' shop opposite."

"Barry!" Jim grasped his shoulder. "Wake up, man! You are daydreaming."

"Watch until she comes out," the monotonous whisper went on. "Don't let her see you, for God's sake. But follow her, Jim—don't lose sight of her—until you find out where she is living."

"But, Barry," Jim began, a note of profound anxiety in his voice, when:

"Quick! There she goes!" he was interrupted.

He looked across the street. He gasped audibly; then:

"Wait for me here!" he said tersely.

Zalithea, carrying a small parcel, had just come out of the shop and was walking away!

Jim Sakers experienced a sense of sudden acute exhilaration. The wildly unforeseen had happened! And at last he was going to be of real use to his friend! What it all meant was outside the province of his mental powers. Who this mysterious girl really was who had so hopelessly bewitched Barry he had never been able to understand. Nor could he comprehend how she could possibly have reached Paris without the knowledge of the American authorities.

But unmistakably it was Princess Zalithea and none other who walked along before him. Her lithe figure, her graceful carriage, the very turn of her head when she paused to look in a shop window were familiar to the man who had met her many times in New York.

From the crowded boulevard into which she had turned on coming out of the perfumers' she entered a side street. Jim didn't know the name either of the street or the boulevard. His bump of locality was low. But he knew that he wasn't going to lose sight of her if he had to follow her around Paris all day!

He was turning a problem over in his mind as he tracked the trim, leisurely figure. What should he do if she saw him?

Zalithea came out onto another boulevard and waited at the corner of the street for a moment. Evidently she was going to cross. She did so, and Jim was delayed by the eccentric Paris traffic. When he finally ran over, for a moment he lost her. Then, just disappearing around the corner of the next street along, he saw the smart figure again.

He hurried to the spot, swung round the corner—and saw Zalithea entering a discreet-looking hotel on the same side. He was in the lobby a minute later—and she was talking to a clerk at the desk!

Jim turned his back and stared out into the street through the glass doors. The lobby was small. He could hear every word spoken at the desk. And what he heard gave him the crowning surprise of the morning.

"No, madam—" the clerk spoke perfect English—"no American mail has come in yet."

"Thank you. If any comes later will you please send it right up?"

The speaker was Zalithea!

Astounded—thrown off his guard—Jim turned and met Zalithea face to face!

"Princess!" he said. "You remember me!"

The girl's white teeth closed sharply on her lower lip. She nearly dropped the parcel she was carrying, but just managed to recover it. She flushed and as quickly paled. But she looked at him unflinchingly— and he knew her long, dark eyes.

"You have made a strange mistake," she said, evenly. "I am not a princess and I don't know you."

Jim wondered if he were going mad. The clerk was watching him dubiously, so was a hall porter.

"But—" he floundered—"but—" The dark eyes remained fixed upon him inscrutably. "I'm sorry. Forgive me. But it's miraculous."

She turned and walked out of the lobby. Jim did not afterward remember having seen her leave. It was the scrutiny of the officials that brought him to his senses and sharpened his ready wits. He turned to the clerk, taking a card from his wallet. It was the card of a member of the agency recently employed by John Cumberland!

He tossed it on the desk, and:

"You no doubt wonder what I'm up to?" he said breezily. "There's the answer!"

"Oh!" muttered the clerk, glancing at the name. "I see. But you were wrong, weren't you?"

"I'm afraid so," Jim confessed—"quite wrong!"

He stared at a menu that chanced to lie near and learned that he was in the Hôtel Chatham. "Nothing for the Chatham to worry about!" he added reassuringly. "But I should like to make my apologies. *We* have a reputation, too!" He drew a pencil from his pocket. "What is the name of the lady I so unfortunately insulted?"

"She is a Miss Marguerite Devina of New Jersey, U. S. A."

"Thanks," said Jim, making a note of it. "Here alone?"

"Yes. I believe she is expecting relatives today."

"Much obliged."

Jim nodded in a brusque fashion based upon that of the lawful owner of the card and stepped out into the street.

The street gained, his assured manner deserted him. He was the most hopelessly bewildered American in Paris. What in the name of sanity should he tell Barry? That this *was* Princess Zalithea he would have been prepared to declare upon oath. Besides, good actress though he granted her to be, she had failed to hide her surprise at sight of him. He had seen her bite her lip—to check what? A sudden utterance of his name? Probably. Her changed colour, her trembling hands, proved that she had recognized him.

It was she. But what did it mean?

How could he face Barry with such a story?

Turning these problems over in his mind, he plodded back to the café. From afar he saw Barry—watching. At sight of Jim he jumped up and ran to meet him.

"Tell me!" he cried, his eyes feverishly bright. "Where does she live?"

"At the Hôtel Chatham."

"Thank God! And she didn't see you?"

"But she did!"

"What!"

"Come back and sit down, Barry," Jim urged. "Get a grip on yourself. We're together in this thing. Let me order you a glass of good cognac."

"You're hiding something!"

"I'll give you the story word for word when you have sat down and had a drink and lighted your pipe. Not a damn' syllable before!"

He had his way, for he could be very truculent at times; and poor Barry Cumberland was a parody of his old masterful self. So, while Barry smoked furiously the story was told—a stranger story than any Jim had ever expected to have to tell. In conclusion:

"If you are mad," he said, "I'm mad, too! Because Miss Marguerite Devina is Princess Zalithea. But Princess Zalithea only spoke *gazoobi* or *swahili*—and Miss Devina speaks perfect English. Now search me! *Garçon, deux cognacs!*"

The chairs about them were becoming filled with loungers, as the day wore on to noon. A cosmopolitan crowd thronged the street and the neighbouring boulevard. Somewhere nearby an orchestra had begun to play a melody very popular in New York. Newsboys shouted. Drivers of carts shouted. Everybody shouted.

But Barry was silent. At last:

"Well?" Jim inquired. "What do we do now?"

"I have just decided," Barry replied quietly. "It will be best for you to stay where you are at the Meurice. We don't want to frighten her. But I shall transfer to the Chatham, at once."

CHAPTER XXXI

THE MEETING

If Barry Cumberland had his weaknesses—and who has not?—he had one marked virtue. He knew what he wanted, and always headed straight for his objective. In fact, his impulsiveness was excessive and sometimes overrode his practical common sense.

He was wise enough to know this, for he was well stocked with imagination; and, safely lodged at the Hôtel Chatham that afternoon, he made a direct move, which was characteristic, but one that allowed of safe withdrawal in the event of failure. This was sound strategy. His tentative advance was suggested by the name of the mysterious guest—"Devina."

John Cumberland sometimes spoke of a Madame Devina, a once famous operatic soprano of the Metropolitan Opera; an idol of New York who had disappeared from the musical world at the height of her success. She had been entertained at the Cumberland home more than once during a brilliant season notable for her singing of Thaïs—the role which had made her reputation. Those days Barry could just remember and no more. They belonged to the dreams of childhood in which his dainty mother figured as the centre of a wonderful world.

Now, those memories served a good purpose, and, seated in his room, he wrote the following note:

DEAR MADAM:

Please forgive an impulsive countryman for intruding. But I chanced to see your name in the register today, and it reminded me of the fact that my father, John Cumberland, and my mother, were formerly friends of Madame Devina. As the name is an unusual one, I venture to ask if you are related to that lady. If you are, I should be more than happy to make your acquaintance, and my father, I know, would be delighted to hear of you.

Respectfully,
BARRY CUMBERLAND.

This he directed to "Miss Marguerite Devina" and gave to a page to be delivered to her in person.

His letter dispatched, Barry restlessly crossed to the window, which he threw open. It overlooked a garden courtyard, which for some reason cast his memory back to Shepheard's in Cairo. Many balconies looked down upon this sheltered oasis, and he allowed his imagination to tell him that one of them belonged to the room of Zalithea. . . .

Zalithea! Was there any such person as Zalithea? Had there *ever* been a Zalithea?

Once, this thing which had happened would have frightened him and set him questioning his own sanity. But now, as Jim had said that morning, "If you are mad, *I'm* mad, too!"

Would she answer? Would she consent to see him? If she refused, what next?

His anxiety and impatience made it impossible for Barry to keep still. He walked away from the window; paced the room; listened at his door for the footsteps of the returning messenger; then went across to the window again.

For long minutes he stood there, moving restlessly. He lost track of time. A knocking on his door recalled him to reality. He turned, his heart leaping.

"Come in!" he cried.

The page entered. At a glance Barry saw that he brought no note.

"Miss Devina will be downstairs at four o'clock, m'sieur."

No doubt the world went on as usual during the next hour, and Paris lived and loved and laughed as Paris has done from time immemorial; but to Barry the interval afterward appeared to have been a blank—a hiatus in existence. Four o'clock came at last. . . .

She was seated in a cane chair before a little round table set for tea. She stood up as he crossed to her.

"It was nice of you, Mr. Cumberland," he heard her saying in Zalithea's unforgettable voice!

He found himself seated beside her. A waiter was serving English tea and handing little dishes of cakes, biscuits, and sweetmeats. This Barry saw and heard through a sort of fog. Everything was muffled. His sensations were almost identical with those he had known toward the close of his farewell college supper. Presently, in a voice not unlike his own:

"You have not told me," someone said, "if my guess was right. Are you related to Madame Devina?"

"Devina was my mother."

The fog was cleared away by that definite, simple statement. The merciful numbness which alone had enabled Barry to behave himself rationally thus far left him. He looked into long, dark eyes.

"You know that we have met before?" he said.

Marguerite Devina watched him unflinchingly.

"You had an accident some months ago right outside my door," she replied. "But I didn't know that you saw me. You were unconscious when we found you."

Barry clenched his teeth. An insane desire to laugh came to him. He knew he must fight it.

"You are referring to my crash in New Jersey?" he said evenly, tonelessly.

"Yes. You must have wondered why we behaved so oddly afterward. The fact is that my guardian and I were booked to sail for Europe, and we realized that if we appeared in the matter it would almost certainly mean delay. We couldn't afford that, you see."

"Your guardian? Mr. Brown?"

"Oh, no!" she laughed—Zalithea's beloved laughter!—"Mr. Brown was the man who drove you to the hospital and took care of your car. We were tenants of his." She hesitated, bit her lip, and: "When did you see me?" she asked—"before or after the accident?"

"Before," said Barry. "On the balcony."

"Yes," murmured the girl, bending to pour out tea—"It's a queer thing to admit, but I'm fascinated by lightning. Do you think—it was seeing me there that—caused you to crash?"

"No," Barry replied promptly. He was watching the slim hands, the turn of her wrists, the line, seen below a smart little hat, of her creamy neck. "You were dressed very oddly."

She stooped forward over the sugar bowl.

"Yes; I was—trying on a fancy costume." She glanced up quickly. "Two lumps?"

"One, please." He watched her dazedly. "It's amazing to think that my father knew your mother. I have heard him speak of her singing Thaïs."

"The critics said she did not merely *sing* Thaïs, she *was* Thaïs."

"Is she—?"

"She died when I was a baby," the girl replied simply. "Here, in Paris."

"You were born in Paris?"

"Yes."

"How did you come to live in America?"

"My foster-father is an American. He was once engaged to marry my mother, you see. But she changed her mind—unfortunately."

As she spoke the final word, an expression of such implacable hatred crept over her beautiful face that Barry flinched. It was so that he remembered her on that night in the *wâdi!*

"It's dreadful to say and dreadful to hear," she went on; "but my father ruined my mother, in every sense of the word. She would have died in a pauper's hospital but for Paul Ahmes."

"Who is Paul Ahmes?" Barry asked, a sort of new awe in his voice.

Marguerite Devina glanced up at him, and her eyes were very bright.

"He is the greatest-hearted soul in the world," she answered in a queer tone of challenge. "My mother brought him nothing but sorrow. Yet he spent all he had to try to make her happy—at the end. And he took the place of my father—afterward."

"And is he, also, an operatic artist?"

She gave a little choking laugh.

"No," she replied. "He is, or used to be, a vaudeville artist! He retired years ago. He was known throughout Europe as 'The Great Ahmes.' He was an illusionist. Not so famous as Houdini, but equally clever in his own way."

Watching her closely and trying to steady his voice:

"Ahmes is surely an Egyptian name?" said Barry.

"Yes," she replied composedly. "He used to work as an Egyptian. There is Arab blood on his father's side. He was always billed as 'The Wizard of the Sphinx.'"

With a curious eagerness she poured out these confidences. Obviously she wanted to do so. She watched Barry with those long, lovely eyes, as if inviting further and closer cross-examination; as if challenging him to put her upon trial.

"Is—your guardian—in Paris?"

"I expect him today."

"Did you expect *me?*"

The abruptness of the thrust startled her, Barry determined. But if it were so her defence remained impregnable.

"No," she replied, laughing; "how could I?"

And even as she lowered her dark lashes and looked in her bag for a cigarette, sanity whispered: "How could she? This girl, whose every movement, every expression, every feature, and every mannerism are familiar, yet is not, cannot be, Zalithea!"

Memory plays odd tricks at times, and as Barry struck a match to light their cigarettes, a hitherto forgotten remark of Professor Blackwell's flashed, intact, through his mind. It had been made on the evening that the Professor had examined Zalithea. "There is a small scar under the hair, just above the right ear, which suggests that the theory—now generally accepted, I believe—that surgery was practised by the ancients is not without foundation."

"Have you a small scar under your hair above the right ear?" he asked suddenly.

At this Marguerite Devina unmistakably grew pale.

"Yes," she answered, and looked at him with half-veiled alarm. "How strange you should know that!"

"Professor Blackwell told me."

"Is he a clairvoyant?"

"No," said Barry, and laughed without mirth. He met the glance of the dark eyes. "I once thought *I* was, though. Now—I don't know what to think. But there's something I must tell you. Perhaps I should have told you right away. You are the living image, a miraculous double, of someone—"

"Someone?"

"Someone I love very dearly. There! I've told you! I came here, to Paris, to find her. And when I saw *you*—"

His voice failed him. He turned his head aside miserably.

The girl was silent for a time; then, very gently:

"Do you mean," she asked, "that you have come from America to—look for her?"

Barry nodded.

"What made you think you would find her in Paris?"

"I don't know. We were—very happy in Paris. But I'm on my way to Egypt."

"To Egypt!"

"Yes. That was where—we met."

"And you really expect to meet her again, in Egypt?"

"I don't dare to expect. But if I left off hoping—"

He did not complete the sentence. Marguerite Devina had abruptly stood up. Her head was averted.

"Please forgive me," said Barry. "I didn't mean to hurt you."

Even as the words left his lips, he remembered where he had last uttered them—and to whom. She turned to him impulsively, and the memory was complete. Her lashes were wet with tears.

"You haven't!" she said. "But I must go."

Barry reached out a detaining hand.

"Please," he pleaded, "let me see you again!"

She averted her head once more, and:

"If I can," she murmured. "I'm sorry—but I must hurry away now."

And, stumbling in her haste, she walked around the little table and ran across the lobby. . . .

Back to his room Barry went in a state of mind which he found himself incapable of analyzing. Was it possible, in the natural order of things, for two human beings to be so absolutely alike? As well ask himself if it were possible for a girl to live three thousand years! One being possible, why not the other?

He was curiously reluctant to leave the hotel. Therefore Jim dined with him in the grill room whose chef has been preserved for posterity by Orpen's brush. Of Marguerite Devina they saw nothing. At the end of dinner:

"If I don't stop thinking about this muddle," Jim declared, "I shall become completely cuckoo. It's the Folies Bergères or a lunatic asylum for mine. Make your selection."

The selection was made. And it was at a late hour (Paris time) that Barry returned to the Chatham. The night porter handed him a letter.

In his room he tore open the envelope. He began to read. Then, rushing to the telephone, he banged the lever up and down in a frenzy of impatience. At last:

"Hullo! Hullo!" he called, in a high, unnatural voice. "Ring Miss Marguerite Devina!"

"Miss Devina left this evening, m'sieur."

And when dawn came it found Barry haggard, wild-eyed, pacing the room, ever and anon taking up a crumpled letter and reading and rereading it.

CHAPTER XXXII

THE GREAT AHMES

"BARRY DEAR:

"I don't ask you to forgive me. I never meant to see you again. But when Jim spoke to me today I realized, somehow, that *you* were here. And I knew you would come. And I knew I would have to see you. I didn't know how hard it would be—because I never believed you cared, like that.

"I don't know how to tell you what I see now, I *must* tell. It all began, really many years ago, when I was a baby, and when Paul Ahmes was giving up everything to make my mother's last days bearable. She had never loved him, but they had one thing in common. It was their passion for Egypt. She made her great success in an Egyptian opera and he as an Egyptian performer. He used to buy Egyptian antiques with all he could save. He knew more about these things than any dealer in Europe. Most of his stage properties were real. They inspired him.

"One day my mother read that a ring which had been the property of the real Thaïs was being auctioned at Sotheby's in London. This ring had once belonged to her. She never sang Thaïs without wearing it.

But poverty had forced her to sell it. Paul Ahmes, knowing what happiness the recovery of this ring would give her, went to London to buy it. This was like him. He did not bid, himself, as all the auctioneers knew him. He sent someone.

"Barry—your father was at that auction—and he has the ring today! When Ahmes heard that John Cumberland had secured it, he wrote to him, and without mentioning my mother's name told him all the circumstances. Your father did not believe him.

"My mother died the night after Ahmes returned.

"Soon after that, before I can remember, we left Paris and went to live in America. I grew up to look upon Ahmes as my father. I was always surrounded by things belonging to Egypt, for my guardian had left the stage and become a professional dealer in antiques. He was sometimes away for months together, in Egypt, where he had agents now that his business had grown so big. He had changed his name. John Cumberland was one of his clients.

"But, Barry, very few of the wonderful and beautiful things he received from Egypt ever left Ahmes's possession. They went into his own collection—which is priceless; for this was his ruling passion now that my mother was dead. He sold copies, or restored originals mostly, to his wealthy customers. Some of the most famous museums in the world contain his work! His love of everything belonging to Egypt simply wouldn't allow him to sell a genuine piece. His genius for making duplicates (for he is, truly, a genius) made it easy for him to keep them.

"And all the money he earned in this way was spent acquiring more and more rarities for his private museum.

"Then—this was years ago—he stumbled upon the tomb of Zalithea. He reached it through a long narrow passage cut at some time by Arab robbers. He found there the great stone sarcophagus, and he raised and wedged the lid. The sarcophagus was empty.

"Thinking that one day this discovery might profit him, he reclosed and concealed the opening. This opening, I must tell you, came out in another valley, *behind the tomb*, and it led, through a hole in the roof, into the *shaft* between the first and second portcullis. You remember where the roof had fallen? This second portcullis the thieves had broken, and also the door of the chamber where the sarcophagus was.

"I unknowingly inspired him to what followed—I and his wish to score over John Cumberland, whom he had taught me to detest. He said I had the true Egyptian profile. The showman in him came to life—this part of his strange nature was only sleeping; and he thought of the wildest plot that surely any man ever attempted to carry out.

"He said to me, 'I will sell *you* to John Cumberland! And if you play your cards properly you will marry a millionaire!' I was completely under his influence, Barry. I had never known any other kind of life but this commercial use of Ahmes's genius as an illusionist. I don't want to excuse myself. I prepared for the thing with enthusiasm!

"This was when we came secretly to New Jersey. Mr. Brown, who took the house, was formerly Ahmes's stage manager. His wife acted as cook. There were other members of my guardian's old company there as well. For no one who had ever worked for Ahmes wanted to leave him.

"Here for a long time I lived like a nun. No one outside our small household ever saw me. When I went anywhere I was always heavily veiled. Ahmes taught me to speak *Coptic*. This was the mysterious language of Zalithea! Arabic I knew, because I had had an Arab nurse from childhood—an old member of Ahmes's company—Safîyeh!

"A year before the papyrus was brought to your father, Ahmes went to Egypt. He erected the screen, as you know, his agent, Hassan es-Sugra, having traced the real, or front, entrance to the tomb. He broke through as far as the first portcullis, which he knew was intact. Then he reclosed and hid the entrance as you found it. The hieroglyphic of 'She Who Sleeps' he himself carved in the rock.

"By the other tunnel, the one he first discovered, he took in lifting gear and swung up the stone sarcophagus lid. The painted sarcophagus, which he had made in New Jersey and shipped out, he put inside. Then he lowered the stone lid again. The tables, lamps, couch, and other things he set in place. Some of these were genuine. Some he had made. He also added the cartouche of 'She Who Sleeps' to the ancient inscriptions painted on the wall.

"He cemented the door and, from the tunnel above, blocked the secret entrance. Then he came back to America. The stage was set for his last and greatest illusion.

"The 'Zalithea Papyrus' and the 'Formula' Ahmes had been at work upon for two years. They were the biggest achievements of his career! The materials had cost him no end of research. But no other man in Europe or America could have written them—to pass Horace Pain and Dr. Rittenburg!

"Yes, Barry! I'm proud of him! Until you came, it never occurred to me to question his way of life. Besides, he had taught me to hate the name of Cumberland. It was a mania with him. I believe for a long time he held John Cumberland responsible for my mother's death.

"The Zalithea dress, the strange ingredients mentioned in the Formula, and all the other things, he got from many sources, working patiently for months and months. He put his whole soul into the affair.

"Then, just as we were ready, you had an accident right outside the house!

"We were in an awful panic. But Ahmes was always at his best in an emergency. You know how we managed to keep out of the matter. The household was dispersed. Only Mrs. Brown stayed to clear things up. I was hidden in my guardian's apartment in New York. And I nearly ruined everything one evening by going out to our old garden in New Jersey to get some flowers. Yes! I was there that day when you came!

"As soon as the date of departure was fixed, Safiyeh and another Arab, called Omar, were sent to Egypt. Soon afterward I went, also. I sailed on the same ship, to Cherbourg, as Professor Blackwell! But it didn't matter, because we had arranged that I should stay in my stateroom all the way.

"I remained hidden with Safiyeh in Luxor until the night before the tomb was opened. That night I was smuggled across—and you heard my voice as I stumbled in the little valley where Omar was waiting for me! Omar you saw once. He is tall and thin, and you thought he was a ghost!

"In a ruined tomb in that little valley I was dressed for the part of Zalithea. Safiyeh was there with me. But she went back to Luxor in the early morning.

"You understand, now, that when you first discovered the painted sarcophagus I was not in it? He carried me up to the tomb during *the second watch* on the night before the lid was raised! I was placed inside. Then the lid was fastened down! I was frightened, although the gold mask allowed me to breathe freely and there were lots of air holes in the sarcophagus.

"I had to lie there for nearly three hours! But I had been training to do this for months before.

"Never shall I forget my relief when you came at last to unwrap me! Of course I had been prepared in all sorts of ways for the ordeal. And you will remember, Barry, that none of you had a chance to touch me or even see me properly up to the time that I opened my eyes.

"Yes! You were in the hands of a master illusionist!

"As for the rest—I was prepared to hate you! But on the night you came to my tent and said, 'Forgive me. I didn't mean to hurt you,' I couldn't hate you, somehow.

"Ahmes, too, had changed his mind about John Cumberland. He had learned to respect him; in fact, to love him. But he had to go on then! So did I!

"Sometimes it was good fun. Sometimes, when your father talked to me, not knowing I understood, I couldn't bear it. But we didn't know how to end it!

"You ended it! The night when you found me with that pig Edwards I knew it must finish. While you were asleep I went to Ahmes and told him.

"He was sorry—for me; but glad that we were through. Safiyeh went to Montreal and sailed, under her own name, for England, three days later. I was here, in Paris, before you allowed the news of my disappearance to be published. Ahmes wrote the hieroglyphic letter to relieve your mind. It was delivered by the same messenger who brought another letter. He is here, now, with the others. That is why you failed to trace him.

"That's all, Barry dear. We have a house in Paris. It had been closed, though, and so I stayed at the Chatham for a short time. But Ahmes arrived today, and I am going to join him. He knows I have told you.

"Do what you like. But I shall be punished enough.

"You see—I love you.

"MARGUERITE."

CHAPTER XXXIII

A FLASH OF LIGHTNING

"Jim," said Barry miserably, "what else can I do?"

"Well," Jim replied, thoughtfully rapping on the café table to attract the waiter's attention, "you can order another half bottle of this very good wine, and then perhaps ideas may come."

The order given:

"It's Kismet," Barry went on. "If she had confessed to murder I should still have wanted her! In fact, mad as it may seem, I love her better, now, knowing her to be what she is, than I did before."

"Not mad in the least," Jim commented. "Taking into consideration the way she was brought up, I, myself, harsh though my judgments of frail humanity notoriously are, should feel the same. I could both love and respect the Marguerite who wrote that brave letter. I don't think I could ever have worked up any real enthusiasm for a living mummy."

"I *know*," said Barry emphatically, "that one day I shall find her again. When I do, I'm going to marry her if she'll have me!"

"Strong, sound sentiments," Jim replied. "It is men such as you are who make men such as I am love men such as you are! But the old problem arises; your father."

"I have made up my mind on that point," Barry declared. "He must not know—yet. It's hateful, but I mustn't shatter his illusion. I shall write and tell him I have met the girl of the balcony, and that she is the double of Zalithea—and the daughter of Devina. Those who knew Zalithea will soon forget the resemblance when they hear Marguerite speak. Then, one day, he shall know the truth. Nobody else must ever know."

"We shall have to lie like the Brothers Ananias," said Jim sadly, "for a time. This prospect appalls my proudly virtuous spirit. But it's up to you. What you say, goes. Meanwhile, a full week has elapsed and our patient inquiries have merely yielded, No, sir. Shall you go on advertising in the Paris papers?"

"Yes," was the answer. "My advertisement means nothing to anyone else. It might as well stand. Who knows?"

"Nobody knows," Jim murmured. "It is ignorance and not knowledge which makes us lose faith in Santa Claus. And this afternoon? Shall I scour the district in and about Batignolles as you so kindly suggest?"

"Jim, you're a brick! This 'scouring' is no sort of way to enjoy a holiday in Paris. Just say you're tired, and I'll do that part myself tomorrow."

"No, no, Horatio. Batignolles appeals to me because I can't pronounce it. And have I not said many times that I long for the life of a detective? 'All forms of shadowing undertaken. Your pay roll guarded by machine-gun experts (in uniform). Missing relatives traced by our special staff of lady searchers. Our watchword—'"

"Jim! I love you, but—"

"Guilty! Dismiss the jury. We reassemble at the Chatham at six for cocktails."

And so the quest went on. Barry had in mind a neighbourhood he had noted during a drive on the outskirts near the old fortifications. Here were discreet villas sheltering behind little gardens which, like the *yashmak* of a Turkish beauty, merely provoked without concealing. He felt sure that the house he sought would have a garden.

Barry had considered the idea of engaging a detective agency to trace Zalithea, so strangely found only to be lost again. But, in the circumstances, he had decided that to do so would be unwise.

Marguerite's letter he almost knew by heart. At first, the shock of it had stunned him. The readjustment of perspectives which it entailed appalled his brain. But out of all the chaos one fact emerged—a fact brooking no denial. He loved her. He could not imagine life without her.

His eagerness was eternally conjuring up mirages. A group at a café table would suddenly come into view—and *she* was there. As he drew nearer, all resemblance would disappear. He hated those unconscious mimics, some of whom were astoundingly unlike Marguerite at close quarters. Perfumery stores he unfailingly explored. And a hundred times he had run like a madman to overtake some girl seen in the distance—only to alarm a stranger.

More than one gendarme had eyed him with suspicion. A tall, distinguished-looking old gentleman, wearing the ribbon of the Legion and escorting a very pretty girl whose figure and carriage certainly resembled those of Marguerite, demanded the name of his hotel and promised to send his seconds to Barry in the morning.

And now he was on the outskirts of the woods. Just ahead lay the group of villas which had attracted his attention on the previous day. He proposed to pursue a plan adopted on other occasions: viz.—to call at a likely-looking house and ask if Miss Devina and her father were at home. Being assured that he had come to the wrong address, he could inquire if two Americans resided anywhere in the vicinity.

Following an unseasonably hot morning, clouds had begun to gather shortly after noon. Now, it was growing very dark. The woods on his right were haunted by ghostly shadows. From somewhere beyond the western outskirts of Paris echoed ominous rumblings, to remind good Parisians of that black day when Von Kluck's Prussians came hammering at their gates.

Then, suddenly, the downpour started. In sight of a charming little villa whose green shutters and green balconies were visible above a guardian row of dwarf acacias, Barry darted to cover. His back against the trunk of a tree the dense foliage of which promised shelter, he stood, looking up.

A black thunder pall hung directly above. Except for the sound of falling rain, a profound stillness had come. Then, blindingly, lightning flicked its venomous fang from the heart of the cloud. The house opposite was illuminated ice blue, eerily. Every leaf upon the trees was lent a momentary hard, individual existence. Every nail in the woodwork of the villa gate, every piece of gravel on the garden paths, summoned attention vividly, alone, aloof from the rest. . . .

And a window directly facing the tree beneath which Barry stood was thrown open.

Marguerite came out onto the green balcony!

Her lips were parted in a half-frightened smile. Exultant, like a roll of Titanic war drums, thunder crashed and boomed and beat out its fury in dying echoes.

Across the feathery crests of the acacias their glances met. . . .

Barry uttered an involuntary cry. The storm was forgotten. The world was forgotten. Out into the drenching downpour he ran, across to the gate and on, up the gravelled path, to the discreet, glazed door. She had fled at sight of him. The balcony above was empty; but the window remained open. He rang, but without result. He rang again—and again—and again. He rang continuously.

The door was opened.

And he found himself looking into a wrinkled Arab face.

"Safiyeh!" he exclaimed.

She smiled, unsurprisedly, and stood aside to allow him to enter.

He discovered himself in a little lobby furnished throughout in Egyptian fashion. There were antique tables and figures of the gods of the Nile. There was a fresco of subjects from Der-el-Bahari. A perforated silver lamp hung from the ceiling. And the air was laden with a faint perfume, the indescribable smell of Egypt.

Safiyeh raised a tapestry curtain and again stood aside. Barry went into the room beyond.

This apartment was littered with every imaginable kind of relic, from exquisite enamel necklaces to mummied cats. At sight of the treasures contained there, Barry was transported in spirit to a similar room high above the turmoil of New York, where once he had sat in conference with Horace Pain, Dr. Rittenburg, and others.

Leaning upon a mantelpiece composed of carved red granite fragments adapted to the purpose was a tall man, the collar of whose white shirt fell open at the neck, while the sleeves were rolled up on muscular arms. One elbow rested on the ledge; the clenched fist supported a handsome, leonine head. A scarab ring glittered on his finger, as, raising the other hand to remove a cigar which he was smoking, he bowed in courteous greeting.

"Danbazzar!" cried Barry.

A roll of distant thunder from the moving storm echoed and reechoed over Paris.

"Paul Ahmes, at your service, sir!" Danbazzar corrected him. "But the former, if you prefer it. One's as much mine as the other! Sit down and let's talk this thing over."

Fascinated against his will, as he had always been fascinated by this man's extraordinary personality, Barry dropped onto a divan, silenced—stupefied—by the entire self-possession of the speaker. Here was no recognition of wrongdoing; this was not a detected impostor; this was the masterful man to whom obstacles were merely stepping stones, who was fearless as he was unscrupulous. This was Danbazzar.

"Margot told me what she had said in her letter," he went on. "I agreed. Get that clear. She did nothing behind my back. What she wants goes with me, and she wanted you to know the truth. You'd never have known if you hadn't followed her to Paris. But I'm not sorry, anyway. I have retired from business. Zalithea was my last deal. I regretted it long before the end came, because I found out that John Cumberland was white clean through. So, listen. Tell him if you like. I'll hand you a complete list of all the stuff he's got that isn't right, and he can sell it back to me for just what he paid. I'm not playing tin angels: I've got a market for it at big profit!"

Barry was unable to restrain a smile.

"If you ask me," Danbazzar added, "he'd be happier left alone. But do as you damn' please. There's no committee of experts in the world would say any piece from my workshop was faked—and you can lay your last dollar *I'm* not going to say it! As for the job at the tomb— we're all in the dock together. Pirates can't afford to quarrel! And now I'm going to talk to you about Margot. I'm going to talk straight, and I expect you to talk straight. . . ."

He talked, and talked straight, for the better part of an hour. He displayed a side of his complex, twisted character, that Barry had never suspected to exist. And, at one point, when he spoke of Marguerite's remorse for the part she had played, the words of Hassan es-Sugra recurred to Barry: "Be not angry with her." Finally:

"Now we've got it all set," said Danbazzar. "I've quit the United States for keeps. You know where I stand. We're agreed about the bunch in New York. And I know where you stand. Settle the rest with the kid."

He walked out of the room, stately, unperturbed; the Great Ahmes, master of the situation. Barry stood up. Suddenly, he had grown appallingly nervous. He paced up and down once or twice, among those priceless relics of an age whose loves and hates were forgotten before Paris arose from the forests. On one long, low wall, Pharaohs, gods, and goddesses made mysterious signs to one another, signalling: It was so in our day; it is so in this.

The rustle of the tapestry portiere told him to turn.

He faced Marguerite. . . .

She stood on the threshold watching him. Her long dark eyes held the same expression as on that night when, unseen by Barry, she had stolen to the library door to take her last look at him.

Yet something else was there, and slowly she came forward to where he stood. When she was close to him:

"My darling!" he whispered.

His arms went around her very tightly but very gently—not as in that first fierce embrace. And when he kissed her it was a lingering tender kiss.

THE END

MOON OF MADNESS

SAX ROHMER

CHAPTER I

THE GERMAN LINER

"I should *love* a long glass of iced German lager," said Nanette. "Besides, I refuse to be deserted for a whole morning."

Her Japanese parasol lay along the rail of the veranda, her round bare elbows rested upon it and she cuddled her obstinate little chin in upturned palms. I turned to her with a glance in which I had meant to convey rebuke. But the blue eyes danced with mischief and pouting lips smiled impudently, a smile half childish and half elfin.

"Young ladies of eighteen do not drink beer," I answered paternally. "It isn't done."

Jack Kelton came out as I spoke, saw Nanette, and flushed like a girl. When I say "like a girl" I mean like a girl of Victorian literature. Today one should say "like a boy." I never saw Nanette blush during all the time I knew her. I saw her grow deathly pale; but this was later.

Jack was good to see in the Madeira sunlight; one of those lean-limbed young Oxonians who strip so well and who always look amazingly clean. Nanette turned a slim shoulder in his direction, and stared out pensively across the bay. I thought that she had the most perfect arms imaginable. So did Nanette.

"I want to go out with you two and Mr. Ensleigh to that ship," she said, peering aside at the enraptured Jack. "Please ask Mumsy. She likes you—and I love beer."

Jack and I exchanged glances. We both looked at Nanette; and then beyond to where the subject of controversy lay anchored—a big German out of Bremen, in from the River Plate.

"I *have* asked her," Jack declared. "She's adamant."

"So have I," came a cheery voice—and Ensleigh joined the party. "She says that Mr. Kirby is coming to lunch."

"But I *loathe* Mr. Kirby!" cried Nanette, turning upon the speaker scornfully. "He's one of the reasons why I want to go!"

"Is that so, Nan?"

From a long, awning-covered chair near the corner of the veranda Nanette's mother arose—a gracefully pretty woman who solved the mystery of Nanette's beauty for those who had met only her father.

"Mumsy! Have you been sitting there all the time?"

"All the time, dear—and I have heard every word! So don't attempt to take one back!"

Ensleigh, the well-groomed, became all attention. He became attentive from the crown of his perfectly brushed hair to the soles of his spruce white shoes. He placed a chair for Nanette's pretty mother. He focussed his Zeiss glasses to enable her to view the German liner. She thanked him with a smile that was very like Nanette's.

"So you loathe poor Mr. Kirby?" she murmured, raising the glasses.

"Hate him poisonously!"

"And you love beer?"

"Simply worship it, Mum! Lager is my vice!"

Her mother lowered the glasses and fought with rising laughter, for Nanette was looking straight at her. Then:

"You little devil!" she said. "I don't believe a word of it! But your father simply won't hear of you going on board a German ship. Don't ask me why. You know him as well as anybody."

"I'll ask him myself!" Nanette said, flashing blue eyes rebelliously. "Where is the funny old thing?"

"Nan, dear!"

"Oh, he's a darling! But he *is* funny! He's never forgotten that I was once a baby."

"You are still a baby, Nan—a mere infant."

Nanette threw back her shapely bobbed head and laughed scornfully. Wild canaries were love-making in the palm grove below the balcony, and, being poetically inclined, I suppose, I thought that Nanette's soft rippling laughter was music sweet as theirs.

She turned swiftly. She had all her mother's grace as well as the divine abandon of youth. With never another glance at any of us, she walked in through the open French window. Jack Kelton's glance followed the slim, straight figure. Her mother looked up at Ensleigh.

"Have you a daughter?" she asked.

"No," he replied. "I regret—"

"Don't regret," she interrupted; but her smile belied the Chinese solecism to come: "Pray that you may never have a daughter!"

"Really," Jack began, in his youthful, diffident way, "I don't think there's any harm in—"

He was interrupted. Nanette returned, dragging by the hand a very bored, gray-haired gentleman who carried a copy of the *Times* that was ten days old. The gentleman, blinking through his glasses, was being forced out into the sunshine.

"Now, Pop," said Nanette firmly, "is there really any reason why I shouldn't go with Mr. Ensleigh, Mr. Decies, and Mr. Kelton to see that German liner?"

"Well, dear," her father replied, in his laboured manner, "I am afraid you would be late for lunch, and—"

His glance sought his wife's. I distinctly detected a negative shake of the head from Nanette's mother.

"And," he went on, "your mother thinks that this would be rude, as Mr. Kirby is expected."

He smiled almost apologetically, patted Nanette on the head, and, *Times* in hand, returned to his shady lair in the smoke-room. Nanette stared reproachfully at her mother.

"Don't be huffy about it, darling," said the latter. "Really, you will only have time for a swim and a sun bath, if you are to make yourself presentable by one o'clock."

Nanette looked swiftly from face to face. A number of people had now begun to come out from late breakfast. She checked speech, withered poor Jack with a final, comprehensive look of scorn, and walked quickly into the hotel. The last few steps that were visible, as she crossed the threshold, almost consisted of stamping her little feet.

Following a moment of silence:

"Look here, you chaps," said Jack, "it looks rather mean for us all to desert Nanette. I know we've engaged the launch and all that, but it's beastly tame swimming alone—"

"Don't worry, Mr. Kelton," Nanette's mother broke in. She was smiling. "Nanette will not be swimming alone!"

Poor Jack smiled in return, flushed, and then frowned darkly. His glance constantly sought the entrance to the hotel. But Ensleigh tactfully made the conversation general, and we were discussing the feminine modes of Paris as opposed to those of Buenos Aires when a slight figure arrayed in a pink bathrobe and shaded by a Japanese parasol passed slowly down the path below the terrace; whereupon:

"There goes Nanette!" said Jack, jumping up. "Excuse me. I'll just run and ask her if she would rather I stayed."

He hurled himself in the direction of the steps and disappeared. A moment later he reappeared, running after the girl. We watched.

"Nanette!" he called.

Nanette paused, turned, waved her hand, and went on. She walked under a veritable awning of hibiscus, sweeping some of the blossoms off with her parasol. Rounding the corner, she came into view again on a lower path. Her mother leaned over the balcony rail.

"Go after her, Jack!" she called. "Don't be afraid of her!"

The words reached Nanette. She looked up through flower-laden branches. Her voice came faintly.

"I don't want him to come after me. I want to be alone."

Jack Kelton turned and began to walk back up the sloping path. He kept his curly head lowered, taking out a briar from his pocket and fumbling for his pouch. Nanette's mother glanced at Ensleigh.

"Poor Jack," she said. "He is very young!"

CHAPTER II

RESCUE

We did not take the lift down to the landing-stage. It was busy with bathers; therefore we descended by the rambling stairway cut out of the rock. At the bend, I paused.

Half across the bay, far beyond the waddling group who hugged the bathing pool, where the transparent water showed turquoise blue, I saw a flashing of white limbs and glimpsed a pink-covered head lowered to the swell. Came a rapturous murmur behind me.

"Nanette! Gad! That girl swims like a fish!"

"They should follow with the boat," Ensleigh's voice broke in on Jack's. "There's a beastly current cuts round the headland."

"She is safe enough," said I. "Her fairy godmother was a mermaid—or a siren."

Nevertheless, when we reached the waiting launch, Nanette's daring had attracted attention. I could not see her mother; but there was a buzz of excited conversation all around, and the brown-skinned professional was making urgent signals to the boatmen.

"She's right on our course!" cried Jack. "Come on! Hurry up!"

"Don't worry," I implored him, tumbling into the launch.

"But she'll never be able to swim it!" said Ensleigh, jumping in behind me. "Hullo! What's this!"

He had stumbled over a bulky parcel wrapped up in newspaper. I thought I recognized the *Times*.

"Please leave alone, sir!" cried the Portuguese in charge. "I aska tella you no touch!"

"Oh!"

Ensleigh stared at him suspiciously, and then we were off.

"Pick her up, Decies!" came a shout from someone on shore. "She's overdone it this morning. She can never get back!"

The purr of the motor made it difficult to hear the other shouts that followed us. But excitement was growing intense, and I looked out ahead uneasily. I could not see Nanette.

"Can you see her, Decies?" said Jack hoarsely.

"No."

"There she is!"

The cry came from Ensleigh, and:

"Where?" Jack and I yelled together.

Ignoring us:

"Port, easy!" he directed the man at the wheel. "Now—as she is! Hold it!"

We raced, all out, in the direction of the rash swimmer. A sort of anger claimed me. This crazy performance was a display of girlish pique. I felt particularly sorry for Jack Kelton. He was hanging over the bow in a perfect anguish of terrified expectation. Presently:

"She's still swimming strongly!" he gasped; then, almost immediately: "My God!"

"What?"

Ensleigh and I were peering ahead over Jack's shoulder.

"She's gone down!"

Over the noise of the motor, over the sound of the sea, it reached us dimly—a prolonged, horrified cry from the watchers on shore.

What happened during the next few minutes I am unable to record. I think Jack was fighting with the boatman because he couldn't get another amp out of his engine. Ensleigh, I remember, looked dishevelled for the first time in my experience of him. I was drenched with perspiration—and it was not wholly due to the heat of the sun.

Then, dead ahead, not six lengths away, a white arm was thrown up out of the sea.

"Stop her!" I yelled.

Hot on the words came a splash—and Jack was in. He was fully dressed, except that he had shed his college jacket. He reached Nanette as she came up for the second time.

"Reverse! Starboard!"

We described an untidy crescent; and then—Nanette was being hauled aboard. She sank down on the cushions as Jack came clambering over looking like a half-drowned Airedale.

"Nanette!" he panted, and dropped on his knees before her.

She opened starry eyes, and looked at him.

"Yes?" she said.

"Back to the landing-stage," I heard Ensleigh direct the boatman.

"What's that!" cried Nanette, surprisingly sitting upright. "Not on your life, Pedro!"

We were riding the swell, the motor silent, and from the now-distant bathing pool I heard a sound of great, prolonged cheering.

Nanette sprang up on the thwart, standing there, poised on tip-toe, a slender young goddess. Jack's coat was in her hand; and she waved it furiously, looking back to where moving figures showed upon flower-draped terraces.

The cheering was renewed.

"That will relieve Mumsy's anxiety," said Nanette, sitting down again. "Please go ahead, Pedro—and would somebody pass me my robe?"

"What!" cried Jack.

Ensleigh tore away the pages of the *Times* from the mysterious bundle—and there was Nanette's pink robe!

"Be careful, please!" she said. "My shoes are wrapped up in it." She turned to Jack, at the same time pulling off her pink bathing cap. "I'm so sorry you jumped in," she added. "You were a darling to do it, though."

He had been positively glowering at her; but, at this, he blushed with delight and became a proud and happy man. Nanette shook her tousled head distractingly. Stooping, she pulled out from the folded robe a pair of high-heeled shoes and proceeded to squeeze five tiny wet toes into each of them.

"Nanette!" I said slowly. "Weren't you drowning?"

She looked up at me.

"Of course I wasn't drowning!" she returned. "I was swimming underwater. I was good for another mile!"

"Nanette!" said Ensleigh. "You will come to a bad end, my child."

"Please pass me my parasol," Nanette retorted. "It's in the locker. And be careful. My bag is inside it."

The Japanese parasol was discovered. From it, Nanette took a small bag. Surveying herself disdainfully in a square mirror, she combed her hair. She delicately applied lip salve and powdered her impudent nose.

"You are all wet!" said Jack, feasting his eyes. His case was worse than hers, and I marvelled at the altruism of love.

"The sun will dry me. But, oh! how good that lager will taste! Won't someone please give me a cigarette?"

I held out a yellow packet, and:

"Nanette," I said, "one day a Someone will come who will teach you how to behave yourself!"

"Tosh!" said Nanette, taking a Gold Flake. "I've outlived that sheikh stuff."

CHAPTER III

THE MAN FROM THE RIVER PLATE

As we drew alongside the German, it became evident that we were objects of much interest to her people. I had a good view of the third-class quarters; she had a deck-load of dagoes under her awnings that would have frightened a Chicago bootlegger.

We started up the ladder; and I thought it probable that some of the spectators would either fall overboard or break their necks, so urgently did they crane across the rails.

"They are anxious to see the gallant rescuer," said Ensleigh.

I knew my dago better. They were anxious to see Nanette's pretty legs.

On the deck, I turned and looked across to where Funchal climbed the hill. The sunlight was dazzling. I could trace the steep cobbled street, from point to point, down which one may slide in a wicker toboggan; see the square, too, with its powder-blue trees, and imagine the morning gathering at the tables outside the Golden Gate. Away over the bows I looked, and saw the flower-draped cliffs below Reid's, where, on the lower terrace, over cocktails, Nanette would, I surmised, be the sole topic of conversation.

The lady in question, supremely indifferent to the somewhat marked curiosity of the passengers, was walking aft with Jack, doubtless in quest of the much-desired lager. Jack, his legs encased in sodden flannels, was ridiculously happy because Nanette hung on his arm.

"Leave them alone," said Ensleigh. "God knows he's earned it."

We found our way to the smoke-room and ordered drinks. They were good and cheap. They served to wipe out one more of the old scores I had against our Teutonic friends (*nées* enemies). It was a distinctly mongrel company. Germans predominated, with a big sprinkling of those nondescripts and none-such usually invoiced as Argentines but sometimes mistaken for Greeks.

One man, who sat alone, puzzled me. He was handsome, in a way. He wore his wavy hair rather long and was dressed in a perfectly cut and immaculately white drill suit. With the aid of a black-rimmed monocle attached to a thick ribbon, he read what looked like an official document.

"By Jove!" Ensleigh exclaimed.

Glancing aside, I saw that he, too, was staring at this romantic individual.

"Looks like John Barrymore," said I.

"I know," Ensleigh replied. "But he didn't wear his hair like that the last time I saw him—coming out of the Salient with what was left of the Irish Guards. By Jove!"

He jumped up and crossed the room. I followed.

"O'Shea!" he cried.

The man addressed dropped his monocle and stood up; then:

"Ensleigh!" he exclaimed, and held out his hand. "Can it be Ensleigh!"

"Ensleigh it is!" was the reply; "and I want you to meet"—drawing me forward—"Mr. Decies. Decies, this is Major Edmond O'Shea."

The Major readjusted his monocle and looked me over briefly, as if to determine whether he wanted to know me or not. I found myself looking into a pair of the coldest gray eyes that had ever examined my hidden motives.

But, to tell the truth, I was more than a little flurried. For, as Ensleigh spoke, the fact had dawned upon me that I stood in the presence not only of an Irishman of ancient family, nor merely in that of a distinguished British officer, but in the presence of a mess-room tradition; a thing infinitely more wonderful and holy. This was "The O'Shea"—a synonym for all that's fine under the Colours from Whitehall to Khatmandu.

He dropped his monocle and grasped my hand warmly.

"I am glad to meet you, Mr. Decies," he said. We formed a trio, and there were some inevitable reminiscences—and more drinks; then:

"What, in the name of wonder, are you doing on this ship?" Ensleigh asked.

O'Shea shrugged his shoulders. He had some queerly Gallic mannerisms. In fact, if one had not known better, one must have written him off as an incurable poseur.

"Peace-time soldiering is a dull business," he replied. "I take on odd jobs to keep me out of mischief."

He rang for the steward and ordered drinks in what I believe was unexceptionable German. Following some aimless chatter:

"Are you for Bremen?" asked Ensleigh.

"I don't know," said O'Shea surprisingly. He twirled his glass and stared around the smoke-room. "I may come ashore here."

"You *may!*" I exclaimed and glanced at the clock. "You have twenty minutes to decide!"

"Two would be sufficient," he assured me. "I travel light!"

He smiled—and, in the smile, I met for the first time the real O'Shea. The cold gray eyes were cold no longer; they smiled, too—whimsically, lovably. The cloak of inscrutability was dropped, just for a moment, and the clean, brave soul of the man peeped out. A vague dislike vanished as morning mist, and I knew that men would follow Edmond O'Shea into the thickest and the hottest, if he needed them; women, too, perhaps. A man like that is a man born to suffer. But suddenly I understood why the Guards had worshipped him.

"There goes the first shore signal," said Ensleigh. "We had better rescue Nanette from the lager."

We found her on deck with Jack and another man who had tacked himself on to the party. He was a poisonously handsome none-such, and his heavy-lidded dark eyes were literally devouring the girl's dainty beauty. He had come across Jack in London; and now Jack was the most unhappy man in Madeira. Every time roguish blue eyes met lustful brown eyes, he visibly shuddered.

The dark gentleman was presented.

"Ensleigh, Decies—meet Senhor Gabriel da Cunha."

We met him—reluctantly.

"This," said Ensleigh, "is Mr. Jack Kelton—Major Edmond O'Shea. Doubtless, Senhor da Cunha, you have met already?"

"No," murmured O'Shea, bowing coldly. "One does not meet everybody on board."

"Nanette!" I called.

She had stepped to the rail with Da Cunha. She turned.

"Yes?"

"I want you to know Major Edmond O'Shea." She came forward and I introduced them formally. Nanette gave one quick, startled look at O'Shea—and O'Shea, noting her unusual attire, smiled. Nanette dropped her lashes, said something meaningless, and ran back to Da Cunha.

I heard Jack grind his teeth. When he joined the pair at the rail I stood at his elbow.

"We must be saying good-bye, Mr. da Cunha," he began, but:

"Not good-bye at all!" Da Cunha exclaimed, turning and resting one hand on Nanette's shoulder. "I am undecided until this morning, but now—it is settled! Here, in Madeira"—he indicated distant hills—"I have a bungalow, so charming. Do you know—" he included us all in the conversation—"that in Funchal is what they call a 'blind spot' in radio? Yes. But in my bungalow, high up, I have the most perfect set in the island; and one night—tonight, maybe—" he glanced aside at Nanette—"we shall dance to your Savoy band!"

"You are going ashore, then?"

"But certainly! It is settled. Is it not?"

The question was addressed to Nanette, and:

"I should just *hate* to lose you so soon," she replied. "Let's go and see if your things are in the boat."

Side by side with the radiantly smiling Da Cunha, she hurried forward. She glanced at Jack, at me, at Ensleigh. O'Shea was watching her, but she avoided his gaze. He turned and went in at the saloon entrance.

The last gong sounded. Jack had suddenly disappeared. I stared at Ensleigh. He whistled softly.

"Nanette has been bitten at last," he remarked.

"Yes," I said, "I think she has."

Da Cunha's baggage was loaded into Reid's launch and we all got aboard. We were surrounded by a babbling gang in boats who held up Madeira lace and cane chairs and shawls and bedspreads, desperately inviting bids from the passengers. It was distracting, so that I scarcely noticed a steward coming down the ladder, carrying a suitcase and a valise. Jack sat right astern, his hands plunged in the pockets of his sodden flannels. Then, suddenly, I realized that someone was beside me.

I turned—and met the cold gray eyes of O'Shea!

"Good heavens!" I exclaimed. "Your decision was a sudden one!"

"Yes," he replied, "it was—very."

"Hullo, O'Shea!" cried Ensleigh. "This is fine!"

Nanette bent toward Da Cunha, talking animatedly.

CHAPTER IV

AT THE CASINO

A party of us went down to the Casino that night, consisting of Nanette, Nanette's mother, Ensleigh, and myself. Jack excused himself on the plea that he had promised to play somebody five-hundred up. Nanette had been put through the hoop well and truly for her escapade, but she looked none the worse for this parental correction.

Newly from the seclusion of a French convent, she was learning the dangerous truism that beauty governs mankind.

Da Cunha was waiting at the Casino—and Nanette pretended to be surprised. Her mother really was surprised, and maternally alarmed. She was a woman of the world and she knew her Da Cunhas.

The said Da Cunha wanted to dance. Nanette loved dancing and danced divinely. Therefore she decided to play roulette.

"Please, mumsy," she pleaded—"until I have lost a pound!"

Her mother consented, silently signalling me to sit beside Nanette at the table. Whilst Nanette's mother danced with Ensleigh, I chaperoned Nanette.

The game was dull. Da Cunha constantly urged the superior charms of the ballroom. But Nanette played on. Presently:

"Do you think Jack will come along?" she asked.

"I hope so."

An interval in which Nanette lost five shillings, then:

"Had you met Major O'—what's his name—before?"

"No. I had heard of him."

"Really? Is he famous?"

"I suppose he is—in a way."

"But listen!" Da Cunha exclaimed, "this is *so* boring! Let us dance."

"Not until I've lost my pound," said Nanette firmly.

More aimless play, then:

"I saw your Major man when we first went on board, you know," said Nanette, casually staking her all on a number. "Jack and I peeped into the smoke-room, and—he was in there."

"Really. Is that so?"

"Yes. Wasn't it odd I should meet him, after—seeing him like that?"

"Very odd."

Nanette's fortune was swept away by the croupier. She remained unperturbed. She kept throwing quick little glances all about the room, and now:

"Please take me out on the terrace and get me a long, cool drink," she asked.

We stood up and crossed to the open doors. Da Cunha grabbed Nanette's arm and led her out. As I followed, I glanced aside, and saw Jack coming in. He looked very flushed. He was literally glaring after the pair in front of me. I waved to him, but he swung around and went out again.

It was dark on the terrace and at first I couldn't see Nanette. Then I glimpsed a raised white arm over in a distant corner. She was standing with her back to the railing and Da Cunha stood in front of her, bending forward, one hand resting beside her and his face very close to hers.

"What about that long, cool drink?" said I.

Nanette immediately ran to me.

"Oh, please!" she cried. "I'm simply gasping! Where shall we sit? Somewhere by the windows—where we can watch."

She was excited, and it was clear enough that Da Cunha had been making love to her. He turned, and I heard him snap his fingers. "Why not here?" he suggested. "How beautiful is the view in the moonlight, with the dark groves and twinkling lamps."

"No," said Nanette, selecting a table near an open window. "I feel chilly and I want to watch the dancing."

"If you are cold, let us dance."

Nanette shook her head and opened a tiny jewelled cigarette case. She bent toward me. "A match, please," she begged.

She was quite determined, and so we sat there sipping iced drinks until Nanette's mother and Ensleigh joined us. There were inquiries for Jack, but I said nothing—for the boy had been palpably drunk.

Nanette was unable to mask her preoccupation, constantly looking into the lighted rooms, then, suddenly, halfway through a Charleston, she jumped up.

"Come on," she said to Da Cunha, and threw her wrap to me—"let's dance!"

He was on his feet in an instant and the two went in. Nanette's mother was playing, and as I stood up I glanced toward the table.

O'Shea was standing watching the play.

Nanette and Da Cunha began to dance. Da Cunha danced perfectly, with all the sensuous grace of a none-such; but the look in his dark eyes raised my gorge to a hundred and twenty in the shade. Nanette floated in his arms like a bit of thistledown; her tiny feet seemed scarcely to brush the floor. He talked to her constantly, and sometimes she smiled up at him; but, always, she glanced into the roulette room as they passed. Ensleigh joined us.

"Yes," said he, "little Nanette is in the throes of her first infatuation."

As he spoke, she went past in Da Cunha's arms, and frowned at Ensleigh—because he blocked her view of the roulette table.

"She is," I agreed.

She danced every dance after that with Da Cunha, becoming more and more animated as the night wore on. Then her mother moved an adjournment. Of course, Nanette objected.

"Mumsy," she said. "Mr. Da Cunha has invited us all to drive up to his bungalow. We can dance to the Savoy band. Think of it!"

But her mother refused to think of it. Da Cunha was not defeated yet, however. His car was waiting. He would drive the party to Reid's. In the end this invitation was accepted. Nanette, her mother, Ensleigh, and I elected to go.

"How many can you take?" Nanette asked.

"Oh, six easily."

"I wonder if anyone else is going back?" said Nanette.

Following her glance:

"I might ask Major O'Shea if he is ready," said I. "Do you mind,

Senhor da Cunha?"

"But of course not!" he replied, looking like Caesar Borgia thinking out a new prescription.

O'Shea thanked me. He preferred to walk.

"And I dislike Senhor Da Cunha," he added.

Therefore the five of us packed into a flamingo-red Farman that stood before the Casino. I thought that if brass helmets had been served out, we should have done credit to any fire brigade. Da Cunha, of course, had Nanette beside him in front. I could hear his constant murmur over the roar of the engine. He took us up to Reid's at an average of about fifty-five. Nanette's mother steered Nanette to bed, and Da Cunha did not stay long. I sent a page to look for Jack, but he was not in his room.

At about midnight, O'Shea joined us. We went out on to the terrace, pipes going, and sat watching the fairyland of the gardens below, with the winking lights of Funchal climbing the slopes beyond. Presently I heard a faint movement, and:

"Oh!" said a voice in the darkness.

We all turned—and there was Nanette, distracting in déshabille.

"I can't sleep, and I left my book out here!" she explained.

"Let me look," said Ensleigh.

But he looked in vain.

"May I stay awhile and smoke a cigarette with you?" Nanette pleaded; "or were you telling funny stories?"

She stayed—seated on the arm of my chair. There was not much conversation, but after a while O'Shea got up and disappeared. Nanette began to talk, then, with feverish animation, until presently O'Shea came back, carrying a loose coat.

Very gracefully, he placed it around Nanette's shoulders.

"You must be cold," he said.

Nanette glanced up at him, then down again—and shivered. But it was not because she was cold.

Later, long after Nanette reluctantly had retired to her room, Jack was driven up from Funchal. We put him to bed without arousing anyone.

"I'll kill that slimy Da Cunha," he declared thickly—and went to sleep.

O'Shea surveyed him through the black-rimmed monocle.

"I wonder if cats and pretty girls know how cruel they are?" he murmured.

CHAPTER V

"IN FIVE MINUTES"

The days wore on in that lotus-eaters' paradise and I became an audience of one at a comedy designed to end in drama. There was a mystery that intrigued me vastly, and Ensleigh shared my curiosity.

I could not imagine what the O'Shea was doing in Madeira.

Da Cunha, palpably, had broken his journey to pursue Nanette. He positively haunted the hotel. I found it hard to believe that any such motive had inspired the Major. Ensleigh, with singular density, believed that Nanette was desperately infatuated with Da Cunha. I let him think so, and studied O'Shea.

This strange man spent a large part of every day seated on his balcony, reading and writing. What he read or what he wrote, nobody knew. On occasions, he disappeared for hours: and no one knew where he went.

It was queer, too, how many times Nanette strolled through the unfrequented part of the gardens below this balcony. Sometimes, but rarely, she would be alone, sometimes with Jack, more often with Da Cunha. But, always, she paused to glance in her mirror and powder her nose before she turned the corner. O'Shea, apparently, never noticed her.

She would loiter around the bathing pool for hours in the morning and then suddenly throw off her robe and plunge into the sea with an easy, gliding dive like a young dryad. By this token I would know that O'Shea was sauntering down the steps.

As she went in, Da Cunha and Jack would take the water like twin ducks. It was a miracle that they never tried to drown each other.

O'Shea was a hard man to know; a lonely man. I was honestly proud of the fact that, little by little, he began to unbend to me, to grant me something like friendship. Occasionally he would join me on the cocktail terrace before lunch; and Nanette would ask him for matches and then run back to her mother, Ensleigh, Jack, Da Cunha, and the rest of the party who, amongst them, had enough matches to fire the building.

Da Cunha was ceaselessly persevering in his endeavours to take her for drives, to take her fishing, and to dance with her to the strains of the Savoy band. Her mother negatived these plans.

One day a very (apparently) indignant Nanette came across to where

I was sitting with O'Shea. Jack followed.

"Mr. Decies!" she burst out, "Gabriel wants to drive me out to a perfectly wonderful cliff. You lie on the edge and look down I don't know how many hundred feet. Now, do you see any earthly reason why I shouldn't go?"

"I don't suppose Decies sees any earthly reason why *I* shouldn't," said Jack. "But I haven't been invited."

"You are always quarrelling with Gabriel," Nanette retorted, fixing a cigarette in her holder. Please, Major, would you give me a light?"

As she stooped over the match that he struck for her, I could see her eyes—looking at every wave in his hair, seeking out the hint of powder at his temples, studying his long, sensitive fingers. He threw the match away, and:

"You are such a restless little girl," he said. "Why not spend a few peaceful hours in the garden, reading? Let me lend you a book."

Coming from any other source, this suggestion would have provoked a scathing rejoinder, but:

"Thank you," said Nanette simply, "I will."

She sat for that entire afternoon in a secluded corner of the garden, a comfortable, empty chair drawn up beside her own, reading a Russian novel—and waiting for O'Shea to join her. But he didn't.

That evening the comedy became drama. I was to learn in a few short hours how Nanette's alluring beauty had averted tragedy from a royal house. And this was how it developed:

A rather special dance had been arranged—I forget why; and O'Shea, quite the best-dressed man in the hotel, was last to go to his room and first down. He could get into black quicker than anyone I have ever met. You may know Reid's green and yellow jazz cocktail bar? Well, as I looked in, having changed, there was O'Shea on a tall stool studying a dry Martini through his monocle. The way his bow was tied excited my envy; it was a poem in white pique.

We had the bar to ourselves, and presently: "How long do you expect to stay in Madeira?" I asked.

He shrugged his shoulders and smiled—that rare and revealing smile.

"In the strictest confidence, Decies," he replied—and suddenly his gray eyes grew steely; he was smiling no longer—"until I have in my possession a certain small black dispatch-box."

"What!" I exclaimed.

"It contains," he went on, "some unfortunate correspondence compromising a royal personage; and if it ever reaches the Communist base in London, I hesitate to imagine the consequences."

"Good heavens!" said I, and formed my lips to convey an unspoken name.

O'Shea nodded.

"Exactly," he replied. "That was what took me to the Argentine; but the Reds' man—a dangerous and clever agent—doubled on me in Buenos Aires, and so you met me on my way back to Europe."

"Then you have it!" I cried.

"No, damn it! I haven't!" said he; "or would I be sitting on this stool? It's getting desperate, Decies! There's a British destroyer standing off Funchal waiting my radio that I'm coming on board!"

I said nothing for a few moments. Then I thanked him for his confidence.

"I confide in you with a definite purpose," he replied. "I claim to be a judge of men, and I judge you to be one who would stand by in a rough house. I may need help, after all. If I do, the facts being as we know them, can I call on you?"

We solemnly shook hands—as Nanette came racing in.

She was flushed with excitement, and wearing a new frock. Her blue eyes shone like stars when she saw O'Shea. She looked adorable, and was well aware of the fact. Her happiness was that of the girl who knows herself to be perfectly gowned. It was completed now that Fate had ordained O'Shea to be the first man to see her so.

Jumping on to a tall stool:

"Do you like me?" she demanded naïvely.

"You look as though you had come straight from fairyland," I said. "Let me order you something, to prove you are mortal."

"Oh, no, please!" cried Nanette. "Mumsy would play Hamlet if she caught me drinking cocktails! Give me just a sip of yours!"

She drank from my glass, watching me with roguish eyes; then, turning to O'Shea:

"Am I smart enough to be honoured with a dance this evening, Major?" she asked—but the note of raillery faded as she met his glance, and she dropped her bobbed head, looking down at tiny blue and silver shoes.

"The honour would be mine, Nanette," he said, in the gentle way he had of addressing all women.

Nanette bit her lip and jumped to the floor, as her mother came to look for her.

"Good gracious, Nanette!" she exclaimed. "In the *bar!* And your frock, dear! I see, now, why you wouldn't have me with you to try on!"

"Please *don't*, Mumsy!" cried Nanette. "Will you *never* allow me to grow up!"

The blue-and-silver frock was certainly daring for a debutante. It was pure Paris; but Nanette's sweet shoulders were worth displaying.

"You are altogether too naked, dear!" her mother declared.

"I wear less when I'm swimming!" argued the reasonable Nanette.

"Never mind. Please wear your wrap, dear, or a scarf—at least during dinner."

And so the famous evening began.

Da Cunha had managed to get himself invited to the dinner party that included Nanette, and Jack sat facing him. Ensleigh, O'Shea, and I shared a bachelor table.

When the dancing began, I missed O'Shea. Nanette danced with me, but very abstractedly, alternately watching the door and the open French windows. There are few things more provoking than to dance with a pretty girl who wants to dance with someone else.

Da Cunha claimed her quite often and she suffered his public love-making in a way that nearly led to an outburst from Jack. The storm broke when O'Shea appeared. Nanette had begun dancing with Jack, but she did not finish. She dragged him across the floor to O'Shea, and:

"Please say you will dance," she pleaded. She turned to her flushed partner. "Then we will finish our fox-trot, Jack," she added.

"I hate to refuse," O'Shea replied, and his voice was very gentle; "but I came down to beg you to excuse me. I find that I must go out—on most urgent business. Don't be angry. I mean it, Nanette."

Nanette was not angry—but she was deeply humiliated. Every woman in the room had marked her descent upon the aloof O'Shea, confident in her radiant young beauty.

"I don't want to dance anymore," she said petulantly, when the Major had gone, "at least, not to this silly band."

"It's an excellent band, dear," her mother replied, watching Nanette with a sudden maternal anxiety.

"They play such old stuff," Nanette declared. "'Brown Eyes, Why Are You Blue?' is wildly out of date. They are liable to break into 'Rock of Ages' almost any minute!"

"Then what do you want to do?"

"I want to drive up to Gabriel's and dance to the Savoy band."

"Nanette!"—her mother spoke sharply—"I have already told you that I absolutely refuse. You heard what your father said?"

"No, Mumsy, I didn't," Nanette replied. "*You* told me. I would like to ask Pop."

But "Pop" had retired with a *Financial News* and three old copies of the *Morning Post*.

"Then I'm going to bed," Nanette announced. "I have a headache."

She turned and walked from the ballroom. Da Cunha detained her in the doorway, but only for a moment. Then he crossed the floor and went out on to the terrace. A few minutes later I strolled up to my room to get a pipe. The window was open, and I lingered in the dark for a moment, held by the moon-magic of the night. As I stood there, I heard a soft call:

"Nanette!"

Nanette's room was below and to the left of mine. I looked out. I could see a slender silvery figure leaning over the balcony.

"Is that you, Gabriel?"

"Yes, dear."

"In five minutes!"

CHAPTER VI

THE BUNGALOW IN THE HILLS

Personality is a queer thing. Nobody has quite defined it yet. In my wild quest of a plan to save Nanette from herself, without letting her mother know and without compromising her, I came straight to what looked to me like an inevitable decision—I decided to tell O'Shea.

What I thought he could do that I couldn't do alone, God knows; but the Guards used to feel like that about him.

One fear I had: that he should have started out on whatever mysterious business called him. I raced across to his room. It was in darkness. I went haring down to the lounge. Dancing was in full swing; no sign of O'Shea. I grabbed the hall porter.

"Has Major O'Shea gone out?"

"No, sir. Not this way."

I turned, hope reborn—and there stood O'Shea reading a note that a chambermaid had just handed to him!

"O'Shea!" I cried.

He glanced up. His face was very stern. His eyes glinted icily.

"Go and get Kelton," he said. "Bring him here—alone."

"But Nanette—"

"I know all about Nanette. Bring Kelton to me."

I ran. I was under orders. But it was a service of love.

Jack was in the bar—quite alone. He looked at me in a lowering way.

"Nanette's in danger," I said briefly. He jumped up. "Come quickly."

When we got to the hall porter's sanctum, and he saw who was waiting, he pulled up with a jerk.

"What the hell has *he* got to do with it?" he demanded.

"Mr. Kelton!"

O'Shea was watching him.

"Well, what is it?"

"This!" O'Shea handed him the note. "You read it, too, Decies."

Jack and I read together:

> Have gone to Gabriel's bungalow to dance. If you get this in time, will you join us?
>
> NANETTE.

Jack crushed the paper into a ball.

"My God! The little fool!" he said. "Why did she send this to *you?*"

O'Shea stared the angry lover down, then:

"Because she is very young," he answered, without one note of anger. "Don't blame her, Kelton—and don't blame me. Blame the customs of today. Leave me out. *You* are going to save her from Da Cunha."

"Has she started?"

"I fear so."

"Then where's the chance? That swine has a Farman racer!"

"True, but he can't race at night on those roads. It will take him half an hour."

"We have no car!"

"We don't need one. I happen to know a route—a mere goat track— by which we can climb to the bungalow almost as quickly as he can drive there."

"You mean it?" asked Jack hoarsely.

"As it happens, I was about to take a stroll in that direction when this note reached me."

"Come on!" said Jack.

I have the haziest recollection of that appalling climb. O'Shea knew the way like the palm of his hand. Under a sickle moon that looked so near in its white purity one almost felt one could reach up and grasp it, we climbed, panting and sweating. From the gardens of the valley we broke up through banana plantations where the great bursting pods banged our heads as we stooped to follow that tireless guide. We scaled a sheer hillside steep as a roof. We crawled along a path less than a yard wide, with a gorge yawning hundreds of feet below in which the vineyards shrank to a close green carpet.

We came to the red earth of the uplands. Our feet sank in it as in moss. Pines barred our way, rank on rank. Away to the left, below, beyond, the still sea shone like lapis lazuli.

"Ssh! Quiet!" O'Shea ordered.

We pulled up. I looked at Jack. He might recently have come out of the hot-room in a Turkish bath. His collar was a mere farce; a loop of exhausted linen. I believe I was no more spruce. I looked at O'Shea. That remarkable man appeared to be as well-dressed as usual.

"Single file," he commanded. "Not a sound."

We crept on, breathing heavily; and presently, through those sentinel pines on the crest, it reached us—the music of the Savoy orchestra, playing in a distant Strand!

"Thank God! We are in time!" said O'Shea.

We sighted Da Cunha's bungalow through the thinning trees. Lights shone out from three tall windows fronting on an L-shaped stoop. The windows were open, and O'Shea made his dispositions.

"Kelton," he directed, "take the window on your right front. Keep out of sight. Wait your moment. Time it. We shall not interfere." He held out his hand. "This is your chance. Make the most of it."

Jack grasped the extended hand, and: "Thank you, sir!" he said.

He went off through the pines, stooping warily.

We gave him time to reach his post; then O'Shea and I made a detour and crept up on to the veranda so that we looked into Da Cunha's bungalow from a window opposite to that which concealed Jack.

The room was sparsely furnished. It had a polished floor from which the few rugs had been removed. There was champagne in an ice bucket on a buffet. There was the most elaborate and costly wireless set I had ever beheld. A Moorish lamp hanging from the beamed ceiling gave light. I could see two good pictures—both nudes—and a long, deep, cushioned divan. At the Savoy, they were playing Jerome Kern's "Who," and Nanette and Da Cunha were dancing to it.

I have said that the none-such danced perfectly. His dancing on this night was inspired—inspired by passion. He did not merely hold Nanette, he enveloped her; with his arms, with his ardent, lascivious eyes.

She swam into view and out of view like a dream-nymph hypnotized by a satyr. Her expression was indefinable as I saw it. A sort of exaltation was there, born of adventure and sensuous music. I could not know whether she had tasted the wine; but there was a dawning doubt, too, a doubt of herself that was not yet fear.

Then the music ceased, and we heard remote applause.

Da Cunha disconnected the set and led Nanette to the divan. He seated himself beside her, smiled, and put his arm around her bare shoulders. She made a little whimsical grimace, but did not protest. Then she glanced at him quickly—and he stooped and kissed her. It was a lingering kiss, which she ended by pushing him away.

Their conversation reached us as a mere murmur; but Nanette imperatively negatived further advances and pointed in the direction of the buffet. Da Cunha shrugged, smiled, and crossed to the ice bucket.

I had both fists so tightly clenched that they hurt; but O'Shea's hand held my wrist like a human manacle. Jack's inaction astounded me. Then, under the urge of O'Shea's iron restraint, I began to think. After all, poor Jack held no rights over Nanette, and he was too unworldly to grasp the inwardness of this scene. She had suffered Da Cunha's kiss. Jack was still waiting for his cue.

It came shortly after Da Cunha returned with two beaded glasses. I had watched Nanette whilst the man had poured out the wine; and I knew that, at last, pique, rebellion, having died their natural deaths, she realized her position.

He set the glasses on a little coffee table and drew it beside the divan. Nanette asked him to connect up with the Savoy again. He shook his head and smilingly handed her one of the glasses. She put it down, untouched. Da Cunha drained the other, replaced it on the table, and, suddenly throwing himself on his knees, clasped the girl in eager arms and burst into a torrent of passionate speech.

Nanette shrank back on the divan. Da Cunha followed her. He kissed her hands, her arms, her shoulders. He devoured her with his lips.

She writhed in his clasp, uttered a half-stifled cry, and wrenching one arm free, tried to thrust him away.

Then Jack came in.

He covered the course in four running strides, stooped, seized Da Cunha around the neck, and jerked him on to his feet. Whereon followed—catastrophe.

Jack slipped on the polished floor, stumbled, tried to recover—and fell.

Da Cunha twisted about and kicked him above the left temple.

He lay prone.

"Jack!" cried Nanette. "Jack!"

O'Shea's grip on my wrist was like a vise. "Wait," he said. "The boy's down but he's not out!"

O'Shea was right. Nanette's voice recalled him. Da Cunha wore only light dancing shoes.

Jack rolled over, avoided a second swinging kick, and came to his feet, shaking his tawny head like a terrier with a flea in his ear.

"Jack!" cried Nanette again.

She crouched on the divan, wide-eyed. Her shoulder strap had slipped; and Nanette will never know how beautiful I know she is. Even as I saw, guiltily, she readjusted it—and the fight started.

Blood was trickling into Jack's eyes. He kept dodging and trying to clear his sight. It upset his judgment, beyond a doubt; added to which his skull must have been humming like a beehive. Remember, too, the climb he had put in.

To my intense annoyance, the none-such proved able to box as well as he danced and kicked. He took all a trained fighter's advantage of Jack's double handicap. Some punishment came his way, but it was not heavy—and he kept registering killing body blows on his opponent. Jack might have planted a lucky one before it was too late. But Nanette defeated him.

"Jack!" she cried, a sob in her voice. "Don't let him *beat* you!"

Half-dazed, the boy paused, dropped his hands—and Da Cunha recorded a tremendous right well below the belt. Jack went down—to stay.

"The dirty swine!" I exclaimed.

O'Shea slipped a revolver into my hand.

"I don't think there are any servants about tonight," he said. "But see that I'm not interrupted."

He stepped in through the open window, twirling his monocle on its black ribbon. It was not pose; it was nerves. The man was human. He was fighting for composure.

Da Cunha faced him, and:

"*You!*" came, as a sort of rapturous sigh, from the divan.

The two men confronted each other for an electric moment; then:

"You are a very dirty fighter, Da Cunha," said O'Shea smoothly. "But, as you are probably tired, I suggest that you give me the black dispatch-box that you have locked in your bedroom—and we will say no more about it."

Da Cunha's expression became complicated. My own brain was revolving like a merry-go-round. This sudden revelation was too much for me—that Da Cunha was a Red agent!

"Go to hell!" was the reply. "Who are you?"

"You are very forgetful," said O'Shea.

As he spoke, he reached out a long, lazy left. It looked effortless, but it was perfectly timed, perfectly measured. It started in the ball of his suddenly rigid right foot and from there carried every amp of energy in his body to the point of Da Cunha's jaw.

There was a pleasant snapping sound. Da Cunha went down like a poleaxed ox.

Nanette sat silent, a second Niobe.

"Decies!" cried O'Shea. "The revolver! We have no time to waste!"

I ran in, passing the weapon to him.

"Attend to Kelton," he directed. "We must get him away."

He crossed to a door right of the divan and went into a room beyond, which was dimly lighted.

"Mr. Decies—" Nanette began.

Came the sound of a pistol shot . . . a second! There followed a splintering crash. Nanette leapt to her feet, and turned—as O'Shea came out again, carrying a small black dispatch-box. He put it on the coffee table.

Jack stirred and groaned. Nanette's gaze never left O'Shea. And now, timidly approaching him:

"I was mad," she whispered. "Oh, thank you!" She swayed and sank into his arms, her perfect lips raised to his in offering. "Can you forgive me?"

He held her for a moment, very tenderly, looking into her eyes, then:

"I have nothing to forgive, little girl," he said. "You have been foolish, but I don't think you will ever be so foolish again."

Gently, he set her aside, and:

"Decies," said he, "lend a hand with Kelton. We will borrow the Farman."

CHAPTER VII

A SHORT NOTE

Wonderful to relate, we managed to keep secret the story of Nanette's indiscretion. Her mother never knew that she had left her room. And it was toward dusk of the following day that the first act of the tragi-comedy came to a close.

To Ensleigh's inquiries touching my disappearance from the dance, I had returned evasive replies. Jack kept his room, for good and sufficient reasons, and O'Shea had gone into the town early and had not come back. Nanette remained invisible.

For all the glory of the Madeiran sunshine and the wonder of the flowers, black depression sat heavily upon us.

I was lounging on the terrace at about six o'clock wondering what Nanette was doing and whether her mother suspected anything, when O'Shea suddenly walked out to me.

"Hello!" I cried. "I thought you had gone for good!"

"No," he answered musingly, "not yet."

He sank into a chair, as though dog weary.

"Had a hard day?" I asked.

"Fairly," he replied; "but I've done my job. I suspect there are harder to come." He paused, then: "Have you seen Nanette?" he asked.

"No," I stared at him. "O'Shea, tell me if you resent my frankness—but that girl's madly in love with you."

"I don't resent it, Decies," he answered. "I know she thinks she is. But Nanette is very young. There is something you don't know—that nobody else will ever know."

I looked into the gray eyes. But they were not cold: they were on fire! I drew a sharp breath.

"O'Shea—" I began.

He nodded, and gripped my hand hard.

"Yes!" he said simply. "From the first moment I saw her. I daren't trust myself to see her again. You understand? It's quite impossible."

"But why?"

"For many reasons. Thank God, *she's* young enough to forget."

There was a short silence, which is more memorable to me than many long conversations.

"What shall you do?" I asked.

He pointed across the bay.

Trailing a pennant of smoke in her wake, the greyhound shape of a destroyer raced for the harbour.

"I sail in an hour," he answered. "I can take care of myself, Decies, but Nanette is of an age when a—silly attachment might spoil years of her life. So"—he took a letter from his pocket—"I have done a cruel thing. I have said what isn't true—God knows it isn't true! Her pride will do the rest. Will you give it to her—after I have gone?"

The promise was made. I thought of Nanette's fresh young loveliness, which this man, who wanted her madly, might have taken as an unconditional gift. I thought of certain others I had met. I recalled that we moved in the year of freedom, 1927. And I wondered.

I have known some good Irishmen and some bad. But Edmond O'Shea would be a mighty fine advertisement for any race on earth.

Nanette came down to dinner, and I can never forget her expression when she saw O'Shea's deserted table.

My task was going to be a hard one.

I took her out to the terrace afterward. Away on the distant horizon I could trace a faint wisp of smoke.

"Do you mean," she said, and her voice had changed strangely, "that Major O'Shea—has gone?"

I looked at her, a sweet picture in the moonlight. And little Nanette had grown up. She watched me with a woman's eyes.

I handed the note to her. She ran to the library window, tearing open the envelope as she went. I turned away and tried to trace the slender smoke trail fading, fading on a distant horizon.

A cry brought me sharply about.

Nanette stood before me, her eyes blazing, her face deathly white.

"Do you know what is in this?" she demanded.

"I do not, Nanette."

And indeed I shall never know; but I know what it cost him to write it.

A moment she stood so, glaring at me. Then, frenziedly she began to tear the letter into tiny fragments, and:

"How dare he!" she cried. "Oh, God! how *dare* he!"

Whereupon she burst into such passionate sobs that it was agony to hear them. Dropping into a chair on the deserted terrace, she cried until my heart ached.

It was her first love, and a very big one. An O'Shea inspires nothing petty. But she had courage, and pride.

She conquered her weakness, and stood up. "You are very kind, Mr. Decies," she said. "I am sorry I made a fool of myself."

Then she went in, walking very upright.

I spent a wretched evening, and when I retired to my room, sleep simply would not come. I got up, with an idea of smoking a pipe, but, first, I crossed to the open window. On a moon-dappled path below the terrace I espied a moving figure; and Burns's words flashed through my mind: "The best-laid schemes o' mice and men . . ."

Nanette was stealing among the flowers, collecting tiny fragments of the torn letter that a light evening breeze had blown from the terrace above. It was a hurt, an affront; but it was the only thing of his she had.

CHAPTER VIII

THE CALL

"Telegram, sir!" I sat up with a start. Morning sunlight flooded the large bare room. Wild canaries were singing outside my window. Slowly, facts began to assert themselves. I had been dreaming that I was taking tea at Stewarts with the Duchess of York and Mr. Tom Mann, when Trebitsch-Lincoln had appeared through a window, holding a bomb in his hand. Now, I realized that I had read news of all in a week-old *Daily Mail* recently; but that actually I was in bed at Reid's Hotel, Funchal.

The radio message that the boy had brought up was crisp enough, but it effectually banished my drowsiness.

> Please call on British consul at once. Vitally urgent. Am holding you to our bargain.
>
> O'SHEA.

A bargain based upon the survival of so old an institution as the British Empire is not lightly denied: I thought that perhaps my dreams had been prophetic. Nor was Edmond O'Shea the man to send such a message except under stress extraordinary.

As I hurriedly bathed, shaved, and dressed, I reviewed the position. There was O'Shea, homeward bound with a packet of letters whose publication would further Red anarchy a number of points. There was myself, George Decies, who in a neutral way had helped to secure these. There was Gabriel da Cunha, agent of the nightmare called Communism, nursing a broken jaw as a result of foregoing transactions. And there was Nanette.

Even as her name brought the dainty image to my mind, from under the open window came a soft call:

"Coo—oo!"

I crossed, struggling with an intractable tie; and there on the balcony below was Nanette.

To know that the most provocatively pretty girl one has ever met is madly in love with a better man and to behave sanely in her company is an acid test of what I have heard termed "British poise."

She shaded her eyes with her hands, looking up at me. Her arms were a delicate brown colour on their outer curves where the sun had tanned them, and by comparison ivory white beneath. With a background of flowers against distant sea blue, Nanette made a picture exquisite to remember in old age but disturbing to a comparatively young bachelor. Temptation is sweet only when there is a chance of falling.

"What a horrid tie," she said. "Please wear the gray one with silver stripes, as it's our last day in Madeira."

There was a wistful note in her appeal, and, looking down at little Nanette, slowly a memory came: I had worn that gray tie on the day we had met O'Shea.

I suppressed a sigh, "admirin' how the world was made." At eighteen, there are many things that even Miss 1927 doesn't know. There was one that Nanette did not even suspect. There was another that I knew of; but this not my own secret. I was unselfish enough to wish I could tell her.

"Very well, Nanette," I replied, and lingered, looking down.

"Are you going to swim this morning—for the last time?"

"No. I have to go into the town."

"I don't think I shall swim, then," said Nanette. "May I come with you? Or is it a stag party?"

Before I could reply:

"Please remember your packing!" came a voice from below.

Nanette's mother stepped out onto the balcony and looked up at me in mock severity. Seeing her, beside her daughter, I reflected that the lucky man who won Nanette would acquire a bride who would always be beautiful. "Consider well the mother of thy beloved," says an Arab poet. "In her behold thy beloved-to-be."

"Pop is doing his tonight," Nanette protested.

I visualized "Pop," sole occupant of the family table in the dining room, dealing with a solid English breakfast, regardless of flies, temperature, and the indifferent quality of the bacon.

"He has none to do, dear," was the reply. "I do it for him."

"But, darling," Nanette wheedled, bobbed head pressed against her mother's shoulder, "there are hours and hours. Please let me off."

In the end she had her way, and we set out together along the dusty road. There would be disappointment this morning down at the bathing pool, I mused, peering aside at the piquant face shaded by a Japanese parasol. Nanette wore no hat, and I said to myself that if all the women who were bobbed had such shapely heads as Nanette's, the world would be very beautiful.

"Did you tell Jack you were going?" I asked.

"No." Nanette aroused herself from a reverie. "I forgot."

Poor Jack! And he would have sold his Blue for a smile from Nanette.

The road to the town is very picturesque; and I might have counted George Decies a happy man had I not known that my charming companion loved to be with me only because I formed a link with her memories of someone else. Down the steep slope we walked, talking but little. An old roadmaker doffed his hat, smiled, and bade us good-morning. I sensed his kindly, appreciative glance following us. Funchal is famous for honeymoons.

Past the gardens of the Casino and the flower-cloaked balconies of villas we went. I forced myself to think of my real mission. Common sense whispered that I should have driven down in a fast car. Sense of duty demanded that I should conceal the nature of my business from Nanette.

"Shall you be long with the consul?" she asked.

"I don't expect to be," I replied.

"Then I will go along and have a simply perfect shawl I saw sent up to Mum," said Nanette. "She won't like it. But *I* love it."

We were just about to turn into that steep and narrow street that leads to the square, when:

"Hi! hi! Hullo there!" we were hailed.

We turned. Bumping along in a sledge behind two sweating patient oxen, was Jack.

"Hullo, Jack," said Nanette. "Mr. Decies has to see the consul and I'm going shopping. Want to come along?"

"Rather!" cried Jack. "Jump in."

We proceeded to the consulate in the bullock cart, escorted by a battalion of flies with fixed bayonets.

"Meet you at the Golden Gate," called Jack.

He was absurdly happy when I left him with Nanette and climbed the narrow stairs to the consul's office.

The British consul was a quiet little official automaton who had buried his heart in somebody's grave and had nothing left to hope for.

"Good-morning, Mr. Decies," he said, and smiled rather sadly as I plumped an ornamental object down on the table.

"Good Lord!" said I.

It was Nanette's handbag, a frivolous trifle from Paris, which she had asked me to take care of as we got into the bullock cart. I had been carrying it unconsciously.

"You are early," the consul went on, "and I have not quite finished decoding a dispatch which I am instructed to deliver to you. The main point, however, is this: Major O'Shea arrives in Madeira tomorrow night, and—"

"Oh!" A faint cry interrupted him. "I'm so sorry—"

We both turned and looked up.

Nanette stood in the doorway, her blue eyes so widely opened as to convey an impression of fear.

"I came for my bag," she said. "I didn't mean to intrude."

CHAPTER IX

MOON OF MADNESS

Fifteen minutes later I was in possession of the facts—and faced with a problem.

"This chap Da Cunha," said the consul, "isn't Portuguese, in spite of his name. He's some kind of what-not. He has the biggest radio outfit in the island up at his summer bungalow."

"He's a Communist agent."

"I know," the other returned quietly, "but it wasn't my business to mention it first. He crashed in his car the other day and he's dry-docked for repairs in a house he owns down here in the town. I know the surgeon who's attending."

I did not contradict him, for I was reading once again the body of the decoded message:

> Arrive Funchal Harbour 2 A. M. Friday morning. Please meet me. Arrange for accommodation privately. No one must know. Letters have all been photographed. See Da Cunha does not slip away. Watch Arundel Castle. Try to learn if any associate of Da C. sails. Prevent if possible. I count on you.
>
> O'SHEA.

"Not a ship has cleared for European ports since Major O'Shea left," said the consul. "So there's a good chance."

"He's returning in the destroyer?"

"I don't think so." He glanced at a list of shipping. "Although this dispatch came from her. My idea is that they intercepted the Yeoward boat and put him on board. She's due here at the time stated."

"Devilish awkward," I murmured. "It's late to cancel my sailing. I'm booked in the *Arundel Castle*."

"I'll step across to Blandy's with you," said the consul, standing up and reaching for his hat. "We can get you transferred to a later boat. Leave the finding of private accommodation to me, too."

"Do you know of any one associated with Da Cunha?"

"No. Da Cunha has property in Madeira, but he's rarely here. Nearly all I know about him I have learned officially."

We settled our business at the Union Castle agent's, thanks to consular aid, and, the morning growing insufferably hot, my friend agreed that something icy through a straw was indicated. When we arrived at the Golden Gate this theory proved to be popular. A party from Reid's that included Nanette's mother had arrived, and Jack was sharing Nanette with a stranger whose ancestors had known more about how the Pyramid was built than you or I can ever hope to learn.

He reminded me of my London stockbroker until he was introduced as Macalister. He had a real-estate smile that was not unattractive, and my first, natural impression was that he had recently purchased the island from the Portuguese and was running his eye over the property. Presently, however:

"And how is our friend, Gabriel?" Nanette asked. Then, turning to me: "I met Mr. Macalister with Gabriel da Cunha," she explained.

I forget how Macalister replied, for I was exchanging significant glances with the consul. A few moments later that competent official took the floor.

"So you are leaving Madeira, Mr. Macalister?" he asked.

"No," the other replied, sharing an appreciative look between the cigar that he had just lighted and Nanette. "I had hoped to sail in the *Arundel Castle*, but I have been delayed."

The consul put several more leading questions to Macalister, in a chatty way, but I rather lost track of the conversation. Nanette was in a mood of feverish animation, which I knew, from experience, meant mischief. The party had been over to Blandy's apparently, and had learned that accommodation in the *Arundel Castle* was limited. Nanette and Jack talked happy nonsense about camping out in boats and what not. Then I made an announcement.

"Somebody is lucky," I said. "My berth will be vacant."

This statement was received with gratifying consternation.

"You surely can't mean that you are not coming with us?" Nanette's mother exclaimed.

Two pairs of eyes I particularly noted at this moment—the heavy-lidded brown eyes of Mr. Macalister and the wide-open blue eyes of Nanette.

"Unhappily, yes," I replied. "Unfortunate, very; but I must wait for the Royal Mail boat."

There was a sort of farewell dance at Reid's that night. Quite a number of people were leaving in the *Arundel*. Nanette persistently avoided me; and I doubled-up with Jack in a scowling competition having for target Mr. Julian Macalister, who had dropped in after dinner and monopolized Nanette.

Once, pausing near me:

"Do you know what they call the crescent moon here?" she asked.

"No."

"Moon of Madness."

She laughed and danced on. Jack scowled. I wondered.

At the cocktail bar, during an interval, things bordered on the hectic. I have been honoured in the friendship of some of Mr. Macalister's race who were very courtly gentlemen. Mr. Macalister was not as one of these.

"Don't look so gloomy, my lad," he said to Jack. "It takes a man of experience to please a young girl."

Jack had boxed for his college and was no mean craftsman. I rapidly took in the powerful but fleshy form of Macalister and prepared to mourn his passing. He smiled confidently; but one could have got roughly about the same odds on a peanut in a monkey-house, when:

"Mr. Decies!" said someone at my elbow.

Jack was just descending in a leisurely way from his tall stool. He paused as I turned. The British consul stood behind us.

"A word in private," said he.

I grabbed Jack's arm.

"Come along, too," I urged.

He hesitated, then:

"Perhaps you're right," came with manifest reluctance.

We walked out into the lounge; and the consul handed me a scribbled note.

"Received in code tonight," he explained.

Detain Julian Macalister at any cost.

Jack had left us, going to look for Nanette, and:

"From O'Shea?" I asked.

"No. From Scotland Yard!"

"But he's not sailing!"

The consul met my gaze of inquiry.

"That radio set of Da Cunha's is very well informed," he said. "Macalister knew of this move before *I* did. He only cancelled today."

CHAPTER X

THE ARUNDEL CASTLE SAILS

I cannot pretend that I was a happy man as I climbed the ladder of the *Arundel Castle* on the following morning. All my friends were leaving, and the affection and admiration that I had for Edmond O'Shea could not recompense me for their loss. My only consolation lay in the knowledge that, unhonoured and unsung though I should be, yet, in a modest way, I was doing my job of work toward saving Great Britain from the Reds.

An inward-bound liner, by the time she makes Madeira, offers a ripe crop of studies to the psychologist. The gay Conrads, who have learned the truth of Leonard Merrick's unmoral dictum, "a man is young as often as he falls in love." The anxious-eyed women who have lost what their men have found. A score of flirtations and two or three intrigues, followed with interest by the midnight watch and reported in routine to the purser. The odd men out, too, are always rather pathetic. It was wonderful how many lonely eyes lighted up when Nanette stepped on to the deck. Even some of the Conrads prepared to change their minds.

Baggage was missing, of course. Nanette's mother had lost a wardrobe trunk, nothing less.

"Don't worry," said Nanette's father, in his imperturbable way. "It will turn up."

"It will be Nan's turn to worry," was the reply. "All her things are in it!"

Nanette, the irresponsible, had disappeared with Jack in quest of her new quarters. She professed to be the victim of a dreadful theory that her stable companion was an elderly Boer lady with gout.

Coffee-coloured boys were diving off the boat-deck; vendors of lace shouted themselves hoarse from a flotilla of small craft that clung to the steamer like wasps to a honey-pot; Portuguese lightermen shrieked amiable execrations at one another; nobody could find the missing trunk, nobody could find Nanette; Nanette's father said both would turn up—and the Bay of Funchal embraced it all with peaceful beauty.

When the last shore-signal was sounded, I found Jack beside me. He was plainly in a panic.

"Here, I say," he exclaimed. "I thought Nanette was with you!"

"And I thought she was with you!"

"When did you see her last?"

"When she went to look for her cabin."

"But she came back to fetch *you!*"

"She didn't arrive."

"Hurry up, please," urged the officer on the gangway. "You're last for the shore, sir."

Jack turned and ran in at the saloon entrance. I could see no one else I knew; so there was nothing for it but to tumble down the ladder. Reid's launch had gone, and I took the boat in which some customs people, office men, and others were going ashore.

They had turned steam on to the anchor and the ladder was swinging up as we drew away. I stood in the boat, searching the decks far above me, their rails lined with unfamiliar faces. From the white-capped, gold-laced officers on the bridge, I worked down, deck by deck. I caught a momentary glimpse of some folks I knew and waved automatically; but of Nanette's party I could see nothing.

Then sounded faintly a bell. Straggling boats seemed to be drawn astern of the liner by some powerful current. There was movement in the placid water; a swell rocked us. One could see the churning of the screw in clear blue sea. Renewed waving—and the *Arundel Castle* was homeward bound for Southampton, with mails, mixed cargo, several potential weddings, and a broken heart or so.

As I stepped from the boat on to the stone stairs and went up to the jetty, I paused, looking back. I was shortly to meet Edmond O'Shea, and the thought was pleasurable, but I would have given much to have been aboard the liner now headed for the open sea.

I walked up the tree-lined street, sighing when I passed the shop where Nanette had found that wonderful shawl. The square, you may recall, is planted with those trees that flourish principally in South Africa and bear a light blue blossom. In the sunshine of early morning it seemed to me that all the streets were dim with an azure born of the flowers.

Only two tables had been placed outside the Golden Gate. At one of them a girl was seated, her elbows on the table, her chin propped upon clenched hands. She stirred slightly, and I saw the sunlight gleaming in her hair. . . .

I stood stock still. Then I began to run.

Nanette looked up.

She was pale. Her widely opened eyes were the colour of those flowers—misty blue. And they said, "I am afraid. I am ashamed. Don't be angry with me."

"Nanette!" I whispered.

She bit her lip and turned her head aside quickly; then:

"I was mad to do it," she confessed. "I am sorry—now. Please send a message to the ship. They will be frantic."

"But—your things? You will have to wait for a whole week."

"They are in the small wardrobe trunk. I bribed Pedro to leave it behind. Oh, please, Mr. Decies!" She clutched my arm and I felt how she trembled. "Look after me. I am so frightened."

CHAPTER XI

THE PHOTOGRAPHS

The S. S. *Aguila* of Messrs. Yeoward Brothers dropped her anchor on to the rocky bottom of Funchal Harbour at fifteen minutes after two A. M. under a perfect moon like the crescent of Islam; a true Moon of Madness.

They had the ladder down in a trice, and my boat drew alongside. I ran up to the deck—and there was Edmond O'Shea in a white drill suit, more like John Barrymore than ever with the moonlight gleaming on his wavy hair.

We shook hands in silence, whilst his searching gray eyes looked into mine and mine told him all that I was helpless to conceal. Then:

"It was good of you, Decies," he said. "My message has put you out?"

"I had booked in the *Arundel*; but it didn't matter. My time is my own."

Indeed, already the spell of The O'Shea was on me. There are many names honoured in connection with the Grand Parade, but ask one of the men who knows what happened on the Retreat when Smith Dorrien sent for O'Shea; a company commander then, and only a major now. We all won the war, according to our own accounts; the old Irish Guards—what's left of them—would convince you that Edmond O'Shea helped us.

"What has happened?" I asked him.

He gave me the facts, whilst we enjoyed the hospitality of the captain who was delighted to have been instrumental in helping so distinguished a passenger.

"The original letters are safe in Whitehall, Decies. But I found pinholes showing where they had been stuck on a board—obviously to be photographed! We sent a radio to Captain McPhee here, and I doubled back. The mails will be watched at Southampton; but I don't fear the mails. Some trusted agent will carry the photographs. I wired headquarters for likely birds."

"Scotland Yard replied," said I. "One, Julian Macalister, is under surveillance."

O'Shea's cold eyes fixed me.

"Who's watching him?" he asked.

This brought me to it, and I gulped a quick drink before replying:

"Nanette."

His expression changed; then:

"So they are still here?" he said.

"*She* is still here."

The captain excused himself gracefully, on a plea of duty; and I told O'Shea.

"You think she overheard you in the consul's office?"

"I know she did. She admitted it."

"And so you told her—the rest?"

"Was I wrong?"

O'Shea stood up and paced the room a couple of times; then:

"I don't know," said he. "Let's go ashore."

Fate has playfully set me in some queer situations, but I can recall none stranger than that in which I found myself now. O'Shea, occupying a room in the consul's house, and engaged in private consultations with the military governor and others; Nanette, studiously declining to meet him—although his return to Funchal was the reason of her being there; Da Cunha, incapacitated, and only able to act through Macalister; the latter gentleman dancing attendance on Nanette.

"He doesn't know that I know anything," she said to me. "And he doesn't know that Major O'Shea is here."

We were taking tea on the terrace of Reid's; the adorably pretty girl who had "missed the boat" and my innocent self subjects of much inaccurate speculation. Two frantic radios had been brought out to Nanette: one from her mother and one from Jack.

"Please answer them for me," was all she had said.

"Nanette!" I looked into the childish blue eyes, in which, when O'Shea was mentioned, I had seen the woman-light shine. "I feel responsible for you. In playing with a dangerous man like Macalister you take risks which you don't understand."

"I'm going to find out where the photographs are!"

"Because of—O'Shea?"

She looked at me bravely.

"No," she lied—yet did not know she lied. "Because Major O'Shea insulted my intelligence. I am going to find out for my own sake."

I dined with O'Shea in the town that night. He was frantically worried. That Macalister was the man to whom the task had been assigned of getting the photographs to Red headquarters he could not doubt. But where were they? And how did Macalister propose to smuggle them through?

"Where is Nanette?" he asked suddenly.

"Dining with Macalister at Reid's."

"Damn!" said O'Shea; then: "Go back and look after her," he begged. "I can't stand it, Decies. You shouldn't leave her."

"She dismissed me!"

"Report yourself for duty. 'Phone me here."

I arrived at the hotel fifteen minutes later. The hall porter handed me a note as I ran in. I tore the envelope open in a sort of frenzy. This was the message:

> Photographs are on board a motor cruiser belonging to Gabriel da Cunha. I can't find out where it is. But Macalister goes in it tomorrow morning to Las Palmas and from there by steamer to England. Have gone with him to the Casino. Will keep him as long as possible. Can't do any more.
>
> NANETTE.

When I 'phoned to O'Shea, I heard him groan.

"Send someone from the hotel to stand by her," he said; or, rather, it was an order. "I can find out where Da Cunha's boat lies by using the military wires. It's hell, Decies, but I daren't take chances. Join me here. But make sure she is safe."

CHAPTER XII

THE MOTOR CRUISER

The governor's car, a Cadillac—tribute to the far-flung efficiency of American salesmanship—was driven by the chauffeur over what I took to be the edge of a sheer precipice. I inhaled noisily. Then we were gliding down a cobbled road that, serpentine, embraced a fairy port.

Nestling in a cleft, a volcanic chasm, its terraced roofs silvered by the crescent moon, lay a town asleep. Patches of colour, as though a Titan artist had thrown uncleaned palettes into the hollow, crowded upon and overlay the white walls. Green fronds peeped above pools of shadow. A beautiful auditorium, this town looked down upon the eternal drama of the sea.

O'Shea spoke to the chauffeur in Portuguese. His command of

unpronounceable languages was not the least of his acquirements. The powerful brakes were applied and our switchback descent ceased.

We proceeded on foot.

Where a low stone wall prevented the traveller from falling through the roof of a villa some twenty feet below, O'Shea pulled up, grasped my arm, and pointed.

Displaying her graceful, creamy shape like a courtesan stretched upon blue velvet, a fine-lined motor boat rode in the tiny harbour. Lights shone out from her cabin ports. O'Shea unbuttoned the coat that he wore over dinner kit and began to twirl his monocle to and fro upon its black ribbon about an extended finger.

"There is Da Cunha's boat," said he; "and there, no doubt, is what we are after. But it looks—"

"As though Nanette had failed to keep Macalister?"

O'Shea turned to me, and his eyes gleamed very coldly in the moonlight.

"Decies," he said, "you remind me of an unpleasant truth: that if I succeed in this matter I shall be indebted to a girl."

"She will have done a big thing for England."

"I don't begrudge her that. It would hurt me to think she had done it for me."

For a moment I hesitated; then:

"I think she knows it," I ventured, "and wants to hurt you."

"Why?"

"Because you hurt *her*."

He stared very fixedly out over the harbour for some moments, but he did not seem to have taken offence. At last:

"If I had married very young, Decies," he said, "and God had been good to me, I might have had a daughter like Nanette. Even if there were no other reason, shouldn't I be a blackguard to think of her except as a wilful child?"

But I could find no answer. This man's codes were beyond me. Young though he was in the days of the Big Push, he had won a name that had outlasted those of a score of general officers and more than one field marshal. The fact came home to me and brought with it a great humility; that I was not of the stuff that histories are made of.

"Suppose we go and look for a boat," I said.

O'Shea aroused himself—for he had his dreams even as you and I.

"A boat it is," said he. "As I have no official status whatever, there's nothing for it but frank piracy. Are you game?"

"Every time."

We went on down the sloping cobbled street. Presently it led us through the heart of the little town, where shuttered windows told of citizens asleep and only a zealous dog broke the silence. This until, as we were about to come out on the waterfront, from a high balcony stole the strains of a guitar.

O'Shea paused, looking up. A dim light might be discerned. He glanced at me, smiled, and we passed on. Love is an art with the Southerners.

I have wondered since, reviewing that journey, during which both our minds, I think, were busied with plans for boarding the motor boat and securing the incriminating photographs, that no premonition touched me. "Nanette had failed to keep Macalister," I had said, noting the lighted cabin. Yet Nanette had dared to slip away from the *Arundel Castle* and to remain alone in Funchal. I should have known my Nanette.

Drawn up beside a quay, a red blotch in the moonlight, was a long-nosed French car.

"Da Cunha's Farman," I exclaimed. "Macalister is on board."

But O'Shea did not reply. He was starting out in the direction of the lighted craft, a thirty-eight-foot motor cruiser, very handy in smooth water but a dirty brute, I thought, in a choppy sea. Then:

"I am wondering," he murmured.

"What?"

"Why he is lying out there and not alongside? There is no boat at the stair."

At first, the full significance of his remark missed me. My concern was with the problem of how we were to find transport. Then, something in the quality of that fixed stare with which my companion watched the lighted ports, his poise, as if listening, prepared me for what was to come.

The tones of a coarse voice, raised hilariously, reached my ears, coming from the cruiser's cabin. A trill of laughter followed, youthful, musical. My heart missed a beat. I clutched O'Shea's arm.

"My God!" I said, "he has Nanette with him!"

Involuntarily, my gaze went upward, to where in cold serenity the Moon of Madness raised her crescent lamp.

O'Shea from the pocket of his light coat took a revolver. He placed it in his soft hat and crammed the hat tightly on his head. He began to peel his dinner jacket.

"I'm going for a swim," said he. "Coming?"

But he was not alone in the idea. Before I could frame any reply came sounds of loud laughter, a scuffling of feet—and I saw Nanette run out on to the after-deck. She wore a blue-and-silver dance frock. I heard Macalister call to her and I heard her laughing answer; but I could not distinguish a word.

I saw her raise her arms as though to unfasten the string of beads about her neck. She stooped swiftly, stood upright again—and Macalister was beside her.

There was a shrill cry—half laughter, half hysteria. Nanette disappeared in the shadow of the awning. I heard the man's voice, his heavy tread. . . .

Nanette reappeared at the bow of the boat.

Heroism is always beautiful, whether it spring from love of country or love of man. The dance frock had vanished, shed like the sheath of a chrysalis when the moth is born. A silver moon-goddess stood at the prow. She stooped, once, twice—I thought to discard her shoes. Then, as Macalister came stumbling forward, Nanette dived almost soundlessly into the still blue sea.

And Nanette could swim like a seal.

Macalister craned over the side. For one moment I think he contemplated following. Then the bobbed head came up two lengths away. Behind the swimmer, on a tow-line of beads, floated a flat, square portfolio.

I glanced once at O'Shea—and that man of action was stricken to stone. Fists clenched, he stood, watching a girl of eighteen doing the work he had come to do—and doing it for *him*.

Macalister was hauling in his anchor. The motor started with a roar. Then Nanette saw us. She was halfway to the shore.

"Please throw one of the rugs on the steps," came gaspingly. "And go away! Start the car up!"

When, a few minutes later, a very wet Nanette, wrapped in a light top coat, confronted O'Shea, I don't know quite what happened.

"There are your photographs," I heard her say. "If I never see you again, at least think I was not such a fool as you supposed."

With all her dear bravado, she could not still the trembling of her voice. I saw O'Shea's pale face, and turned aside. That meeting was one I can never forget. Yet the details will always be hazy.

Macalister was in the picture somewhere. I think I knocked him down. I don't remember why. But I fancy it was not because of any attempt to recover the portfolio but because he grossly misunderstood the situation.

Then, I recall, O'Shea stooped, lifted Nanette, and walked up the sloping cobbled street under a smiling moon. He had suffered as only the few can suffer, to make her forget him. His sacrifice had been rejected by the Great Goddess.

Once, Nanette peeped up at him swiftly. I saw her eyes. Then she hid her face against his shoulder. I think Nanette was crying. But I know Nanette was happy.

CHAPTER XIII

THE GRASS ORPHAN

"Public men should never indulge in private correspondence," said O'Shea. "Such indiscretions sometimes lead to war. I understand that all Napoleon's social engagements were made by proxy."

He turned toward me, his arm resting on the rail of the balcony. There were times when O'Shea looked extraordinarily handsome. Today, I thought he appeared almost haggard. In his spruce white suit with Madeiran sunlight making play in the waves of his hair, he had all that curious atmosphere of romance that made him attractive to women and unpopular with men who knew no better. But his eyes were tragically tired.

I saw him glance at a square portfolio that lay upon the table in the shadows of my room.

"Six photographic negatives," he went on musingly, "and twelve prints—as all the letters photographed ran to more than one page. It's odd to reflect, Decies, that these scraps of film and paper might light a bonfire big enough to burn up a whole Empire."

Odd indeed; yet I knew it to be true. For that relentless loom which the Arabs call Kismet had drawn me into the pattern of this human carpet woven of anarchy, love, sacrifice, and God knows what other threads. I knew; therefore:

"Why not destroy them?" said I.

O'Shea shook his head.

"My instructions are to deliver them intact to headquarters," he replied.

"Are you returning in the Royal Mail boat?"

"No. They are sending for me."

"Lodge them in the bank, then."

"Contrary to instructions, Decies. They must remain in my charge."

I met the fixed stare of his cold gray eyes. "In which respect," said I, "your instructions resemble mine."

"And do honour to both of us," he added.

I lighted a cigarette, smiling perhaps a trifle wryly. When a wayward beauty of eighteen deliberately misses the boat home and her parents radio an eligible bachelor that they hold him responsible for her safety, one sits up and takes notice. Traditional English phlegm is called upon to do its best.

On the terrace above the bathing pool, a band was playing jazz. Below my windows a multi-coloured cascade of flowers poured down, wave upon wave, to meet the deep blue ocean. Sounds of laughter came floating up. Little yellow birds darting gaily from palm to palm appeared to find life a thing of song. I wondered. Was it Abraham Lincoln who confessed that he could mould men but not circumstance?

"It seems absurd," said O'Shea, breaking a long silence. "But do you know what I was thinking?"

"No."

"That, after all, Madeira is a very lonely island."

He stared at me fixedly, until:

"What do you mean exactly?" I asked.

"Decies," he said, "the Reds have had a nasty setback in England. But there's propaganda there"—he pointed to the portfolio—"for which Moscow would pay a substantial fortune. They have forty-eight hours to act."

"But only two agents in the island—one out of the ring."

"Gabriel da Cunha has a mysterious radio set in his bungalow. He will be in touch with his chief—and his chief is a dangerously clever man."

The official records of the Irish Guards afford sufficient credentials for the courage of Major Edmond O'Shea. He was watching me with that close regard which seemed to concern itself with one's subconscious self, so pointedly did it penetrate; and, rather fatuously:

"You are surely not nervous about your charge?" I queried.

He continued to watch me for a moment, then:

"No," he replied, and his expression grew abstracted. "Oddly enough, I was thinking of yours."

He turned aside, toying with the black-rimmed monocle that he rarely wore unless he were annoyed. At the Guards' depot in Essex it used to be said that the appearance on parade of O'Shea wearing his monocle made bayonets rattle.

Precisely what he had in mind I found myself at a loss to imagine, and before I had time to ask:

"Please, are you at home?" cried a voice from below.

I crossed to my balcony and looked down.

Nanette stood on the terrace. The sunshine made a glory of her tousled head as she laughed up at me. A stout German seated nearby in a cane lounge-chair found his attention engrossed by the unashamed beauty of a pair of slim legs that had suddenly interfered with his view of the bay. They were delicately sunburned to the knees, which—the brevity of modern frocks and a habit of going stockingless had forced me to learn—were dimpled. One suspects that Cleopatra had dimpled knees.

"Yes, Nanette," said I. "Where have you been?"

"Bathing. You should know that, Mr. Decies. You are sadly neglecting your grass orphan!"

She looked very lovely. The German tourist raised envious eyes to my balcony, their envy magnified by heavily rimmed goggles.

"Please come down and join the party."

"Very well, Nanette," I answered.

But when I turned back and reentered my room, O'Shea and the portfolio were gone. And I knew that little Nanette would be disappointed.

Presently, side by side, we walked down a shady path strewn with fallen hibiscus blossom. Nanette was very silent. An American training ship manned by naval cadets lay in the bay, and, at a bend in the path, Nanette paused. She stared out at the little vessel—"a painted ship upon a painted sea."

"One of the boys from the cadet ship is with our party," she said. "He's nice. I have promised to dance with him tonight. He's from Boston," she added.

"Has he got late shore leave then?" I asked.

"No," Nanette answered in a dreamy voice, moving on. "I don't think so. He just wants to stop. They are going to the Azores from here. Where is—or are—the Azores?"

"Quite a long way," I answered vaguely; for Nanette really didn't want to know.

There was small envy in my heart regarding the cadet from Boston. He was being used as a diversion by a distractingly pretty girl whose heart was not in the game. However, it is the mission of youth to learn, and the poor fellow would "learn about women from her."

I met him in due course. He was being lionized by a group seated around a table beneath a gay umbrella that cast pleasing shadows.

Nanette unblushingly monopolized him, and his joy was ghastly to behold. He would cheerfully have deserted his ship for her.

The sister of the British consul, who was acting as a sort of official chaperone to our grass orphan, kept throwing appealing looks in my direction. But I was helpless, and I knew it. A hundred times Nanette's glance sought the steps. And if only O'Shea had joined us, the eyes of the infatuated young man from Boston might have been opened before he doomed himself to cells for a siren's smile.

But O'Shea did not join us.

When I drifted down to dinner that evening, I missed him. I waited in the cocktail bar in vain. Nanette peeped in, too. At last, there was nothing for it but to dine alone. And constantly the blue eyes of Nanette, who had been "adopted" by a charming couple from the North Country, were turned in my direction. Always she smiled—but only to hide her disappointment.

The cadet blew along in due course, flushed with excitement, and was greeted by a very composed Nanette. Accompanied by her temporary "parents," she bore the young man away to the Casino.

I made up my mind to walk down later. But I was largely concerned with the absence of O'Shea. I hung about until after nine o'clock and was prepared to go out, when I saw him crossing the lounge. He beckoned to me, and:

"They are not idle, Decies," he said. "Da Cunha's radio has been busy."

"Have you picked anything up?"

"No. Conditions in the town are bad. But there's something afoot."

"Short of burglary, what can they do?" He stared at me vacantly; then:

"I don't know," he confessed.

But we were to learn—and very soon.

A disturbance in the lobby proclaimed itself.

"What's the trouble?" said I.

Even as I spoke, the worthy man from Lancashire, whose wife had taken Nanette under her wing, came hurrying in. He was pale.

"My God! Decies," he exclaimed. "Did you send a car to the Casino for Nanette?"

"No!" I replied blankly.

"Damn it! I suspected there was something wrong!"

"Quick!" said O'Shea. "What has happened?"

The other spoke very breathlessly.

"Someone brought her a message—from you, Mr. Decies. She ran out without a word. Young Clayton, the cadet, ran after her."

"Well?" O'Shea urged.

"When I got to the door, they told me that both had driven off in a car that was waiting by the gate."

"Did anyone actually see this car?" O'Shea demanded.

"No. It stood out in the roadway."

"Then who brought the message?"

"A boy idling at the gate."

"You questioned him?"

"Closely," replied the man from Lancashire. "He did not know the chauffeur and only had a glimpse of the car."

"But I don't understand," said I dazedly.

"I followed," the hoarse voice went on, "but just this side of the bridge, where it's so lonely and dark at night, I nearly ran over Clayton! He was insensible. He's out in the hallway now! Nanette—has disappeared!"

Very deliberately, O'Shea adjusted his monocle.

"Decies," he said coldly, "why, in God's name, didn't you stick to your post?"

CHAPTER XIV

THE PORTFOLIO

Born leaders of men do not achieve leadership; men force it upon them. Here was a panic-stricken group, soon augmented by the manager and a doctor who chanced to be in the hotel. One was for communicating with the police; another urged the military; all were anxious to enlarge the news.

We were in a room on the right of the entrance, the medical man bending over an insensible cadet. O'Shea quietly closed the door. And I have since remembered how instinctively we all turned and faced him.

"Doctor," he said, "how soon will he recover?"

The Portuguese physician shook his head.

"Do not count upon him," he answered gravely. "A tremendous blow on the back of his skull. I cannot examine him properly here. He must be taken at once to the hospital."

"An accident?"

"But certainly, no! Foul play. Some blunt weapon. I suspect a sandbag."

"Shall I telephone the police?" the manager asked.

"No," said O'Shea. "Get young Clayton away as quickly as possible. Gentlemen"—he included us all in a comprehensive glance—"let us keep this affair to ourselves."

"What!" I cried.

But indeed, beyond that one word I could not go. Inertia at such a time astounded me.

"There is a well-known policy of war," O'Shea went on: "Masterly inactivity. We have no Service de Sûreté and no Scotland Yard in Madeira. A clumsy hue and cry could serve no better purpose than to drive the enemy into some more remote hiding place."

"But, Nanette!" I burst out.

Then I met O'Shea's glance. I noted the grim set of his jaw. I saw how pale he was.

"Your remark was rather unnecessary, Decies," he said. "I recently pointed out to you that Madeira is a very lonely island. If you can suggest any plan for locating the whereabouts of Nanette, do so."

Then I understood. And I think I groaned.

"There are so many roads they might have taken," the manager explained. "And what means have we of tracing the car? There are no traffic police in Madeira. Such a thing has never happened here before. Certainly not in my time."

"What villain has done it?" came in agonized North Country dialect. "Oh, the poor little lass!"

"Madeiran blood runs very hot," said the physician.

"No doubt," O'Shea agreed. "And Nanette is a lovely child. But do you believe there is any one amongst her acquaintances mad enough to commit such an outrage?"

"Why do you say 'amongst her acquaintances'?" I asked stupidly.

"Because *your* name was used to induce her to go," O'Shea answered. "Ultimately, she must be found. Her abductor knows this. Therefore he is prepared to make terms."

Came a rap on the door.

"Yes?" said the manager.

A hall porter appeared. Major O'Shea was wanted on the telephone. As he went out:

"Come to my room in five minutes, Decies," he directed.

The five minutes that followed form a blur in my memory. There were hushed voices. There was movement; a still figure being carried through the hall to where a car waited out in the scented darkness. Someone kept saying, "We must *do* something. We must *do* something," over and over again. There was a woman who sobbed with a Lancashire accent.

Then I stood in O'Shea's room. He was seated on the side of the bed.

"I was right," he said. "It's a move in the Red game!"

"What!"

My wild, distorted ideas were tumbled over one another by that statement. They fought in my brain, seeking fresh formation.

"I knew that if my theory were sound they would waste no time. That was Julian Macalister on the 'phone. It's the photographs they're after, Decies!"

Whereupon: "Thank God!" I exclaimed.

O'Shea raised his eyes to me.

"I forgive you," he said softly, "for preferring my ruin to Nanette's."

Certainly the swift tragedy of the last half hour must have numbed my brain. O'Shea had watched me, not angrily, for several moments before the full meaning of his words gripped my mind.

I dropped into an armchair.

Gabriel da Cunha and Julian Macalister, Communist agents, had triumphed at the eleventh hour!

"My special duties as a secret service officer end tonight." It was O'Shea who spoke, but his voice seemed to come hollowly from a great distance. "My resignation from the regiment must follow."

I spoke never a word.

"There is just one thing, Decies, you can do."

Then I roused myself. I looked eagerly at O'Shea. I think, in that dark hour, I would have crawled through the hottest alleyways of hell to save him. "Why, in God's name, didn't you stick to your post?" Those words of his would sound in my ears for many a long day to come.

"You can enable me to resign," he went on. "It would be preferable to being gazetted: 'The King having no further use for this officer's services.'"

"Anything," I said. "I will do anything."

A party of serenaders, playing gently on guitars and singing a languorous love-song, passed along the road below. Their voices mingled in perfect harmony. A sea breeze bore perfume into the room. And I thought that this soft island, set like a jewel above the brow of Africa, might once have been the home of Calypso, stealing men's senses.

"It may seem mere splitting of hairs," O'Shea went on. "But it serves my purpose, and so I ask you to do it."

He took up the precious portfolio, which lay upon the bed beside him.

"I forced the lock last night," he said, "but had it repaired and fitted with a key in the town this morning. I removed the seals intact and replaced them. Here is the key." He held it out upon his open palm. "Take it."

I took it, wondering and waiting.

"Now take the portfolio," said he. "You will find it is locked. Hide it where you please. But its security means everything to me, to Nanette, and to England."

"You mean," I began, "that I—"

"I mean," O'Shea took me up, "that *you* may pay this price to ransom her. *I* cannot. You have sworn no oath of allegiance to the Crown. I have."

"Good God!" I cried. "The decision is to rest with *me!*"

"As a private citizen you can choose between the claims of your country, in this very difficult matter, and the claims of a helpless girl who has been given into your charge. As an officer, I have no choice."

He spoke in a low, monotonous voice. But I shall remember every word of his instructions whilst memory lasts.

"You must not tell me where it is concealed. It should be in some place, though, that is quickly accessible."

"But, O'Shea! Are they sending someone to make terms?"

"They are. At eleven o'clock tonight."

"Why not have him arrested?"

O'Shea stared at me, and smiled. But it was a cold smile.

"Julian Macalister is coming in person," he replied. "News of this unfortunate occurrence having reached him and our mutual friend, Gabriel da Cunha, both are anxious to place their extensive knowledge of the island at our disposal. On what charge should you propose to arrest Macalister?"

"Directly he declares his real object, upon a triple charge of blackmail, abduction, and attempted murder!"

"And then?"

"Well, surely—"

"My dear fellow!" O'Shea stood up and sighed wearily. "Racks and boiling oil would never be sanctioned by the civil governor. Personally, I should prescribe them."

I was silenced. O'Shea was right.

"Under Portuguese law the case would take weeks," he added. "It would be adjourned to Lisbon. No. We cannot leave her in unknown hands—"

He turned, the sentence unfinished, and walked across to the balcony.

I knew that if she had never met Edmond O'Shea little Nanette would have been safe in England that night. And I knew that he knew.

Taking up the portfolio, I went out, closing the door very quietly.

CHAPTER XV

TERMS WITH THE ENEMY

I had noted a loose floor board in my room. With the aid of a knife blade, I succeeded in lifting it, revealing a dusty cavity. Here I hid the portfolio. I replaced the board and slipped the key on to my ring with others that I habitually carried.

That I was destined to be present at the interview with Macalister, I foresaw clearly enough. How best to prepare myself it was not easy to determine. Primarily I had to focus upon keeping my temper. O'Shea plainly wanted to be alone.

I looked into the cocktail bar. Two men whom I knew were drinking highballs, and:

"Hullo, Decies," said one, "what's this crazy rumour about your little friend?"

The words offended me. I suppose I was in a mood for it. Since the fateful morning that Nanette had missed the boat, many questionable glances had been cast upon me.

"It's what you say," I answered shortly: "a crazy rumour."

Then I went out.

I crossed the lobby and stood in the porch for a while, breathing the warm perfume of the gardens. A man and a girl were walking down the slope toward the terraces. He had his arm about her waist.

The open road called to me. Lighting my pipe, I set out. Drivers of bullock carts solicited my patronage, but I ignored them and walked on. I had no idea where I was going. I think I was merely running away from myself. I could not banish the illusion that Nanette was hiding behind some tree; that she would suddenly leap out at me with mock reproaches for my neglect of the grass orphan.

Twice I thought I saw her slender figure in the distance.

O'Shea was ruined. This was the idea that ultimately came to the top and stayed there. O'Shea was ruined. The blind love of a child-woman had wrecked the best man it had ever been my lot to know. She had stayed for O'Shea. No one suspected it. But I knew.

This was the sequel.

Lonely in my knowledge of all it might mean—when, willy-nilly, I should have surrendered the portfolio—I tramped on. A great, cold jewel, the moon lighted my way. By a stagnant cistern, green with slime, I pulled up. I had walked half the distance to the Casino.

This cistern was infested by poisonous insects with nasty habits in their tails and a social custom of leaving red-hot visiting cards. I turned back, scratching viciously.

A party homeward bound to Reid's in a car offered me a lift.

I thanked them but preferred to walk.

". . . Having no further use for this officer's services." Yes, I could save him from that.

The hall porter said that Major O'Shea was in his room. Therefore, having a curiosity respecting Macalister, I took up a strategic position on a shadowed bench in that miniature palm grove which commands the porch. I told the porter where he could find me.

I had waited but a short time when Macalister arrived, in the pomp and circumstance of a glorious Farman. A chauffeur, whose pedigree connected with apes more recently than usual, drove the red torpedo in at the gate with much skill and even more noise. I stood up to see Macalister alight.

He entered Reid's proprietorially. He was in evening kit, wore a straw hat boasting a band of well-known colours, to which he was not entitled, and smoked a successful cigar decorated with what looked like the Order of the Garter. If he was nervous he showed no sign of the fact.

One has heard many jokes aimed at the courage of the Jew. Sometimes from members of his own race. In justice to one whom I shall always dislike, I wish to say that Julian Macalister, bearing a Scottish name, was fearless as any man who ever wore the tartan.

Caliban drove the Farman out into the road again, and I settled down with my pipe to await O'Shea's summons.

It came sooner than I had expected. Mr. Macalister was all of a man of business.

"Major O'Shea asks you to step up to his room, sir," said the hall porter.

Knocking out my pipe, I made my way upstairs. On the side of the angels though I might be, I found myself not wholly at ease. I rapped at O'Shea's door and walked in.

Macalister was seated in an armchair, a stump of fat cigar between his teeth. The band was absent. I presumed that he had smoked it.

O'Shea stood, facing me, by the open window. "I hope I have not dragged you from pleasant company. But Mr. Macalister here has presumed to question a statement of mine."

"Cut it out," said Macalister. "This is business."

"Mr. Macalister," O'Shea resumed blandly—and now I noted that he wore his monocle—"is not personally responsible for his defects of education. Forgive him, Decies. The facts, briefly, are these: You may recall that I recently placed in your care a certain portfolio, the contents of which you know?"

"You did," said I.

"My reason," O'Shea continued, "was that I feared an attempt by Mr. Macalister or his friends to recover this portfolio. I mentioned my fears to you at the time."

"You did," I repeated.

"Mr. Macalister," O'Shea turned to him, "Mr. Decies, here, has the portfolio and a new key which I have had made. The portfolio is locked. I don't know what he has done with it. Therefore your proposals are useless."

Macalister rolled the cigar stump. With a thumb and forefinger he removed fragments from his mouth—of what, I cannot say; possibly the band. Then:

"I believe you," he granted. "I never doubted your word. You're damned up-stage but you don't lie."

"Thank you," said O'Shea.

The tone in which he spoke puzzled me at the time. It was so oddly sincere.

"But, you see," Macalister went on, "I know why you've done it!"

O'Shea did not exactly start. But his glance, as Macalister spoke, was dagger-like in its intensity.

"You're an officer and a gentleman. The two aren't always twins, but you happen to be both. I've got to deal with Mr. Decies? If he lets you down, the disgrace is his. You're just branded a fool, but you save your 'British honour.' Am I right?"

By heavens! I knew he was right! And, studying the low brow, the small, Semitic skull, the gross person of the man, I wondered. If a Julian Macalister could read human nature so clearly, small wonder that the cream of his race ruled the Rialtos of the world. So I reflected.

"Very well, Mr. Decies." He diverted the cigar stump in my direction. "As it's turned out, I'm not sorry. You're sweet on the little lady who's disappeared. I don't blame you. I fancy her, myself. But business is business."

Only O'Shea's frigid stare held me in my place. I plunged my hands in my trouser pockets and clenched them tightly.

"Do not permit Mr. Macalister's vulgarity to upset your judgment," said O'Shea. "Also, make due allowances for him."

"I don't say I know where she is," Macalister resumed unmoved, "but I'm prepared to promise that she'll be home by midnight if you, Mr. Decies, will double on the major and hand over to me that portfolio!"

"One moment!"

O'Shea broke in so violently that he startled me.

"Well?" said Macalister.

"You fully appreciate the value of what the portfolio contains?" O'Shea challenged.

"Fully," I answered.

"You know what is at stake—on both sides?"

"I do."

"So do I. Therefore I am going to leave you alone with Mr. Macalister. Make your terms, Decies. I shall never reproach you. Communism is a powerful movement. Tonight it conquers."

He walked quickly to the door and went out.

"Very pretty," said Macalister. "When he's fired from the Guards he should do well in the movies."

CHAPTER XVI

THE HOUSE ON THE CLIFF

I have come to the conclusion that British honour is pretty good stock-in-trade. Macalister accepted my word that no rescue by force would be attempted. And, if Macalister accepted it, I think my promise must be a gilt-edged security.

At twenty minutes before midnight—the time I had arranged to set out—Reid's was moderately excited. The absence of Nanette could no longer be concealed in view of the fact that her worthy foster-parents had created something of a hubbub following her departure from the Casino. Hotel servants had been talking, too.

The arrangement had the charm of simplicity.

In a car containing only a chauffeur and myself, I was to follow the Farman. Any support must be not less than five hundred yards in the rear.

"But," I had objected, "although you trust me, I don't trust you. I might be held up."

"You can arm yourself if you like," Macalister had conceded. "And you will have the driver. Your friends, too, will be close behind you."

I had hesitated, until:

"Damn it!" he cried. "I want the goods! This deal is square!"

I agreed when he spoke thus. Slowly, I was learning my man.

O'Shea elected to follow alone.

"They will stick to their bargain, Decies," he said sadly. "We dare not take the risk, I admit; but Nanette is safe enough. They know how far they can go."

Past a curious group clustering around the hotel entrance, we walked out—Macalister, O'Shea, and myself. I watched a magnificent cigar being lighted in the Farman, wondering how and where Macalister found room to carry more than one at a time.

Then we set forth upon our queer journey.

The Farman led through the outskirts of Funchal, around the flank of the little town and out to that sea road which scales the frowning cliffs.

I am never at my best on roads of this kind. A squat red lozenge in the glare of our headlights, the leading car, from time to time, would disappear over a precipice. Nothing would obstruct my view of starry sky and the still mirror of the ocean far below.

Then, a hairpin turn in the dizzy path being negotiated, there ahead again the Farman would appear.

So it went, up and up, around bend after bend, until the bumping and jolting told me that we had left the road, such as it was, and were digging a road of our own.

We crept over a desolate dome of territory that must have been left behind when Atlantis sank. Upon our topping the crown of this blasted heath, I looked out ahead. I prayed that the brakes had been recently overhauled.

A long, curving, rock-strewn slope swept gracefully down to a sheer edge. And perched close to the precipice like a lonely seafowl was a little, dirty white dwelling—hundreds of eerie feet above the sea, approached by no perceptible path. I exhausted my imagination in endeavouring to invent a reason why any human being should live there.

By means of zigzag maneuvering, the Farman was brought to within fifty yards or so of the place. My chauffeur gingerly imitated the design. Then came the prearranged signal.

Macalister's arm was protruded. He waved his cigar like a field marshal's baton.

"Stop!" I said—and the word sounded like a gasp of relief.

I got out, turned, and looked back.

O'Shea's car had been pulled up on the crest. I could see him standing beside it, a distant silhouette against the sky.

I walked down to where Macalister waited by the house.

There was a low stone wall round the seaward end of the property, enclosing a tiny garden in which bricks were apparently cultivated.

And now I could see over the edge. I gasped. A wooden ladder, connecting with a platform that jutted out just below the house, described a jazz pattern down the cliff-side. In a miniature cove, below, a smart motor cruiser lay, her lighted ports like watching eyes.

"Send your car up to the top," Macalister directed.

I shouted to the man. And, as I watched him painfully tacking back against the gradient, I reflected that if O'Shea's psychology should prove to be at fault, mine was a sorry case. I fingered a revolver that nestled in my pocket.

The climb accomplished:

"Now," said Macalister, "you remember the conditions?"

"Perfectly."

"Halfway between the house and my car."

I turned and mounted the slope. Macalister whistled shrilly.

Spinning about, I watched. I saw two things happen.

Macalister's simian chauffeur leapt from his seat, stripping off his jacket and discarding his cap. From somewhere on the hither side of the building, which appeared to possess no door, three figures came into view. Two were men, thick-set nondescripts; the third was a girl.

And the girl was Nanette!

They held her wrists, but the moment she caught sight of me standing there in the moonlight:

"Mr. Decies!" she cried. "Don't do it! don't do it! I'll never forgive you! They *dare* not harm me, and you are not to do it!"

I made no answer. I had none to make. And so the men led her on until she stood before me.

She was pale, and so slender, between her burly captors, as to look ethereal. Her widely open eyes were fixed in a stare of reproach. My heart thumped.

"You don't understand, Nanette," I said. "There is Major O'Shea—and he wishes it."

One long, lingering glance she cast up to where O'Shea stood watching. I saw a flood of colour sweep over her face. Then her obstinate little mouth quivered. She lowered her head, and:

"I hate myself," she whispered.

"Now," said Macalister, coming forward, "give me the key."

I did so. He placed it carefully in his waistcoat pocket. Nanette never looked up.

"Hand the portfolio to Miguel."

The chauffeur was indicated. I obeyed, and the man handed the portfolio on to Macalister, who narrowly examined the seals.

"Senhor da Cunha," he said sharply.

Whereupon Miguel ran off, carrying the portfolio, and disappeared over the edge where the ladder was. So Gabriel da Cunha was on board the cruiser!

Again Macalister spoke rapid Portuguese.

Nanette was released, and the two men turned and went back to the house. She stood before me, with lowered head.

Macalister raised his straw hat. The colours of the band looked highly effective in the moonlight.

"Miss Nanette and Mr. Decies," he said, "I bid you good-night."

He was not without a certain vulgar dignity. He followed his brace of ruffians to the dwelling.

"Come, Nanette!" I urged. "It isn't safe to delay."

But, as we climbed to the waiting cars, she spoke only twice.

"They told me you had sent for me," she said, "because Major O'Shea—was ill."

"What happened?"

"Poor Tommy Clayton sat in front, and the man with me, who said he was a doctor, reached over and hit him with something. I screamed."

"Did he put his hand over your mouth to stop you?"

She nodded.

"Have they been unkind to you?"

She shook her head.

O'Shea waited until we gained the crest, then he got into his car and drove off. I followed, with an unusually dumb Nanette.

She sneaked into Reid's by the side entrance and went straight to her room. O'Shea was waiting for me in the cocktail bar. I entered very gloomily and he ordered me a double whisky and soda.

"They will have some little difficulty in opening the portfolio, Decies," he said, watching the bartender preparing our drinks.

I stared at him. He was smiling!

"What do you mean?" I demanded.

"I mean that I took the precaution of filing one of the wards before I gave the key to you."

But, even then, I didn't understand, and:

"What for?" I asked.

"Unnecessarily, as it fell out," he replied. "But my idea was to gain time."

"To gain time!"

"Yes. To enable us to get a good start before they forced the lock."

He slid a full glass along the counter in my direction, and:

"Do you play poker?" he asked.

"What the devil are you talking about?"

"I was merely wondering if you did. That portfolio which you have been treasuring, Decies, contains several pages torn from an old copy of the *Sporting Times*. Yet neither you nor I have told a lie about it from start to finish! Chin-chin!"

CHAPTER XVII

NANETTE IS CONFIDENTIAL

"Did you ever hear of Adolf Zara?" said O'Shea.

I shook my head blankly.

"That's the devil of it," he murmured. "He works in the dark."

"Who is he?"

He hesitated for a moment, then:

"He is the immediate chief of those Communist gentlemen," he replied, "whose activities have detained me so long in Madeira. One good thing I owe to him. I shall be returning to England with you in the morning."

"What!" I exclaimed gladly. "By the *Union Castle?*"

"Yes." He turned, staring at me in that coldly penetrating way which was so disconcerting and so misleading. "By a sheer coincidence, Mr. Zara is on board and I am instructed to look out for him."

"But the ship is full, O'Shea."

"There is always room for three more passengers in any British liner," he replied: "a diplomatic agent, a King's Messenger, and a pretty woman."

"What are you expected to do?" I asked.

"I am expected to prevent him landing!"

"But"—doubtless my expression became more blank than ever— "surely the authorities at Southampton—"

"The authorities at Southampton don't know in what name he is travelling. Neither does Capetown, apparently. They merely know that he's on board—with a false passport. He made South Africa too hot to hold him. Moscow's idea seems to be that another Boer war would add to the gaiety of nations. The Boers don't seem to think so."

He stirred languidly in the cane lounge chair and, raising his monocle, surveyed a number of ants performing mysterious evolutions on his white drill suit. It was very still and peaceful in the little palm grove. A faint breeze carried perfume from the gardens, a sound of distant voices and soft laughter. Outside the cool oasis in which we sat, shaded, Madeira sunlight blazed on a million gay flowers, and the low mossy walls were alive with lizards.

"Have you ever seen this man?" I asked.

"No," O'Shea turned his head lazily. "I haven't the slightest idea what he looks like. Unless I get some further news by radio, my chance of identifying this Red sportsman is a bad hundred to one."

"But you say he has a false passport?"

"So I understand. Probably issued in Paris or Milan or even New York, and in perfect order. Thousands of undesirables travel about the world annually with other people's passports, Decies. The appended photograph is the only snag, and you might be surprised to learn how easy it is to replace it and duplicate the official stamp."

Presently I went hunting for Nanette. My guardianship of this dainty, wayward ward was soon to cease; and whilst I lacked the courage to think about saying good-bye at Southampton, I had learned that for a man of my age and temperament the role of official uncle to a beautiful girl was no sort of job.

Tea was in full swing on the terrace, but Nanette was not there. I thought she might be on the tennis courts, and I strolled down the steps and along the sloping, flower-gay path sacred to basking lizards.

Halfway down there is a sort of abutment, overhanging the lower gardens and possessing a stone seat. Here, in a lounge chair, her parasol propped against the low wall, I saw Nanette.

Her little feet tucked up on the chair, to protect her bare legs from the ants, she sat manicuring her finger nails.

She neither saw nor heard my approach. And I stood still watching her. Quite mechanically she was polishing away with a chamois burnisher, but her blue eyes were staring, unseeingly, out over the bay.

As I studied the charming, pensive profile, I wondered, as I had wondered too often, what fate had in store for little Nanette. My more immediate wonder was concerned with the problem of how she had contrived to be alone.

Suddenly she turned and saw me.

"Coo-ooh!" she called. "Have you come to take me to tea?"

"Yes," I replied, walking down to her. "What has become of everybody?"

"I don't know," said Nanette. "I wanted to be alone."

"To think?"

"I suppose so."

I dropped on to the stone seat beside her. "Whom did you want to think about, Nanette?"

She lowered her lashes, and polished busily.

"Oh—Pop and Mum—and folks."

I lighted a cigarette, and presently she looked up. Her clear eyes regarded me wistfully for a moment, and:

"You know," she said. "Don't you?"

"I am afraid I do, Nanette," I confessed.

"Isn't it strange," she went on, staring away over the sea, "that I should be so crazy about someone who avoids me?"

"Very strange," I answered dully.

When a girl thus makes a confidant of a man she has never kissed, if he knows the rules of the game he retires hurt. Then:

"I suppose I shall get over it," she said, and smilingly packed up the manicure implements. "We have to be on board at a fiendishly early hour tomorrow. I don't know whether to go to bed at nine o'clock or sit up all night. Let's have tea."

As I helped her out of the cushioned chair:

"I have some news for you, Nanette," I said. "Major O'Shea is coming with us."

Her eyes opened very widely; and she stared at me in a frightened way that I always associated with any sudden reference to O'Shea. Then she turned swiftly, taking up her parasol.

"Really," she said. "How often he changes his mind."

But as we walked up the long path to the terrace she talked animatedly. And glancing aside at her flushed face, I realized with almost a shock of surprise how very young she was—and how sweetly incapable of hiding the excitement that my news had created.

CHAPTER XVIII

SUSPECTS

That run home to Southampton did not begin auspiciously for Nanette. Her happiness at being on the same ship with O'Shea was distinctly blunted by the presence of an official chaperone.

Her father had some sort of pull with the line, and by dint of industrious cabling, he had contrived to get in touch with a lady he knew who was returning from South Africa: One Mrs. Porter, a really formidable matron, deep-chested, heavy-jowled, and contemplating a sinful world through spectacles of an unnecessarily unpleasant pattern.

"Pop is mad!" said Nanette. "This woman must die."

Excluding O'Shea and myself, Nanette had come on board with a male escort of three devoted dancing partners. Lacking the society of Nanette, these were three very lonely young men, divided by a mutual distrust but united in their dislike of O'Shea.

Unreciprocated passion renders its victims clairvoyant; and each one of these three knew what the rest of the crowd at Reid's Hotel had never suspected: that Nanette only emerged from a land of dreams when O'Shea was with her. Now, to crown a troublous situation, Mrs. Porter presented a protégé—Captain Slattery. She made it pointedly clear that no other follower would be tolerated.

I resigned my staff of office with a sigh, and settled down to be sorry for Nanette—and Slattery.

O'Shea and I stood at the door of the smoke-room watching the coast of Madeira melt into a blue distance. Nanette, in a short, sleeveless frock, came along the deck, linked between two men, one of whom was Slattery. She pretended not to see us. But right in front of the door she pulled up insistently, leaning on the rail and pointing out something to her companions. Nanette knew she had very beautiful arms. But she wanted O'Shea to know.

He smiled at me, sadly, and turning, went into the smoke-room. The girl's dainty naiveté was hopelessly disarming. We sat down facing one another across a table, and:

"There is something I want you to do for me," said O'Shea.

"About—Nanette?"

"No." He shook his head, and that tragically hungry look came into his eyes that I had seen there before. "Don't let us talk about her, Decies. I have a valuable portfolio in my stateroom."

"Surely you will hand it over to the purser?"

"Impossible. Contrary to the rules of the game. The ship might sink. But a certain Adolf Zara is on board. Therefore—"

He paused, staring at me significantly.

"You want *me* to take charge of it?"

"Yes. Lock it in your trunk. I don't expect any move on this gentleman's part. He is stalking bigger game and therefore anxious to avoid publicity. But he *might* take it into his head to pay me an unofficial visit. I have a room to myself. You are sharing a cabin with a representative of the *Cape Times* whom, luckily, you chance to have met before."

"Very well," said I. "Of course, this man, Zara, will know you are on board?"

"Naturally," O'Shea returned. "His associates in Madeira will have advised him—although absolutely nothing to afford a clue to his assumed identity happened at Funchal. He is a dangerously clever man."

"Have you taken a look around?"

"Yes. Have you?"

"I have. But no likely candidate for the honour of being Adolf Zara has presented himself."

"I agree," said O'Shea quietly. "But I have an appointment with the purser in an hour's time. I am going carefully through the declaration sheets."

When O'Shea left me, I was joined by the journalist, my stable-companion; a substantial Scot whom I had met in London two years before. He proposed a promenade. And just as we started the faithful three came into the smoke-room, together, and ordered drinks. Their aspects were mournful.

Then, in a shady corner outside, we discovered the explanation. Nanette was coiled up in a deck chair, her charming head turned in the direction of her neighbour on the right—Slattery. In a chair on her left, enveloped in an unnecessary rug, Mrs. Porter slumbered soundly— and almost noiselessly.

Nanette beckoned to me. As I paused, she threw a venom-laden glance at the unconscious chaperone, and:

"I do not like you, Mrs. P.," she murmured. "The reason why is plain to see—and hear."

Slattery, his gaze fixed upon her, smiled admiringly. He had very even white teeth. Then he looked up at me.

"I hear that your friend is the famous O'Shea," he said. "I thought he was a movie actor."

The words told me plainly that this was another victim of the distracting Nanette. Therefore I forgave him.

"His appearance is certainly deceptive," I admitted.

"We were on their right at the time he was recommended for the V. C.," Slattery went on. "I was only a pup, but *we* saw some dirty work, too. The crack regiments always get the limelight, though."

Nanette glanced at him under suddenly lowered lashes, and:

"Please, Mr. Decies, lead me to a cool drink with lemon in it," she said.

She was on her feet in one graceful movement. Her ability to disentangle herself from complicated poses resembled that of an antelope. Grasping my right arm and the left of my startled Scottish companion, she moved away.

"Captain Slattery is so good-looking that he bores me," she whispered in my ear.

O'Shea found me some little time later.

"I have ventured to have you put at a table among strangers," he said. "Your immediate neighbour is a certain Dr. Zimmermann." He stared at me.

"I'll do my best, O'Shea," said I. "Where are *you?*"

"At the purser's table," he replied, "facing one John Edward Wainwright, of Halifax, Nova Scotia. These two birds may prove to be black swans, but there isn't another query in the passenger list."

I experienced Dr. Zimmermann at lunch and later at dinner. Apart from his audible enjoyment of the soup, I found his table manners genial. He had been studying the neolithic fauna of South Africa on behalf of some learned Munich institution blessed with a name that only Dr. Zimmermann could pronounce and that I shall never attempt to spell.

My report to O'Shea was unsatisfactory.

"He seems fairly true to type," I said. "If he is not what he professes to be, he carries it well. How about your man?"

O'Shea shrugged in his curious way.

"He obviously knows Halifax," was the reply. "His line appears to be steam trawlers. Having unaccountably neglected the subject of steam trawlers, I am rather at a disadvantage here."

"I am equally rusty," I confessed, "upon the neolithic fauna of South Africa."

There was dancing on deck that night. Nanette danced with the faithful three in turn and with Slattery. Slattery secured more than his fair share because of the powerful backing of "Mrs. P."

Nanette was dancing with me, in a curiously abstracted way, when suddenly she grew animated. Her eyes sparkled. She floated in my arms lightly as a feather.

Following her glance, I saw O'Shea watching us.

When I had deposited Nanette with the guardian Mrs. Porter, I returned to find O'Shea; for he had signalled to me. He was standing just inside the smoke-room door.

"Adolf Zara is active," he said in a cautious voice.

"What do you mean?"

He glanced around the smoke-room warningly. I took the cue and looked about me. Dr. Zimmermann sat in a corner, fast asleep. Wainwright, the other suspect, formed one of a bridge party.

"Two dispatch-cases have been forced open," O'Shea went on, "by someone who entered my cabin tonight!"

CHAPTER XIX

DR. ZIMMERMANN CALLS

"You have my authority to take any steps you may think fit, Major O'Shea," said the Captain. "I have received the usual instructions and of course I shall do nothing without consulting you."

We came down to the nearly deserted promenade deck. Three young men were doing a midnight route march there—and Nanette, coiled up, squirrel-like, in a furry cloak, occupied one of two chairs. The other accommodated Slattery. "Mrs. P.," leaving her charge in selected company, had presumably retired.

Slattery was obviously elated. The chairs were set very near to the foot of the ladder communicating with the bridge and the commander's quarters. Slattery didn't know that Nanette had seen O'Shea go up and that she was patiently waiting to see him come down.

We crossed to the rail, and leaned there, watching the clear water and the strange phosphorescent shapes glittering in its depths. And presently a slim bare arm was slipped under mine. I turned, startled—to find Nanette beside me.

"Please may I stay for five minutes?" she said. "Or do you want to go to the smoke-room?"

She stayed, and for longer than five minutes. Slattery had disappeared; and the threesome had terminated around a table decorated with tall glasses. We began to pace up and down, Nanette clinging to my arm.

Presently, as we turned, very timidly she slipped her other arm under O'Shea's.

"Is it true," she asked, "that there was nearly a mutiny at a reinforcement camp where you were toward the end of the war? And that a company sergeant-major called Meakin was court-martialed?"

O'Shea looked down at her in his gravely gentle way.

"It is not true, Nanette," he answered. "Where did you hear the story?"

"I didn't believe it," she answered indignantly, "but someone told me."

O'Shea caught my side glance and smiled—the happy, revealing smile that had grown so rare. But after Nanette had retired, over a final pipe in O'Shea's room:

"Queer thing," he murmured. "That that story should have leaked out."

"What story?" said I.

"The trouble with a group of N.C.O.'s at that camp, which rumour would seem to have expanded to a mutiny." He stared at me coldly. "It was the long arm of hidden Moscow," he added. "We had agents of theirs in our ranks. Did you ever hear of it?"

"Vaguely, now that you remind me."

"The ringleaders managed to slip away. But it's odd Nanette should have got hold of the thing. Well!" He lay back on the sofa berth and regarded me with raised brows. "There is nothing more to be done tonight."

"Are you satisfied about Zimmermann and Wainwright?"

"About Wainwright, yes. He had been playing since dinner time. Zimmermann nobody seems to have noticed. How long he had been in the smoke-room I can't discover. We may safely count steam trawlers out, Decies. Focus on the neolithic fauna of South Africa."

"Shall you turn in now?"

"No," said O'Shea, reaching up to the rack above his head for a pipe and tobacco pouch that lay there. "I am going to spend an hour with the young gentleman from the Marconi Company. Radio operators are sometimes inspiring."

To reach my cabin I had to pass the smoke-room door, and, just as I came to it:

"Either of them is old enough to be her father!" I heard.

I stepped in. The faithful three alone kept a resentful steward from his bed.

"Whose father?" said I.

"Hullo, Decies!" the speaker hailed me. "Sit down and let's have a doch-an'-dorris. We were talking about Nanette."

"Oh!" I remarked, dropping into a chair. "What seems to be the difficulty?"

"Well," another explained, "she has fallen flat for that chap Slattery; and we were saying that he's old enough to be her father."

"He is about thirty-five," I hazarded—"a dangerous age for a girl of eighteen."

"Piffle!" was the retort. "Why, when she was only thirty he would be nearly fifty!"

"Have you pointed this out to her?"

"Rather not! Suppose *you* have a shot. You are well in with her ladyship."

"I should prefer to be excused," said I.

The profound slumbers of my Scottish friend proclaimed themselves to the ear as I walked along the alleyway leading to our stateroom. A sleeping partner who snores is difficult. When he snores in Gaelic he is nearly insupportable.

I undressed to a ceaseless accompaniment that I found the reverse of soothing. Slipping on a dressing gown, I lighted my pipe, determined to go out on the deserted deck; for the night was hot as Sahara; the sea a burnished mirror.

Off I went, and met not a soul. For half an hour or so I wandered aimlessly. When, at last, my pipe burned out, feeling sleepy enough to face the snore barrage, I retraced my steps.

Rounding the corner of the alleyway, I pulled up short.

Dr. Zimmermann had just come out of my room and was quietly closing the door behind him!

I stepped back swiftly. But I was too late. He turned and saw me.

He wore an appalling red gown and a really incredible nightcap. Through the thick pebbles of his spectacles he beamed apologetically, and:

"Mr. Decies—my *dear* sir!" he said, coming forward. "I can never forgive myselves—never!" He held up a huge pipe. "I did not know that you had a companion. I knock. I think I hear you sleeping. And I venture to come in. I am restless. The smoke-room steward is retired. I know you are a pipe lover, and"—he indicated the yawning bowl—"I have not tobacco, so, I venture."

I stared him fully in the eyes for a moment, then:

"Don't apologize," I said. "You are welcome to a pipe."

Opening the door, I stood aside for him to enter. My pouch lay, conspicuous, on the bed cover, but:

"I see it there," Zimmermann whispered, stuffing about an ounce of expensive mixture into his incinerator. "But you are not here."

Thanking me profusely in a thick undertone, he presently took his departure. I listened to his receding footsteps, then I stooped, pulled out my trunk, and examined the lock.

It was fast. Nor could I find a scrap of evidence to show that anything else in the cabin had been tampered with.

What was I to believe? Could Dr. Zimmermann really be the formidable agent, Adolf Zara? If it were so, he had cool courage enough to justify the faith of his employers. In any event, I determined that O'Shea must be informed without delay of this suspicious occurrence. Sleep was not for me.

CHAPTER XX

FOG IN THE CHANNEL

Toward dusk on the following day—our last evening afloat—things began to move to that strange revelation which solved the Zara mystery.

O'Shea had been missing quite often. Several times I saw him coming out of the radio cabin, and he had had two long interviews with the commander, at the second of which the purser had attended. Then, having got into dinner kit, I was making for the smoke-room when I met him.

"Hello!" I called. "Any news?"

He took me aside, and:

"No reply yet," he answered.

"Perhaps the authorities in Munich don't realize the urgency of your message."

"Perhaps not," he said absently. "Let's explore a cocktail."

In the smoke-room we found Slattery and my Scottish piper; so we formed a quartette.

Slattery's attitude toward O'Shea was not friendly. I excused much of it, feeling the real cause to be, not professional jealousy, but Nanette. However, O'Shea was senior and Slattery never allowed himself to be openly rude.

I was seated with my back to the door, when suddenly I saw a change of expression on three faces. I turned.

Nanette was peeping in at us. She looked adorable in a dainty lace frock and I saw Slattery glance aside at O'Shea in a way that was twin brother to murderous.

For it was to O'Shea that Nanette was appealing.

"Would it be perfectly horrible of me to come in?" she asked.

"It would be perfectly delightful, Nanette," said I.

She came in, to the marked perturbation of the smoke-room. She sat between O'Shea and myself. The three musketeers, who had been talking loudly in a neighbouring corner, grew suddenly silent.

"If you see Mrs. P.," said Nanette, taking a sip from my glass, "please hide me until I get under the table."

Dinner that night was something of an ordeal for me. Dr. Zimmermann talked continuously about fossils, took two servings of every course, and generally seemed to be in high good humour. I think my own share in the conversation was not marked by any unusual brilliancy.

O'Shea's mood rather defeated me. He was by habit a lonely man, with a way of sinking into himself. Tonight, this phase of his temperament, which had expressed itself in his evasive talk, for some reason I found irritating.

On the morrow we should dock. The identity of Zara remained a mystery. The result of O'Shea's radio message was unknown to me. And O'Shea had become a sphinx.

A group having for its nucleus the faithful trio had got up an extempore dance on deck. A victrola belonging to Slattery provided the music. Mrs. Porter presided over the instrument, and Slattery and Nanette did most of the dancing. A few others joined for a time and then retired, presumably to cope with the important job of packing.

I discovered myself to be the victim of a rising excitement. Something was afoot. I determined to find O'Shea.

It was a longish quest, but I found him at last. He was pacing up and down the deserted boat-deck. As I came up the ladder he stopped and stared at me, then:

"Hullo, Decies," he said. " Forgive my odd behaviour. But it's a race against time, and time looks like winning."

"What do you mean?" I asked blankly. "Have you had no reply?"

"That's it," said he, "and I can't afford to make a mistake. They expect fog, though. It may save the situation."

I was not at all clear on this point, but O'Shea immediately resumed his promenade and I perforce fell into step beside him.

"Zimmermann is in his cabin," I said.

"Good," O'Shea murmured. "Where is Nanette?"

The question surprised me. Very rarely indeed did O'Shea speak of

Nanette.

"I left her with Mrs. Porter and Slattery," I replied.

He nodded, but made no comment. Presently:

"If this dangerously clever devil slips through my fingers," he declared, "Whitehall will disown me!"

And suddenly, as he spoke, an explanation of his recent behaviour presented itself. To the world he remained the aloof O'Shea; something of a poseur; a man unmoved by the trivial accidents of life. With me he felt that he could be real. He had treated the matter lightly enough, hitherto. But now, England all but in sight, and the enigma of Zara unsolved, he showed himself a desperately worried man.

"If I get him," he began abruptly, after long and taciturn promenading, "do you know to whom the credit will belong?"

"No," I returned, puzzled.

"To Nanette," said O'Shea.

This silenced me effectually. For what Nanette had to do with the matter was about as clear as pea soup.

I left him, toward one o'clock, promising to return. I had abandoned the idea of sleeping; and I wanted to change. No message for O'Shea had come up to the time of my departure from the boat-deck. The wireless operator on duty was unable to conceal his intense excitement. Just before I came down, leaning over the half-door of his room:

"Fog in the Channel, sir!" he announced gleefully.

"Good!" said O'Shea. "Go and change, Decies."

I managed to effect a change of costume without arousing my Scottish friend. He snored harmoniously and uninterruptedly. When I returned to the deck, no trace of mist was visible. The sea looked like oil and the heat was oppressive. I lingered at the rail for a moment, staring forward to where the Cornish coast lay veiled in distance.

Right ahead, I discerned a faintly moving white speck. Then I became aware of someone beside me.

I turned. The Captain stood at my elbow. "No rest for me tonight, Mr. Decies," he said. "The Channel is a mass of soup."

"So I have heard," I replied. "What's that ahead?"

"I have been wondering," he murmured. "It looks like a motor boat— and right on our course. Excuse me. I might as well go up."

A few minutes later, as I rejoined O'Shea, the ship bellowed her warning to the small craft ahead.

O'Shea was in the operator's room.

"What's that?" he asked. "Not fog already?"

"No," said I. "There's some kind of boat in our way."

"Oh," said he. "Fisherman?"

"No. It looks like a pleasure cruiser."

He stared for a moment. I had never seen him look so ill groomed. His wavy hair, since he had gone hatless all night, was wildly disordered. Then the instrument began its mysterious coughing.

O'Shea placed his monocle carefully in position and lighted a cigarette. The operator adjusted the headpiece.

"Here it is, sir!" he said. "At last!"

"Excellent," said O'Shea calmly.

And, whilst this long-awaited message came through, the horn began its disturbing solo—and mist crept, damply, into the cabin. We had struck the outer fringe of the Channel fog.

At this moment I saw Nanette. She stood at the door, wide-eyed, wrapped in a furry coat. I ran out to her.

"Oh!" she exclaimed, and clutched me—"where is—Major O'Shea?" She was trembling.

"Nanette!" I said. "What is it? He is there—in the operator's room."

"Thank God!" I heard her whisper. Then "I have been so frightened!" she went on, clinging to me. "Mrs. Porter sleeps like a log—and Captain Slattery came to our room a few minutes ago and knocked. I opened the door, not realizing who it was."

"Yes?" I said, clenching my hands tightly. "He was—insane. He said— he was going to kill Major O'Shea—"

"What's that?" came in a cool voice.

O'Shea stepped out on the deck. He held a slip of paper in his hand. The mist had closed down, now, like a blanket. Even the deep note of the fog-horn was muted.

"I've got him, Decies!" said O'Shea.

"What!"

"He sent off two code messages before my eyes were opened; and he received one reply. I don't know the code."

Dimly, through the fog, a queer, high siren note reached us.

"Major O'Shea!" Nanette released her grip and grasped O'Shea's arm. "Are you talking about Captain Slattery?"

The Marconi operator joined our party as:

"Yes," O'Shea replied, "thanks to you, Nanette! Only the Bolsheviks knew so much about our trouble in that camp as Slattery confided to you!" He turned to me. "I acted on that slender clue, Decies. The name of a company sergeant-major—and I was right! The *real* Captain Slattery is in hospital at Ladysmith!"

"Good God!" said I. "Then this man—"

"Is Adolf Zara! I told you he was dangerously clever!"

Then, muffled, ghostly, it reached our ears on the boat-deck—that most thrilling of all sea dries:

"Man overboard!"

Already the ship's engines were running dead slow. Now they were rung off.

Helter-skelter we went hounding after O'Shea—to Slattery's stateroom. It was empty. One of the lifebelts was missing. Out in the fog, that queer high siren note persisted. I thought of the white motor boat—and of Slattery's radio message.

O'Shea fixed his monocle in place. The sleeping ship was awakening to a growing pandemonium.

"Have you a cigarette, Decies?" he said. "I have smoked all mine. It needs a brave man to do what Adolf Zara has done tonight. If ever I have the pleasure of meeting Captain Slattery again, I shall tell him so."

CHAPTER XXI

A MISSING PICTURE

"Oh, I say!" cried Jack. "This is topping!"

His admiring gaze was set upon a photograph in my portfolio of Madeira snapshots. It represented a slender girl, arms raised, poised in the act of diving from a rock into the clear water below. In justice to the beauty of the model and not out of any desire to fan my artistic vanity, I agreed with Jack.

The original of the study, seated on the edge of a table, slim legs swinging restlessly, surveyed the work with less enthusiasm.

"I look painfully bare," said Nanette severely.

"Can I have a copy, Decies?" Jack asked.

"Please say no," came promptly from Nanette. "If you want a photograph, Jack, I had several good ones taken in Switzerland."

We examined other items of my collection.

"Hallo!" said Jack. "Who is the sportsman with the toothy smile?"

He was frowning at a snapshot of Nanette coiled up in a deck chair. Seated very near to her, in smiling tête-à-tête, was a man whose white sun helmet cast a dark shadow upon his features.

"Captain Slattery," Nanette replied. "You don't know him, Jack."

She turned over the print, giving me a swift glance. Its full significance rather missed me at the time. I merely supposed that this picture of the man we had known as "Captain Slattery" conjured up memories of O'Shea. And memories of O'Shea almost invariably brought about sudden changes of mood in little Nanette.

Later, however, having induced Jack to telephone to somebody about something or another, she drew me aside.

"Captain Slattery is in London!" she said, speaking with suppressed excitement. "This was what I really came to tell you."

"What!" I exclaimed.

In the days that had lapsed since the disappearance of the notorious Adolf Zara, alias Captain Slattery, I had begun to share O'Shea's view that this greatly daring man had perished at sea.

"I received this note from him last night," Nanette went on. "And I don't know what to do."

Opening the envelope which she handed to me, I drew out a single sheet of unheaded, undated paper having a cutting pinned to it. The note read as follows:

> I learn from the appended picture that you are in London. If you can forgive me for my behaviour and will consent to see me for a moment before I leave England, put a message in the Personal Column of the *Daily Planet* and I will arrange the rest. I can never forget you—so try to be kind.
>
> J. SLATTERY.

The picture referred to was cut from the *Daily Planet*, and showed Nanette as one of a group at a dance party—I forget where.

"How did he learn your address?" I asked.

"He didn't," said Nanette. "Look at the envelope. It was forwarded from the office of the *Planet*."

She watched me almost pathetically, and I divined the nature of the problem that was disturbing Nanette's mind.

"I simply couldn't do it!" she burst out. "It isn't as though he were really a criminal. He is a criminal, I suppose, in a way. But political crimes leave me rather cold. And, you see—he trusts me."

"Do you mean, Nanette," I asked, "that you don't want me to tell Major O'Shea?"

Nanette shook her head.

"Of course I don't," she replied. "I shouldn't have mentioned it if I had meant that. What I mean is—that I am not going to do what he asks."

"Yet he begs you to be kind," said I, feasting my eyes on Nanette's charming face which, now, wore an adorably wistful expression.

"I am being kind," she retorted; then: "Oh!" she exclaimed, and, suddenly silent, watched the open door.

Jack's voice might be heard. He was returning from the telephone downstairs and had evidently admitted visitors. A moment later they came in—O'Shea and an inspector of the Special Branch whom I had met before. He was a burly man with a rat-trap jaw, and I thought it probable that he could trace an unbroken descent from the first Bow Street Runner in criminal history.

Nanette greeted O'Shea with disarming nonchalance. But the only person in the room who believed that she had not expected to meet him there was Jack. The detective, a peculiarly efficient man-hunter, as events were to show, smiled grimly and stared out of the window.

O'Shea held Nanette's hand for a moment, and then turned aside, twirling his monocle string around an extended forefinger.

"Come along, Jack!" cried Nanette gaily. "Mumsy will be tearing the Berkeley down!"

Jack was only too ready to depart. His admiration of O'Shea was something he could not hide, and, whilst he was no psychologist, this very hero worship inspired distrust—where Nanette was concerned. In other words, he was not clever enough to know that Nanette loved O'Shea, but he was modest enough to wonder how any girl could spare him an odd glance whilst O'Shea was present.

Nanette's vivacity became feverish. She literally danced down the stairs, calling farewells to everybody. But, finally, from a long way down:

"Good-bye, Major O'Shea!" she cried.

"Good-bye, Nanette," he said, and shook Jack's cordially extended hand. "Look after her, Kelton. She is well worth it."

"You're right, sir!" Jack replied with enthusiasm—and was gone.

"Now," said O'Shea, and fixed one of his coldest stares upon me— "are the snapshots developed?"

"Yes," I replied, almost startled by his abrupt change of manner. "The prints came in this morning."

"And are there any of Adolf Zara, sir?" asked the inspector.

"There is one. Unfortunately, his features are in shadow."

"Let me see," said O'Shea.

Once more my portfolio of snapshots was produced.

"This could be enlarged," said the inspector eagerly. "It is quite sharp."

"Does the face seem familiar?" O'Shea asked.

"Vaguely. I think I have seen him somewhere. But it's very much a case of a needle in a haystack. Of course, he's far too clever to go to any of the known centres—always supposing he's alive, and, being alive, that he's in London."

"He is alive, and he is in London," said I.

"What!" O'Shea rapped out the word in a parade-ground voice. "How the devil do you know that, Decies?"

In a very few sentences I told him.

"That settles it," said the inspector. "The rest is routine. Find the woman and your case is won."

O'Shea adjusted his monocle. It was a danger signal, but the Scotland Yard man was ignorant of this fact.

"Explain yourself, inspector," he directed, with ominous calm.

"Well—it's clear enough," was the reply. "I shall insert a paragraph in the *Planet*, and when Mr. Zara turns up, he will be met by someone he's not expecting."

"You will do nothing of the kind," said O'Shea coldly. "The assistance of the Special Branch has been asked for because of the facilities that you possess in cases of this kind. But on no account must the name of any friend of mine be dragged into the matter."

The atmosphere grew oppressively electrical for a moment; then:

"As you wish, sir," returned the inspector. "But you are going to lose him."

"I trust not. But even so, I decline to use this lady's name as a bait to trap Zara."

No doubt the man from Scotland Yard thought the speaker mad. No doubt he wondered why cases of this sort were placed in charge of distinguished soldiers handicapped by such preposterous scruples. But he did not know how Fate had intertwined Nanette in this affair so that at every turn success or failure seemed to lie cupped in her little hands. He took it like a good sportsman, however.

"Might I look over the other photographs?" he asked.

"Certainly," said I, and spread them before him. "The negatives are in the wallet. You will want the one of Zara."

But when, later, I found myself alone, and began to arrange my photographic gallery, I missed not one negative, but two. Search availed me nothing. The negative of Zara was gone, but so also was that of Nanette in the act of diving from a rock.

"Jack!" I exclaimed. "Jack must have taken it!"

But I was wrong.

CHAPTER XXII

PORTRAIT OF A GIRL DIVING

On the following morning Nanette's mother called. One great disadvantage of this era of freedom is that it has taken all the kick out of life. Without prohibitions there can be no thrills. If a pretty married woman had called upon my father in his bachelor days he would have immediately consulted his solicitor.

She looked more like Nanette than ever. Her shapely arms were sunburned, and (I thought) were very beautiful so. But, as Nanette had done, she declared that she was ashamed of her gipsy appearance. But she had come with some more definite purpose than merely to chat, and presently the truth popped out.

"Really, you know, Mr. Decies," she said, "I don't think it was quite playing the game."

I suppose I stared like an idiot.

"You know quite well what I mean," she added, and smiled in that way which was so like Nanette's.

"On the contrary," I assured her earnestly. "I really haven't the faintest idea to what you refer."

She stared at me very unblinkingly, then nodded.

"I can see you haven't," she confessed. "Perhaps you didn't think there was any harm in it—and, of course, I admit the excellence of the charity. But I'm afraid it will get her talked about. At least, you might have consulted me."

"Please—please!" I entreated. "Take pity upon me. You are clearly referring to something of which I have no knowledge whatever."

"Mr. Decies," she interrupted—and held out a newspaper which she carried—"I am referring to the picture in the *Daily Planet.*"

"But what have I to do with the pictures in the *Daily Planet?*" I asked blankly.

"Since you took the picture in question, the connection in this case is obvious."

Dazedly, I opened the copy of the *Planet* which she handed to me—and there, prominently featured, was a large reproduction of my snapshot of Nanette diving! The caption read:

A charming study of a charming diver. No wonder Madeira
grows more popular every season. The original photograph

is on view in the Modern Gallery, Bond Street, amongst a collection offered for sale in aid of St. Dunstan's Institute for Blinded Soldiers.

To say that I was staggered is to convey but a feeble idea of my frame of mind. I stared at the picture until I seemed to see it dimly through a haze. When, at last, I looked up and met the reproachful gaze of Nanette's mother, I was temporarily past comment.

My innocence must have proclaimed itself, for:

"Mr. Decies," she said, and I saw her expression change, "I must apologize. You evidently are as surprised as I was. But this only deepens the mystery. Did you develop this film yourself?"

"No," I answered. "It was on one of several spools which I brought back. The Kodak people developed it. But—"

I stopped short. The truth had presented itself to me. One of four people had taken this unaccountable liberty with the photograph. Jack, the inspector, O'Shea, or Nanette herself. For I had no evidence to show which of these four had removed the negative from the wallet.

"Yes?" Nanette's mother prompted.

"The firm in question certainly knows nothing of the matter," I went on. "You see, I missed this negative yesterday."

"You mean that someone stole it?"

"Stole it or borrowed it."

"But with what object?"

"Presumably a philanthropic one," said I, very blankly. "Nobody profits—except the charity."

"It resembles the work of an enemy—if one can imagine Nan having an enemy. Unfortunately, it is a perfect likeness. In fact, it was brought to my notice by someone. Personally, I don't read the *Planet*."

"What does Nanette think about it?"

"She doesn't know. That is, she had already gone out when the paper was shown to me. She may know by now. I am afraid it will earn her a rather unenviable notoriety."

I promised that I would thresh the matter out, but as I had a luncheon appointment all I could hope to do immediately was to ring up the *Planet* and speak to the department responsible.

This led to nowhere.

The art editor was out, and apparently no other member of the staff knew anything whatever about the photograph—or about anything else.

I lunched that day at the Savoy Grill. So did nearly everybody who had been in Funchal whilst Nanette was there. The room appeared to be decorated with copies of the *Planet*, and my reception would have gratified Gene Tunney and overwhelmed Douglas Fairbanks. I grew stickily embarrassed.

Finally, I made my escape—and in the lobby ran into Jack.

"I say, Decies," he exclaimed, "it's hardly good enough. Nanette kicked at the picture from the first. Now you go and publish it!"

"Stop!" I said sharply. "This is the last time I shall explain the fact to anyone. But I did not send Nanette's photograph to the *Planet*. Except that someone stole the negative from the portfolio at my rooms yesterday, I know nothing whatever about the matter."

"*Stole* it!"

"Exactly."

"But when?"

"I missed it just after you had gone. In fact, Jack, I thought at the time you had borrowed it to have a copy made."

"Good heavens, no! She didn't want me to have it."

"Then the mystery remains a mystery."

"It's so objectless!" cried Jack. "A photograph like that is just good fun amongst friends, but one doesn't want the million readers of the *Planet* to see it. This defeats me! Have you rung up the office?"

"Yes. I could get no satisfaction. I am going along to the Modern Gallery now."

"I'll come with you!" said Jack.

CHAPTER XXIII

FIASCO

A curious episode marked our arrival at the gallery. On the opposite side of Bond Street, you may recall that there is a block of offices and showrooms, occupied by beauty specialists, modistes, and others. Well, at the entrance to the gallery, where an announcement stated that an exhibition of modern drawings and art photographs was being held in aid of, etc., we bumped into one of Nanette's Madeira conquests.

"Hallo, Milton!" said I.

The young man, who had been leaning against the doorway and staring abstractedly across the street, became galvanized into sudden action. He gave a swift look at me, a second look at Jack, and then:

"Hallo, Decies," he returned in an oddly guilty way.

Immediately he stared across the street again. At which moment came a cry from Jack. "Gad! There's Nanette!"

"Where?" I asked.

"In that window, on the first floor there. She has seen us, I think."

I followed the direction of his gaze. The window indicated belonged to an expert organizer of female hair. An attractive wax bust was visible but no Nanette. I turned to Milton.

"*Is* Nanette there?" I asked.

"I couldn't say," he replied evasively.

Jack gave him a venomous glance and started across the street.

"We can see for ourselves," he snapped.

I looked inquiringly at the young man in the doorway, but he returned my regard with so high a challenge that I wondered, checked the words on my tongue, and followed Jack.

We mounted the stairway to the first landing, and Jack threw open a door bearing the simple legend "Pierre" with quite unnecessary violence. We found ourselves in a discreet waiting room delicately perfumed. A stout French gentleman, whose wavy gleaming locks were a credit to his professional acquirements, greeted us. He bowed.

"I have called for a lady who is here," said Jack. "Please tell her Mr. Decies and Mr. Kelton."

"But there is some mistake," Pierre replied—assuming that this was none other than the maestro in person. "No one is here at the moment—unless you mean Mlle. Justine, my assistant." He raised his voice. "Justine!"

A trim figure in white appeared at the door of an inner sanctuary sacred to hair.

"M'sieur?" said Justine, and bestowed upon us a swift glance of roguish dark eyes.

"You are alone?"

"Yes, m'sieur. I am waiting for Lady Rickaby whose appointment is at three."

She bit her lip, suppressing a smile, and disappeared.

"You see?" M. Pierre extended apologetic palms. "There is no one."

"What's afoot?" Jack asked as we regained Bond Street. "That fat bird was lying. The girl gave it away. Nanette is hiding from us."

We stared at each other, badly puzzled. Then we looked across to where Milton lounged in the entrance to the Modern Gallery, seemingly oblivious of our existence.

"Come on!" said Jack savagely.

We joined the waiting Milton.

"Have you seen the famous picture?" I asked.

"No," he replied, "I haven't."

Jack made a snorting noise, then, paying a shilling each, we went into the exhibition. We found it to be far from crowded, and, indeed, the artistic donations were not of outstanding merit. Quite the most interesting exhibit was the lady in charge of the sales department. And, at the end of a ten minutes' quest, we sought her aid.

"Perhaps you could tell me," said I, "where the picture is that was reproduced in today's *Planet*—a portrait of a girl diving."

Whereupon the lady addressed began to laugh!

Jack's expression was worthy of study. In the eyes of poor Jack, anything touching Nanette was sacred, and this was the second time in one afternoon that inquiries concerning her had provoked merriment.

"I wish I could!" was the reply. "Really, it's most absurd. But all the same the publicity has done the exhibition a lot of good. Forgive my laughter, but, you see, we know nothing whatever about this picture!"

"What!"

Jack's exclamation was not merely rude; it was explosive.

"It has never been here," she went on. "Dozens of people have asked about it. But we have never seen it. The secretary 'phoned the *Planet* this morning and was told that they had used the photograph in good faith."

"But who sent it to them?" I asked.

"I am afraid I can't tell you," was the answer. "All we could learn was that it had been sent in by a responsible agency. Personally, of course, we are rather grateful."

In silence Jack and I departed. Milton was standing in Bond Street just outside the doorway.

"Good-bye, Milton," I said. "Let's hope it keeps fine."

"Good-bye, Decies," said he, jauntily imperturbable.

Jack glanced sharply up at M. Pierre's windows; but only the wax bust rewarded his scrutiny.

"I am beginning to hate your friend Milton," he confided.

"He is not so popular with *me*," I confessed.

"Come round to the club," Jack suggested. "This thing calls for cool reflection."

I left him at four o'clock. We had telephoned Nanette's mother, only to learn that Nanette had not returned. The whole thing was provokingly mysterious. It had entirely diverted my thoughts from the more serious problem of the capture of Adolf Zara. In fact, I could not shake my mind free of it.

That Nanette had been hiding in the establishment of M. Pierre, I no longer doubted. And that Milton had some part in the comedy was clear enough. Poor fellow, I regarded him in a more charitable spirit than Jack had at command. Nanette had been using him—for what purpose I could not imagine—and his reward would be small.

Some association between Nanette, at M. Pierre's, and Milton, in the entrance of the Modern Gallery, seemed to be established. But since Nanette's photograph was not in the gallery, why this association—and conveying what?

Nothing—in so far as my bewildered brain served me.

So I mused, as I drifted along Pall Mall. I determined to hunt up O'Shea, when, suddenly, I saw something which called me to prompt action.

A taxi turned a corner at the very moment I was about to cross. In it sat Nanette—and Adolf Zara!

It is in such moments of stress as this that vacant cabs magically disappear from the streets. No fewer than five taximen had solicited my patronage during the few minutes that had elapsed since I had left Jack.

Now, with a dangerous agitator wanted by the British Government disappearing in the distance, from end to end of Pall Mall not a taxi was in sight!

When at last one crept into view, pursuit was out of the question.

If I had been perplexed before, perplexity now gave place to consternation. The comedy of Bond Street had been no more than a gay curtain draped before a stage set for drama. I tried in vain to allot the actors their proper roles. What part did the missing photograph play? How came Zara in the cast? What of Milton? And what of Nanette?

It was not far to my chambers, and I hurried back, with the intention of 'phoning O'Shea. I met him at the door.

Those who enjoyed the privilege of seeing Edmond O'Shea in action relate that when things were going hopelessly wrong he would fix his monocle immovably in his eye and retain it there, contrary to regulations, throughout the hottest fighting. He was wearing it now.

"Hallo, O'Shea!" I called. "This is lucky! I want to see you badly."

"I came to see *you*, Decies," said he. "There is something I wish you to know."

Having opened the door and hurried him upstairs:

"Don't jump to conclusions," I began. "But Nanette met Zara this afternoon."

O'Shea stared at me incredulously.

"Where?" he demanded.

"I don't know where. But I saw them together not ten minutes ago."

He hesitated for a moment; then:

"Tell me all about it," he said calmly.

In as few words as possible I outlined the events of the day, terminating with my glimpse of Nanette and Adolf Zara together in Pall Mall.

"It is a blank mystery to me, O'Shea," I said. "I simply cannot understand what it's all about."

"To me," he replied, "it is equally, but painfully, clear."

"What do you mean?"

"In the first place," said he, "our friend the inspector borrowed your negative of Nanette."

"The inspector! In heaven's name, what for?"

"Because he happens to be a clever man at his trade. I declined to allow him to insert a paragraph in Nanette's name. But he was by no means defeated. He employed certain official channels and secured the publication of her photograph."

"With what object?"

"You recall the words that appeared under the picture?"

"Clearly. But the original was *not* in Bond Street."

"Quite unnecessary that it should be, Decies. Our friend the inspector was in Bond Street, however."

I think I was gaping like an imbecile.

"You are simply confusing me, O'Shea," I managed to say.

"Yes," he admitted. "No doubt the scheme is difficult to grasp. You see—the inspector banked on Zara's infatuation for Nanette. He judged it, no doubt, by the risk that Zara ran in communicating with her."

"Good heavens!" I cried. "I see it all! He hoped in this way to lure Zara to the gallery?"

"Certainly. He thought that Zara would probably come, first, to secure the picture, and, second, possibly to obtain a glimpse of Nanette in person."

"And you say the inspector was there? I didn't see him."

"I did!" said O'Shea grimly. "He was in an office at the end of the gallery—with the door ajar. The girl in charge knew he was there on some police business, but she did not know that it had any connection with the missing print. I gave him a crisp five minutes. But, officially, he was within his rights—and he knew it, dash him!"

"O'Shea," I said, "I can't fit Nanette and young Milton into the picture."

O'Shea's expression changed, softened.

"I wonder?" he murmured. "She has a high spirit, and, I am beginning to think, a keen brain. Decies!"—he suddenly grasped my shoulder—"how happy some man is going to be, some day!"

He turned aside abruptly, and walked into the inner room where my modest library formed a haven of refuge. Vaguely, as we had talked, I had grown aware of voices below. My man was one of the speakers; the other voice had been inaudible throughout.

Then I heard the door open behind me. I looked. And there was Nanette!

But, even as I was about to greet her, I checked the words. I had seen Nanette merry; I had seen her sad. I knew her moods of coquetry and of contrition. But, always, save once, I had thought of her as a child. I did not know her as I saw her now.

"I thought you were my friend," she said. "I thought I could trust you. If I had had one little doubt I would never have told you—"

"Nanette," I began—

But she checked me with a sad, angry gesture.

"You are no better than *he* is," she went on bitterly; "for you helped him. Heavens, what a fool I have been! And he only thinks of me as a *bait* for his traps!"

"Stop!" I cried. "For heaven's sake, stop, Nanette!"

"He was right," she pursued, stonily ignoring me, and looking unseeingly, miserably, before her as she spoke. "Captain Slattery came. But I had arranged to warn him."

I remembered Milton and his watch upon the window of M. Pierre. Then, abruptly, her mood changed. The blue eyes, which were so sweetly childish, blazed at me.

"No man, however bad he is, shall ever be lured to ruin by *me*. Tell Major O'Shea that Captain Slattery is laughing at him!"

"He is entitled to laugh, Nanette," said a grave voice.

O'Shea came out from the recess and stood watching her.

A moment she confronted him, then: "Good-bye!" she said.

Turning, Nanette ran from the room. I heard the street door slam.

"O'Shea!" I cried. "Why didn't you tell her?"

"It is better she should think as she does," he replied. "Fate has done what I failed to do. Now she will forget."

I have often wondered, since, if he believed it would be so. I have tried, knowing the man's honesty of soul, to conceive that he hoped it would be so. What *I* believed or what I hoped I cannot pretend to record. But, at some hour past midnight, I learned that Nanette was unwilling to ignore the promptings of her heart.

Dejectedly, I sat smoking a lonely pipe, when the 'phone bell rang. I took up the receiver. I think I knew who had called me, even before I heard her voice.

"Is that you, Mr. Decies?"

"Yes, Nanette."

"I am so miserable, because—"

She hesitated.

"Because of what?" I prompted gently.

"Because I never gave you a chance to explain. Oh, Mr. Decies! Tell me—*is* there something I don't know?"

"Why, yes—there is," I replied. "You don't know that Major O'Shea and I were totally ignorant of the plot to trap the man you call Captain Slattery."

"Oh!" came, as a sort of sigh, broken by a sob. "And I told him—Mr. Decies, do you think you can ever forgive me?"

"I *do* forgive you, Nanette."

"And do you think— Good-night!"

"Nanette!" I called. "Nanette!" But there was no answer.

CHAPTER XXIV

PETER PAN

A delicious haze hung over the Serpentine, by which token I knew that a warm day might be expected. Votaries of Peter Pan were few, for the morning was young as yet, but I sat watching him in his green temple and I thought how puzzled some archaeologist of the future was going to be.

Strange to reflect that a Scotsman should add to the ranks of the gods; stranger still that his immortal child should find himself so completely at home upon Olympus. More and more strange the reflection that none of the older gods were jealous.

Children of course came to pay tribute, and I think it was this morning I learned for the first time that there are many juvenile citizens whose day is incomplete unless they have made offering—a laugh, a pointed finger, a fleeting glance—to the god of that dear world which is hidden from most of us behind the gates of innocence. To many an exile under palm and pine, the coming of spring means dreams of crocuses and Peter Pan in Kensington Gardens.

I was suffering from a fit of physical and mental restlessness. I could not clear my mind of the idea that some imminent peril threatened O'Shea. That Nanette was involved, I feared, but tried hard not to believe. Experience of that Red organization known as the S Group had shown its members to be frankly unscrupulous; and Nanette had blindly involved herself with one of them. I knew why she had done it, but the man, Adolf Zara, could not know. For Nanette, Zara had ceased to exist. I doubted that the reverse was true.

The peace of the morning and the beauty of the lake mocked me. In the long encounter between O'Shea and the S Group, honours had gone to the enemy. But the battle was not yet over. Instinct and common sense alike told me that the worst was yet to come.

My ceaseless meditations along these lines had earned me a sleepless night, and I think I had sought out this spot beside the Serpentine with some vague idea of finding peace.

Now, coming out of a brown study and looking up, I observed a figure approaching along the path. It was that of a girl very simply dressed in a gray walking suit, and wearing a tight-fitting hat, which I should have described as claret-coloured but for which the fashion journals no doubt have a better name. Her fingers listlessly interlocked, she came slowly along, looking down at the path and sometimes kicking a pebble aside. Never once did she look up, not even when she arrived before Peter Pan, until:

"Good-morning, Nanette!" said I.

Then she stopped as suddenly as though a physical obstacle had checked her.

"Good heavens!" she replied, tore herself from a land of dreams and stared at me, smiling. But her smile was not exactly a happy one. "It's like a musical comedy, isn't it?"

"Why?" I asked.

"Well, everybody turning up at the same place for no reason!"

"Not everybody," said I.

"Well—no." Nanette hesitated, and then sat down beside me on the bench. "Not everybody."

"Curiously enough," I went on, " I was thinking about you."

Nanette stared at the point of her shoe.

"Must be telepathy," she murmured.

"Why? Were you thinking about me?"

"Yes." She nodded. "I shall never forgive myself for what I have done."

"You mean—about Adolf Zara?"

"About Captain Slattery, yes." She turned to me. "You see, I always think of him as 'Slattery.'"

"Does that make you like him any better, Nanette?"

"No," she admitted; "I have never liked him. But, well—you know how I felt about him? Does Major O'Shea know that I know?"

"You mean," I suggested, "does he know that you no longer suspect him of using you as a lure?"

Nanette nodded without looking up.

"I have had no opportunity of telling him," said I. "But I expect to see him today." I rested my hand upon hers, which lay listlessly on the seat beside her. "May I talk to you quite honestly?"

"Of course," said Nanette, but still did not look up.

"I want to tell you," I went on, "that the man you call Captain Slattery, but whose real name is Adolf Zara, is not as civilized as he appears to be. He is a member of a very dangerous organization. I hope you will make a point of avoiding him."

"I am never going to see him again," Nanette declared.

She spoke abstractedly, and it dawned upon me that her interest was centred less upon this matter of her perilous acquaintance with a member of the S Group than upon the passers-by. I attached little significance to the fact at the time, and:

"I am only anxious about your personal safety," I said. "Anything you care to tell me, I shall keep to myself. Are you sure that Captain Slattery does not mean to see *you* again?"

Nanette looked aside at me.

I thought that, since Adolf Zara was human, my question had been rather superfluous. O'Shea, who was no alarmist, had admitted that the secret organization of these people was extensive and efficient. Wild ideas assailed my mind, but:

"Of course, we are no longer in the lonely island of Madeira," I went on, "but in the capital of a civilized country. All the same, Nanette, I should be glad to know that Zara was no longer in England."

"So should I," she admitted, and looked away again.

The words were simple enough, but, from what I knew of Nanette, I detected an unfamiliar note in her voice. I was not sorry to hear it, although it was a note of fear. It told me that my warning had been unnecessary. Nanette knew that Zara was a dangerous man.

"I have been wondering what I should do," she began suddenly. "But now I have made up my mind."

She opened her handbag and took out a twisted scrap of paper. Smoothing it carefully, she passed it to me, and:

"Captain Slattery dropped this yesterday," she said, "while he was with me in a taxi. I think, perhaps—"

She hesitated.

"Yes?" said I, glancing at what was written on the paper.

"It's so odd that I think, perhaps, you should show it to—your friend."

Watching her as she spoke, I wondered at the scheme of things; wondered whether she would outlive a romance born in a jewelled island, or whether, despite her youth, it was real, for good or ill, this love of hers for O'Shea.

I suppressed a sigh, and bent over the writing. This was what I read:

Book from Charing Cross to the British Museum. From the

Mansion House also it is no distance to the British Museum. Hyde Park there is a station. Change at Charing Cross for Piccadilly. Bond Street is merely Bond Street, and two London Bridges are better than one Bond Street. But the Mansion House and the British Museum are national institutions, and Berkeley Square pulled down or Berkeley Square blown up would only lead to the Old Bailey. Residents at the Crystal Palace rarely moved to Berkeley Square, and the Tower Bridge is new whilst London Bridge is old. Meet you in Bond Street.

I raised my eyes. Nanette was stifling laughter. Now she stifled it no longer. And Nanette's laughter was very sweet music.

"Of course," she confessed, "I know it *seems* perfectly idiotic! But one never knows. It may mean a general strike or something. But whatever it means, I shall have to be pushing along. I am meeting Mumsy at Marshall's."

She stood up, looking sharply to right and left, and I wondered what this might portend. However, we took the path to the Gate, walking very slowly, and from there proceeded in a taxi.

I dropped Nanette at her destination and was standing outside the shop wondering whether to walk over to the Club or to hunt up O'Shea, when an explanation of this chance meeting presented itself.

O'Shea, I recalled, had once said, in Nanette's presence, that when he had a difficult problem upon his mind, he varied the ordinary routine of a London morning. Other duties permitting, he walked as far as Peter Pan, and in the presence of the little god not infrequently discovered a solution of his difficulties.

Nanette had been unfortunate. This morning O'Shea had not come.

I reentered the taxi which I had kept waiting, and:

"Lancaster Gate," I directed.

Why I did so I have no idea; but experience has taught me that the motives which prompt many far-reaching actions are so obscure as to defy subsequent research.

Discharging the man, I set out along that path beside the Serpentine. The hour was now approaching noon, and platoons of white-capped nursemaids promenaded with the younger generation. I found myself surrounded by future society beauties; statesmen who would be making laws when I was an old man; great soldiers destined to save the British Empire from enemies yet unborn; actresses whose reputations might overshadow the memory of Sarah Bernhardt; princesses, dukes, vagabonds, thieves; some in perambulators, others in miniature automobiles, some toddling; a fascinating crowd.

Then I awakened from my daydream. Standing squarely in front of Peter Pan, and watching that youthful deity with a fixed stare, was O'Shea! He remained unaware of my presence until I touched him on the shoulder.

He turned swiftly. And I saw a far-away look in his gray eyes instantly change to one of close scrutiny; then:

"Decies," he said, "I am glad to see you. I learned something last night."

"What?" I said.

"I learned why Adolf Zara has come to England! The president of the S Group—a person with the mentality of a Tomsky and the morals of a baboon—is one Schmidt."

"Well?" said I.

"Schmidt is in London!"

CHAPTER XXV

THE SECOND MESSAGE

"Of course," I said, "it may mean nothing." O'Shea raised his eyes from the extraordinary communication that I had handed to him, and:

"Or it may mean everything!" he added.

We sat on that bench by the water's edge where I had met Nanette. O'Shea continued his scrutiny of the message, and, looking over his shoulder, I read it again for perhaps the twentieth time. Its absurdity fogged me. Passers-by ceased to exist, and I forgot Peter Pan.

"Perhaps," said I, "it is some kind of code."

"Since it is otherwise meaningless," O'Shea murmured, without raising his eyes, "your suggestion is excellent. You will have noticed that there are three references to the British Museum and that the expression 'Two London Bridges' occurs?"

"I had not particularly noticed this," I admitted.

"Two London Bridges," O'Shea went on musingly. "Very interesting— very interesting. You see where I mean?"

He indicated the passage with the rim of his monocle.

"Quite," said I eagerly. "But Charing Cross, Berkeley Square, and Bond Street also occur several times."

"But only Bond Street and Berkeley Square crop up in pairs," he replied, "if we exclude the brace of London Bridges."

And now, as we sat there pondering over this nonsensical piece of writing, came a strange interruption.

"Have you seen Comrade Zara?" said a guttural voice.

I looked up sharply. A stout German obstructed my view of Kensington Gardens. His ample face was draped in a pleasant smile, and he surveyed O'Shea and myself through a pair of spectacles that resembled portholes. No doubt I was gaping like an imbecile but O'Shea rose to the situation lightly.

"He is here," he replied calmly. "Are you from Comrade Schmidt?"

"I am," said the German. His smile disappeared. Relieved of it, his face was frankly sinister. "Have you seen Comrade Wilson?"

Perhaps it is unnecessary to state that emerging from a perusal of the letter about Hyde Park, Bond Street, and Berkeley Square, and finding myself plunged into this apparently inane conversation, I began to doubt my own sanity; but:

"*This* is Comrade Wilson," said O'Shea gravely, and waved his hand in my direction!

The German nodded in a very brusque way.

"Show me the order," he demanded.

O'Shea held up the demented document we had been reading; whereupon:

"Good," said our eccentric acquaintance. "Quick! The order for tonight!" He passed an envelope to O'Shea. "I am followed. Good-morning."

He moved off hurriedly, and I was still staring in speechless astonishment when a thick-set man wearing a blue suit and a soft hat, and who, without resembling a straggler from the Row, might have been a Colonial visitor, came along the path. One keen side-glance he gave us, and then disappeared in the wake of our Teutonic acquaintance.

"O'Shea—" I began; but:

"After all," he interrupted me, "one must admit that the Scotland Yard people are efficient. That was a detective-inspector of the Special Branch."

"Do you mean he is following the German?"

"Undoubtedly."

"But why should he follow him? Who was the German?"

"I haven't the faintest idea!" O'Shea replied.

"But he mentioned Zara! And you seemed to know him."

O'Shea adjusted his monocle and looked me over in a way that I didn't like.

"Really, Decies," he replied, "considering the admirable assistance which you have given me in this matter—for which I shall always be grateful—there are times when you defeat me. Why our German friend reposed his confidence in us I have no more idea than the Man in the Moon, nor why he confided this letter to my keeping. But his reference to Zara brands him a member of the S Group, without the significant fact that he is being followed by an officer of the Special Branch, whom I chance to know but who does not know me. The weary arm of coincidence is not long enough to embrace all these happenings, Decies. There is some other explanation. Let us see if it is here."

He tore open the envelope and withdrew a single sheet of paper. I bent forward eagerly, and over his shoulder read the following:

Charing Cross, London Bridge, Hyde Park, and the Strand are all worthy of a visit. Kingsway is modern, but the British Museum, Tower Bridge, the Mansion House, especially the British Museum, must not be neglected. Hyde Park merits several visits. The Mansion House, or the British Museum, can be done in one day, but Hyde Park is the only Hyde Park, whilst Piccadilly and the Strand are merely thoroughfares. The British Museum exhibit 365A is not in the National Gallery. The Crystal Palace does not resemble Buckingham Palace and Bond Street is not the Station for the Crystal Palace. Shepherd's Market is a survival. But book at Kingsway. Meet you at the Mansion House.

"And now," said O'Shea, "you know as much as I do!"

I stared at him blankly, and, as I stared, heard clocks, near and remote, strike the hour of noon. O'Shea suddenly thrust the second letter into his pocket and began to study that which Nanette had given to me.

He looked up, staring intently at the figure of Peter Pan, then:

"Twelve o'clock," he muttered. "Does the fact that it is twelve o'clock convey anything to you, Decies?"

"Nothing," I confessed, "except that I feel thirsty."

But it had conveyed something more to O'Shea. A distinguished officer is not relieved of his ordinary duties and dispatched to the Argentine upon the toss of a coin. He is selected for his special qualifications. That O'Shea's qualifications were extensive I had already learned; that they were also peculiar was beginning to dawn upon me.

CHAPTER XXVI

THE CRYPTOGRAM

Nanette was with a party at the Hippodrome that night, and I had promised to look in during the interval. The curtain had just fallen and the orchestra was playing as I entered with O'Shea. The manager met us at the top of the steps.

No doubt you remember him. He is unforgettable, being the best-dressed manager in Europe. He was delighted to meet O'Shea and much happier in greeting an officer of the Household troops who had come in for a drink than in endorsing a plebeian check for the use of the Royal box.

Nanette came running out ahead of her party and stopped dead on seeing O'Shea. He bowed in his grave, courtly fashion. She glanced at me swiftly, and then:

"Oh, Major O'Shea," she said, "I want to ask you to forgive me!"

"And I want to thank you," said he.

"To thank me?"

Nanette looked up at him and then down again very swiftly. She began tapping her foot upon the rubber-coated floor.

"To thank you," he repeated, "once more. It seems to be my happy fate, Nanette, to be always thanking you."

"But what have you to thank me for?" she asked, industriously studying the point of her shoe.

"For giving me an opportunity of redeeming my many failures."

Nanette looked up—she was quite calm again—and met his eyes bravely.

"Some of them," she said, "have been my fault."

"You are wrong," O'Shea assured her. "The fault has been mine from the very beginning."

"What do you mean?" she asked; and I turned aside, joining some friends who had just come out from the stalls.

In spite of my determination about Nanette, it still hurt a little bit to see that light in her eyes.

"I mean," I heard O'Shea reply, "that I have tried to do something that is impossible."

I heard no more, nor did I want to.

That bell which indicates the rise of the curtain releases from the bars of a London theatre certain characteristic types. The wet man returning guiltily with guarded breath to his dry wife in the stalls, having stepped out to "smoke a cigarette." The bored man, who is present under protest, and who goes to his seat like a martyr to the stake. The victim of jazzitis who dances with his girlfriend in the lobby, and post-mortem examination of whose skull reveals the presence of several perfectly formed saxophones but nothing else.

The curtain was about to rise and practically everybody was seated when I learned that Nanette had straggled. She stood with O'Shea in the opening at the back of the stalls. And I thought that I had never before seen her so animated in his company.

Envied model of her girlfriends, Nanette was a paragon of self-possession in the company of all men, or had been until she had met O'Shea. Never, hitherto, had I seen her at her ease with him. But tonight she was—realized that she was—and her happy excitement will be good to remember when I am ten years older.

One hand resting upon his arm, she looked up, talking gaily. He, too, had relaxed, as any man must have done finding himself in the company of an adorably pretty and spirited girl who loved him so much that she didn't care who knew. He was laughing like a schoolboy.

The curtain was up before Nanette tore herself away. She was very flushed, and I know her heart was beating wildly. I pitied her escort, foreseeing that she would be abstracted throughout the remainder of the evening.

O'Shea turned to me, and his eyes were still glistening happily.

"Well, Decies," said he, "what are you thinking?"

"I am thinking," I replied honestly, "that we are about of an age. That if Nanette had looked at me as I saw her looking at you, I should have asked her to marry me before I let her go back to her seat."

He stared very hard, his expression changing from second to second; then:

"Being Celtic," he said, "I suppose I am superstitious. At every turn since I have met her Nanette has intruded in my life. I am beginning to wonder."

"About what are you thinking in particular?" I asked.

"About the letter that Zara dropped in the cab and that Nanette gave to you."

"Have you fathomed it?" I asked excitedly—"and the other?"

"Both are in the same code. But without the first I doubt that I should have been able to read the second."

"Then you *have* read them?"

"I have," O'Shea replied; "and this time Nanette has dealt me a full hand."

His suppressed excitement communicated itself to me.

"What have you learned?" I said eagerly. "Can I be of any assistance?"

"Your assistance is indispensable!" he returned. "Are you game?"

"Every time!"

"Good enough. Let us go along to your rooms, and I will explain what tonight has in store for us."

As the taxi that we presently hailed threaded its way through the traffic of Cranbourne Street, and on through that of Piccadilly, I glanced aside several times at my silent companion. I wondered if his abstraction might be ascribed to the problem of the S Group, or to that of Nanette. Not being an O'Shea, I hesitated to judge. But my vote was for Nanette.

Arrived at my rooms and having sampled the whisky and soda:

"Now," O'Shea began, "the mantle of Edgar Allan Poe not having fallen upon my shoulders, I doubt that I should have solved this cipher but for the happy coincidence of meeting our German friend in the very shadow of Peter Pan. You will recall, too, that at the moment of his departure, the clocks were chiming the hour of noon."

"I remember," said I.

"I turned it over in my mind, considering the thing from every conceivable angle. Before I tackled the cipher—for of course the messages were palpably written in some kind of cipher—one fact was plain enough to me."

"What was that?"

"The fact that Zara, an important member of the S Group, was not known by sight to the member who spoke to us! He mistook *me* for Zara, and he mistook *you* for one Comrade Wilson, of whom I had never heard, and respecting whom I have no instructions."

"So far I agree," said I, "but what I simply cannot make out is why this deranged German should walk up to two perfect strangers seated in Kensington Gardens and take it for granted that they were the people he was looking for."

"His opening remark was non-committal," O'Shea reminded me, reflectively sipping his whisky and soda.

"Certainly it was; but am I to assume that the man was walking about London addressing the inquiry, 'Have you seen Comrade Zara?' to every male citizen he met on his travels?"

"The very point that led me to a solution of the problem," O'Shea returned. "I realized, of course, that the routine which you indicate would have been insane, and I do not look for insanity of this kind from members of the S Group. I recalled that we had been sitting by the statue of Peter Pan, and that I had drawn your attention to the presence of 'Two London Bridges' in the message. I noted that the double bridges were preceded by a reference to Bond Street—or, rather, by two references to Bond Street—and followed by another. I remembered that the hour was noon.

"Treating the message as a cipher, I assumed, as a basis of investigation, that the various well-known spots mentioned represented letters and that all intervening words might be neglected. Now, I had two almost certain clues to work upon.

"First, that our German friend clearly expected to meet Zara and someone called Wilson by the statue of Peter Pan. Second, that he expected to meet them there at noon. Think for a moment, and you will realize that this must have been the case."

"It is clear enough," said I, "now that you point it out to me."

"His handing me a second message in the same cipher," O'Shea went on, "suggested that the first related to the appointment which we, by bounty of the gods, had accidentally kept. I therefore assumed that the first message conveyed something of this sort: 'Be at the statue of Peter Pan at midday.'

"I began to examine it with this idea in mind. Particularly, I was looking for a sequence to fit the name, Peter Pan. As you can see—" he spread the original messages on my table before me—"it appears unmistakably at the very beginning. Charing Cross is the first point mentioned; four other London landmarks occur, and then Charing Cross again. I assumed as a working theory that Charing Cross stood for the letter P.

"This suggested that British Museum was E as it occurs next, is followed by Mansion House, and then occurs again.

"Assuming Mansion House to be T, we get P-e-t-e. Calling Hyde Park R, we get Peter. Charing Cross then crops up in its correct place. Reading Piccadilly as A and Bond Street as N gives Peter Pan."

He laid his cigarette in an ashtray and bent over the writing enthusiastically.

"This enabled me to cross-check, for Bond Street occurs again immediately, with the two London Bridges which first attracted my attention, followed by another Bond Street.

"Bond Street being N, it was reasonable to assume that London Bridge was O, making—Peter Pan, Noon."

"By gad!" I exclaimed. "It's wonderful!"

"On the contrary," O'Shea assured me, "it is elementary. To continue: we now have Mansion House again, or T, followed by British Museum— E, and two Berkeley Squares, hitherto unmentioned. Old Bailey and Crystal Palace crop up next—very defeating—followed by a third

Berkeley Square. Then Tower Bridge. This is followed by London Bridge, O, and Bond Street, N. Remembering the name of the Comrade for whom you were mistaken, Decies, I very quickly determined that Berkeley Square stood for L and the word following 'Noon' was 'Tell.' This gave me a pair of blanks, then L, another blank, and o-n. Wilson was clearly indicated, and I had my complete message. 'Peter Pan noon, tell Wilson.'

O'Shea replaced his cigarette between his lips and turned to me, smiling.

"You mean," said I, "that you have read the second message?"

"Naturally," he replied. "It is childishly easy, once having got the idea of the nature of the cipher. Without bothering you with details, such as the letters implied by Buckingham Palace, Shepherd's Market, and Kingsway—places that don't occur in the first message—I may say that it reads as follows: 'Porchester Terrace 365A—which I assume to be the number of a house—midnight.'"

"Good heavens!" I glanced at the clock. "And he said the order was for tonight!"

"Tonight," O'Shea returned, glancing up. "We have two hours."

"We have two hours?"

"Precisely," said he, and his gray eyes surveyed me unblinkingly. "There are certain chances, but there is no game without chances, and we shall be covered by a raid squad from Scotland Yard. Whether Comrade Schmidt is more familiar with the appearance of Comrades Zara and Wilson than his emissary seems to be, I cannot say. But tonight at twelve o'clock I suggest that you and I present ourselves at number 365A Porchester Terrace, as Comrades Zara and Wilson! It is asking a lot, Decies, but are you game?"

"Good God!" I said, hesitated for one electric moment, and then held out my hand.

O'Shea grasped it.

CHAPTER XXVII

THE COMRADES GATHER

"Nanette has gone on somewhere to dance," said O'Shea.

"I know." I stared out of the window of the taxi. "I take it that she doesn't know where *we* have gone on to?"

"No."

O'Shea's reply was little more than a whisper, but it told me that which made me at once glad and sorry. For good or for ill, Nanette was winning.

"Two things are rather worrying me," O'Shea confessed. "It is obvious enough that Zara is afraid to visit any of the known centres of the S Group, hence the appointment at Peter Pan. He probably received the letter—or 'Order'—at some post office, under an assumed name. But if he had read it and decoded it before he dropped it in the taxi, where was he at noon today?"

"Unable to approach Peter Pan," I replied promptly, "because we were there, not to mention the man from Scotland Yard who was following the German."

"Yes," O'Shea mused. "Zara's reaction to this check is one of the points I am wondering about. It may prove to be a snag. The second snag—"

But as our taxi had turned into Porchester Terrace and was now pulling up, I did not learn what the second snag might be.

We alighted, and I looked up and down the street. Save for O'Shea's assurance, there was nothing to show that our movements were covered by the squad from Scotland Yard. Porchester Terrace proclaimed itself empty from end to end, or for as far as I could see.

Number 365A was a prosperous-looking mansion set back beyond a patch of shrubbery and approached through a sort of arcade guarded by handsome double doors. What appeared to be a large room on the first floor was brilliantly lighted, but otherwise the house was in darkness.

"Pull over to the other side of the street," O'Shea directed the taxi driver, "and wait. We shall not be long."

"Very good, sir."

As the man turned his cab:

"Now," said O'Shea, "we are going over the top! Are you fit?"

"All ready," said I.

O'Shea pressed the bell button.

In the interval that elapsed between the ringing of the bell and the opening of the door, I conjured up a picture of Nanette dancing with somebody or another somewhere, perpetually glancing abstractedly about the room, as I had seen her do so often, in hope of catching a glimpse of O'Shea.

It was hard to believe that this doorway before which we waited represented a frontier which, once crossed, shut us off from the life of empty gaiety which the name of London conveys to so many; difficult to regard it as the porch of a grim and real underworld, controlled by enemies of established society, remorseless, almost inhuman in their bloodthirsty fanaticism.

A saturnine foreign butler admitted us. We had shed our dinner kit and were wearing tweeds.

"Comrade Zara and Comrade Wilson," said O'Shea with composure.

The man nodded and stood aside. We entered the arcade, which was bordered by plants in pots, and saw ahead of us some carpeted steps, lighted by a hanging lantern.

As the double doors closed behind us, I experienced one of those indescribable moments compounded of panic and exhilaration. Then somewhere, very dimly, I heard a clock striking midnight. We were going upstairs.

"Comrade Zara and Comrade Wilson."

I found myself in a large room, very simply furnished in library fashion, and in the presence of six or seven rather unsavoury human specimens, some of whom bowed curtly, and some of whom did not bow at all.

Our Peter Pan acquaintance was present; and a short thick-set man, who had incredibly long arms, and who generally resembled a red baboon, came forward to greet us. He had incomplete teeth, and those that survived badly needed scaling. His accent opened up wide possibilities.

"Greeting, Comrades," said he. "You are welcome. My name is Schmidt."

And as he spoke, fixing his piercing glance first upon O'Shea and then upon myself, I recognized beneath that uncouth exterior the primitive, formidable force of the man.

He presented the other comrades, by names which are not to be found in Debrett, and I reflected that impudence is indispensable to success in this sort of game.

It became evident that, from Comrade Schmidt downward, nobody in the room was familiar with the appearance of either Zara or Wilson!

An appalling-looking bearded creature attached itself to O'Shea.

"We are anxious, Comrade," it said, "to hear your personal account of the state of the work in South Africa."

"I am not too hopeful," O'Shea replied gloomily, and glanced aside at me.

"But," said Schmidt, turning his dreadful little eyes in my direction, "Comrade Wilson brings us news from the United States which will be like new blood in our veins."

Somehow or another, O'Shea managed to shake off the Missing Link, and to secure a word aside with me.

"Very full bag," he murmured. "If we make no mistakes, we shall purge England and America of some unsavoury elements. But the second snag which I had foreseen rests on the fact that another steamer from Madeira has reached Southampton since we returned. There is one member of the S Group whom we left behind. He knows us both. He might quite conceivably have been in that steamer! His appearance here would raise the temperature considerably. And—"

He was interrupted. The door of the room was thrown open and the foreign butler entered.

"Comrade Macalister," he announced.

"The snag to which I referred!" said O'Shea.

CHAPTER XXVIII

THE RAID

I suppose that at some time during his life every man who has anything of the boy left in him has thought that he would like to take a fling at the great adventure of Secret Service. I feel called upon to assure these aspirants that a comfortable armchair is the better choice.

Accident, or that Higher Power which the Arabs call Kismet, had cast me into the path of Edmond O'Shea. He had honoured me with his friendship, but had quite failed to recognize that I was a man of lesser stature than his own. Whilst granting every honour to marshal and statesman, personally I am disposed to believe that it was men such as O'Shea who steered the Allies to victory; and perhaps, hitherto, I had been inclined to look upon the Secret Service as a job for highbrows rather than for soldiers.

This error was to be corrected.

Conceive a large room filled with enemies of established order; fanatics, whose collected scruples would have left a thimble empty. Conceive that I and O'Shea, posing as members of their bloodthirsty organization, were amongst them as spies, pledged to bring about their ruin.

Now, conceive that a "Comrade," who knows us and has fared ill at our hands, is suddenly announced.

Perhaps I shall be forgiven when I say that I remembered with gratitude how Edmond O'Shea had rallied a company of the Guards during the great retreat, how his presence of mind and consummate self-possession had helped historians to chronicle Cambrai with pride rather than with humility.

He edged up beside me. I saw him fumbling for his monocle and saw his change of expression when he realized that he had left it behind;

then:

"Get near the door," he murmured. "My fault, Decies, to have let you in for this. But I had hoped to learn things that police examination can never bring out."

Macalister came in.

He was in dinner kit and he smoked a cigar which, to my disordered vision, appeared to be decorated with two bands. His superb self-possession was worthy of Tom Mix. He did not merely own the room; he possessed the property.

"Take the left," said O'Shea.

Unerringly, instinctively, Macalister's glance settled upon us at the moment of his entrance. He had advanced no more than one pace beyond the butler, and his mouth was agape for excited utterance, when O'Shea's revolver had him covered.

Overwhelmed with a sense of utter unreality, I covered the group of four on my left which included the formidable Schmidt.

Glibly, as though born of long familiarity, the words leapt to my tongue:

"Hands up!"

The command was obeyed. And I have since thought, paradoxical though it may appear, that violent men, in these matters, are more tractable than men of peace. Assessing human life lightly, they credit the brain behind the gun with compunction no greater than their own.

"By God!" I heard Macalister say—and I hope I shall always find time to take off my hat to a good loser—"I had you wrong all along, Major!"

Schmidt looked dangerously ugly for a moment; then:

"Line up," said O'Shea sharply. "Jump to it. Fall in on the left of Schmidt."

Came inarticulate mutterings, but without other audible protest the group obeyed, forming a line having Schmidt at one end and the saturnine butler at the other.

"Now," O'Shea continued, "if any man lowers his hands, I shall not argue with him. Decies, will you go down to the street door and whistle? Pass behind me. Keep a sharp look-out. I don't know who is in the house."

I obeyed, the sense of unreality prevailing. But I know I shall always remember that row of sullen-faced men with raised hands, who watched as I crossed behind O'Shea.

There was no one on the stairs, and no one in the long, glazed passage that led to the street. This gained, I ran the length of it, and throwing open the double doors beheld a seemingly deserted Porchester Terrace.

I whistled shrilly. The result was magical.

Springing from what hiding places I know not, men appeared running from right and left! This was the raid squad from Scotland Yard, and I realized that I was helping to mould history.

Our taximan, who was waiting on the other side of the street, and who had been peacefully smoking a cigarette, jumped down from his seat and watched the proceedings with an expression of stupefaction that was comic in its intensity.

Everything was carried out in a most orderly manner. The members of the Group were arrested without unnecessary fuss. The whole thing might have been "produced" by David Belasco. A six-seater car appeared from somewhere or another, in which the gang was canned as neatly as tinned sardines.

The police handled the job with such discretion that chance passers-by never dreamed that anything unusual was going forward. They do these raids much better on the screen.

Macalister was the last to come down from above, his cigar still held firmly between his teeth. He was unperturbed. Deportation was the worst he had to fear, and he knew it quite well. He was smiling slyly. He paused, looking hard at O'Shea and at myself.

"Listen," he said, "you two boys have doubled on me pretty badly, but I don't bear no malice." His grammar at times revealed the influence of the Cubist school. "Zara is different, and he's still loose. Take my tip and watch out for Zara. If he's seeing red, don't try to pet him. Goodnight!"

He entered the car, urged by two detectives. "Good-night," murmured O'Shea thoughtfully, and turned to me.

"You know, Decies," he went on, "if that man had had our advantages, he would have made a damned good sportsman."

There were certain formalities to be attended to, and I suppose it was close upon two o'clock when O'Shea and I found ourselves outside my rooms. I suggested a doch-an'-dorris.

"If I were superstitious," O'Shea declared, "I should refuse."

He smiled, glancing up at the tall ladder beneath which we must walk to reach my door.

"Oh!" said I, "they are mending the roof, or something."

"I suppose we might risk it," he replied; and we went in.

The incident stuck in my mind, not so much because of any superstitious significance that I attached to it as because of what actually happened later.

O'Shea dropped on to the settee in my big room and sighed rather wearily as he watched me preparing drinks.

"You know, Decies," said he, "I am both glad and sorry that this job is over. I have blundered through by sheer good luck. Without your aid, and the aid of someone else, I should have crashed badly."

"Perhaps not," I returned. "If you had not succeeded in one way, you might quite easily have found another."

"Or I might not," said he. "No. I am a poor policeman, and peace-time soldiering is no sort of game."

"What do you mean, O'Shea?"

"I mean," he replied, holding up to the light a glass that I had handed to him, "that I am infernally restless."

I sighed as loudly as he had done and stooped over the syphon. Then:

"Decies," said O'Shea, "we live in a generation that grows up very early."

"We do," I agreed.

"I should like to talk to you seriously. There are many men I have known longer, but none I could sooner trust. Yet in this matter somehow I don't feel . . ."

"Yes?" I prompted.

"Well, I don't feel quite at liberty to discuss it with you."

There was a silence that might have been awkward. O'Shea was watching me almost pathetically; and:

"I know what you want to talk about," I said. "Nanette is a witch. But there is only one man in the world for her now. It might be fair, though, to give her a year to think it over."

"You don't doubt *my* attitude in the matter," O'Shea murmured.

"No," I replied, "I know it."

He looked at me very fixedly, when:

"Coo-ooh!" I heard.

O'Shea's expression changed; and, turning, I crossed to an open window, looking down into the street.

Standing just in front of the ladder which disfigured the front of the premises, was Nanette, staring upward. A two-seater with several people in it stood at the curb.

"Hello, Nanette," I called.

"Saw your light," she shouted, "as we were passing. May we come up, or are you going to bed?"

"No," I replied, and hesitated to tell her what I knew she hoped. "Come right up and bring your friends. I have only just got in."

"Right-oh!" she cried.

CHAPTER XXIX

ADOLPH ZARA

The party that presently invaded us proved to consist of Nanette and a brunette girlfriend whom I had not seen before. They were escorted by a young medical officer on leave from Mesopotamia—a very charming type of Scotsman—and Milton, one of Nanette's Madeira conquests, whom, you may recall, I had met again recently under rather odd circumstances. I thought that this evening was probably his reward for the weary job of scouting that he had performed on that occasion.

He was not a happy man. The fact was beginning to dawn upon him that at the Savoy, the Hippodrome, and wherever else they had gone, he had been wasting his fragrance on the desert air. I pictured him driving to my apartment as one consciously heading for his doom.

The poor fellow was rather pathetically young, and, regarding every acquaintance of Nanette's as a serious rival, he had awakened to the fact that he had three score or so of deadly enemies in London. Presently:

"Whisky and soda?" said I; "or have you reached the Bass stage?"

"Neither, thanks," he returned, and glared around my modest bachelor apartment as one who finds himself in the chamber of Bluebeard.

Nanette had sped to O'Shea like an arrow to its target. As I turned aside from the peevish Milton, "I hadn't dared to hope I should see you again tonight," I heard her say.

The other man and the pretty brunette were jointly occupying my most comfortable armchair, therefore, conquering a perfectly stupid pique which Milton had inspired:

"Well," said I, holding out my cigarette case, "we seem to have no alternative but to—look on, Milton."

He rejected the olive-branch, and, rudely ignoring my proffered case, crossed to the settee where Nanette and O'Shea sat side by side.

"I say, Nanette," he exclaimed, "what about going on to Chelsea?"

Nanette barely glanced up as, she replied:

"No, I don't want to dance any more tonight, Jim."

"Why not dance here?" cried her friend, pointing in the direction of the piano. "Do you play, Mr. Decies?"

"Not dance music," I confessed gladly.

"But Jim does," she went on. "Go on, Jim! Just one."

"Jim" crossed to the piano, offering an excellent imitation of an ox approaching Chicago. He crashed into a piece of syncopation that put years on the instrument. I had never heard the item before and trust that I shall never hear it again. I saw O'Shea smilingly shake his head; then Nanette ran across to me, and off we went around the furniture, I wondering which would burst first, a wire in my reeling piano or a blood-vessel in the empurpled skull of the player.

Nanette danced because she was too happy to keep still, even with O'Shea beside her. I danced because I had no choice in the matter. It was an odd business, pointedly illustrating the part that Terpsichore plays in this modern civilization of ours.

Nanette was dancing with me, but she wanted to dance with O'Shea. The other pair didn't want to dance at all. They just wanted to be alone together. And Milton didn't want to be the band. In fact, the whole thing was a sort of neutral territory, or sanctuary, in which the various protagonists found temporary refuge.

I don't know what momentous decision Nanette's girlfriend was shirking, but when Milton threatened to weaken:

"Go on, Jim! Please go on!" she cried, avoiding the ardent gaze of her partner.

Milton, the most ferociously reluctant musician I have ever seen at work, made a renewed assault upon the keyboard. He was watching Nanette, who rarely took her eyes off O'Shea; and a vein rose unpleasantly upon his forehead. He perpetrated some discords that set my teeth on edge.

How long this might have continued I hesitate to guess. Milton's gorge was rising tropically. I doubt that his destruction of my piano would have ceased while life remained in the instrument, but an interruption came.

Nanette and I had navigated an awkward channel behind the armchair and were beating up toward the settee and O'Shea. The man from Mesopotamia had ingeniously steered his partner into a little book-lined recess at the farther end of the room. I had my back to the open window and Nanette was facing it. Suddenly she grew rigid.

Her face became transfigured with an expression of horror that I can never forget. She pulled up dead—staring, staring past me, into the darkness of the street beyond.

"What is it, Nanette?" I began, when the music ceased with a crash and I saw Milton bound to his feet.

Unconsciously, I had gripped Nanette hard. But, in the next instant, she wrenched herself free from my grasp, turned, and with a queer sort of smothered cry threw herself upon O'Shea!

I twisted about.

Not two feet behind me an arm protruded into the room! The hand grasped a strange-looking pistol—for at that time I had never seen a Maxim Silencer. I heard a muffled thud. Something came whizzing through the air in my direction. (I learned later, when clarity came, that it was a valuable Ming vase that had stood upon the piano.)

"Hold him, Decies!" yelled Milton.

It was Milton who had hurled this costly projectile at the dimly seen arm in the window. The vase went crashing out into the street. I heard a second thud. Milton fell forward across the instrument—and then slid down on to the carpet. The hand clutching the pistol had vanished.

A sort of vague red mist was dancing before my eyes. Came a rush of footsteps. Nanette was slipping from O'Shea's arms. His face as he looked down into hers was a mask of tragedy. I heard her utter a little moan and I saw a streak of blood upon one white shoulder.

Then followed chaos.

A very weak voice, which vaguely I recognized as that of Milton, said:

"Don't worry about me, Doc. Look after Nanette."

I saw O'Shea stoop and lift Nanette. I saw her pale face. When, cutting through the tumult like a ray from a beacon:

"The window, Decies! Watch which way he goes!"

Automatically, I obeyed O'Shea. I strained out, looking to right and to left of the ladder. It was boarded over, but I realized that a desperate man, given sufficient agility, could have climbed the rungs from underneath, as evidently the assassin had done.

At first, the street seemed to be empty from end to end; then I saw the figure of a man emerge from shadow into a patch of light cast by a street lamp—one who walked swiftly in the direction of Berkeley Square. I withdrew my head and stared, only half believing, about the room.

Milton, looking deathly, lay propped up against the piano. He met my glance, and: "Seen him?" he demanded.

I turned, as the military surgeon who had been bending over Nanette looked up at her friend, who stood beside him.

"Know anything about nursing?" he jerked.

The girl was very pale, but:

"Yes," she answered bravely, meeting his eyes, "a little. Tell me what to do, and I will do it."

He nodded, smiling, whereat I was reassured, and then:

"Have you a manservant in the house, Mr. Decies?" he asked.

"Yes."

"Dig him out. I can manage. You fellows are in the way. Get after the swine who did this." But O'Shea had already started for the door. His expression was one I had rather not have seen. There is a savage hidden in every Celt, if one digs deep through.

The other members of the group by this time were safely housed in cells. I thought that if we were destined to overtake Adolf Zara, he was likely to enjoy the distinction of spending the night in a morgue.

CHAPTER XXX

MEMORIES CAN SAVE

As Milton's car, driven by O'Shea, raced around the corner into the square, all question of the fugitive's identity was settled.

Just vaulting into a two-seater that had been parked over by the railings was the man whose retreating figure I had seen as I leaned from the window! I prayed that he might be unable to start. But my prayer was not answered. Off he went, heading for Piccadilly.

One swift glance back he gave over his shoulder. And in the light of the street lamp by which the car had stood, I saw the face of Zara!

I glanced at O'Shea beside me. His pale features were set like a mask. I looked to right and to left; but not a soul was in sight. Berkeley Square was apparently deserted. Often enough I had wondered how certain notorious burglaries had been accomplished with all the resources of civilization at beck and call of justice. This was the answer.

We had no means of arranging for Zara's interception—although a constable was on duty at the corner of Bruton Street! We could only hope to keep him in sight or else overtake him. The merest hitch, or slightest traffic delay, would deliver him into our hands. But the betting was equal. Such an accident might as well befall us as him; and, the quarry once out of sight, our chances fell below zero.

O'Shea spoke never a word. His mind held but one single purpose. That purpose, I firmly believe, was to wreak justice upon Zara with his own hands.

Momentarily, I wondered about Milton. Of Nanette I dared not think. But a cold fury was growing within me, and I fingered the pistol that had been in my pocket since the raid upon the house in Porchester Terrace.

Zara whirled round into St. James's Street. The traffic in Piccadilly was not great but there were a number of pedestrians about. I even saw policemen in the distance. It all seemed utterly grotesque. Then, hot upon the fugitive, we, too, were dropping down the slope. Far ahead I could see the clock above St. James's Palace. The hour was a quarter past two.

Our speed was outrageous. We crossed Pall Mall at about thirty-five, and came out into the Mall, heading for Buckingham Palace in Brooklands fashion. We were gaining slightly. We crept from forty-five to fifty. Broad thoroughfares, brightly lighted, offered no obstruction; and we flew around the sharp bend by the Victoria Memorial and headed east.

"Westminster Bridge!" I muttered.

O'Shea did not speak. Past the barracks we sped, and, undeterred by a certain amount of traffic in Parliament Square, shot on to the approach to the Bridge. We were now three lengths behind Zara, and on the gradient began to improve upon it. Zara drove on the inside of the car lines, hugging the pavement. And at about the centre of the Bridge we passed outside him. I heard someone shouting.

"Cover him, Decies!" said O'Shea grimly. "Shoot if he doesn't pull up!"

I turned and gave a loud cry. Zara had slowed down and was already twenty yards behind us!

"Stop, O'Shea!" I cried—"stop!"

He obeyed so suddenly that I nearly dived through the windshield. Then we jumped, one on either side, and started to run back.

Zara had already dismounted, and I saw him peeling his coat. A picture arose out of the recent past: a foggy night off Ushant: and I seemed to hear again that eerie cry, "Man overboard!"

So it was that Zara had eluded us once before. Undoubtedly he was going to do so again; and for all the cold hatred in my heart, I could not entirely withhold admiration as I saw him bound upon the parapet, raise his arms, and take that appalling dive into the Thames far below.

I knew now, however, what I had not known formerly: that Adolf Zara's courage was the courage of madness. His was that disease of fanaticism which, when it does not cough up a Tomsky, floods the criminal lunatic asylums.

As we both craned over the parapet, peering down at the uneasy water, I heard the sound of a runner and then the flat note of a police whistle. "There he is!" said O'Shea.

I stared but could see nothing, when:

"Hello, there! What's the game! Who was it that went over?" cried a loud voice.

We turned, as a breathless constable came doubling up.

"A very dangerous criminal," O'Shea replied, "and we were chasing him. Quick, officer! on which side of the Bridge shall we find a boat?"

The manner of one accustomed to give orders is unmistakable, and:

"West, sir," the constable answered promptly. "There's a boat at the pier."

"Good," said O'Shea, and started to run to the car. I followed.

As we jumped in, turned, and headed back to where Big Ben recorded the fact that only seven minutes had elapsed since we had passed St. James's Palace, I saw the constable coming after us. But, leaving the car by the foot of the clock tower, O'Shea raced across to the gate at the head of those steps that lead down to the pier. It was locked; and here I thought that the chase ended. But I had counted without O'Shea.

London, unlike New York, normally is a very empty city at two o'clock in the morning; but now, as if conjured up by a magic talisman, a group began to assemble. I looked to my right—from which the constable was bearing down upon us. Even as he ran, his bearing was ominous. It occurred to me that he regarded O'Shea and myself with justifiable suspicion, and I foresaw complications.

It was odd, I reflected, that we stood almost in the shadow of Scotland Yard—representing Law and Order, the forces of Empire against those of disruption—but that the very powers that should have backed us were likely now to aid and abet a dangerous conspirator and assassin in escaping the meshes of justice.

The constable rather windily began to blow his whistle again.

A resolute-looking man, clean-shaven, and of a very hard-bitten countenance, suddenly appeared at my elbow.

"What's the trouble?" he inquired—and challenged me with keen eyes.

An official note in his voice was recognizable. O'Shea turned quickly. The ever-increasing group drew more closely around us. A second constable was making his way across from Parliament Square.

"The trouble is," said O'Shea, "that this gate is locked, and I want to get on to the pier."

The man, whose face seemed to have been chiselled out of seasoned teak, stared in a curious way. Then the breathless constable burst upon us.

"Just a minute!" he began. "I want to know some more about this business!"

He became uneasily aware of the presence of our weatherbeaten acquaintance. He stopped in the act of laying his hand upon O'Shea's arm. O'Shea, watching the man who had accosted us, spoke, and:

"Sergeant Donoghue!" he said.

The expression on the grim face changed. The man so addressed drew himself smartly to attention. It was automatic—second nature;

but his smile was good to see.

"Thank you, sir," said he, "for remembering me."

O'Shea held out his hand.

"Stand easy, Sergeant," he replied. "I gather that you have left the Army and rejoined the Police."

Donoghue's eyes were glistening as he grasped the proffered hand.

"I have that, sir," he said, "and without loss of rank. I am a detective-sergeant now."

He glanced at the two constables—for the Parliament Square reinforcement had come up.

"Carry on," he directed, "there's a man drowning. Leave this to me."

"Donoghue," said O'Shea, "do you hate the Reds?"

"I do, sir!"

"Well, one of them has just jumped off the Bridge. He is a powerful swimmer. I want to get on to the pier and into a boat."

"You are in luck, sir," Donoghue returned enthusiastically, "for tonight I happen to have the key."

When, a minute later, we pushed out into the stream, watched by an ever-increasing group of idlers, I thought how proud a man must feel to see a light like that which had crossed Donoghue's face as he had recognized the officer he had served under. One such silent tribute is worth more than a thousand cheers.

"Do you remember the night behind the farm, sir?" Donoghue asked.

And O'Shea in reply merely laid his hand upon his shoulder and gripped hard for a moment. But this apparently simple question had a far-reaching result, as I was presently to learn.

A fairly strong current was running, which, together with O'Shea's recollection of the swimmer's position as seen from the Bridge, sufficiently indicated where we should lay our course.

Certain official steps had automatically been taken, and we were not alone in our quest. Apparently, even at two o'clock in the morning, it is contrary to County Council regulations for anyone to bathe from Westminster Bridge.

Looking up from that unfamiliar viewpoint at certain London landmarks outlined against the clear sky, I wondered why Fate always seems to put a brake upon our joy-rides.

Untrammelled by an intense anxiety on account of Nanette that obsessed me tonight, this queer adventure must have been definitely enjoyable. But, like so many human experiences, it was less exciting in the doing than it is in the telling. For exploration of unfamiliar by-paths, as I have already mentioned, there is no vehicle like a cosy armchair.

That Zara would head for the nearest landing place, it was fairly reasonable to suppose. Therefore we pulled hard across in the direction of the County Hall, eagerly watching the surface of the water. Suddenly:

"There he goes!" cried Donoghue.

But, even as he spoke, I had seen the swimmer—close in, under the right bank, heading powerfully for the stairs. We raced for him and made land almost simultaneously.

In the act of landing Zara stumbled and slipped back into the river.

He came up by the stern of the boat. O'Shea's hand shot out, grasped him by a soddened collar-band, and hauled him in against the side. Dimly, I could see O'Shea's face as he looked down at the upcast eyes of Zara. I think I knew what was in his mind, and in those upturned eyes was recognition of it—and acceptance.

Still grasping the helpless man, O'Shea glanced quickly at Donoghue.

"Yes, Donoghue," he said coldly, "I remember the night behind the farm. You have reminded me that I once had decent instincts. Sergeant, here's your prisoner."

CHAPTER XXXI

HIATUS

I find that my memory holds no proper record of the hour that elapsed between this time and our return to Nanette. There were certain unavoidable formalities to be gone through; but within ten minutes of the arrest of Zara, I was on the telephone to my rooms. My man answered; and his replies, whilst reticent, were reassuring.

"Mr. Milton has been removed to hospital, sir. A very narrow escape, I understand. It will be a long job, but he is in no danger. Yes, sir, the lady is"—pause—"still here."

"Why?" I asked uneasily, and glanced at O'Shea, who was standing at my elbow throughout this conversation.

"They—didn't like to move her, sir. I 'phoned to Sir Frank Leslie, in Harley Street, sir, by request. He is here."

"But where is—the lady?"

"Sorry, sir, but she is—in your room. Her mother is with her, sir."

"Is she dangerously ill?"

"I don't really know, sir. Both the medical men are with her now."

As I replaced the receiver, I stared at O'Shea. He had moved away from me and was pacing restlessly up and down the bleakly furnished room in New Scotland Yard from which we had been speaking.

"You understand?" I said. "She is—rather badly hurt."

"I understand." He nodded grimly. "She saved my life, Decies, perhaps at the price of her own. I can't bear to think of it."

He turned abruptly and stared out of the window at a vista of empty Embankment below, lighted by many twinkling lamps.

"I have been a self-reliant man all my life, Decies; it may be aggressively so. Perhaps this is poetic justice. Since the moment that I set foot in Madeira, up to this very hour, she has done my work for me, step by step. You admit it, Decies? You admit it?"

"I do," said I. "It's true, but no discredit to you."

He shook his head and resumed the restless pacing. I saw him groping for his monocle, which he had left at his rooms prior to setting out for the raid on the S Group, and I saw him snap his fingers irritably as he realized how enslaved he was to this habit.

"I have placed independence above every other virtue in man," he went on. "I have fought for it and suffered for it. I suppose she has been sent to teach me that independence and loneliness are inseparable. Do you know," he turned and looked fully into my eyes, with an expression almost of humility, "I don't think I could bear that lonely path any longer, Decies. And if—" he paused and squared his jaw for a moment—"and if I have to follow it, there won't be very much left."

"Shut up!" I said. "You are talking nonsense. If you elect to be lonely in future, the choice is yours."

"Unless . . ." he smiled wryly.

"Don't think of that!" I replied. "She is young and full of stamina. Besides, she wants to live."

"And I want her to live," he added softly. "Yet, even now, I can't believe it—and I can't quite condone it."

"Condone what?" I demanded.

"The acceptance, by a man of my age, world-worn, a little disappointed, more than a little cynical, of such a sacrifice, from a girl with all the world to choose from. I can find no justification."

"I see," I murmured. "And can you find any for leaving her, now that you know? Because you can't shut your eyes to the fact that this is not a schoolgirl's infatuation, but the real thing. Can you condone that?"

My voice was not quite steady.

"She was ready to die for you, O'Shea," I said. "It would break her heart to lose you. Damn it!" I pulled out my cigarette case, "I am talking like your sentimental aunt."

O'Shea smiled, this time more happily, and grasped my shoulder in characteristic fashion.

"I believe we are both behaving rather idiotically," he admitted. "Let's hope for the best."

"I don't believe you would recognize it if it came to you," I returned.

He shrugged his shoulders and we went up to a room on the floor above, where some sort of superior official was waiting. Throughout the interview that followed O'Shea became again the steely-eyed, square-jawed soldier whom I knew so well; the traditional O'Shea, whose name had been a tonic to many a man during those black days when the shadow of Prussia lay over Europe.

CHAPTER XXXII

THE HEART OF NANETTE

I seemed to detect an ominous air of hush as I opened the door for O'Shea and myself to go up to my apartments. Nanette's mother met us. I could scarcely bear to look at her. Almost immediately, she fixed her eyes upon O'Shea.

"Major O'Shea," she began bravely, "I have known for a long time how Nanette felt about you. . . ."

"And I suppose you have reproached me," said he.

"I have not," she returned. "I have had many opportunities of watching, and I know that your behaviour has been admirable, if . . ." she hesitated.

"Yes?" O'Shea urged gently.

"If she has really meant anything to you. Be frank with me, Major O'Shea. Has she?"

"She has," he replied gravely. "I didn't know, but I know now."

"It is frightfully hard to say," she went on, "but . . ." she turned to me impulsively. "Can you help me, Mr. Decies?"

"I think I can," said I. "There is no reason why my friend, Major O'Shea, should not marry Nanette, unless there is any on your side. Personally, he thinks he is too old for her!" This last remark I added in what was meant to be a facetious manner, for the situation was difficult to cope with. "But please tell us—how is she?"

"She will recover," was the reply, "thanks to the speedy attention that she received. Failing this, it might have been—otherwise. I am afraid she cannot be moved for some time, Mr. Decies. It will be a dreadful inconvenience for you. . . ."

"And a great honour," I added. "Is it possible to see her?"

"I don't know if it is advisable. But she is asking to see"—glancing at O'Shea—"someone."

O'Shea bit his lip—the nearest approach to a display of emotion that

I had ever observed in him—and turned quickly aside.

Then followed a period of waiting. Nanette's girlfriend came down, having been relieved by a professional nurse. She smiled at O'Shea, and blushed furiously; an unusual accomplishment in a girl of her type and age. But the smile and the blush told me more of the state of Nanette's heart than a long dissertation could have revealed.

The young medical officer appeared at last, and his expression was reassuring.

"Can we go up?" I asked.

"Yes," he replied; "I have Sir Frank's permission to admit you for three minutes, but no more than three minutes."

He stared significantly at O'Shea.

In a queerly furtive fashion I began to mount the stairs of my own house, treading softly as upon holy ground and going with bated breath. O'Shea moved equally silently. I cannot say what his feelings were at this moment, for I did not even look at him. But when we came to the door of the sick room that had been my bedroom, it was opened by a white-capped nurse, and we entered, catlike as burglars.

Nanette lay propped up in my bed, with closed eyes. She was pale, but, in that hour, more adorable than ever. Her mother sat over by an open window, watching, and Sir Frank Leslie stood beside the bed. We crept forward, abashed as detected criminals. But Nanette did not stir, until:

"Someone has come to say good-night to you, dear," said her mother.

Then the drooping lids quivered, and she raised her blue eyes. I cannot say if she saw O'Shea, or merely pretended that she did not see him; but admittedly he was standing behind me. She laid her hand in mine, and:

"Thank you, Mr. Decies," she murmured, in a pathetically weak voice. "I am going to be a frightful nuisance to you. In future, I shall try to arrange to be shot in my own bedroom."

She closed her eyes again, wearily, and dropped her hand upon the coverlet. Sir Frank beckoned to me to step aside. I did so.

O'Shea drew nearer.

"I have come to thank you, Nanette," he said.

He sat on the chair beside her, bending forward. Slowly, she turned her head, raised weary lids again, and looked at him. She stayed so for what seemed a very long time; just looking—looking—and questioning. He stooped nearer and nearer, until suddenly, but very weakly, a white arm crept around his neck and little trembling fingers were plunged into his hair.

Nanette drew his head down upon the pillow beside her, sighed, and closed her eyes again happily.

I turned away, staring at her mother. Then I caught Sir Frank's glance. He began to tiptoe toward the door, nodded significantly to the nurse—and shepherded us out of the sick room!

The last to leave, I looked back, guiltily, for one moment. Nanette was fast asleep, for they had given her an opiate. And she lay with her head nestling upon O'Shea's shoulder.

I shall always remember her smile.

THE END

Sax Rohmer Bibliography
(1983-1959)

Pause! (1910) [essays, monologues & dramatic sketches, published
    anonymously]
Little Tich (1911) [autobiography of the Music Hall entertainer ghost-written
    by Ward]
The Sins of Severac Bablon (1914; stories)
The Romance of Sorcery (1914; nonfiction study of the occult)
The Exploits of Captain O'Hagan (1916; stories)
Brood of the Witch Queen (1918)
Tales of Secret Egypt (1918; stories)
The Orchard of Tears (1918)
The Quest of the Sacred Slipper (1919)
The Dream Detective (1920; Moris Klaw stories)
The Green Eyes of Bâst (1920)
The Haunting of Low Fennel (1920; stories)
Tales of Chinatown (1922; stories)
Grey Face (1924)
Moon of Madness (1927)
She Who Sleeps (1928)
The Emperor of America (1929)
Yu'an Hee See Laughs (1932)
Tales of East and West (1932; stories)
The Bat Flies Low (1935)
White Velvet (1936)
Salute to Bazarada (1939)
Egyptian Nights (1944; US Title: Bimbashi-Baruk of Egypt; stories)
Hangover House (1949)
Wulfheim (1950; originally credited to Michael Furey, later printings listed
    as by Sax Rohmer)
The Moon is Red (1954)
The Secret of Holm Peel and Other Strange Stories (1970)
The Green Spider and Other Forgotten Tales of Mystery & Suspense (2011)
The Leopard Couch and Other Stories of the Fantastic & Supernatural
    (2012)
The Complete Cases of the Crime Magnet (2012; stories)

Fu Manchu series
The Mystery of Dr. Fu-Manchu (1913; US Title: The Insidious Dr. Fu-
    Manchu)
The Devil Doctor (1916: US Title: The Return of Dr. Fu-Manchu)
The Si-Fan Mysteries (1917; US Title: The Hand of Fu Manchu)
The Daughter of Fu Manchu (1931)
The Mask of Fu Manchu (1932)

The Bride of Fu Manchu (1933; original US Title: Fu Manchu's Bride)
The Trail of Fu Manchu (1934)
President Fu Manchu (1936)
The Drums of Fu Manchu (1939)
The Island of Fu Manchu (1941)
The Shadow of Fu Manchu (1948)
Re-enter: Fu Manchu (1957; UK Title: Re-Enter: Dr. Fu Manchu)
Emperor Fu Manchu (1959)
The Wrath of Fu Manchu and Other Stories (UK: 1973; US: 1976; 12 stories
    including four previously uncollected Fu Manchu stories)

Gaston Max series
The Yellow Claw (1915)
The Golden Scorpion (1919)
The Day the World Ended (1930)
Myself and Gaston Max (a series of six BBC radio plays, 1942)
Seven Sins (1943)

"Red" Kerry series
Dope (1919)
Yellow Shadows (1925)

Paul Harley series
Bat-Wing (1921)
Fire Tongue (1921)
The Voice of Kali: The Early Paul Harley Mysteries (2013)

Sumuru series
The Sins of Sumuru (1950; US Title: Nude in Mink)
The Slaves of Sumuru (1951; US Title: Sumuru)
Virgin in Flames (1952; US Title: The Fire Goddess)
Sand and Satin (1954; US Title: Return of Sumuru)
Sinister Madonna (1956)

Related Works:

Bianca in Black by Elizabeth Sax Rohmer (1958; Rohmer's wife)
Master of Villainy: A Biography of Sax Rohmer by Cay Van Ash and
    Elizabeth Sax Rohmer, edited by Robert E. Briney (1972)
Ten Years Beyond Baker Street: Sherlock Holmes Matches Wits with the
    Diabolical Dr. Fu Manchu by Cay Van Ash (1984)
The Fires of Fu Manchu by Cay Van Ash (1987)
The Terror of Fu Manchu by William Patrick Maynard (2009)
The Destiny of Fu Manchu by William Patrick Maynard (2012)
The Triumph of Fu Manchu by William Patrick Maynard (2015;
    unpublished)

More exotic tales of mystery and suspense by

SAX ROHMER

"...thrillers, supernatural tales, borderline science fiction, occult novels, and crime stories, most of them exhibiting the same atmosphere of strangeness and menace and the same inventiveness of exotic detail that characterize the best of the Fu Manchu stories."—Robert E. Briney

Bat Wing / Fire-Tongue $15.95
"The nearest approach to the pure detective-story that Sax ever made."
—Cay Van Ash & Elizabeth Sax Rohmer, *Master of Villainy*

The Yellow Claw / The Golden Scorpion $15.95
"... sets up an intriguing mystery that titillates the reader with its strong hints of sordid drug and sex scandals among the upper class..."
—William Patrick Maynard

Brood of the Witch Queen / The Quest of the Sacred Slipper $15.95
"...fast-paced, clever, ingeniously contrived and thoroughly enjoyable... with vampires, black magic and occult powers that have lain dormant since the days of Ancient Egypt."—*Vintage Pop Fictions*

Grey Face / Green Eyes of Bâst $15.95
"Sax Rohmer has written a dozen thrilling books, but none of them of greater power or interest than this one."—*The Boston Globe*

The Haunting of Low Fennel / Tales of Secret Egypt $17.95
"...a nice collection of shorts which should entertain those who appreciate old style mysteries based in the post WWI landscape of rural England."—Stuart Dean

"Although it was Dr. Fu-Manchu who made Rohmer's reputation it was his entire output that cemented his fame around the world, and it has barely dimmed over a century later."—Mike Ashley

Available in trade paperback from:
Stark House Press · 1315 H Street, Eureka, CA 95501
Starkhousepress.com